Rise of the Aligerai

ALSO BY KIRA R. TREGONING

The Aligerai Series

Rise of the Aligerai
A Shadowed Soul

Find out about new releases by signing up for the Aligerai
newsletter at:
http://eepurl.com/3mLh9

Rise of the Aligerai

Kira R. Tregoning

ISBN-13: 978-1492304944

Cover design and photo: Regina Wamba of www.maeidesign.com.

First print edition © 2016

To the Fellowship—you know who you are—and especially to Sam and Michelle.

To my brilliant beta readers and idea-bouncers: Stevan, Melissa, Michelle, Renee, Lyn, Kelly, Neha, Chris, Lauren, and even Derrick.

Thank you.

Chapter One
Puzzles and Pictures

Darkness engulfed the city. Pinpricks and pockets of light scattered across town shed some light, but the violence of yesterday's storm left downed trees and power lines, debris everywhere, and standing water in low-lying streets that had yet to drain.

Robert rubbed at his aching eyes. As it was, it felt like nothing more could be tacked on to the end of a long and tiring day. He had been rushing everywhere today, traveling around to meet with various people on the whims and orders of his employer. So much fetching and carrying, searching and spying . . . and the lack of electricity in an already steamy summer only made things worse for everyone.

He groaned and sat up. "I'm only in my twenties," he said to no one. "I shouldn't hurt this much already." A single candle burned on his rickety table, throwing out a little bit of light. It felt nice, to wallow in the dark after a hard day. For once he couldn't be sucked into the Internet or computer games—no electricity meant no Internet, and no Internet meant no games. Instead, Robert appreciated the view from his apartment's window—with the city so dark, the stars in the sky shone brilliantly.

Suddenly a voice from nowhere boomed throughout his apartment. "Robert!" The great voice lingered, and when it faded, Rob put a hand to his aching temple. His boss wanted to see him. He could feel a headache coming on. *I really hate that scrying bowl of his, and his voice trick.* Sighing, Robert climbed from his couch and shuffled into the middle of his small living room, losing sight of the sky. A quick glance around the apartment showed that his door was indeed locked, and he was far enough from the window that he couldn't be seen through it. Feeling secure, Rob breathed deep and slow.

A blue halo gathered around both of Rob's hands. He raised them to just in front of his body and traced shapes in the air, the blue glow fading into nothing. The light around his hands extinguished. Rob closed his bloodshot eyes.

In front of him now stood the hazy outline of a tall upright rectangle, the air and space contained within warped just enough to look like a desert mirage. The thought made Robert smirk. *I have a mirage in my apartment.* He took one regretful glance at his comfortable old couch before stepping forward into the magical doorway.

The sensation of passing through the door woke him up with a shock of cold air and momentary weightlessness. A second of utter darkness studded with globes of starlight, and he was through the door.

Robert emerged into the brightly lit entrance hall of a manse. His pupils shrank and he flinched, the light hurting his eyes. Candelabras stood guard around the walls, and an elegant golden chandelier hung from the ceiling over a scarlet runner rug. The air felt much cooler here than it did at his home on Earth—even though this world had never been introduced to electricity, the room temperature was cooler and much more comfortable than his air conditioner could have produced. It made him shiver just a little, his body still used to the height of humid summer.

A tall man stood in the middle of the rug, waiting for Robert to regain his equilibrium. "Welcome back, Mr. Gordon. Mr. Knight is expecting you." He waved his arm and inclined his head toward the stairs. "Please follow me."

"Thank you, Joe," Robert said. He brushed off his wrinkled shirt and followed Joe up the grand staircase. Joe's navy and charcoal suit blended in with the much gloomier halls in such a way that Rob felt the man was more a ghost than a human, transparent and colorless. Even his dark brown hair blended with the surroundings.

Joe led Robert down the burgundy rug of the second floor hallway, past closed brown doors on both sides. He stopped outside a door decorated with ornate brass swirls and wooden carvings on the left and knocked. A muffled voice came from inside. Joe responded. "Mr. Knight, Mr. Gordon has arrived and is here to see you, sir." The muffled voice came again and Joe opened the door to usher Robert inside.

Rob nodded to Joe in thanks and walked in, tugging on his still-rumpled shirt. Joe stayed outside and closed the door behind him. "Mr. Knight, sir. I have come as requested," said Rob.

Robert's employer sat behind a wide wooden desk, papers stacked around the workspace. The man was still fairly young, but prematurely graying. Bright brown eyes glanced up at Robert from over the top of thin reading glasses. "Robert, thank you for joining me. How did the meeting go today with the Earth suppliers?"

"As expected, sir. The smugglers met with Mr. Alan to move the shipments in secret to Alan's warehouses in the south." Robert summoned his report from home with a twitch of his fingers and it popped into existence in his hand. He removed the spell on the pages that transformed the words into gibberish to all but him and laid the report on the desk. "I believe I was the only spy in the meeting itself—I know there were two others watching from outside. I also believe Mr. Alan will not use those smugglers again. Whatever it is he's up to here in Corá, he's trying to keep it very quiet on Earth."

Mr. Knight pulled the report closer and skimmed through the first page before adding it to his stack of papers. Then he changed the subject. "I have a long-term assignment for you that will have top priority. It is the only thing you will be doing from now on."

The older man passed Robert the paper he held. Robert read it, his eyes widening and eyebrows spiking up into his floppy hair when he saw the picture. His heart beat faster and he could feel nerves building in his chest. "That's Roxie. What does she have to do with this?" A shiver of apprehension overtook him.

"Your friend is going to college."

"I know." Robert curled the fingers of one hand and picked at a fingernail. *How does he know this?* His heart still beat against his ribs, as if in warning. "But I ask you again, *sir*, what does she have to do with this?"

Mr. Knight frowned, the lines of his face deepening into displeasure. "Your tone is insolent, Robert, but I shall let it pass for now. You are too protective of this girl." His eyes narrowed. "Do not worry, my boy, she is not the assignment. She is the means to an end, so to speak."

"I don't understand."

The man picked up another sheet of paper, removing his own coding spell as he did. "Roxanne is going to college in a few weeks." He handed Rob the paper. "With this girl."

This paper had no picture, only a name and some information. "Sita Newbury? I've never heard of her. What does she have to do with my assignment, sir?"

Mr. Knight stood up, his movement graceful and fluid, and he ambled over to a cabinet near his desk. "She *is* the assignment. As it happens, she is going to the same school as your Roxie." He knelt down to reach in the cabinet and pull out a black mirror. Something inside the cabinet shone an ethereal white, bright enough to make Robert squint. Before he could see what it was, Mr. Knight closed the cabinet and held up the mirror. Mr. Knight carried it to the desk and set it in front of Robert.

Rob looked from Mr. Knight to the mirror and back. Mr. Knight's eyes grew hard, and Rob felt his apprehension grow the longer the meeting went on. Sweat beaded on his palms, but Mr. Knight spoke once more, his voice quiet but colder than before. "Your assignment, Robert, is to watch Sita. Learn about her. Report back to me everything you find out. She may be exactly the person I have been looking for."

"How so, sir?"

The older man gave him a brittle smile. "You will find out later. For now, it is not necessary for you to know why I am interested. In fact, you will likely find out before I even tell you. You're a smart boy. Use that brain of yours." Knight held his hand over the mirror's glass, closing his eyes. Dark green light gathered at his fingertips and dipped onto the mirror, making its surface cloud over, the green absorbed into the black.

An image formed in the scry glass. A young woman gazed up at them: beautiful, young, blonde-haired and green-eyed, with a wide and engaging smile. Rob's nerves subsided a moment, pushed out by curiosity, and his heartbeat returned to a more normal pace. He examined the face closely, trying to memorize every detail. "That's her?"

"That is Sita Newbury. Find her, Robert. Track her. It would be highly beneficial if your Roxanne could befriend her, but I do not have such high hopes. Just being at the same school will be enough." The mirror went blank.

Robert heard the finality in his employer's tone. He stood up, enspelling and folding the papers into his pocket as he did. Joe opened the door from the outside. Knight said one last thing as Robert walked to the door. "Robert, I remind you, this is your *only* assignment. I place a great deal of importance on this project. I expect results, and in as timely a manner as possible. You know the rules: she is not to know of your profession. You are just another college student. A friend. Try that photography thing you like so much, she might believe you as a photographer, you have the grungy, artistic look." Knight smirked and sat back into his chair.

Robert nodded and gave a half-hearted smile before walking out the door. "It will be taken care of, sir," he said under his breath. Joe led him back down the stairs into the entrance hall, clearly waiting for him to disappear. Rob took a deep, steadying breath and closed his eyes for only a moment. It was a bad idea to let Joe see any of his nerves—he would report back to Mr. Knight anything unusual. *How can I not be worried?* he thought. *Somehow Knight knew about Roxie . . . I've never mentioned her.* The implications of that unsettled him even more, and he knew he needed to find Roxie.

He wiped the bit of sweat from his face, using a yawn as his pretext. Then he redrew the magic blue door and disappeared back into his lonely apartment, leaving Joe to stare at an empty hall.

∞

Sita Newbury set aside her book. Her silent home, nestled in a cul-de-sac in a quiet Maryland town, sheltered only her at this hour. Yet something didn't feel quite right to her. A sense of unease swept through her fluttering heart and stomach and she rose from the couch, unsure of what to look for or where. It couldn't be her sister home already—school wasn't even close to being finished for the day.

A shape outside the front window drew her to sneak a peek outside. She stepped close to the drapes and carefully peeked out the corner.

No one was there.

A creak in the kitchen. The sound of rustling cloth. The hiss of breath being released all at once as someone moved.

Sita let go of the drapes, spun on her toes, and crouched to the floor, just in time to avoid a punch to the head. The man's fist landed on the wall instead and he cried out in pain. Sita didn't wait for him to recover. Her hands moved before her brain did. She clutched the man's shin and poured magic into him, overwhelming his body and making him faint. He slumped to the floor, head banging on the linoleum. Sita sniffed and scrambled to her feet, back to the wall.

The first man was forgotten as a second man came around the corner. He was more cautious than the first—this one waited. So she studied him. The two men dressed similarly in black clothing with half-masks covering their faces. She didn't see any obvious weapons, but that didn't mean much when they wore long-sleeve shirts, gloves, and pants. Sita rolled her eyes. "What do you all want? And how'd you get in here, anyway?"

But the moment she opened her mouth, the second man attacked. A knife headed her way, followed by a second and third. Sita raised her left hand, palm out, and blocked the knives with a shield of violet magic. "Don't make me ask again," she said.

More knives whizzed through the air, and Sita blocked them all without breaking a sweat.

Now he began to annoy her. So she stopped talking. She knew there was a third man somewhere around her, and she wanted to make one of them talk. Since this man clearly wasn't interested in speaking . . .

Sita dodged to the right out of the man's immediate line of sight. She pulled out a thread of her magic, rolled it into a ball, and threw it at the man's right shoulder. She made a second that hit him in the chest as the first orb knocked him back, and a third that hit him in the left shoulder as he spun. Finally, he fell, stunned.

A hand grasped her shoulder from behind, but Sita was ready. Instead of trying to escape, she made her magic course through her body all at once, and little sparks of power ran over her skin. The man grunted and let go when the sparks shocked his gloved hand.

Now Sita did turn, a violet-sheathed fist aimed at the man's gut. But he blocked her with his arm, knocking her off balance. Sita let herself fall, pulling the man down with her. She kneed him in the groin as he fell on top of her. He groaned and rolled to the side, but still managed a grip on her wrist. "Let go!" Sita said through gritted teeth. Another jolt of magic through her arm into his hand made him release her.

Sita sat up onto her knees and watched the man lay there in pain. "Alright, who are you?" He growled at her.

She ripped his mask off, making him cry out. He wasn't very old—certainly not much older than her. His brown hair fell into his eyes. If he hadn't just attacked her, Sita might have found him handsome. As it was, she wasn't very inclined to be nice to him right now. Her breathing began to return to normal after the slight exertion of fighting off three men. "What do you want? Who are you?"

Sweat ran down his forehead and pain knitted his brows together. Sita moved her knee onto his groin and pressed down, just enough to cause some pain. He cried out. "OK, OK! I'll talk! Just move your knee!"

"About time." Sita moved off, resuming her position beside him. She raised a shield around the both of them, to keep him in and to keep anyone else out. "Talk."

"I'm Allen. From Imbri Mors."

"Never heard of Imbri Mors."

"Your problem, not mine."

Sita grimaced. Her knees began to ache from kneeling. "Who or what are Imbri Mors and why did you attack me?"

The man, Allen, shrugged. "Orders. Following orders. Dunno beyond that."

The pain must have started to wear off—he had stopped sweating. Sita kept an eye on his hands, which were beginning to creep toward his pockets. "Fine. How did you get around my shields?"

"What shields?"

She shifted and threatened to lay her knee into his groin again, but he cringed and curled up protectively. "Relax, geez! I dunno how, you'd have to ask the other two. But the shields around the place let us through."

Sita cursed under her breath. She had thought something was off in the shields lately. Clearly, there was. Knees aching, she leaned back and considered the man. She couldn't kill him—too messy, and she had nowhere to hide a body right now. Besides, her sister would be home in a few hours. She couldn't clean up the house by then if she killed them all. With a sigh, she reached out and touched a finger to Allen's temple. He gasped as if about to say something, but Sita's magic rolled into his brain and knocked him out.

He would stay asleep for a few hours now. Sita crawled over to the other two men and did the same to them, making sure they would stay asleep.

Then she rose to her feet and looked out the front window, scanning the yard and cul-de-sac for any sign of people. But no one moved around outside. No one walked anywhere. The children were all still in school, their parents at work. So Sita grabbed her car keys, backed the car into the yard, and hauled the three men into the back seat and trunk of the car. They barely fit, and they were heavy, but with a touch of magic, Sita managed to get them all in. Then she hopped in the driver's seat and started down the road.

She drove a few miles away to the local park. Only one or two people were around at the moment, so Sita drove down behind the soccer field and turned the car around to hide the trunk. Each man she carried out of the car and into the woods, propping them up against a tree out of sight of the field. No one would see them, and when they woke in a few hours, they could find their own way out and back to where they'd come from.

When she finished, Sita huffed and wiped her hands on her jeans. "That's done. Now to fix those shields around the house when I get back there." She checked her watch.

Her sister would be home any minute.

Sita cursed and hopped back into the car, gunning the engine and tearing off down the field to the road. Her sister would be pissed if she found the house torn up, and their aunt would be even more furious since she would now be staying with the younger girl while Sita was at college.

Sita groaned. Her sister would have one more thing to scold about. Sita was supposed to leave for college tomorrow.

And she hadn't started packing at all.

Chapter Two
Suite 400, East Hall

Her back felt itchy.

Sita would have tried to scratch the itch, but she knew it wouldn't help. There was only one solution. With a frustrated sigh, Sita threw off the bed covers and sat up, legs dangling off the side of her loft bed.

Darkness engulfed the room, with just enough moonlight filtering in to see a little. Sita's roommate, Vanessa Yeager, made soft, delicate snoring sounds from her side of the room.

I thought my first night of college would feel way different than this. Sita jumped down from her bed. Vanessa slept on, so Sita rooted through one of the last of her boxes until she found what she sought: a floor-length black robe with silver buttons from mid-chest to mid-thigh. Two slits as long as Sita's forearm were permanently sewn into the back, each one beginning above her shoulder blades. She took off her pajama top and pulled the knee-length robe on.

In near silence, Sita slipped from her dorm room. She closed her door and tip-toed past her other two suite-mates, Roxanne Dalton and Ariene Sanford. Earlier they had fallen asleep on the couch in the common room watching a movie. Sita chuckled as she reached over and clicked the television off, which plunged the room into black.

Once free of her suite, Sita walked more freely. She made her way to the left down the hall, the itch in her shoulders growing stronger. Her heavy long blond hair, left free to hang down almost to her waist, swished against the robe.

A fire escape waited outside the hall window. It took a bit of tugging to get the ancient window to move in its frame, but at last Sita managed to raise the window and climb through onto the red platform. A breeze would filter through the window into the hall, but this late at night Sita thought no one would be around to notice.

A tall ladder stretched up to the roof. Sita set her bare feet on the chilly metal rung at the bottom and began to climb. Twenty rungs later, she edged onto the tiles of the roof and let go of the ladder. Sita crouched down, exhaling with contentment as she finally eased the ache in her shoulders.

The long slits in her robe served a very useful purpose. Slowly, so she wouldn't injure herself, Sita unfurled her great wings, sliding them through the slits of the fabric and stretching them out to the wind. The slits sewed themselves up to fit snug around the base of her wings, holding her robe closed.

Moonlight glowed down on her fluttering white feathers, making Sita smile in pleasure. She reached between the feathers to scratch at the skin around the base. If she held her wings in for too long, her skin began to feel painfully tight and itchy. She lifted her face to the moon and hummed a soft melody to herself, enjoying the quiet and darkness of the night.

Standing slowly so as not to lose her balance, Sita stretched her wings to their fullest span, loving the feel of her sore muscles stretching. Flapping to loosen and warm her flight muscles, she stepped to the edge of the roof, looked down with a smile full of triumph and adventure, and jumped off into the night.

Staying up all night flying probably had not been the best idea in the world. Sita's jaw creaked from the giant yawn that overtook her. *Maybe not the best idea, but it did help.* She folded up her flying robe and stuffed it under her pillow so she could pull on real clothes for the day. *No point in trying to sleep now.*

As she pulled on a pair of jeans, Sita shot a reserved glance to her roommate. Vanessa remained asleep, snoring softly, her head resting on a silk-covered, down-filled pillow and the rest of her cushioned by her expensive mattress from home. All of which Sita had heard about extensively yesterday during the second day of move-in. Sita had arrived on the first move-in day, two days before classes started, but Vanessa, Roxie, and Estelle had arrived yesterday on the second move-in day. Vanessa had dominated their room for an hour so her daddy's movers could place her things just so. Part of the reason she needed to fly last night was Vanessa. Her new roommate had tried to boss her around as she moved her suitcases in, and had given Sita a headache from the complaints about the room.

Sita rolled her eyes, grabbed her keys, and left her room. It wasn't until she had shut the door that she remembered she hadn't turned off her alarm. She almost went back in. *Ah, forget it,* she thought. *Consider it payback for yesterday, Vanessa!*

Her other two suite mates still lay on the sofa and couch, fast asleep. Sita grinned, then yawned again. Talking with the roommates would have to wait until after breakfast.

While Sita ate a bowl of cereal and sipped at some hot chocolate, someone asked to sit at her table. Sita nodded hello and her assent, but didn't recognize the girl who asked. *I'm sure I would remember someone with such curly hair. It's kind of pretty.*

The unknown girl offered a gentle smile. "I think I recognize you. Are you in 400?" Confused but more awake now, Sita nodded again. Relief infused the young woman's brown eyes. "Oh, good, I thought you looked familiar. I saw you yesterday during move-in. I live across the hall in a double." She smiled again while she buttered her bagel. "My name is Skylar."

"I'm Sita. What year are you?"

"Junior. I'm in Art. You're a freshman, right?" Sita cocked an eyebrow. Skylar interpreted the look correctly and chuckled. "You can usually tell the freshmen apart from the upperclassmen by who sits alone the first few weeks until the freshmen start making friends."

Sita laughed. "Well, when you put it that way it seems so obvious." Her hot chocolate was almost gone, regrettably, but she felt much more awake. "I thought the hard work of moving day would help me sleep better, but nope! My headache kept me up all night. And I think my mattress has lumps."

"Mm. Get a foam mattress pad, it's worth it. Moving gives you a headache?" Skylar ate her bagel in neat bites.

More people began to flow into the dining hall now. Sita thought she spotted Roxie, but the flash of red hair disappeared. "Not moving. My sister's whining and complaining about helping me move. That's what caused the headache." Skylar laughed.

A shadow and then a plunking down of a tray announced Roxie's arrival. "Sleeping on the couch after moving in yesterday wasn't my best idea." She sat in her chair and a groan escaped her lips. "I should have moved in Saturday instead of Sunday. More time to recuperate before classes." Roxie began shoveling food into her mouth.

Between bites of toast Sita introduced Skylar to Roxie and kept up a somewhat sleepy conversation about the day of classes ahead. Roxie had an early class on Mondays—hence the shoveling of food—but she stuck around at breakfast long enough for Ariene and Vanessa to join them, as well as Skylar's roommate, a plump, squeaky girl named Estelle. Sita thought Estelle nice enough, but the squeaking of her voice grated on her nerves. Vanessa scowled at Sita, but said nothing. Sita merely smiled to her roommate.

Roxie's rushed departure for class triggered an exodus. Everyone else at the table also ended their breakfast, but only Roxie had a class to go straight to. The others went back to their rooms for a bit. Sita only stayed long enough to grab her bookbag and leave for Shakespeare class.

That class filled her brain almost to bursting. The professor plunged right into the material, and to her surprise Sita found herself taking notes on the first day of class. Then she met Vanessa in World History, a fact that had the potential to be troublesome. But she pushed the thoughts aside and snatched some lunch after History before she hurried to Psychology with Roxie and Ariene. By the time Sita took a seat in Algebra, her last class for Monday, she questioned her decision to come to college in the first place. Climbing the three flights of stairs of her hall, she thought to herself, *I didn't think we would really do work on the first day—this is different than I thought it would be.*

Dinner that night was a confusing, loud, but leisurely affair. Sita and her suitemates again met Skylar and Estelle, but this time a new girl asked to take the last available seat at their table. Introducing herself as Darci, she said little aside from her major—Psychology—her freshman status, and her dorm room, which was at the end of Sita's hall. The group welcomed her into their new circle, and she looked nice enough, but she said very little as she watched them all with her big brown eyes.

Skylar's sophomore roommate, Estelle, spoke very little as well, for which Sita was grateful. Roxie and Ariene carried most of the conversation. "How did we get saddled with two freshies, Ari?"

said Roxanne. "I mean, we're sophomores, we've already been through the freshmen hell. Now we have to go through it again vicariously?"

Sita threw a fry at Roxie, who deflected it with her napkin and a laugh. Sita rolled her eyes. "Come on, we won't be that bad. Well, I won't. Can't speak for Vanessa, I don't know her well enough. Except that she snores."

"I do not!" Vanessa frowned. "You're making that up!"

"Am not!"

"Oh yeah, they won't be too bad," Ari said. She shook her head and took another bite of lasagna.

∞

Sita returned from her second day of classes to find Vanessa's stereo blasting pop music through the suite. "Vanessa," she called. "Vanessa!" But Vanessa, hidden away in their room, couldn't hear over the music. Grumbling about rude roommates, Sita hoisted her backpack onto her shoulder once more and returned to the hallway.

At the end of the hall, in front of the fire escape Sita had used the night before, sat Ari and Roxie. Sita ambled over and let her bag drop to the floor next to them. "Hey guys." They raised their faces to her, smiles on their lips. "Enjoying the musical selection in the suite?"

Ari snorted. "Oh yeah, totally." She popped a cookie from the bag set between her and Roxie. From the smell, they were chocolate chip. "Wanna join us out here?"

Sita sank to the stained carpet and folded her legs beneath her. "Definitely." Both Rox and Ari had open books on their laps and notebooks out. "Homework already?"

Roxie scrunched her nose up. "Sad but true. You?" With a grin, Sita pulled a textbook from her bag and opened it to the right page. Ari passed the cookies and they sat together in companionable silence. From time to time someone would turn a page or Sita would hear the scratch of a pencil, but mostly they were quiet. The hall was quieter than she had thought it would be, too. But with the suite's door closed, the music stayed contained behind walls, and she could study in relative peace.

After half-an-hour of study, Sita stood and stretched. Roxie yawned and slammed her book shut. "I'm done!" she said. "I'm done with this for today."

Ariene shoved her roommate's shoulder. "The second day of class and you're already burned out? That's lame." Roxie stuck out her tongue and shoved her back. Sita laughed and rescued the cookies as they shoved back and forth on the floor.

The door at the end of the hall opened and Darci stuck her head out. "What's going on out here?" she said. Her soft voice almost didn't register in Sita's ear, Roxie and Ari were being so noisy. Sita nudged them both with her foot until they stopped their shoving and looked around.

Darci leaned against her door frame, arms hugged to her body across her chest. "Hey Darci," Sita said. "Sorry, did we bother you?"

"No, no, I was just curious." And Darci began to back into her room again.

Sita walked slowly over, her hands clearly visible at her sides. Something about Darci just screamed "frightened animal" to Sita. Darci's eyes especially grabbed at Sita's instincts—there were shadows in those eyes that hinted at deeper pain. Sita approached slowly. "It's OK. Why don't you join us? We have cookies. We were studying, until Ari started the shoving, but we could play a game or something." She smiled at the girl and waited.

Darci froze halfway in the door, her arms still hugging her body, and her eyes still unsure. Her gaze flitted from Ari and Roxie on the floor to Sita standing before her and back again. Sita waited. Then Darci gave a tentative smile and walked from the room, her arms dropping to her sides. "OK. What kind of cookies?"

That was all the cue they needed. Sita handed Darci the bag while Ari cleared a space for her on the floor between books. Soon Darci began to laugh with them as Ari told jokes and Roxie ruined the punch lines, and the shadows in her eyes retreated. Ari soon had Darci sitting next to her, a protective arm slung over her thin shoulders, as they played a rousing game of poker with Sita's deck of cards.

∞

The next night, Sita flew over the town, her great white wings beating steadily. Cool September air slipped over the skin of her face, arms, and legs, and her hair tangled as it streamed behind. This high up, with the town very small below, the air had little smell. She felt the chill in her lungs with every breath, but the exertion of flight kept her warm.

Light from the moon filtered down through wispy clouds above her. Sita glanced to her right to see the nearly full moon illuminating her way. She banked to the left and flew lower, back toward the school. This was the tricky part—getting back without being seen. The moonlight didn't help, either.

A dog barked. Cars swished by and beeped below. Sita coasted above it all, a silent dark shadow. Houses with glowing golden windows flashed under her as she flew closer to the school. Tall buildings, taller than any of the houses around them, with brownish-red roof tiles marked the school to her from above. She scanned the ground below, but saw no one wandering the grounds around her building. With care, she spiraled down to her rooftop and backwinged to a soft landing.

The fabric of her flying robe settled around her as she paused for breath and to regain her bearings. Walking always took a slight adjustment after a long flight. *Oh, but I needed that exercise*, she thought. *My wings were starting to itch again.*

After a deep, bracing breath, Sita retracted her wings into her skin. They settled between her shoulder blades, with the skin melding back together into a seamless whole. The entire process itched, and the pain of it made Sita grimace. It had hurt so much more the first time. Now she rarely noticed the ache except occasionally.

With her wings safely hidden once more, Sita crouched at the edge of the roof and peeked over. The coast outside was clear, but she saw movement inside the hall window. Leaning further over the edge, Sita craned her head to see inside and groaned. Roxie, Ari, and Darci sat in the hall.

Sita leaned back to sit on her heels. This window was the only one by the fire escape, and the only one on her side of the hall. The next fire escape was at the opposite end of the hall. She would have to cross the roof to the other side of the building to get there, and no guarantee that the window on that end could be opened from outside. *I don't like those chances. Plus, I might be seen.* With a sigh, Sita did the only thing she could think of. She used a bit of magic to hide the slits in the back of her robe and climbed down the ladder.

Metal clanged as she landed on the platform. Three heads swiveled to face her, their mouths agape. "Sita?" said Ari. "What are you doing out there?"

"Hey guys." Sita clambered into the hall through the window, nearly falling on Roxie in the process. "Sorry!"

"What were you doing out there?" said Roxie. She helped Sita move out of the way and sit down. "Why are you just wearing a coat? Aren't you cold?"

Ari leaned out the window and looked up. "Were you on the roof?"

Sita laughed and fluttered her hands at them. "If you'll stop asking questions, I'll answer them. Yeah, I was on the roof. I'm not really that cold, and it's not a coat, it's a robe." Roxie wrinkled her nose at Sita's correction and Sita wrinkled her own nose back at her. "I was up there relaxing and watching the stars."

A hand tugged on her sleeve. It was Darci, feeling the material. "Where did you get this? I want one."

Sita felt the beginnings of a blush creep into her cheeks. "Um, I made it myself. I could make you one when I have my sewing machine again."

Darci's eyes lit up. "Would you? Oh, thanks! It's so pretty, and I love black."

"It'll go great with your hair," Ari said with a smile as she tweaked Darci's short dark brown locks.

The warmth of the hall banished the lingering chill from Sita's skin as she sat with her suitemates and Darci. No one noticed the slits in the back of her robe—Sita's magic held up. As their questions waned, Sita fell silent and let the others carry the conversation for a while. They talked about class and movies until Roxie turned to Ari and said, "You know, I haven't heard from Mel at all. Do you hear from her?" Ari just shook her head.

"Who's Mel?" said Darci, her dark eyes agleam. Sita leaned forward to hear better.

Roxie shrugged before she leaned back on both hands. "She's our old roommate from last year. She had Sita and Vanessa's room. Mel—Melanie—was pretty cool, but she decided not to take the suite again this year. I haven't heard from her at all, I don't even know if she's back in classes this year, actually."

Sita finally noticed there was no sound coming from the suite. "Speaking of roommates, is Vanessa here?"

Ari shook her head. A predatory grin stretched from corner to corner of her mouth. "Nope. She decided to make herself scarce for a while."

"What did she do now?" Sita said.

Roxie studied her nails through lowered lashes. "Oh, she just decided she liked our room better and tried to make us trade rooms. Something about ours being bigger."

Sita and Darci's jaws dropped. "You're kidding," Darci said.

"Nope!" Ari spoke again. The grin still sat on her lips, reminding Sita of a satisfied cat. "I told her we could trade rooms the day she got a heart."

"Then she threatened to make Vanessa's life a living torture by never letting her sleep again and slammed the door in Vanessa's face," said Roxie.

Darci's giggles were drowned out by Sita's burst of laughter. Ari and Roxie joined in, and they had all managed to calm down when they heard footsteps coming toward them from the stairwell.

Vanessa turned the corner into the hall. She saw her suitemates and Darci staring at her from the floor and paused. Then she turned on her heel, tossed her long hair over her shoulder, and returned the way she came.

They erupted in laughter and remained in the hall for hours after, hoping Vanessa would come back for a second round.

Chapter Three
Secrets

For a suite and four people, the bathroom felt terribly small. Sita washed her hands and face at the bathroom sink on her side of the cramped quarters. Their bathroom was divided into three spaces—the first sat against the back wall, a full shower, toilet, and sink, with a dividing wall and door to cordon it off from the second part. This second area was what Sita considered the bathroom hallway. It was only a walkway between the door to Roxie and Ariene's room and the door to Sita and Vanessa's, with the dividing walls of the bathroom on either side. The other divider sectioned off the third area, which held another shower, toilet, and sink, as well as the door to the common area. All in all, by the end of the first ten days of dorm life, it felt very cramped to Sita.

The side that belonged to her and Vanessa was the one against the back wall, furthest from the common room. Sita was fine with that—she only had one door to worry about locking. She dried her hands on the towel and opened the door to the bathroom hall.

Voices coming from Ari and Roxie's room made her pause. *I thought they were out?* Sita quietly closed the door to her bath chamber and leaned in closer to Roxie's door. A small slit between door and frame betrayed that the door stood ajar.

About to leave, Sita heard a snippet of soft conversation that forced her to freeze. "Where are the ward stones Rob gave me?" said Roxie.

Ward stones? Sita felt a chill run through her. *Ward stones are magical—why would Roxanne and Ari know anything about ward stones? And who is Rob?* She felt only a little guilty about eavesdropping but the feeling filtered away as she leaned in closer to listen.

"They're on your bed." That was Ari. It sounded like she was preoccupied with something. The sound of cloth hitting hardwood floor indicated she was probably still unpacking. "And do you really think we'll need them?"

Roxie sighed, the sound so exasperated it brought a smile to Sita's lips. "Yes! Why do you think Robbie gave them to me in the first place? You know we can't ward ourselves, we don't have that kind of magic. So he gave me these. Do you want just anyone to come banging on our room and find us out?"

A muffled thump reached Sita's ears. Ari must have dumped a box of clothes out somewhere. "Then keep your voice down and hurry up and get them set. You're the one who wants to practice, not me. I'm perfectly fine without them, thank you."

Sita heard Roxie shuffle around the room, but she didn't come near the bathroom door just yet. "Just because you think you don't need the wards doesn't mean you actually don't need them. You really do—you can't transform without some kind of shielding . . . *put the claws away!*" Sita almost jumped at the fierceness of Roxie's low snarl. "The windows are wide open, what if someone looked up, or looked in, or came through the door?"

"You worry too much."

"Check the doors!"

That was Sita's cue to exit. She snuck out the bathroom hall and through the door into her own room just as Ariene's footsteps approached the bathroom door. Sita left her door halfway open so it didn't look like she had been sneaking around.

When she heard Ari close her door all the way, Sita relaxed. Vanessa wasn't in their room just then—Sita thought she remembered Vanessa had class at this time on Fridays—which meant she could ponder what she had heard in peace. *Only the first week of being here and I learn something new. And very, very interesting.* She jumped up onto her loft bed and lay down. *What kind of power does Roxie have? Ari maybe has some kind of transforming power, but Roxie? And who is Rob, and how does he make his ward stones so that Roxie and Ari can activate them?*

She knew she shouldn't snoop. She knew she might not even be able to hear anything because of whatever shield had been erected, and she knew the wards might alert her suitemates to eavesdroppers. But the temptation to sneak back into the bathroom and try to figure out the puzzle of the wards grew too overwhelming.

Sita climbed down from her bed and tiptoed across the hardwood floor. She eased through her bathroom door and across the tiles. No sound escaped from Roxie and Ari's room. If she hadn't just heard them talking, Sita would have thought neither young woman was in the room at all. *But that's the point of a shield ward. And this is so far a pretty good one.*

The tile felt chill on her bare feet. Leaning closer to the door, with one hand and most of her weight pressing against the wood, Sita stretched out her senses to feel for the wards. Whoever this Rob person was, he was good at creating wards—he might even be better than Sita herself. The term "ward stones" was actually incorrect, as the "stones" were not stones at all—the wards and shields had been placed in a small pile of earth, which then hardened and condensed into a small circle or square until it became rock-solid. Hence the name "stones." Sita had been able to make them since the age of ten.

No indication of a ward reached her. *This Rob guy is really good at these kinds of wards. I don't know if I can break this . . .* Sita was just reaching for her magic when the door popped open.

Sita sprawled on the floor, smacking her hands and elbows on the hard wood. "Ow!" she said.

Her suitemates stood above her, stern expressions on their faces. Ari held one hand behind her back, and Sita felt fairly certain that it held a weapon of some sort. "How much did you hear?" said Roxie, her voice cold.

"Not much. Your wards are good."

Roxie's eyes narrowed and her face flushed. "How do you . . ."

"Rox, lay off. We'll get better answers if she's not on the floor." Ari reached down a hand and helped Sita stand. She, too, looked serious and reserved, not at all the funny friend she had been at meals.

Sita brushed off her pants. "I'm not going to hurt you or say anything to anyone else. I was just curious."

"Why?" Roxie hadn't relaxed at all.

"I did hear you mention ward stones when I was in the bathroom earlier, before the shield went up. That made me curious, since I know what ward stones are, I've made them before, and I know what it normally costs a mage to make one. They aren't easy or cheap to the caster."

Ariene and Roxanne shared a significant look. Ari took over from Roxie. "Who are you, how do you know about magic, and whose side are you on?"

Sita took a little time. Instead of answering right away, she glanced around the room. Mostly it was neat—on Roxie's side anyway. Ari's side had clothes strewn on most surfaces and boxes shoved under the bed. "I'm not hiding under any false names or stories. I'm Sita Newbury, from Maryland, freshman English major, one sister, and no parents." Shoving some shirts off Ari's chair, Sita sat down.

"We need more than that. You know about our magic use. How do we know you aren't some kind of spy, here to take us in for study or something?"

A door slammed. "Vanessa," Sita said. Ari moved to the bathroom door and closed it quietly. The three of them waited in silence, listening for Vanessa's movements. When Vanessa didn't enter the bathroom or knock on the room's door, Ari returned to the conversation.

Sita sighed. "Look, I'm not a spy. How three magic users ended up in a suite together, I don't know. That doesn't sound like coincidence to me, so you should probably not be suspicious of me, but of the people who assign rooms." Roxie paled, but Ari growled. Sita held up her hands. "Just sayin'. Anyway, I'm a mage. Look."

And Sita called on her power. Her hands lit up in purple, an aura of violet-colored magic around both hands.

Shock rippled across both Ari and Roxie's faces. "It's purple," said Roxie, her voice hushed. "I've never seen or heard of a purple mage."

"Neither have I," Ari said.

The halos faded. Sita smiled. "That's only part of my appeal. Look, we're going to be living together for the next nine months. I want you to trust me. And I know so few magic users that I'd rather be friends than enemies. I'll be straight-up with you two—I trust you can keep secrets." Turning around, Sita magically created two slits in the back of her shirt and showed her suitemates the rest of her secret.

An already cramped dorm room felt much smaller when two enormous white wings suddenly burst into being. Sita glanced over her shoulder and saw why Ari had been holding one hand behind her back—the hand was not a hand, but a furry paw, with large claws extended. Both Ariene and Roxie stared in utter shock. "Wow. I . . . wow." That was Ari.

"Your hand is a paw."

"And you have wings popping out of your back," Ari shot back. Clearly the surprise was wearing off. "So you're a mage and you have wings. That's interesting."

Roxie chuckled. "I think we can relax, Ari. I don't think she's going to hurt us."

Ari sighed and relaxed. "She's told us everything, I think. So we should return the favor."

Sita waited, but Roxie didn't keep her waiting long. Rox climbed up onto her bed and crossed her legs. "You're right." She focused on Sita. "We're mages too, but not the same way you are. We didn't make the ward stones—which you probably heard. But we do have magic." Roxie gestured to Ari, who held up her paw. "Ari is a shapeshifter. She can take on just about any shape, as long as it's living. And I'm an animal-speaker. I have the magical ability to talk to animals—any animal, and I know what they say when they 'talk' back to me."

"How long have you had them?"

"How long have we been able to use magic?" Ari said. Sita nodded. "I think we've both been able to use our talents since we were kids." Roxie agreed. "A friend of Roxie's helped train us up a few years ago. He's the one who made the wards."

Sita raised one eyebrow. "Would he be the 'Rob' person I heard about earlier?"

Roxie scowled. "You didn't mention you'd heard that bit." Sita just grinned. "But yes, that's him."

The wings shrank and retracted under Sita's skin. After a slight grimace, she sewed up the back of her shirt. "Sorry. But now we're even, I think. I've told you everything about my abilities. And I won't tell anyone if you don't."

"We won't tell." Ari transformed her paw back into a more normal hand. "We're too worried about staying out of sight of any government agencies that might want to lock us up for the rest of our lives for scientific study."

Sita grimaced, but acknowledged the truth of that. A knock on the door startled them all. Ari checked that everyone was safe to show to normal people before she opened the door. Vanessa stood there, white-blond hair covering part of her face. She sauntered in, grinning from ear to ear, and draped herself over the last chair in the room. "I like this place; there are a ton of cute guys here. Do you all want to go to dinner? I've invited the girls across the hall also."

The trio glanced to each other and nodded. Roxie answered for them. "Might as well."

Vanessa stood up, heading for the door. "Well then, let's go. The dining hall opens in fifteen minutes."

The three young women followed her out into the hallway and down to the noisy and crowded dining hall. Their hall mates were already there, claiming a table with enough seats left for the four arrivals. Two unknown people had joined the group: Samantha, an acquaintance of Estelle's who also lived in East Hall, and a friend of Ari's from class named Jack. Vanessa and her friends soon joined them, eating their way through mediocre cafeteria food and sharing stories of their day. Roxie, Ariene, and Sita, of course, completely omitted the revelations of their magical powers.

Sita would have felt guilty about lying to these new friends, but somehow she couldn't muster the emotion. Her secret was no longer her own, and the same was true for Ari and Roxie. Talking about her own powers would potentially lead to a discussion of theirs, and a breach of confidence. Significant glances shared between the three of them made Sita feel like she was in a secret club—which she supposed she was, in a way.

Soon they had all finished eating. The group gathered their trays and began to leave. Vanessa halted them. "Wait! I almost forgot! We're doing a movie night in our suite if anyone wants to come! Suite 400 in East Hall. Starts at eight!" Skylar, Estelle, and Darci all said they would come, but Ari's friend had work and Estelle's friend had homework to finish.

After the quartet got back to their rooms, Ariene turned on Vanessa, a fearsome scowl on her face. "Why did you invite all those people without even asking us first? We live here too, you know!"

Vanessa's eyes widened. "I'm sorry, I didn't think you'd mind. They're our friends, aren't they? I thought they would be welcome," she squeaked in defense.

Roxie glared at her. "That's not the point. If you're going to make a habit of inviting a bunch of strangers to our rooms, then you should at least give us a little warning. What if one of us was sick and didn't want visitors? Or our rooms were a mess and we wanted to clean up? You were really rude to us."

Vanessa crossed her arms and rolled her eyes. "All right, fine, I'm sorry, I'll remember that next time. But can they still come tonight? I think it'll be fun, and they're already invited."

Sita nodded. "It's fine for tonight. Let's just rearrange the couch and chairs around the TV so everyone can see. Vanessa, you get to make the popcorn."

At eight o'clock on the dot Estelle and Skylar knocked on the door, popcorn and soda in hand. Sita opened the door and let them in. Darci slipped in a few minutes later, carrying her own snacks. Everyone arranged themselves while Sita and Roxie pulled out the collective hoard of movies. Debate erupted over what to watch, but finally a choice was made.

Sita put in the movie and turned the lights off. She sat down next to Roxie and Vanessa, curling up under her own blanket. Popcorn was passed around every so often, the group entirely wrapped up in the movie.

But before they even reached the end of their second film, all were beginning to fall asleep, so they called an end to movie night. Estelle, Skylar, and Darci gathered their things and left, yawns overtaking them. Ariene turned off the television and they went to their separate rooms, calling goodnight to each other as the lights flickered off for the night.

Lying in bed, Sita stared at her ceiling, her arms cushioning her head. *I'm glad now that I'm here. I think I'm going to really like this.* She pulled her pillow into a more comfortable place. *I wonder if I'll dream of him tonight . . .* And with that thought, she fell asleep.

Vanessa tossed and turned, trying to get comfortable still with the idea of sharing her room with someone. *I should ask Daddy for a single room next semester. But he insisted I try it this way first. Ugh!* Turn to the right. *My roomie seems OK, but she's really quiet.* Turn onto her stomach. *The others are OK too.* Turn to her left side. *But I can't let them know* . . . She drifted off to sleep.

In the other room, Roxie and Ariene stayed up talking. "What do you think of Vanessa? She seems kind of . . . well, arrogant," said Roxie.

Ariene shrugged in the dark. "I don't know. I think it's really more an act than anything. You know, the 'I'm better than you and so you can't really hurt me' thing. And there's something about her that doesn't seem right. Like she's hiding something."

"Yeah, I got that too." Roxie propped herself up on an elbow. She could just barely see her roommate across the room in the shards of yellow lamplight coming through the window curtains. "That Darci girl, though, she worries me. She seems OK, but still . . ." She raised her eyebrows. "She scares me some, and I don't know why."

"And you don't scare easily. I should know, I've tried."

Roxie grinned in the darkness and chuckled. "We should keep an eye on Darci. There's something not right about her. She might be the one Robbie warned me about."

"He's coming down soon?"

"Next week, he said. He wanted to give us some time to settle in first."

Ariene sighed. "That's good, we can ask him about the others. Darci is probably going to be a problem. Estelle and Skylar are nice. I don't get a sense from them at all, I think they're normal." She turned to her friend. "And Sita was a surprise. I didn't get any hint of power around her, and then bam! it shows itself. Like a freaking lake that's been dammed up, and then suddenly let go. She's well shielded, whether she knows it or not. And those wings . . ."

"She's powerful. A good ally. And I think a good friend, if you're on her good side. If you're on her bad side, though . . ."

"It could be really bad."

"Right." Roxie lay back down. "But I don't think we'll be on her bad side. I like her. She's nice. I think we'll get along with her."

"I think so, too."

"G'night, Ari."

"'Night, Rox."

Chapter Four
Observations

A few nights later, Roxie followed Sita and Ari onto the rooftop, pulling herself up inch by inch. Ariene transformed into a bird and flew to the roof from their window, where she was now perching at ease in her eagle body. Sita climbed to the very top and sat next to Ari, waiting for Roxie to join them. Rox glanced up at them, then back at her hands and feet. "I can't believe you two are so comfortable up here. What if you tripped and fell, or just toppled right over?"

Sita laughed. "I usually do just 'topple right over.' That's what my wings are for."

Roxie sat next to the others, gripping the roof tiles with both hands and very determined to not let go. Or to look too far down. Sita tapped her on the shoulder and then spread her hand out, inviting Roxie and Ari to look.

All three felt chills of pleasure shiver across their shoulders. Moonlight bathed the town in silver, lending its glorious radiance to the otherwise ordinary rooftops. Stars winked down at them, seductively inviting the three young women to fly up into the dark night sky and join their celestial dance. An occasional cloud would fly past, but the stars chased it away so as not to hinder or hide their dancing. The small wind teased their hair and feathers, tugging and pulling and pleading for them to join in its own form of dancing. Crisp, cold September night air burned their lungs, making their noses and chests ache with every breath. Roxie gawked at the magnificent sight. She looked over to Sita. "I understand, now." Sita beamed and lifted her face to the moonlight, letting her wings fan behind her in the breeze.

Ariene fluffed her feathers and changed back to her own form. Sighing, she pulled her knees to her chest. "This is beautiful, Sita. Thank you. I never get to see this sort of thing, since I don't really like to fly at night. I worry about getting lost or caught."

"You're welcome. I come up here as often as I can. I like rooftops. No one can see us from this angle, I've made sure of that. But I can just be me up here, and let my wings out. If only I could do that all of the time." Sita shifted to face Ariene. "When you change forms as often as you do, how can you be sure of your original body?"

Ariene chuckled. "Actually, I do sometimes have trouble with that." She pulled something from her pants pocket. "Since whatever I'm wearing when I change will stay with me—it's supposed to be part of my skin, really—I always keep a small picture of my true body in my pocket. That way, if I have any trouble remembering, I just transform as close as I can, then pull out the picture and change into that shape." She slipped the photo back into her pocket. "I update it every so often, just so it's not out of date."

"Good idea," Sita said.

"But there's a cost to my power that makes changing back into my 'true' body hard."

"What's that?"

"The magic eats up my youth."

Sita's jaw dropped. "What? *Why*? How do you know?"

Ari stared into the distance. "I figured it out when I was thirteen. I changed back into my body one day and found that it was older than it should be. My skin looked more like an older teen's than a young teen's. My hair was a little darker and duller, and my hands felt sore. Every time I change into something, the magic eats up a little more of my youthfulness. How often I change seems to determine how fast the deterioration goes."

"That's horrible! Are you sure?"

Roxie interjected. "We asked Robert about it when we met and figured out each other's powers. He agreed that it was likely, since she has no other symptoms from using her magic, and magic always has a cost." Sita had nothing to say to that.

They sat in silence for a while, until Roxie changed the subject. "You know, I'm supposed to be finding a job. My parents expect me to find one by next week, at the least." She groaned. "So thrilled. It's not that easy finding a job!"

Sita tugged on her lip with one hand. "I need to find one also. I have an allowance of sorts, but it's only enough for basics. I should still find a part-time job." She grimaced. "Probably in retail, too."

"I'm lucky," Ariene said. "I don't need to find a job. My parents are giving me an allowance. They want me to completely focus on my studies, and a job would definitely interfere with that."

"Lucky duck," grumbled Sita. Ariene grinned back. "It might sound a little melodramatic, but when I had my last retail job, I died a little on the inside every time I went in for a shift."

Roxie swiveled around to look at Sita, surprised. "Me too! I know exactly what you're talking about!"

"It's because you're not really cut out for that kind of job," commented Ariene.

"It's torture, even if I am making good money," added Sita.

A strand of moonlit russet hair drifted across Roxie's nose. She tucked it behind her ear. "You know, it's kind of weird. How three people with magic ended up in one school. Don't you think?"

Sita cocked her head to one side. "You know, you're right. I wonder how that happened."

"Maybe we just got really lucky?" Ari said beside them. "I mean, the odds of not just two, but three people ending up here must be huge." She smirked. "Must've been fate. I mean, all my other friends either stayed at home or moved really far away, like, across the country."

"Same," said Roxie. "I just thought it was odd, is all. What do you think, Sita?"

Sita's head bobbed. "It's weird. Especially since I mostly picked this place at random. And I don't know where people at my high school went. I didn't have that many friends there."

"What? You?" Ari asked.

Her lip quivered. "You guys don't understand. I'm shy, I don't have very many friends. The ones I do have live far away. I don't have many fun times like this." She leaned back on her hands. "It feels good."

Roxie scooted closer to put an arm around Sita's shoulders. "You have friends now, Sita. We'll be here for you, Ari and me. We magical types have to stick together." Ariene scooted closer to the two of them as well. "I know you haven't really known us that long—about a week, actually. But I think we're going to be really good friends. So you can always count on us, Si."

She broke into a smile and squeezed Roxie's hand. "Thanks."

The three of them returned to their moonlight view in silence.

∞

Robert walked down the hallway to suite 400, taking slow steps to try to catch his breath. *Climbing sixty stairs was not on my to-do list for today*, he thought. He stopped in front of the door, breathing deep. He straightened his shirt and knocked. A tall skinny girl with long blond hair opened it, her blue eyes gazing at him in suspicion. "Um, hi. Who are you?"

He gave her his best grin. "I'm a friend of Roxanne's. She's expecting me, is she here?"

The girl studied him. "Are you Robert?"

"Yeah," he answered.

She lost most of the suspicion and opened the door wider. "Oh. Come on in. I'm Vanessa, one of her suitemates. Roxie's in her room over there."

Robert nodded a thank you at her and walked to the closed door. Clearing his throat, he called, "Hey, goofball, you in there?"

A thump, footsteps, and then the door flew open, Roxie framed in it. She stood there for a moment, staring at him, then grinned and threw herself at him. "Robert!" she yelled as he engulfed her in a huge embrace. "You're here! I didn't expect you for another day or two!"

Robert picked her up and twirled her around. "Well, I couldn't wait to see you! And to meet your friends. And see your school. And all that other stuff." He grinned at her stupidly. She hugged him once more, squealing, and then wiggled out of his embrace. He let her go and flopped onto a couch. Both young women joined him. "So how's it going?"

Roxie sat next to him. "It's going great so far. You know my roomie, Ari, we're getting along still. Classes are going OK, they're kind of boring. The professors seem fair and kind of nice. At least they aren't professors who torture their students. My friends are nice, too."

Vanessa bounced a little, her face reflecting sly curiosity. "So where are you from, Robert?"

He turned to her. "I'm from Maryland, like Roxie. I work as a photographer and a journalist, sometimes. I mostly do research for a private foundation." He chuckled. "As long as I make my deadlines and don't do anything illegal, they don't care what I do or where I go."

"Are you staying at a hotel?" Roxie asked.

"Yeah, it's just down the road. I'll give you the info before I leave."

Vanessa caught his attention again. "How long will you be here?"

Robert stretched out his legs, relaxing. "Probably a while. I have some time to kill before my next deadline is due, and some money to spare. I won't mind being here with you ladies for a while."

Vanessa giggled. "Then I guess I should clean my room up a little, if you're going to be here a while." She sauntered into her room and closed the door.

Roxie rolled her eyes and glanced at Robert, who was struggling to hold in laughter. "Yes, she's always like that. She's a big flirt." Robert sighed theatrically, making Roxie chuckle. "The other two should be here soon, I don't know where they are. Their class ended fifteen minutes ago."

As if they heard her, Ariene and Sita walked through the door, laughing at some joke. They both paused when they saw Robert sitting on the couch. Ariene threw her book bag into a chair and broke into a smile, holding her arms out for a hug. Robert rose from his comfortable seat and hugged her tight. "Ari! You look so different! Have you been . . ."

She snorted and leaned back to slap him on the shoulder. "No! You know I stay as natural as possible." Ari turned and waved a hand toward Sita. "And this is Sita, Vanessa's roommate. You can talk in front of her, she knows about us."

Robert raised an eyebrow. "She knows? You do remember what I said about secrecy, don't you?"

Ariene glared at him and crossed her arms, trying to stare him down and failing. She chose sarcasm instead. "No, we're going to tell the world. Of course we remember! But she's . . ."

Roxie stood up quickly, cutting her off. "Ari! Vanessa's still here!" Rox walked to her room and opened the door. "In here." They followed her in and she shut the door behind them. Relaxing, they chose seats around the room or on the beds.

Turning back to Robert, Ariene continued her previous thought. "She has power, too. And wings! They're really cool!"

"Oh, really?" said Robert. "And just what can you do, Sita?"

Sita jumped down from her perch on the bed, smirking. She held out her hands, allowing them to glow a soft purple. She allowed her shield on the door to be seen. Robert looked to the door, noting that the other two girls ignored it. Sita understood his glance. "If we're doing magic in here, I always put a shield on the door and the walls. Since we're just talking, there's only a shield on the door. If we were practicing, the entire room would be covered in a containing, muting shield. Plus the ward stones they've already got, just in case."

Robert nodded in approval, a silent signal that she could drop her magic for now. "And your wings?" he asked.

"They're part of me—they actually grow out of my shoulders. So my bone and muscle structure is somewhat different. Can you imagine what it was like going to the doctor as a kid?" She chuckled. "I couldn't hide them until I started figuring out my powers. I can hide them now, making them shrink inside my skin—I'm not going to try and explain it, I'm not sure I could." Shrug. "But give me a second, I need to slice my shirt in the back to make room."

She turned around and moved her hair aside so he could watch as she split her shirt with her power. "If I know beforehand that I'm going to be taking them out, I wear a long black robe that's already split—makes it easier on me. If I don't, though, I have to do this." The splits were done and her wings began to show. She was silent as they continued growing, looking over her shoulder at Robert until her left wing hid him from view.

Robert gawked in amazement. *I've never seen anything like this! And I've seen quite a bit!* He set his chin in his hands. *Knight will definitely be interested in this. Maybe I can get her to let me take a picture.* He watched as the wings finally stopped growing and Sita flapped them in slow motions.

He wanted to reach out and touch those glossy white feathers. They shone in the bright sunlight coming through the open windows, making him squint. As large as Sita herself, they looked as soft as goose down but deadly as a knife. He didn't miss the fact that those powerful wings could easily blow a grown man over, and one hit would wind him, at the least, if not break a rib or two. Mostly, though, he just wanted to feel those beautiful feathers . . .

Roxie broke him from his trance. "See? Told you. She has wings."

Someone knocked on their door. "Roxie? Robert? Are you in there?" called Vanessa. Sita hid her wings in a rush, a hiss of pain escaping her as Vanessa knocked again. She turned her back to the nearest wall to hide the slits. Sita checked to make sure everyone was ready before dropping the shields and nodding to Roxie. Roxie rose and opened the door, making it out of the way before Vanessa floated in, wearing something red and silky that she hadn't been wearing a few minutes earlier.

She smiled at Robert and sat down next to him. His lips curled into the semblance of a wooden smile, and he began inching away from where her hand was trying to touch his. Roxie, Ari, and Sita tried in vain to hide their smiles and laughter. Vanessa batted her eyelashes at Rob, who was trying to think of a nice way to refuse her.

Ariene took pity on him and stepped in. "Vanessa, why are you wearing that shirt? That red makes you look like a washed-out hooker."

Sita and Roxie snorted, just managing to hide their grins of glee. Vanessa whipped around, staring wide-eyed at Ariene. "What do you mean? This looks good on me!"

Ariene eyed her up and down, then shook her head. "No, dear, it definitely makes you look like a pale, desperate hooker. Bright red is not your color."

Vanessa stood up in a flash, trying to make it look as if she were unconcerned, and left the room as fast as she could. The others erupted in laughter once the door was closed and the shields replaced. Ariene was almost rolling on the floor in absolute, slightly-malicious glee. Sita doubled over, hanging onto a bedpost to keep herself upright.

Robert could only sit there and grin, delighting in watching them laugh. *I've missed this*, he thought.

Once they calmed down enough to talk coherently, the young women reclaimed their seats. Roxie wiped her eyes on her blanket, turning back to Robert. "So we know that Sita has powers. We think there may be two more people who have powers, but we waited for you to test them before we talk to them about this."

He nodded. "And these two would be . . . ?"

"Darci . . . and, believe it or not, Vanessa," answered Ariene.

"Vanessa?" he asked with a raised brow. "You really think *she's* got power? Somehow I doubt it, but I'll test her anyway."

Roxie sighed. "Thank you. And I have to tell you, there's one of them that kind of bothers us. All three of us have picked up on it by now." Ariene and Sita nodded in wordless agreement. "I noticed that Darci has power, but there seems to be a lot of darkness around her. She makes me really scared. And kind of depressed. As if my soul had died a little and would never see the light again." She wrapped her arms around her shoulders and shivered. "She scares me," she repeated.

Robert moved beside her to wrap his arms around her shoulders, trying to warm the chill he could see she felt. "It's all right, Rox, I'll check it out. If she has dangerous powers and doesn't know it, I'll be able to tell. If she's using her powers for dangerous or evil ends, I'll know that, too." He looked to Ariene and Sita. "I'll meet them over the next few days and observe. I'll know if they have powers or not." He regarded them. "What you're saying about Darci makes me think she might have strong, but dark, powers. You might not want to bring her into your group if that's the case."

"We understand," Roxie said.

"Good." He rubbed his hands and looked at them all with a silly smile on his face. "Now, what is there to do around here that's fun?"

∞

Darci massaged her temples, hoping the headache would go away soon. She sighed. *Not much for it, I guess. I have to practice, and the headaches are part of that right now.* She allowed herself a brief moment of self-pity, then raised her hands for another try. She closed her eyes and let her magic travel to her hands, where it pooled in her palms. It felt like there were a hundred needles pricking her skin, over and over again. She shivered from the sensation of it.

Taking a deep breath, Darci willed her power to flow from her fingers and fix the cracks in the mirror. It was broken because a stray branch of her power had gotten away from her earlier and cracked it, and now she was trying to repair the damage. But it wasn't working. In fact, if anything, the cracks deepened the more she tried to repair them. She asked her power to flow from her hands and fix the mirror, but it was as if some kind of barrier blocked her palms. Her power would go as far as her skin, but once it got there it dammed up and refused to move forward.

She grimaced and stopped the flow of magic. *My power was working fine when I broke the mirror by accident. Why won't it work now?* Setting the mirror down on her desk, Darci stood and stretched, dissipating her power back into the deep well inside of her. Then she grabbed her pillow and threw it across the room, where it landed on the floor with a soft thud. Darci cursed and began to pace back and forth, running her fingers through her short hair, trying to puzzle out the problem.

Feeling some of the effects of using her power, Darci sank into the nearest chair and massaged her temples once more. *It's no use. I just can't do it.* She looked at the mirror and grimaced. *So much for Mom's birthday present. Now I have to buy something else.*

She looked out her window, enjoying the feel of the sun's warmth on her face. *I wish Joshua was here. I miss him.* She wrapped her arms around herself at the thought of her boyfriend back home. Darci began to drift off into a daydream when there was a knock on her door. "Darci?" someone called.

"Coming! One minute!" she called back, hiding the broken mirror in a desk drawer and checking her appearance in the sink mirror. She walked to the door and opened it wide, revealing a man she didn't know and Roxanne. "Hi, Roxie." Darci said in a subdued voice.

Roxanne smiled at her. "Darci, this is my friend Rob. I'm introducing him to all my friends. Rob, this is Darci."

Robert held his hand out to the girl. "Hi, Darci. Nice to meet you." Darci took his hand and shook it. His eyes narrowed a bit when his palm touched hers. "So where are you from, Darci?"

She tucked her short hair behind her left ear. "I'm from Ohio. You?"

"Maryland, same as Roxie."

"Oh, right. How long will you be down here then?"

"Probably a week or so. Maybe longer, I'm really not sure." He shifted his weight. "What are you majoring in?"

Darci leaned against the door. "Photography. But I'm thinking about switching to graphic design." She glanced back into her room. "Sorry, would you like to come in?"

Roxie and Robert looked at each other, then took Darci's invitation and walked in, each sitting in a spare chair. Darci left the door and jumped up onto her bed, the only available perch left to her. "You should join us for movie night, Robert. We always have a lot of fun. It's on Friday this week. Do you like mystery movies? I think this week's pick is a mystery."

He smiled, though Roxie noticed he looked a little pale. "I might come over, it sounds like fun. Not really into mystery movies though. Are you?"

"Not really. My boyfriend, Josh, is really picky about movies, so I usually end up watching whatever he wants to watch. I'm not a big fan of mysteries, either."

Roxie pointed to a picture of Darci and a plain young man on the desk. "Is that you and Josh?" The Darci of the picture sported a huge grin, and the happy light in her eyes was clear even in the photo.

"Yep." Darci smiled, the expression softening the lines of her face, as she reached out to touch a finger to the frame. "That's us on our one-year anniversary, last January. He's back home right now. He has a job at my uncle's carpentry shop, but he wants to go to school next year."

The bells outside rang for three o'clock. Darci jumped down from the bed in a rush, grabbing her bag and glancing at the clock. "Sorry, but I've got to get to class! It doesn't make a great impression if you're late in the first few weeks!" Roxie and Robert filed ahead of her as she grabbed her keys and locked the door after them.

Robert turned to Darci. "Well, Darci, it was nice meeting you. I hope I'll see you again while I'm here."

Darci smiled at him and shook his hand. "Thanks, Rob, you too." She waved. "I'll see you guys later." And she ran off down the hall.

Roxie led the way back to the suite, locking the door behind Robert. Making sure Vanessa wasn't in the room, Roxie sank into a chair with relief. Robert did the same. After a minute, Roxie looked to Rob. "So, she has power, right?"

Robert sat up, lacing his fingers under his chin and resting on them, thinking. "I knew when I walked in the room that she has power. I could feel it in the walls, the chairs, everything in the room screamed of magic." He sighed. "But not good magic. And she has a lot of it, too. She unnerves me. You and Ari were right; she has a lot of power, and its dark, twisted." His eyes were sad. "She's trying to fight the darkness, I can tell that much."

"What do you mean?" Roxie asked.

He hesitated. Then he leaned forward, palms pressed together in front of him. "Some mages have magic that can only be used to destroy. They can't create, they can't heal, and almost anything they touch is broken. If they don't know this already, they think something is wrong with them, and they try to make their magic do what it can't. They think that with practice, the magic will come more easily." He frowned. "But it would only become 'unblocked' when the mage destroys something. It just won't work for anything else." Rob sighed and bowed his head. "A lot of the mages who had this kind of power in the past didn't understand, or fought the power so much that they ended up destroying themselves. They still tried to do good things."

Roxie's eyes reflected his sadness. "So we can't help her, then. We can't change the nature of magic. Eventually she'll leave us."

Robert leaned back into the cushions and closed his eyes. "Afraid so. I don't know of any way to change the inherent nature of power. She'll eventually go to the darkness, and there is no real way to stop it." His hands dropped useless into his lap. "The only way to try and ensure safety is to befriend her and be as genuinely kind to her as possible. Be a friend to her as much as you can, so that when she does turn from the light, she won't forget what it was like to have true friends, to be loved. Maybe then she'll spare you when nothing else would."

She thought for a minute, then flashed him a half-hearted grin. "You sure you aren't a seer, Rob? That sounded pretty prophetic to me."

He grimaced. "I'm sure. That's just common sense."

The door opened to admit Ari and Sita. The two of them dropped their school bags and flopped onto the sofa with Roxie and Robert. "So, what's goin' on?" asked Ariene.

"Oh, not much," replied Roxie. "Just trying to figure out how to keep a future diabolical betrayer from being completely evil, how to protect ourselves, and how to figure out the rest of our little group."

Sita lounged on the sofa and grinned. "It's going to be a good year."

Chapter Five
Families and Discoveries

Professor Alan smiled at his students, meeting the eyes of the fifty or so people crowded into the small hall. "I know they're predicting snow, people, but I've lived in these mountains for forty years; it won't happen. It's still early September, that system won't come anywhere near us, and if it does, it will drop a couple inches of rain, not snow. So unless you have a broken leg or are bleeding to death and have to be rushed to the hospital, don't miss my next class and try to cite the storm as an excuse." The students laughed. "I'll see everyone in two days."

He watched while they all grabbed their bags and began to stampede for the door. Professor Alan kept an eye on a group of three young women, two of them tall and one of them shorter. He was curious about those three, and the friends he sometimes saw them with outside of class. They were different from his other students—very secretive, clinging to each other as if their lives depended on it. The group intrigued him, and especially those three. The two tall girls were blonds, with one having waist-length hair, and the third was a shapely, animated little brunette.

The trio climbed the stairs as he watched, chatting with each other. Once they had walked through the lecture hall doors, he went back to watching his other students, waving and smiling at a few who looked up at him in farewell. When the last student left, he gathered his books and papers and walked out the door behind the dry-erase board. He went down the hallway, into an adjacent building, down the stairs into the chill basement, and into a small room hidden from common view.

Someone waited for him there, another professor, but female. She turned toward him as he walked in. Dark hair matched her dark eyes, though she was beginning to gray at the temples. She held out her hands to him and smiled. Her dangerous smile raised the hairs on Professor Alan's neck. "Ray. Glad you could make it," she said in her rich voice.

Professor Ray Alan took her hands in his and kissed them, a predatory grin flashing back at her. "Professor Sandara Cane. How good of you to meet me here."

She sat down in a chair across the small room, arranging her elegant dress to the best advantage. Professor Alan sighed to himself. She may be wicked, heartless, and entirely too beautiful for any man's good, but she was powerful and a genius, and his faction needed her on their side. He tried not to let his eyes roam over her figure, which was still fine despite her age, instead fixing on her eyes as he sat in his own chair. "You know why I asked you here, yes?"

Sandara nodded. "I do, Professor."

"Well, Imbri Mors needs your assistance. We realize that you have been seeking admission to our fellowship for some time now." His eyes sparkled in the dim light, though otherwise he showed no sign of his excitement. "If you help us, we will admit you at the end of this year, on the longest night. You will be bound to us for all time; you will be unable to leave us, not even when you die—your soul will be ours as well, so make your choice with care. Once bound, you are bound for eternity. Try to leave, and the bond you formed with us will kill you."

Sandara leaned back in her chair, studying her nails, which were painted a bright red. "I confess to having a question."

Alan hid his annoyance. "Which is?"

"Why are you doing this?"

He frowned. "Doing what?"

"Leading Imbri Mors." One eyebrow quirked upward. Sandara saw it and continued. "You are a successful man, a respected man, and yet you are willing to give it all up without any hesitation. That makes me wonder why. It makes me wonder what Imbri is offering you that you do not already have."

Alan's lips curved into a tiny, wolfish smile. "Ah, I see. You want to know my motives for this venture." She nodded. "I am a man of means, it's true. I don't lack for wealth or comforts." The professor leaned forward in his chair and steepled his hands in front of his face. A curious gleam came to his eyes. "The world is full of people unfit to live in it. Stupid people, ignorant people, violent people. They overrun the world and infect all they touch with their ineptitude. Those kinds of people are unfit to live and prosper, and especially unfit to reproduce." His lip curled. "I have a means of ridding all worlds of such heathens. And in addition, when I have cleansed Earth of all who are unfit to live in it, I intend to raise myself up farther than ever before. I intend to make myself not only rich, but powerful." Alan's fingers found their way to an amulet which hung around his neck. Two diamonds vertically bracketed a small sapphire set in gold and swung on a gold chain.

His fingers played gently with the amulet, stroking the small round stones and circular gold setting. His gazed unfocused, and his voice lowered to almost a whisper. "I intend to have everything I have ever wanted. I will have them back." Of a sudden, Alan remembered he spoke to a dangerous woman, and refocused on his impromptu speech. A grin twisted his lips. "Imbri Mors is the way to fulfilling those desires."

Sandara closed her eyes and smiled. "So what is this mission you have for me?" She looked up through her lashes, her nails looking more like claws as she stared at him.

Ray dropped his hands to the armrests. "There is a group of young women on this campus. They are very close-knit and secretive. I have noticed great power around all of them, but two in particular. One of them seems to have very dark power, but she's denying it. The other powerful one I sense is devoted to the lighter side; I don't think she can be corrupted, but we have to try. Having the darker one's power will be a great asset; having them both will open phenomenal possibilities to Imbri Mors."

"And," her brow quirked, "I ask again, what is it that you require of me, Professor?"

His teeth flashed in the light as he grinned like a cat about to eat a fat mouse. "I want you to bring the dark one to us. Subvert her will to ours, make her one of us. Do the same to the other if you can, but I don't hold much hope for her." He shivered in horror and disgust. "She seems too clean and pure for corruption. But try it anyway; if you fail with this clean one, I will not hold you responsible, I assure you." His hands folded under his chin as he thought. "Also, try to cause as much discord in the little group as you can; the more trouble you can sow among them, the better for us all."

Sandara stood, brushing the folds of her skirt smooth. Her eyes shone with malicious anticipation. "I will do as you command," her curtsy was flawless and absolutely sensuous, making the professor shiver inside, "Master."

Ray nodded at her as she walked out, watching her leave from the corner of his eye. He waited until she left the hallway to unfold his hands and rise from the chair. "Very good, my dear." He chuckled as he closed the door behind him.

∞

"I can't believe I've been here more than a week!" said Sita, plopping down on the couch. Roxie joined her a moment later, soda in hand. "Where are the others? It's a Saturday, they should be around somewhere."

"Hmm. Ari is hanging out with her friend Jack, Vanessa is shopping with Sarah, Darci is somewhere, and Estelle and Skylar are out doing some art thing, and Robert went out to do some research," Roxie replied. "I think they're all supposed to be back here later tonight for a movie night again." She handed Sita a bottle of soda.

She took it and broke open the seal, gulping the dark liquid. "I know soda's bad, but it just tastes so good." Roxie laughed. "Ooh, we're going to have to start getting ready for the dance at the end of next month. Are you going?"

"Maybe, I'm not sure yet. Outfits and dates and stuff, it's so complicated," Roxie said. "And besides, Rob's still here, and I think that he'll *still* be here for Halloween. I don't want to leave him all alone while we go out and party that night."

Sita eyed her with a sly look. "Why don't you ask Rob to the dance?" she suggested.

Roxie's eyes were huge when she looked over at Sita. "Eww, that's gross! No way would I ever do that!" she said, disgusted.

"Why not?"

"Rob and I are just friends."

"Really?"

"Really," Roxie replied. "He's like a big brother to me, but better than my actual brothers. He's practically family. And I know he feels the same about me."

Sita's grin didn't leave her face. "OK, OK, if you say so. Speaking of family, are your parents coming down for parent's weekend next week?" she asked.

Rox's head bobbed in affirmation. "Yep. They figured they'd come down with my brothers since they didn't come down with me when I moved in. They'll be here all three days." She leaned her head back on the couch's armrest. "Is your family coming?"

"Nah. My sister Marie didn't want to come down again so soon—it's a long drive," Sita said. "I wish she would, though. I kind of miss her." She smirked. "Even if she is the annoying little sister."

Rox shook her head, smiling. "I miss my brothers. I have no one to tease and pick on now!" Her fingers played gently with her hair, knotting it accidentally. "I'm not so excited to see my parents, though. I mean, most of why we come to college is to get away from our parents, right? Not keep running back to them."

Sita half-grinned and laughed. "Yeah, I kind of know the feeling."

Rox looked at her friend from the corner of her eye. She hesitated, unsure if what she would ask was too intrusive, but decided to take the chance. "Sita, where're your parents? I remember what you said, on the night we found out about each other, that you have no parents. I mean, if it's something sensitive, you don't have to tell me, but I was curious . . ."

Sita's gentle hand rested on Roxie's, halting her babble. "Rox, it's OK." She sat up, but her face was closed and sad. "It's fine that you ask, but it's not really something I want to talk about. Not yet."

Roxie touched Sita's wrist. Sita shook her head, a half-smile in place. "It's OK, Rox. It's gotten better, and my sister and I are doing fine now, but it's still kind of a raw wound, you know?"

The smile on her face convinced Roxie that it was true. Rox averted her eyes. "I couldn't imagine growing up without my parents. I mean, I know my dad's a major jerk, but at least he's there." Her shrug was half-hearted. "My dad and I don't really get along. He's always tried to control what I chose for my career, and I hate that."

"One of the reasons why you're not looking forward to parent's weekend?" asked Sita.

"Yep. That's going to be oh-so-much fun," Roxie replied, her voice laced with sarcasm. "Next weekend is going to be interesting."

Sita laughed. "If you say so."

∞

A week later, Roxie opened the door of the suite to see her parents and siblings standing there. She squealed in surprise and hugged them all. Her brothers squirmed when she hugged them, still in the stage where they thought girls had cooties. Roxie grinned at her mother, who held her daughter tight. "I've missed you, Roxie, dear," her mother said in her ear. Rox hugged her mother tighter.

Mr. Dalton hugged his eldest child after she extricated herself from Mrs. Dalton's embrace and turned to greet him. "Roxanne," he said, his simple greeting as stiff as his embrace.

Roxie's bright smile faltered. She turned away from her family to lead them into the suite. "Ari! Sita! Vanessa! Rob!" she called as she closed the door behind her younger brothers and pushed them toward the chairs. Her friends came out of their rooms, surprised at being called. Rox indicated her family. "Guys, these're my mom, my dad, my brother Michael, and my other brother, Tony." She pointed to each of them in turn. "Family, this is Sita," Sita waved, "Ariene, and Vanessa." The other two girls nodded their heads. "And you already know Rob." Robert waved and smiled a hello, eliciting answering mischievous grins on her brothers' faces. Roxie shrugged her shoulders, her eyes darting around the suite. "And this is our suite. It's small, but we like it."

Mrs. Dalton ran a hand through Roxie's hair. "It looks homey, dear. You've done a great job with making it comfortable, all of you." The two boys looked bored. They both propped their heads up with their arms, while Mr. Dalton kept his eyes aimed at the floor.

After a minute of uncomfortable silence, Roxie spoke up again. "Well, guys, should we go get some lunch? We can go to the cafeteria. The food isn't so bad, for cafeteria food."

Her parents looked at each other. Mr. Dalton shrugged. Mrs. Dalton answered for them all. "Sure, dear, that sounds fine. What do they usually have?" she asked. Roxanne told her while she led her family and friends down the stairs and into the bustling cafeteria, filled to the brim with students and families. They found an empty table and lay claim to it, gathering their food and choosing seats. Robert attempted to make conversation, but most of their meal was strained and tense, despite his best efforts.

When everyone finished eating, they left the cafeteria and Mr. Dalton pulled Roxie aside. "Go on back to the stairs. We'll be back in a minute," he said to the others. Mrs. Dalton looked concerned, and shot her husband a warning glance. Roxie and her father left the hall, walking outside in the cool early October air.

Mr. Dalton walked beside his daughter, his heels scuffing the sidewalk. "How's the job hunt going? You know you need to find at least a part-time job."

Roxie counted to five before speaking. "I know, Dad. I'm looking. There's not much available right now."

He continued, his voice hard. "Roxanne, what are you ever going to do with this art thing? You're never going to make something of yourself doing this, this doodling and playing around on a computer all day." He ran his hand over his mustache, scowling. "You're going to be a poor, deadbeat artist on our hands long after you should've left home and established a good career."

Roxie watched the sidewalk under her feet as they paced, hearing all the usual arguments and rants that she had heard before.

"What if you never get a good job? What marketable skills will you have when this falls through?" he barked.

She continued to walk, letting her father's cold, angry words float through her skull, remembering all the harsh words over the years.

"Artists never have any money, and are never happy. They never make anything of their lives, and only end up as a disappointment to their parents, their families, and to society . . ."

Roxie snapped. "What about da Vinci? Michelangelo? Van Gogh? Were they nothing, a disappointment to everyone?" she demanded, finally having had enough of her father's words. "If I am a disappointment to you, *father*, then I'm sorry, but I'm going to do what I love, and I'm going to make something of myself whether you like my career or not."

Her father's jaw slackened and his eyes bugged out of his head. He stood still in the middle of the path, listening to his daughter refute everything he said. He opened and closed his mouth, but no words came out. Roxanne never talked to him like this. He held out his hands, making shooing motions to get her to calm down. "Roxanne, I just think this art idea is nonsense. Why don't you go into business? It's profitable, satisfying, respectable work. And you'll always be in demand."

"No!" Roxie wiped at her face, aware of the hot tears trickling down her cheeks. "I'm not going to be *you*, Dad. I'm going to find a career that makes me happy." Her voice cracked. *Please, for once, understand what I'm trying to say.* "I can't be the person you want me to be, because I'm *not* that person. I never have been. And as long as you expect me to be someone I'm not, you'll never like me." She flared her hands at her sides. "I can't change that, Dad. All I can do is be me. That's all I can offer, so that will have to be enough." She turned around and ran back to the building.

Mr. Dalton watched his daughter run away from him, unable to do or say anything to make her stay.

Later that night, Roxanne kissed her mother and brothers good-bye before they went back home to Maryland in the morning. Mr. Dalton had decided to leave earlier than planned rather than stay the whole weekend. When her father tried to hug her, or even explain anything, she turned away with a quick good-bye to run into the suite, where she closed the door behind her. Roxie didn't see the death-glare her mother gave Mr. Dalton when the door closed, or how her brothers turned their backs on their father and stalked away to the car.

Roxie leaned on the door, nearly in tears. Sita came to her, concern etched into her face. Their suitemates stayed away, thinking Roxie would want the privacy. Robert had needed to leave early for more research. "Rox?" she touched her friend's arm. "You OK?" Roxie shook her head. Letting go of the barriers in her mind, she allowed the tears to finally break free, streaming down her ashen face. Sita gathered Rox in her arms and led her friend to her room, where they sat until Roxie cried herself out.

The next morning, Roxie stalked out of her room and gave her suitemates glares that warned them all away for the morning. Each of them left Roxie alone. They edged around her on the couch until they could make a quiet break for the door. Samantha came by the room looking for Estelle around noon, but Roxie sent her away.

When Ari returned from doing homework in the park, Roxie still sat on the couch, her arms wrapped around her folded knees. Ariene dropped her bookbag by the door and sat down next to the silent girl. "Rox?" Ari asked. "Rox, I know it was a bad Friday, but you can't sit here and stew over it. You need a distraction."

Roxanne shifted slightly. "I know." She turned to her friend and gave her a tight smile. "Why do you think I want to get out of here? I'm going for a walk. You can come along or let me get lost all by myself."

Ari chuckled. "I'll get lost with you. Where are we going?"

Roxie gave her an exasperated look. "Ari, I think you're missing the point . . ."

Ari just laughed. "We could go for a walk around town. You wanted to check out that old church on Westpointe, we could walk over there and see if there's any good photography to be had."

But Roxie shook her head, reddish-brown hair flying. "I don't want buildings, I want nature. Buildings are . . . I just don't want to be inside right now, OK? Let's get outside." She sprang to her feet and back to her room to grab her camera and a jacket, then joined Ari at the door.

On the way out, they bumped into Sita as she was about to open the door. Surprised, she jumped back into the hall. "Hey guys, what's up?"

Without a word, Ari and Roxie both grabbed Sita's arms and hauled her along with them. Sita protested, but as they neared the stairs she relented and let them lead her down. Soon they were free of the campus buildings and walking toward the wood nearby. Ari and Sita trailed after Roxie. She heard them crashing through the woods behind her.

No one really came into the woods here. Underbrush threatened to tangle feet and clothes with almost every step. There were no "cool" places to hang out in the woods on this side of the school, so most students avoided the tree line. The woods were quieter, calmer, and more relaxed than the world beyond the trees. Roxie felt her shoulders relax and her tension ease as she walked further into the trees.

After a short while, she stopped. Ari and Sita stopped behind her, their breath coming a little quicker than normal as they'd fought to keep up. Birds chirped in the trees, but stayed away from the intruders. Squirrels had frozen or scampered off as the trio approached, and now Roxie wanted one or two of them to come back. "Just stand there and be quiet for a few minutes," she told her friends. "I want a squirrel or a bird to come back."

"Then just call one," Ari grumbled. "It's not like it's hard for you."

Roxie mock-glared at Ari over her shoulder before she closed her eyes and sent out the call. No animals answered her right away, but she wasn't really surprised. Instead, she kept her eyes closed and just listened. A slight breeze tumbled through the trees. The leaves whispered against each other as the branches swayed. Birds chirped and sang, and some of the songs sounded closer. Squirrels and rabbits rustled in the underbrush and the plants in their search for food. A family of chipmunks chattered at the squirrels when the squirrels threatened to steal their food. Roxie almost laughed. The smell of green permeated everything. It was the smell she always associated with woodland—bark and loam and the barest hint of water or rain.

At last, she felt a tug on her jean hem. Roxie looked down. A pair of squirrels blinked up at her, their tails fluffed out in curiosity. Rox giggled. "Hi there." She spoke to the squirrels in their high-pitched chitter, and they answered back. Soon one squirrel scampered off, but the other squirrel climbed up Roxie's jeans and shirt to sit on her shoulder. One paw grasped her shirt collar while the other tugged on her ear for balance. Roxie turned slowly to face her friends, careful not to unbalance her new squirrel friend. "Come on," she said to Sita and Ari. "He says he knows a neat place to rest. It's nice and cool, and pretty. It sounds like a cave."

"A cave? Here?" Sita cocked an eyebrow. "Are you sure? I didn't think there were many caves in the mountains here, and none close by."

Roxie shrugged the shoulder not serving as a squirrel perch. "I guess there's at least one. He says he can lead us there and back. Let's get moving so we can get back before dinner."

So the two humans followed Roxie and her furry guide deeper into the woods. The college and its town actually sat within the mountains, and the college had been built on top of a hill that was almost a mountain. It wasn't inconceivable to the trio that a cave could really be nearby, since the school was in the mountains. It would be a pleasant surprise to find the cave. Roxie ambled on at an easy pace, her friends following behind.

The squirrel squeaked in Roxie's ear. He sometimes tugged on her shirt or her ear when he wanted her to turn left or right, even though he told her in his language what to do as well. But it made her smile, so she let him keep doing it. He kept up a running commentary on the woods they passed through. A family of squirrels they passed were his cousins, and he squeaked a greeting to them. He made some nasty comments about the chipmunks—Roxie laughed and couldn't repeat what he'd said when Ari asked what was so funny. The squirrel didn't much like birds, and would chitter in anger or fear when a bird flew overhead. He did, however, like the rabbits.

An hour of walking brought them to one side of the mountain. The walk had been mostly downhill. "It's going to be a pain to walk back up," she said to her friends.

The squirrel scolded her.

Roxie chuckled and shook her head. "I'm not fat among my kind, you know."

The squirrel paused, then agreed. He said he'd been fed by humans much larger than she. Then he tugged on her ear and told her to go left.

"Are we almost there?" Ari shouted from behind.

Roxie realized she had gotten too far ahead, so she paused and waited for them to catch up. The trees had thinned out a little here, and there was a bit of flatter surface that looked like an outcropping of rock ahead. Roxie pointed. "That way. We're almost there." Even the breeze had changed, becoming stronger and crisper.

Carefully, Roxie stepped over more and more rocks as she made her way to the outcropping. There she could see a wide ledge to the left, and as she approached, she saw the shadow of a cave's mouth. "It's a cave! It really is a cave!" she shouted back to her friends.

Ari and Sita picked up their pace, but followed Roxie's example and stepped over the rocks carefully. When they joined her, they saw what she now gazed at.

A small, shallow cave tucked into the earth gaped at them, its shadowed entrance partly hidden by pine trees. The walls of the cave glittered faintly in the afternoon sunlight. Roxie approached with caution, her footsteps careful on the rocky ledge. She was far enough away from the edge that falling wasn't much of a concern, but she didn't want an animal to come out of the cave suddenly and scare her toward the edge. Her magic detected no animals inside, however, so she continued toward the mouth.

She peeked into the darkness. The cave truly was shallow—she could see the back about thirty feet away, the back wall just barely lit by the sun's rays. Her magical sense had been right—no animals, not even bats, inhabited the cave at the moment. Roxie carefully sat on the ground and let the squirrel down from her shoulder. He scampered off to the pine tree on the left in search of food. Rox saw her friends eye his passage with unease. "Don't worry. He'll come back. He promised."

Ari sat next to Rox, but Sita wandered over to the walls. She ran a hand over the uneven rock. "I think there's raw quartz in the walls." She squinted and peered closer. "That's why they're shiny. Little pieces of quartz are in the rock."

Roxie watched as Sita examined the walls, but soon lost interest and looked out over the ledge.

Beyond the cave lay the forest, like an ocean of trees. The wind caused waves as the trees swayed and undulated over the ground. Orange and yellow sunlight nearly blinded them as the sun moved toward the horizon, but Roxie didn't mind. She even found it relaxing to close her eyes and let the sun warm her face and the breeze tousle her hair.

Sita sat on Roxie's other side, braced on her arms behind her. "Feel better, Rox?"

The tension eased from Roxie's shoulders and back. She hadn't even realized she had been so tense. As the squirrel returned and the sun traveled on, Roxie found herself smiling, just a little bit, and found that her heart ached less and less.

"Yeah. Much better."

∞

Two days later, Sita waved a letter in the air. "I got a letter!" she cried, startling Roxie and Ari from their homework.

Ari put down her pen and closed the textbook she had been squinting at. "Who's it from?"

"My sister." Sita plopped down into the spare chair, tearing open the envelope. "I love getting mail."

Roxie twisted around in her own chair, curious. "Your sister sends letters? Why doesn't she just send e-mail like other normal people?"

The letter was out now, and looked to be very long. Sita glanced up before beginning to read it. "Well, Rox, you should know by now that my sister and I are not normal." She smiled. "Sometimes it's nicer to get a letter in the mail than an e-mail."

She lapsed into silence while Ariene and Roxie waited for her to finish it. Unable to wait any more, Roxie interrupted. "So what does she say?"

"She says that her teachers suck, her job at the mall is horrible, and she can't wait to see me for Thanksgiving. In fact, she's practically begging me to come home early!" Sita laughed. "Oh, and she broke up with her boyfriend. But that's really not a shock. She hasn't been able to keep a guy for more than three months, and the latest guy was a loser, so I didn't really think he'd be around very long."

Roxie snorted in laughter. "Wow, Si, that's very sisterly. You didn't tell her that, did you?"

"No!" Sita said. "Of course not. But I'm glad she didn't say she was in love with this one, because I couldn't stand him. I barely put up with him over the summer." She shrugged. "But then, I'm not the one kissing him, so I guess I don't really have to put up with him, do I?" The three of them laughed.

"Can your sister do any magic? She's doesn't have wings, too, does she?" asked Ariene as she reclined in the desk chair and twirled a pen in one hand.

Sita shook her head. "Nope, no wings and no magic. She used to ask Mom why we were so different, and Mom would tell her that she couldn't do what I could do because she was meant to do other things. I don't think Marie really understood—she was only like, five or six, I think."

"Aw, that's cute!" said Roxie. "I wish my brothers were as cute as your sister. They'd be easier to handle." They all chuckled. "But seriously, it would be cool if you both could do magic, I think. Think of all the trouble you two could get into together."

Sita's eyes widened in alarm. "No! We'd wind up in jail or something!"

Ariene laughed. "But isn't that where you belong?" A pillow soared from Sita's hands and smacked Ari in the face with a thump and a muffled squeal. Roxie giggled as Ariene pushed the pillow away. "Well, if you're going to resort to that, I'm just not gonna talk to you anymore!" Ari said in a huff as she turned around to her desk.

"Humph. That's fine, sourpuss," teased Roxie. She returned to Sita. "What does your sister want to do? Is she going to college?"

Sita rolled her eyes in exasperation. "She's not sure. I don't think she wants to go past high school, but she doesn't really know what she wants to do. She's going to come down here for a visit sometime, I think. Our aunt and uncle are acting as her guardians while I'm not there. I'm not technically legal, anyway, so I'm not really qualified to be her 'guardian.'"

Ariene whirled back around to face them. "It's really too bad she doesn't have magic. We could have included her in our secret magic group."

"Well, you never know," Roxie interjected. "Maybe she'll develop them later on." She paused and looked between the two of them. "Can that happen, do you think?"

Shrugs and blank stares all around. "I don't know . . ." Sita said. "We should ask Rob. I mean, I guess anything's possible . . ."

∞

Robert knocked on the old man's blue door, tugging at his shirt. He hated asking the old man for help, but it was necessary. *He has to help. She needs to be evaluated.* He knocked again, shivering in the late September chill. *I should have brought a jacket . . .*

The door swung open and Ka'len Lera stood there, beaming at Robert. "Robert, my boy, come inside. You really should bring a jacket with you everywhere." He stepped aside and Robert hurried into the warmth.

Ka'len closed the door and turned to embrace the younger man. They parted and Ka'len smiled down at him. "I am always glad to see you, Robert. You are such a pleasant fellow." He walked into the living room, easing himself onto the couch. "Now, why don't you tell me what you came here for," he said as he waved Robert into the chair opposite him.

Robert studied the old man. A full thick gray beard hung from his chin, and gray hair fell to his shoulders. Ka'len kept himself impeccably groomed with not a wrinkle on his tunic or trousers. The paleness of the white room only made the man's tanned skin stand out more, though there was a startling lack of corresponding wrinkles a man his age should have. Hazel eyes, deep and knowing, twinkled back at Rob from the strange face.

He sighed and looked down from Ka'len's gaze. It was probable the old man already knew why Rob had come to him, but he would make Rob say it. "Alright, Ka'len, I'm here to ask you to teach a pupil, maybe more than one."

Ka'len smiled, but there was an edge to this one. "Go on."

"Well, my friend Roxie made friends with some . . . interesting . . . girls at school. They all have some kind of magic in them." He leaned forward, resting his arms on his knees, his face intent. "One of them is very powerful, and has a lot of sorceress potential. She needs training." This time Rob looked up into Ka'len's burning eyes. "Ka'len, she's stronger than me. And I'm at light blue! I can't train her, I don't have the experience to train someone like her."

Silence took hold of the living room. Robert shifted in the easy chair. Ka'len merely sat on his couch, thinking and watching Rob.

Finally he spoke. "Is this coming from you, or the man you serve?"

Robert said nothing for a full five heartbeats before he answered. "From me."

Ka'len's face lost its hardened look, allowing Rob to relax. "So you came to me. But there is something you are not telling me, Rob. What is it, your trump card. Tell me, lad."

Robert winced. Of course he couldn't fool the old man. Even Rob, strong in his magic as he was, paled in comparison to Ka'len.

Still he hesitated, unsure of what to tell him. "Ka'len . . . this girl . . . she has wings . . ." he began.

Those powerful hazel eyes widened, and slipped toward a tall brown cabinet set against the far wall. His chin quivered before he regained control. "Wings?" he rasped. "Real wings, growing from her back? You have seen them yourself?"

The young man nodded. "I've seen them. She can use her magic to force them inside her skin, and keep them hidden from everyone." He paused, chewing on his lip. "She's amazing. But I'm afraid of what she could become if she's left untrained." Rob gazed back up at the man.

Ka'len bowed his head, sighing in regret. "Just as I was beginning to enjoy my retirement, too."

Robert grinned. "Ha! You've never enjoyed idleness, my friend. Admit it, you're looking forward to this."

The man half-smiled. "Yes. I have needed some excitement. I will train the girl. Send her here during her next school break."

Rob nodded once in agreement. "I'll send Roxie with her. This girl can be a little shy sometimes. Her name is Sita, by the way. Sita Newbury."

A flash of pain traveled over Ka'len's face at the name. "Sita," he echoed, his voice far away and soft. "Yes, I know that name . . ."

Silence descended again until Robert rose from the chair. "I'm sorry I can't stay longer, Ka'len. But I need to get back to my work." Ka'len stood and embraced the young man again, leading him to the door. "And I'm sorry I pulled you out of your retirement."

Ka'len smiled at him. "Not to worry, my boy. If I know these things, I am needed once more. I do not believe I will regret teaching this young woman."

Rob smirked and stepped out the door. Between one step and the next, he had disappeared in a spark of bright blue light. Ka'len shut the door on an empty yard.

Chapter Six
Halloween

Vanessa walked around the rack of costumes, passing through them and disregarding each. Sita followed her roommate, looking for her own costume. Roxie and Ariene were doing the same on the other side of the small store. "I'm glad we're doing this early," said Vanessa. "Or screaming kids and giggling little teens would be everywhere. They annoy me." She held up a maid costume and put it back, turning her nose up in distaste.

Roxie laughed. "Find anything yet, Vanessa?"

She scoffed. "Are you kidding? I haven't even gotten started."

"You've been through the store once already. Pick something!" called Ari.

Vanessa threw up her hands in frustration. "Well, it's not that easy! I want something that fits me perfectly—something royal and beautiful. I'm going to be a queen!"

Roxie grinned. "You want something perfect for you?" Vanessa turned to look at her. "Well, here's something." She held up a nurse's outfit of questionable modesty, making everyone but Vanessa howl with laughter.

"That's not funny! I am not a whore!"

"You're not? Wow, that's news to me," Sita said with wide, innocent eyes. She avoided Vanessa's slap on the arm. Sita snickered and went back to perusing the costumes. "So what are you going to be, Rox?"

Roxie examined a cat costume. "How about a cat? I always liked kitties. Ari?"

Ariene shook her head. "Who says I'm dressing up?" She winked. "I'm just looking for accessories. But I think I'm going to be some kind of cat too."

Sita held up a medieval dress. "I think I'm going to do a medieval theme."

"Well, I think you should be an angel, it's perfect for you," called Ariene. Sita threw her an amused glance over the racks.

"I found it!" shrieked Vanessa in triumph.

Everyone, including the saleswoman nearby, roared with laughter.

Sita took her costumes into the dressing room, the others waiting for their turn in the three other occupied ones. Roxie called through the door, "So, Sita, you going with anyone to the dance?"

"I don't know. I haven't really found any guys that I'd want to go with. All the guys I know are . . . well, typical college guys. Drink too much, sleep around too much, half of them smoke . . ." she replied.

Vanessa twittered. "We know, we know. But Halloween is a week away, and you can't go to the dance without a date."

Ariene shoved her from behind. "Why can't she? I am. Guys are stupid. I'm going alone, so why can't she?"

"You're not going with Jack?" Sita asked.

"No!" Ari sounded scandalized. "That would be like going out with my brother. Jack and I are just friends."

Sita grimaced. *She really doesn't know he's infatuated with her, then.*

The doors opened on two of the other rooms and Roxie and Ariene took their chance. Vanessa scowled outside and waited for the last room. "Thanks guys, it's going to take me forever to try this on, and I'm going to make you wait for me."

Sita yelled over the door. "Nah, we'll just sneak off one by one while you're in the dressing room. Then you'll come out and wonder where we are, and you'll look out the window and see the car gone."

Vanessa banged on the outside of Sita's door. "You wouldn't dare!"

"Hey, I drove! I'll be making the driving decisions around here!" said Roxie.

Ari, Roxie, and Sita all stepped out of the rooms to model their costumes for each other. Sita wore the medieval gown. Ariene chose the pirate to try on for fun, and Roxie stuck with her cat costume. Vanessa looked over them all and sniffed, her nose turned up. "Well, I think my costume is going to be the best, personally, but you guys look nice."

∞

Allen James and Eric Madison walked down the sidewalk outside their dormitory. "So you going to ask her to the dance, Eric? You don't have much time left you know, it's tonight."

Eric shoved him. "I know! And of course I'm going to ask her! If I can ever find her alone, anyway. She's so hard to find, and when I *do* find her, she's always in the middle of a group!"

"So go pull her away and ask her that way! It shouldn't be that hard!"

Eric glared at Allen. "So why haven't you asked Roxie yet, huh? You've been doing the same thing I have!"

Allen let the accusation roll off his shoulders in a shrug. "At least I've talked to Roxie once or twice. You haven't even talked to Sita." He spotted a group of four women coming around the corner and grinned. "So if you get Sita alone long enough to ask her, what would you say?"

"I'd ask if she's going, first, then if she's going with anyone. Then I'd get down on one knee and ask if she would honor me and go to the dance tonight with me."

Allen smirked. "That's great you finally worked that much out, 'cause here's your chance. She's coming this way."

"Wha-" said Eric. "Oh no. Don't say a word, or I'll beat you bloody," he snarled into Allen's laughing face. The group of chatting young women walked closer. Allen waved to them and they came over to the two boys.

Vanessa smiled at them. "Hey, Allen, Eric. What are you guys doing here? Are either of you going to the Halloween dance tonight?" She squeaked when Roxie and Sita both poked her in the side. "What was that for?" she asked, ignoring Sita's blushing face.

Allen grinned at the girls while his roommate stared at Sita. "Actually, that's why I waved you all over. Roxie, are you going?"

Roxie looked up at him, startled. "Yeah, I am. I'm dressing up as a cat. You?"

"Are you going with someone, or are you fair game?" said Allen, his lips curled into his most charming smile. He kept tabs on Sita from the corner of his eye while he spoke, but she didn't seem to recognize him, or even glance in his direction at all. He breathed a little bit easier.

She crossed her arms and shot him an annoyed glare. "Fair game, huh? First off, I'm not some piece of meat for you jackals to fight over, and I won't be treated that way. And second, no, I'm not going with someone, I'm going with my friends." Roxie continued to glare at him until he looked shamefaced.

"You're right, I'm sorry. Well, since you're not going with someone, would you do me the honor of being my date?" He bowed with a little flourish of his hand.

The girls turned to look at Roxie, who tried with all her might to keep a straight face. Allen saw Sita glance over at Eric, taking advantage of the distraction. She blushed and looked away, and Allen tried his best not to smirk. The other blond, Vanessa, winked at Allen when he accidentally met her eyes. Allen returned to watching Roxie pretend to think it over. Finally, Roxie could resist no longer. She snorted and uncrossed her arms. "All right, all right, I'll go with you. What's your costume?"

His brown eyes twinkled with laughter. "I was thinking about being a ghost. Meet you at eight?"

"Sure. Where? Outside the front doors?"

"Why don't I meet you at your door? It's the more gentlemanly thing to do."

That got grins from everyone and a few of the girls chuckled. "OK, outside my suite at eight. It's suite 400 over in East. See you then!" Allen and Eric watched the ladies chatter and laugh as they walked away down the hall.

Allen turned to Eric. "Why didn't you ask her? You didn't even say one word!"

Eric gave him a sheepish smile. "Well, she was in the middle of the group, and she looked so pretty. I got all nervous and couldn't say anything!"

Allen sighed and clapped Eric on the shoulder, dragging him in the opposite direction of the girls. "Well, then, I guess you'll just have to wait until tonight, won't you, and hope she's going," he chided as they walked away.

∞

Ari smiled to herself when she caught Sita looking behind them at the two boys for the second time. She slipped up next to her and put an arm around her shoulders. "So, why didn't you talk to him?" she asked as innocently as she could.

Sita tried to escape, but Ariene had a firm hold on her shoulders. "Talk to who?" she replied, just as innocent.

"Eric."

Ari winked at her. Sita turned red and stared at the ground while she walked. "Why would I talk to him? I don't even know him, except for his name and what he looks like." Sita's hands worried at the edges of her jacket. "He probably doesn't even know who I am, I only know him because he's in my class, and . . ."

Ari interrupted. "That's why you introduce yourself and start a conversation."

The others finally heard what was being discussed in the back of their little group. "Talk to who?" asked Vanessa.

"Eric," Ariene said, ignoring Sita's wince.

"Oooh!" chorused the group, knowing smiles coming to each of their lips.

Sita reached out to smack Ari on the arm. "Ari! I'm not interested in him! I don't even know him."

"That's what dating is for," said Vanessa.

The women began climbing the stairs to their rooms. "But, guys . . . what about Roxie and Allen! Huh? Aren't you going to tease *her* about going out with a guy?" Sita said in desperation.

Gleams of amusement could be seen in every eye but Sita's as they dropped the subject and turned instead to teasing Roxie. Sita breathed a sigh and listened with half an ear to the conversation, deep in thought.

Ariene pulled Roxie's arm and she dropped back to talk to her roommate. "It looks like Sita needs some friendly help tonight," murmured Ari.

"Yeah, it does," said Roxie.

∞

At eight o'clock, on the dot, Allen and Eric showed up at suite 400's door. Eric tugged at his pirate shirt and knocked three times on the blue door. A muffled shout of "Coming!" came from inside and footsteps approached. Allen fixed the collar on his ghost outfit and glanced over at his friend, clearly amused. "Dude, calm down. Just remember why you're here." Eric could only nod and swallow hard as a blond girl answered the door.

Vanessa rolled her eyes and let them in. "The others are still getting dressed, you're early. Just sit on the couch and watch TV or something until we're done," she ordered. She almost made it back to her room when she paused, turned on her heel, and studied Eric. Then she gave him a sly smile and lowered her lashes. "Hey Eric, do you have a date for tonight?"

Caught off guard, Eric blinked and said, "No."

Allen felt the urge to slap him.

Vanessa sidled closer, away from her door and toward Eric. A gleam in her eye made Allen shudder. "Well, I'm free. How about you be my date?" She winked at him and gave a wide, slow grin.

Eric had the grace not to look disgusted, but only barely. "Sorry, but I'm hoping to go with someone else."

Vanessa immediately dropped the act and stalked to her room. "Roxie, Allen is here!" she yelled before she slammed the door closed behind her.

Thanks to the walls being paper-thin, the men could hear everything that happened in the next room hiding the women. Roxie squealed, and the other two shushed her. Allen smirked and traded an amused glance with Eric. "I'll go entertain them, since you two aren't ready yet," they heard Sita say. Eric was tapping his foot in a fit of nervous energy when they heard the door open. Eric turned, and his breath froze in his chest.

Sita stepped out, closing the door behind her. She looked stunning in a velvet-like renaissance gown, the deep purple, black, and silver colors highlighting her fair features, and the cut of the costume flattered to the best advantage. The pieces of her long blond hair not contained in the intricate braided hairstyle fell over her shoulders in soft waves. The make-up on her face only brightened her blue-green eyes. Eric couldn't take his eyes off her face.

Allen saw the effect she had on his friend and took control. He smiled at Sita, holding his hand out to her. "Hello, my lady. How are you this evening?" he asked.

Sita took his hand and blushed. She grinned, playing along. "Just fine, m'lord. Your lady will be out soon, I swear. She's just fixing her face," she declared.

Allen affected shock and consternation as he dropped her hand. "My lady, do forgive my manners, but I haven't introduced my friend here. May I present Sir Eric, a pirate in my ghostly employ?" He waved a hand at Eric, bringing him from his reverie. Eric managed to smile at Sita, who returned the expression.

Roxie came out of the room to appear behind Sita. "Well, hey there, charming, you asking Sita to the Halloween dance?"

Sita whirled around to grab Roxie's arm. "Roxie!" she cried. She turned back to Eric. "You can ignore her, she's . . . um, kind of crazy and . . ."

Eric interrupted her, finally finding his voice. "Sita, it's OK, I was about to ask you." He copied Allen's earlier gallantry and bowed with a flourish of his hand. "So, Sita, would you honor me with your presence at the Halloween dance?"

She peered at him through her lashes and nodded, blushing bright crimson and trying to hide it. "OK, I'll go with you." Eric grinned at her, glancing away only once to say hello to the two other girls who finally joined them. Roxie introduced everyone to the two dates before leading them all out the door. No one noticed Vanessa's sour glare from the back of the group as she closed and locked the door, her eyes boring into Sita's back as the group met Darci, Estelle, and Skylar at the stairwell.

Allen shook his head as Roxie introduced Eric and the group began to walk down the central stairs of the dorm. Eric was besotted with Sita. Allen didn't see what was so great about her— she was nice, and intelligent, and certainly pretty, but no more than that to him. But Roxie, on the other hand . . . he found her irresistible. She may only be pretty, but he thought her beautiful. *Probably as beautiful as Sita is to Eric.* That made him chuckle. Roxie looked back in inquiry and he smiled at her. She grinned and continued to walk down the stairs and out the doors.

The group reached the enormous and crowded ballroom of the student union five minutes later. They showed their student cards and squeezed inside, amazed despite themselves at the number of people crammed into the decorated and dark ballroom. Music pumped from two large speakers at the front, and a DJ controlled everything from the middle of a stage. Streamers and balloons in Halloween colors lined the walls and the ceiling. Fake cobwebs and spider webs hung on the walls or partly covered doorways, and a fog machine gave the ballroom a surreal feeling. Colored lights added to the sense of mystery and excitement. After taking in the scene, they split into smaller sections at once—Roxie and Allen went to dance, while the single girls began to scout the territory and search for single guys to commandeer. Sita followed Eric to the refreshments table for drinks.

Allen pulled Roxie onto the crowded dance floor. Students jumped and spun and swayed to the beat, or shuffled awkwardly if they didn't know how to dance but had somehow been coerced onto the floor. Roxie, however, knew how to dance and matched Allen's movements. He grinned when she laughed in delight as he spun her around. Her smile sent an electric shiver down Allen's spine, and the touch of her skin made his heart beat faster. She seemed to be feeling the same effects, as she arranged their dancing so they moved much closer to each other. When a rare slow song wafted through the air, Roxie cuddled closer and rested her head on his chest. Allen held her close and smiled.

Later that night, as the group arrived happy but tired back at their rooms, Sita allowed herself to give in to the heady exhaustion she felt. She had initially wanted to be the wallflower, talking with Eric and watching the dancers, but Eric asked her to dance. She said yes, and after that first dance, there was almost no break for them until the night ended with the last slow dance and Sita in Eric's arms, sighing with regret that it was over so soon. They met the others, who she had barely seen all night, and followed them back to the hall with Eric holding her hand. Allen caught her eye for a moment—something about him looked very familiar, but she couldn't place it. So she shrugged the feeling off and squeezed Eric's fingers.

Sita stopped a few feet away from her room to give Roxie a private good-bye with Allen. Blushing again, she turned to Eric. "Thank you for inviting me. I had a great time," she said, suddenly turning into the tongue-tied, awkward teenager she had been in high school. Eric was still holding her hand.

His face lit up and he smiled down at her. "I should be thanking you. I had the best time I've ever had at a dance. I normally hate dances. But I really did have a great time." He squeezed her hand. Sita looked up into his dark chocolate eyes and suddenly couldn't remember how to breathe. He apparently was in the same situation, though he actually did something about it. Eric leaned down and kissed her, wrapping his arms around her when she showed no inclination to pull away.

Sita returned his kiss, so sweet she wished it would never end. Then he pulled away, and she sighed. "Hmm, bold, kissing on the first date." But she smiled up at him. "Guess it's lucky for you I kind of like bold guys," she said.

He grinned again, kissed the hand he held and said in a low voice only for her, "You know, I'm really not much for kissing on the first date. Too much of a chance of being shot down. But you're different." He sounded confused. "But in a really good way, I promise. Good night, Sita. I'll see you tomorrow." Eric turned and walked down the hall to where Allen waited before heading down the stairs and out of sight.

"Good night," she managed to squeak out, finding herself breathless. Holding a hand to her flushed cheek, Sita faced her door a few feet away only to find that she had an audience.

∞

Roxie lagged behind most of the group as they chattered their way into the suite or into their rooms further down the hall. Only Sita and Eric were still behind her—everyone else was now out of sight. She turned back to Allen after pulling the door slightly closed behind Ari and Vanessa. He looked so comical in his ghost costume, not frightening at all. He grinned down at her. "Have a good time?" he asked.

She nodded and smiled. Her heart still raced from the touch of his hand in hers. "Absolutely. I had a great time. We should do it again."

Allen's eyes sparkled. "Well, I wouldn't say we should do a repeat of the dance—there's only so much dancing I can take!" Roxie grinned. Elation made her stomach feel light and flip-floppy. "But I would definitely be up for another date. Just you and me this time." He took her hand in his and leaned against the wall on his other free hand. Now Roxie's pulse quickened and her breathing shortened. She looked up into his eyes through her lashes and enjoyed the effect that look had on him. "What do you say? Will you go on a date with me?"

With a mischievous grin, she answered the question in a very deserving way. Rising onto her toes, Roxie leaned forward and planted a soft kiss on Allen's waiting lips. He returned the kiss, deep and passionate, one hand tangled in her lovely red-brown hair. Allen reluctantly ended the kiss.

Roxie remembered to breathe. "I'll see you tomorrow?" she asked.

Allen nodded. "Absolutely." He gave her a final swift kiss and walked down the hall to wait for Eric, who caught up with him soon enough. They left together and walked down the stairs. Roxie saw Sita in much the same state she herself was in. Grinning, she motioned the other girls out of their hiding places where she knew they waited. When Sita turned to the suite, she saw her friends lying in wait, suppressed laughter in the lines of their mouths and eyes.

Roxie let the others tease Sita. She was on too much of a high of her own to notice much else. She almost began to hum to herself as she made her way to her room, changed into pajamas, and fell into a deep, happy sleep.

Chapter Seven
Boulesis

Loud knocking on the suite door early the next morning woke Vanessa from a deep sleep. Still groggy, she jumped down from her loft bed, yawning and stumbling out into the common room. She squinted through the eye-hole and groaned, then opened the door. "Robert, why don't you just have a key to this place or something? It'd save us the trouble of having to open the door this early in the morning."

Robert grinned. "Well, I would, if it weren't against school rules that you give out keys." He stepped inside and closed the door. "Thanks for opening it, Vee. Go back to bed."

Vanessa glared at him over a huge yawn. "It's pointless for me to go back to sleep now. I've got to leave in almost an hour."

"Going where?" he asked.

"Shopping with some friends from class. If the others ask, tell them I'll be back sometime this evening." She didn't wait for his answer, but walked back into her room to change. Robert took a seat on the couch and pulled out a crossword book. Not even ten minutes later, Vanessa closed the door to her room and started to walk from the suite, but she stopped behind Robert. He almost turned around to see what she was doing when he felt her cold hands on his shoulders.

Rob nearly jumped out of his skin. Her hands had begun to slide down his chest before he sprang to his feet and spun around. "What are you doing?"

Vanessa cocked an eyebrow. Even he had to admit she was beautiful, but in a cold, distant kind of way. She just didn't have the warmth that her friends had. Her gaze was calculating as she looked him over. "I just thought I'd give you a shoulder massage. You looked tense." Then she half-smiled. Rob couldn't believe what she was doing. "We're all alone, you know. Just you and me. The others are still sleeping, and will stay asleep for a while. We could . . ."

He held up a hand to cut her off. "Whoa, Vanessa, hold on. I'm, what, four years older than you? That's not a good idea. Besides, don't you have somewhere to be?"

With a huff and a frown, Vanessa sauntered out the door without saying another word. The chill she left in her wake made him shiver. He sat back down on the couch and continued his crossword puzzles.

Almost a full hour after that, Ariene stumbled from her room, heading for the cereal and milk. She fixed herself a bowl of cereal and walked back. Rob watched her, waiting for her to notice him sitting there. He grinned as she wandered to the door, stopped, and edged back around, staring at him through bleary eyes. "Rob. What are you doing here?"

"I'm doing a crossword," he replied.

"You're too awake for this early in the morning," she grumbled through a mouthful of Fruit Loops.

"It's nine, Ari."

"Yeah, that's early." She walked into her room, eating her cereal and shaking Roxie awake. "Rox, Rob's here." Roxie groaned and tried to burrow under the blankets. Ariene pulled the blankets off. "If I 'ave to be up and talking to him, then so do you! Get up." Grumbling and moaning, Roxie got up and dressed. She stumbled out into the common room and pounded on Sita's door.

Roxie could hear Sita throw herself out of bed. Half awake, she pulled open the door. "What?"

Roxie raised an eyebrow. "Rob's here." She watched, amused, as Sita's face went blank, then she glared at Rox, and then she slammed the door. Roxie stood there, waiting. "Well, I guess she's not a morning person." Thuds and grumbling came from Sita's room until she opened the door, fully dressed and more awake.

Robert watched the whole process with an internal grin of amusement. When the commotion began to settle down, he decided to speak up. "Hello, ladies. I see you're all awake now," Robert commented. Three sets of glares turned in his direction as Ariene joined the other two, now fully clothed. Robert tried to suppress a laugh and failed. He continued his crossword. "Surprise! If Roxie would get dressed, we can start practicing."

Once Roxie changed, the girls moved the chairs and tables out of the way against the walls. With a few grumbles and death glares at Robert, Ari began, practicing on changing forms at higher speeds. Roxie started next, focusing on the open window and door in her room and calling as many animals as she could, sending a few away in a steady stream as the little animals began to form a crowd. She was up to three squirrels and four birds when Sita began her practice. She kept her wings hidden and instead called her magic to the front to build and create shields.

Robert watched the trio try to practice their talents in the confined space of the suite's common room. He studied each of them, watching as they used their powers and seeing how they funneled that power through their bodies. Noticing something odd, Robert closed his eyes, summoned his enhanced sight, and opened them again to focus on Roxie. This trick was useful in watching students work. By enhancing his sight with his magic, he could see the flow of magic through his students' bodies as they practiced: how it worked, its strength, whether it was blocked or flowed too freely in places. Nodding in thought, he went back to watching.

He could see they had each become accustomed to working around the others, and had also learned how to anticipate their friends' reactions if something went wrong. *But there simply is not enough space in here for them to practice as they should,* he thought. Whistling, he caught their attention and they stopped. Crossing his arms across his chest, he said, "You know, there really isn't enough space in here for the three of you to practice. You need somewhere bigger."

Roxie wiped a hand across her forehead, tired and sweating from exertion. "We've tried to find somewhere on campus, but there isn't anywhere big enough that we can safely practice in."

"What about off campus?" That stopped them. He chuckled. "I noticed a bunch of warehouses down the street when I went on my walks in the mornings. If they're abandoned, you could use those. They're definitely big enough, and they're the perfect place to let loose." He spread his hands. "How about it?"

The girls looked to one another and shrugged. "We can check them out," said Ari slowly.

He spoke again. "And Rox, I noticed something about your power that hasn't been there before."

She stopped. "What's wrong with it? I haven't noticed anything different."

"Well, I don't think you would have noticed this. It isn't your magic, exactly, but more like your *will*, or what is sometimes called '*boulesis*.' Your *boulesis* has grown, and has become something you can control." He saw her confused expression and stopped. "Um, lemme try explaining differently. Everyone has will power, but some have more control than others, right?" She nodded. "Ari uses her will every time she changes, since it's linked with her gifts. Sita *must* control her *boulesis*, or her magic would be scattered and uncontrollable." They all nodded at this, following his train of thought. He continued. "But your *boulesis*, Rox, isn't as necessary to your power. At least, I didn't think it was in all my observations. But as it turns out, you *have* been using it, and as your power grows, so does your will—or your *boulesis*—and your control of it. Sort of like saying that using your magic more frequently fine-tuned the control of your will. You can do more than just summon, control, and banish animals now."

Roxie tilted her head, thinking. "What can I do, then?"

Robert shrugged his shoulders. "Anything you want. That's the beauty of willpower. It's up to you." He corrected himself. "Most of the time. You can't make your magic do something it simply can not do, like do good when its nature is to be bad. No amount of willpower will change something like that."

"I understand." She brightened. "That's so cool!"

Rob laughed. "Come on, grab some jackets, it's a little chilly outside. Let's go check out the warehouses." Sita and Ariene declined, citing the need for a little more practice. Rob and Roxie walked out, letting them divide up the extra space between them.

An hour later, Robert and Roxie stood in an unused warehouse, filled with empty crates and boxes stacked to the ceiling. Rob held a globe of magical energy in his hand, his magic lending the steel gray walls a blue tone. Roxie followed him and tried not to bump into anything. "Do you think this will work? What if someone is really using this place and we get caught?"

He shook his head. "All of these boxes are empty. My guess is it's strictly for storing these boxes and crates until they're needed, if ever. You could practice here for months with no one finding out. With your group's gifts, you all can sneak in with no problem."

Roxie nodded, looking around and thinking of all the possibilities with this space. "I think this will actually work, Rob. Now we just have to get the others to admit their own powers!"

He put an arm around her shoulders and led her from the dark warehouse. "Well, that will come in time." Rob made a quick decision to tell her the idea he had been concocting for a while now. "You know, Rox, once you and your friends get used to working together, I think it would be a good idea for you all to go out on missions for my organization. The practice would be good, and you'll be helping get the bad guys too." He glanced at her from the corner of his eye. "What do you think?"

She tilted her head to grin up at him, the breeze teasing her hair into her eyes. She brushed it away. "I think it's a great idea. I'll ask the others once we get everything set up. But, you know, I don't really know anything about your 'organization.' Don't you think you should tell us a little more?"

A small frown touched the corner of his mouth. "You're right. I'll figure out what I'm allowed to tell you and let you know, OK?" He smiled and hugged his arm tighter around her shoulders, walking back to the campus together.

The next day, Roxie brought Sita and Ariene back down to the warehouse after classes. She showed them the space, asking if they thought it would work. They both agreed and Roxie laughed in delight. "Well, that's settled. We can work out a practice routine, and develop our skills and all. When should we start?"

Sita and Ari looked at each other, grinned, then turned back to Rox. "Today!"

They came up with a routine, bickering with each other over the details. Once they worked it out, the practice began. Two of them were chased by the third until both were captured, then they switched who hunted and who hid. Each used some magic, but mostly they practiced simple evasion maneuvers, made up from watching too many crime and detective shows with chase scenes on television. After an hour of running and mock-fighting, Sita lay on the floor, panting, wanting nothing more than a shower and sleep. "Are we done for today?" she gasped.

Ariene propped herself up on a box, breathing hard and wiping away sweat on her brow. "Definitely. I'm pooped. Roxie?"

Roxie could only nod. "Let's get back. Sita, light?"

There was no answer from Sita's side. Roxie lifted her head. "Sita?"

Still no answer. Ari scrambled to her feet and hurried over, Roxie following closely and fighting back her hunger and exhaustion. Sita lay on the floor, eyes closed, body completely still except for her breathing. Roxie crouched down beside her friend. "Sita?" She grabbed the blonde's shoulder and tugged gently.

Sita opened her eyes. She blinked a few times, as if coming back to wakefulness from a deep sleep. Her bleary eyes focused on Roxie and Ari. "Did I pass out?" They nodded.

Roxie bit her lip. "Si, are you OK? You scared us."

"Sorry about that. I probably should've warned you before." Sita pushed herself upright, Roxie helping support her back. "When I use a lot of magic in a short amount of time, like I did today, I can fall into a coma-like state. It's not really a coma, it's just the best word I've found to describe it. But it's the cost of using my magic."

"Why a coma?" Ari asked. "That seems like a weird price."

Sita shrugged. "I think it's because my power is partly fueled by my own energy. The more I use, the more my own energy is sapped. I used a lot today, to light the warehouse, set things up, and then fight you two. It took a lot out of me."

"So . . . this might not be the best idea."

Sita grimaced. "It's just going to take some time, that's all. I think that as my endurance rises and I get stronger, the less energy I'll use up at one time. But in the meantime, it's going to cost me. If I use too much energy, the magic forces my body to shut down to recoup. It leaves me vulnerable."

Ari frowned. "So you knew this would happen and you just forgot to tell us?" Claws popped in and out from her fingernails.

Sita's face flushed. "Sorry. I guess it slipped my mind when we started."

Roxie helped Sita to her feet. "Well, now we know. We can help you in the other practice sessions until you get your endurance up. We could even set up a little bed or something in a corner."

"No, that's not necessary. When I pass out, it doesn't matter where I am, it'll just happen. In my 'coma,' I can't really feel what's under me until I wake up. No, just let me sleep it off and then help me back to the rooms. That's all I'll need."

Ari grabbed Sita's other arm and held her steady. "OK. Our powers have different effects on us. We can help you without costing ourselves anything, so you don't need to worry about being a burden."

"Thanks, Ari."

Without another word, they made their slow and painful way back to their rooms, where they passed out on their soft warm beds for an extended nap that night.

∞

Robert appeared once again in the foyer of his employer's mansion. He tugged on his shirt, trying to make sure he caught all the creases and rumples. He cursed himself for being lazy and not going home to change first.

Joe walked out of the shadows. His appearance, of course, was spotless, and only made Rob scowl more. Joe granted him a slight bow. "Mr. Gordon, a pleasure to see you again. Follow me." The butler led Robert to the stairs.

Mr. Knight's office remained the same, the wooden door barring entry. Joe knocked and opened the door on some invisible signal from his employer. Rob nodded to Joe and walked inside.

The butler closed the door behind Robert, leaving the two men alone. Mr. Knight waved Robert into a seat. "Good afternoon, my boy. I trust you are here to report?"

"I am, sir."

"Then please do so."

Rob swallowed. Knight was not in a good mood. He kept his gaze on the papers Mr. Knight glared at, instead of on the man himself. "Sir, there are five young women in the college who have powers, including Roxie and Sita. Sita herself is a color mage, and there is one other color mage, but the rest are all type mages." His fingers fidgeted with the hem of his shirt. "Only two have been confirmed so far. I am waiting for a time to confirm the others."

Mr. Knight did not look up. "What are the confirmed powers and their names, and what are the suspected powers and their names?"

Robert told him, listing them in the order he asked for. He hesitated when he reached Darci, however. "The other color mage . . . sir, I was only around her for a few minutes, but I know this girl is not only very powerful, but very dark as well. I did not see what color her power is, but it's definitely not of the lighter variety."

The focused gaze of Knight flicked away from the papers and now scrutinized Robert. The young man's fidgeting increased. "Dark? How so?"

Robert swallowed, trying to avoid the piercing gaze. "I felt suffocated when I was in her room, like everything was pressing down on me. Her power is probably suppressed, or not being expressed as it should. It is also likely to be dark, as I only get these feelings around those with darker powers than green. The stronger the feeling, the stronger the mage. And I felt like I could barely breathe."

"I see." Knight set the papers down and leaned back in his chair. "If this is all the information you have on her so far, then this report will do for now. But I would like you to keep an eye on her. She may be trouble."

"Yes, sir."

"Now, what else have you learned about Sita? She is your original task, you remember."

"Yes, sir, I do," Robert said in a quiet voice. Mr. Knight's gaze softened and Robert relaxed a trifle. "Sita Newbury is from Maryland and now shares a two-room suite with three of the young women I told you about earlier: Roxie, Ariene, and Vanessa. Sita is a very nice person, from what I have seen, and is very intelligent." Mr. Knight began to frown. Robert hurried along to the important things. "Her power is incredible. She's a color mage of the highest variety. Her magic expresses itself in purple shades, usually very dark, and it's benevolent power." Rob hesitated again, hoping his boss didn't think him crazy. "And she has wings."

Knight's stare was suddenly very intense, boring into Robert's eyes. "Wings. And purple magic."

The younger man swallowed, his fingers now very still. "Yes, sir. I've seen them both myself. Her wings are legitimately a part of her, and her power really is in purple shades. There is no mistake."

The chair creaked as Alexander Knight leaned forward. His expression intensified until Robert likened him to a hawk contemplating how to get the juiciest prey. "Purple and wings, you say . . ." His voice trailed off. Robert waited in silence, his fingers resuming their fidgeting along his hemline.

Alexander Knight snapped out of his reverie. "Excellent work, Robert. Please continue to watch Sita, as well as these others. And keep me updated as you can."

"Sir."

"Is there anything else?"

"No, sir, that is all the information I have for you at the moment."

"Then I have some information for you." Robert sat straighter in interest. Knight leaned back again. "I want you to be extra vigilant, even around the school. My network has informed me that there is a possibility Imbri Mors could have someone inside the school."

Robert felt his eyebrows arch, his mouth go dry. "Inside the school?"

"Yes. These informants have told me that the organization is not behaving as they should. They aren't in their usual places, they aren't showing up where they used to. Something is brewing, and the only place we have not yet looked is at your Roxie's college. So I want you to be careful, even when you think you are safe."

"I understand."

"Good." Knight looked up as Joe opened the door. "You are dismissed. Keep up the good work, Robert."

Robert bowed. "Thank you, sir. Have a pleasant day." Rob walked through the doorway, only allowing his worry to show when he reached the foyer and Joe could no longer see his face.

Chapter Eight
Revelations

Saturday afternoons were lazy days, no matter what else the young women might have been doing. They all made time to just be together, watching television or listening to music. Most of the time, they sat in the suite and talked. The early November weather made the rooms chilly—the heat had yet to be turned on in the dorms.

The women reclined on the sofas, opening their mail that had just been delivered and devouring a large bowl of popcorn. Darci opened her letter, laughing at Vanessa's joke. The others continued their joking as Darci pulled out a beautiful, ornate white card. Still smiling, her brow furrowed as she opened the card. Her smile faded fast, and she grasped the card in two shaking hands. She read it once, then read it again. The others stopped their joking to watch her, waiting for the bad news. Dropping her hands, Darci turned and left the room without a word, her face shocked.

Roxie glanced at the others. She stood and followed Darci, trailed by Ari, Sita, and Vanessa. She knocked on Darci's door and shushed the others with an impatient wave of her hand. "Darci? Is everything OK?"

A muffled thump sounded on the other side of the door. "Darci?" Rox called, knocking again. Something crashed and they heard the tinkle of breaking glass. They heard a soft sob in the silence. "Darci? Open the door, Darci."

Soft shuffling footfalls came toward the door, and the lock snicked free of the frame. Darci opened the door, still sobbing, holding the white card in a clenched fist. Roxie stood still, her arms open. Darci fell into them, speaking between her sobs. "Joshua . . . Josh . . . is . . . is . . . getting m-m-married!" She tried to throw the card away from her but couldn't throw it very far while encased in Roxie's arms.

Darci yanked herself free, her sobs taking on an angry tone as she ripped the envelope to shreds. She was starting on the card when Sita tugged it from her. "Darci, let us see. You can rip it apart in a minute." Sita opened the card and read it through, then passed it to the others. Each scanned it and Ari gave the card back to Darci, who promptly ripped it to shreds.

Suddenly they all began to feel as if there were an enormous power bearing down on them, seeking to smother them underneath its rage. Roxie put her hands to her head, trying to get rid of the feeling of despair that washed over her, but unable to block it from her mind. Darci continued to sob and tantrum, oblivious to her friends standing frozen in her doorway.

Dark blue-black magic sprouted from Darci's hands. She burned the torn up card to ashes. Turning to her bed with a sweep of her arm, Darci's power lanced out at the teddy bear on her pillow, making it explode into tiny pieces, and then burning the pieces into ash that was blown away on the cold wind coming through the open window.

Darci flung open the closet door. An expensive leather jacket went up in flames, incinerated almost instantly. "He was my *boyfriend!* He was with *me!* What the hell was he doing all these months? He was lying to my face, and cheating behind my back!" Darci ranted. "Bastard! How could he!" Black lightning caressed the walls, leaving great black streaks smoking in its wake. "He was *mine!* That lying, cheating, manipulative, stupid little *weasel!*"

The carpet smoked until Darci suddenly collapsed on it, weeping hysterically, her magic contained again. "He was mine. I loved him, I love him, I love him," she cried over and over between her sobs. Another minute and she stopped crying and curled up on the carpet, her arms around her knees. "He's gonna be married," she whispered.

Everyone sighed very, very quietly in relief—the oppressive despair and rage vanished with the death of Darci's fury. Sita stepped forward this time, wrapping the broken girl in her arms. She made soft soothing noises while exchanging a glance with Roxie and Ari, the same thought passing between them. Darci's magic was as terrifying as her use of it.

In that second, a knock on the door startled all but Darci. Ari cracked the door open and peered outside. "Is she OK?" said

Skylar. Roxie heard the shuffling of feet outside the door, as if Sky or Estelle tried to look inside.

Ari nodded and replied in a soft voice that Darci was fine, just upset, and didn't want more visitors. So Skylar and Estelle left quietly and Ari shut the door again.

Darci's sobs quieted, and soon she began to nod off. Roxie watched her eyelids become heavy as the crying wound down. The magical and emotional expense of the ordeal looked like it took a similar toll on Darci as magic took on Sita. That, or the heartbreak just was too much for Darci to deal with. Either way, Roxie thought it best that the other young woman sleep it off now.

With great care and gentleness, Ari and Sita gathered Darci from the floor and lifted her into her bed. Roxie pulled the blanket over Darci while Vanessa closed the blinds of the windows. Then they filed out the door.

Roxie closed the door and leaned against it from the outside. "That was . . ."

"Scary," said Vanessa. The normally pale Vanessa had turned even paler after seeing Darci's magic.

That was when Roxie realized Vanessa had witnessed the magic. Her eyes widened. "Oh crap. Vanessa . . . Darci, um . . . Darci worked . . ."

But Vanessa held up a hand and smiled just slightly. "Don't worry about it. I know what happened. Darci is a mage. But how do you know?"

At the same time, Ari blurted, "How do you know that?"

Sita tsked at them all. "Guys, I think it's time we told the truth."

The other three stared at her, then at each other, then back again. Sita grinned and shook her head. "Vee, we're mages, too. We kind of figured you are as well. We've just been waiting for you to tell us."

Vanessa regained her normal color and composure. "Oh. Well, great. Yeah, I have magic. I work with plants. What do you do?"

"Animal-speak," said Roxie.

"Shapeshifter," said Ari.

"All-around mage and winged human," said Sita.

They waited while Vanessa absorbed the information. But then she smiled, and her eyes shone bright. For the first time, Roxie thought she looked beautiful instead of haughty. "Awesome! So what now?"

Ari took over from there. "You should join us for practices. We have practice space in a warehouse down the road. We practice our gifts there with each other. It's fun, but hard work."

But Vanessa nodded, her eagerness plain. "I'm in."

Roxie clapped her hands and began walking down the hall. "Then let's get started."

Ariene pushed open the huge sliding door of the warehouse. "Here she is! Home sweet home!" she cried. Vanessa peeked inside, peering into the darkness while the other three walked in.

"It doesn't look like much," said Vanessa.

"But that's the beauty of it!" Roxie called over her shoulder. "With our gifts, we can make it into the perfect practice arena." Sita let fly hundreds of tiny clear lights to settle around the large room, making the three newcomers gasp. Each of the little lights was as bright as a lamp, and illuminated the enormous room enough to see with ease. Ari shoved the heavy door closed.

Vanessa joined the trio in the middle, between the huge stacks of apparently empty boxes and crates. Ariene eyed the stacks, thinking while she explained. "What we do is use our powers to attack and try to capture the prey, which is one of us running around the room. We don't use anything fatal or lethal; this is only practice for reflexes, summoning, and just basic practice with our skills. Also, our 'prey' is trying to take us out while evading our attacks. Once she gets us all, or we capture her, we switch to a new target and practice until everyone has had a turn at being the prey."

Vanessa shivered. "Would you stop saying 'prey'? You make it sound like you're going to eat us or something once you catch us."

Ariene chuckled. "Sorry. But that's what you are. Especially when I shift."

"Please tell me that you're still human when you shapeshift. You aren't a total animal, right? You're still you? Because if when you turn into a bear, you really are a *bear*, I'm leaving now."

Ariene shook her head. "No, no, no, only my body shifts. I'm still me inside." Vanessa's shoulders sagged in relief. Ari resorted to considering the room. "It looks like the boxes are still in place. Do we want to move them around or leave them?"

"Did we move them last time?" asked Sita.

"No."

"Then let's leave them. We can still get some use out of this course, and Vanessa hasn't done it yet." Roxie and Ari nodded their agreement.

Vanessa stepped forward. "Well, what do we do now?"

Roxie pointed to Sita. "Sita's going to be our first target. The rest of us will be using our abilities to try to capture her, but try not to inflict any injuries. We've already had to come up with an excuse once when Ari twisted her foot last week." Ariene nodded. "Sita can fly, remember, so she can aim from above as well as on foot. We start by running off to find good hiding places. Sita waits here for a count of twenty seconds, then starts off."

Roxie grinned in pleasure. "The game stops when we catch her, she takes two or more of us out, or we play for thirty minutes without gaining ground. I've got the stopwatch, so if thirty minutes pass and we haven't caught her, I'll let everyone know it's time to switch targets."

Nods all around. Sita popped her wings out of her shirt to stretch and warm her muscles. She looked at her friends. "I'm ready when you are."

Ariene glanced at Roxie, who grinned and held up the stopwatch. "Right. Everyone head out. Twenty seconds starts . . . now!" The others scattered while Sita waited, flapping her wings in slow movements to warm up her flight muscles.

When twenty seconds passed, she began to run. Weaving in and out of the stacked boxes, she spread her magic out across the room, invisible to all but her eyes. She smiled as it told her where each of the other players waited, their locations lit up in her mind as if they were beacons. *OK, Vanessa, here I come.* She veered to the right, her wings tucked in close to her back to avoid the boxes and narrow turns. Vanessa appeared around the corner, peering around a towering stack with her back to the oncoming affront. Sita put on a burst of speed, surprising Vanessa into acting too soon. Vines appeared from underneath the concrete floor, shoving themselves up through the solid concrete.

Sita jumped into the air, wings beating furiously, and fired a beam of magic at Vanessa. The beam crackled as it split into smaller threads, forming a net that hit Vanessa and wrapped her up tight. She struggled to break free, but even her hands were bound. She teetered and began to fall backward, but Sita caught her before she hit the hard floor. Smiling, Sita stood up and patted her roommate on the shoulder, a smirk on her lips. "Don't worry, you won't be like that for long. I'll come and free you when my turn is over." Sita sent a purple ball into the air to hover over Vanessa high enough that it could be seen above the crates and boxes.

Apparently someone else had seen it, too, since Sita heard a cry of surprise from the opposite end of the building. Sita headed that direction and found Roxie lounging on a stack of crates. "That was fast," she said as Sita winged her way in for a landing.

"Yeah, well, Vanessa's got a disadvantage. There aren't many plants here."

Roxie tapped her chin with one finger. "Maybe we can bring in some potted plants . . ."

"Something to think about, at least," Sita said. "Alright, you're 'caught', so I'm going for Ari."

Roxie waved her onward and Sita jumped back into the air. Ari waited for her at the back of the warehouse. She copied her roommate and lounged on a stack of crates, though she had changed into a tiger. Her feline head rested on furry paws.

Sita tapped her on the head. "Got you!" With the last person captured, Sita sent a hail of fireworks into the air, signaling the end of the round. She pulled her magic from the web and back to her, allowing the net to collapse and free her "victim."

Sita grinned in triumph as the others joined her in the middle of their jungle. Roxie studied Sita. "How are you feeling, Si? Still OK? Feel like you're going to pass out yet?"

"I feel great!" Sita grinned. "Who's next?"

Later that night, Roxie closed the door of her room, a towel wrapped around her and her hair dripping wet. She turned around and nearly jumped out of her skin, squeaking in surprise. "Robert!" He grinned at her from her desk chair. She leaned against the door, trying to settle from the sudden surprise. "Geez, Robbie, you should have said something!"

He chuckled. "Sorry, but you just walked in." She was tempted to throw the nearest object—which happened to be the lamp—at his head. "I'll turn around and close my eyes." He held his hands up and turned around.

Roxie glared at him and growled, "That's a horrible excuse." He waved a hand at her. She eyed him for a moment, making sure, and turned her back to him, hurrying to change into something presentable and talking while she did. "Well, you were right about Darci, you know. She has a lot of power, but it is *not* good power."

"What color is it?"

"Black."

He jerked around. Luckily for him, Rox already had her shirt on. "*Black?*" She nodded. "Great, you've got a dark mage on your hands."

"Excuse me?"

Robert collapsed into the nearest chair, visibly shaking. "It's worse than we thought. You know that only a magician's power is visible to others, right?" She nodded, still confused. "Your power, for example, is not visible, but Sita's magic is. That's because she's a magician, a mage, and you aren't, not in the same sense." He closed his eyes. "If Darci's power is visible, it means she's a color mage, not a type mage like you. And the darker a power is, the more powerful they are."

Brow furrowed in thought, Roxie asked, "Sita's magic is that dark purple color. What does that mean?"

"Dark purple magic hasn't been seen by anyone before. Most magicians' powers range from red to blue. It skips over yellow—no one knows why. There are two ways to distinguish power—for instance, if one mage has light or pale red and another has dark red, the dark red magician is stronger.

"The second way is moving down the color spectrum. The dark red mage may be more powerful against other reds, but that mage is weaker when facing an orange, or green, and so on. The further along the spectrum, the stronger the mage."

"So the spectrum is from red to black, skipping yellow, right?"

He shook his head, eyes still shut tight. "From red to black, yes, but there's also silver. For some reason, magic does *not* like to show up in yellow or gold; no one has ever seen any variation of yellow or gold. The oranges are all distinctly orange. Anyway, silver trumps black and any other color. It is the strongest, the highest and purest form, and makes an extremely strong magician." He opened his eyes at last. "I don't like the idea of fighting a black magician, but given the choice between black and silver, I would choose black. At least then I might—*might*—stand a chance, but against silver I would loose before the match even began."

Roxie nodded her understanding. "Your magic is light blue, right?" Robert nodded. She flopped onto her bed, thinking in the silence. "So if we end up fighting with Darci, Sita would still loose. Even if you two teamed up and fought her together, Darci's magic would still overpower yours?" He nodded again. Rox sighed. "Well, I guess the only way we might stand a chance is to stay her friend. What other choice do we have?"

"We have none if she chooses to destroy us. There are no silver mages—there haven't been for hundreds, maybe thousands, of years."

Rox massaged her forehead. "We need to let the others know all this," she said, her voice subdued.

"Get everyone in the common room. I'll tell them now."

Roxie brought the others out, most still with wet hair and in their pajamas. Robert sat in the middle of the suite's common room, leaning against the kitchenette table from his position on the floor, studying each of his girls while they absorbed his news in silence. Sita seemed the calmest, as if she was hearing something she already knew. She waited for the others to process Rob's information, hands steady in her lap. Slowly, the rest came out of their trance. Rob scrutinized them all, his voice soft when he spoke. "Do you all understand? She could be dangerous, but you have no choice if you want to protect yourselves. You've already seen what she can do."

They all grimaced but nodded, their faces solemn. "We understand. We can do this, Rob. You don't need to worry," Sita said into the silence.

Robert glared at her, his mouth drooping into a frown. "I always worry, Sita. Besides, you're the one that has to be most watchful. If Darci does something, you're the one that will have to try and contain her, or you could all die," he said, his voice quavering at the end.

Sita lifted a brow. "I know, Rob. We all know. We can handle it."

He decided to let the matter rest, though he still thought Sita took it too lightly. Taking a breath, he spoke again, but the worry didn't leave his fine face. "Don't relax just yet, there's more. I'm going to have to leave you all for a while." Groans and cries of protest erupted, but settled again at his glance. "I know, we only started the training, but you all, thankfully, have one thing that many of my other students have had to learn—discipline. You've already mastered that fairly well, so I know I can leave you for a while and you *will* continue to practice as if I hadn't left at all."

His face and voice softened when he saw their consternation. "I have faith that you can do this without me, all of you, and that you'll continue to progress and build your teamwork just fine. I even have some missions lined up for you. I'll get those to Roxie as they come up." He climbed to his feet, his sleeping knees creaking in sudden protest. "There's one more thing; I need you all to be on the watch for the enemy inside this school."

That news froze each and every one of them. Roxie spoke up. "I thought we were safe here. It's a university, after all, there's *some* security. I thought we could fade into the crowds and hide. When did that change?"

Rob sighed. "I was . . . recently informed that the enemy group we've been tracking, Imbri Mors, is nowhere near their usual places." He spread his hands wide. "The only place we haven't looked thoroughly is here. We never expected them here. Now we have to consider the possibility." He sighed again, the unconscious tension leaving his shoulders and making them sag. "Just please be alert. And trust no one outside of the group. Not until this is over with and done. Please?"

Sita's brow furrowed and her eyes changed from bright blue-green to a cloudy dark blue. "Rob, did you say Imbri Mors?"

"Yeah. Why?"

"I think . . . I've heard that name before."

Rob tensed again. "Where?"

She closed her eyes, as if she needed help remembering. "Men attacked my house before school started. I got one of them to talk, and he said he worked with Imbri Mors. He said . . ." Her eyes opened wide. "It was Allen," she said in a whisper. "That's why he looked so familiar! *Allen* attacked my house!"

Roxie gasped. "Impossible. It couldn't have been him." She looked to Rob. "Right? It couldn't have been him."

The news didn't help Robert relax. Instead, he grimaced and closed his own eyes. "I can't say for sure, Rox, but I can do some digging and find out what's going on." She opened her mouth again to protest, but he silenced her with a comforting hand on her shoulder. "I'll look into it, I promise. I need you all to promise me that you'll stay safe and alert and careful. OK?"

Roxie's eyes darted from friend to friend and she answered for them all. "We swear, Robbie. We'll be careful."

"And on the watch?"

"And on the watch."

His sudden grin startled them. "Thank you. That's all I ask." He glanced at his watch. "And now it's time for me to go. Take care, and I'll see you all soon." Rob left them to their quiet examination of his news and left the suite.

∞

Robert appeared in the empty hallway his girls were on and walked down the hall to find someone waiting for him at the end of it. He stopped short, and everything around him, including time, simply stopped, as if the world held its breath.

The man waiting for him was someone Robert knew quite well. Still, he was not pleased to see him, and made his displeasure known. "Still working for *them*, are you?"

"Yes," the man said to him. "They've got me working two jobs at the same time, did you know that?"

"Of course I knew that," snapped Rob. "I know all about you. One employer is too tame for you, you have to spy for everyone, and on everyone. You sell your services to the highest bidder—" The man opened his mouth to protest. "—and you've been spying on our enemy for years now, and managed to make it convincing." Robert narrowed his eyes and tried to look as formidable as possible, which was formidable indeed. "I also know you've been spying on my girls. *That* doesn't make me happy at all. By the way, Sita remembered your attack on her house. What the hell were you thinking?"

The man yawned and stretched. "Oh, *why* do you always treat me with such hostility when we meet? We're brothers in this spy game, after all."

Rob stepped closer, wondering if he should try to take him on now, or wait until later. "You know why. Back to the subject. What do your people want with them? My girls are on the good side, you know that."

Silence.

He stepped closer, his teeth bared in a snarl. "If you *dare* to hurt any of them, and especially Roxie, I will hunt you down and never stop until you're dead. You understand?"

Silence again.

Robert growled under his breath and moved back, glaring at the man until the other finally looked away from the challenge. Satisfied, Rob crossed his arms. "So why are you here anyway? As a simple spy? You're too intelligent for that. A warning? Which employer sent you after me this time?"

The man raised his eyes back to Robert. "I have a message for you. He says to tell you you're late. Which, by the way, you are. Very late." Robert sighed and rolled his eyes, rubbing his temples as a headache sprang to life. The man continued. "He also says to tell you that you were right, the enemy is here, and both your group and mine have guards posted and watching. If at all possible, we will protect 'your' girls, as you call them, as much as we can until they're ready." He slumped into an easier posture. "That's all, Rob."

Robert looked back at him, studying. He let his ice toward the man melt—but only a little. He still disliked him. "You should get more sleep. You look like the living dead."

The man grinned. "Maybe, but sometimes so do you, *brother.*"

Rob had to grin and shake his head. He turned toward the stairs, looking back at the man. "I meant what I said about Roxie and *my* girls. Make sure you remember, brother." He walked down the stairs and time resumed again, the world releasing its breath of tension in a rush.

Allen James watched him go. He smiled to himself as he disappeared like a ghost from the hall and headed back to his own missions.

Chapter Nine
The House of Awle

Sita reclined in her chair, thumbing through her Psychology textbook. *I should really be trying harder to read this, it's due next week. But it's so boring! Stupid core classes* . . . She wrapped her blanket closer around her shoulders. The chill in her room had gotten worse since November began, and the heater in the room refused to work in an ongoing fit of stubbornness. She glared at the heater, which popped and fizzed and groaned, but gave off no warmth.

Grumbling, she tried to sink lower into the bucket chair and wrap the blanket even tighter. *Lucky Vanessa, she gets the nice warm electric blanket from Daddy.* Calming herself, she tried to summon her magic to her so she could warm up, but the cold had gotten to her magic as well, which put her in an even worse mood.

Suddenly Robert popped into her room. Sita squeaked, almost falling from her chair as he appeared out of thin air. "Robert!" she exclaimed, clutching the blanket around her. "What are you *doing* here, you're supposed to be gone!" She shot him a glare.

Robert grinned and sat down in the spare chair. "Nice to see you too, Si. Yeah, I'm gone, but remember that research I was doing last month? I forgot that I hadn't told you what I'd found, so I thought I'd pop in when I had a free minute." He put his feet up on a pile of books and relaxed. "By the way, how's the job search going?"

Sita regarded him and scooted back into her chair. "It's going. Don't change the subject. Why would I need to know whatever you're not telling me? Why aren't you telling anyone else in the group?"

"Because it's about you. You can tell them if you want to, but it's up to you." Smiling again, he sat straighter in his chair, Sita unconsciously copying him. "People with wings aren't exactly common, you know," he began.

Sita glowered at him, arms crossed. "Yeah, I think I know that."

Robert chuckled. "Of course. Well, what I meant was, they aren't common in magical society, either. So I got curious. How do you have wings? Is it pure magic, or maybe a combination of magic and genetics?" He pulled some papers out of his coat pocket. Unfolding them, he lay them out on the low table Vanessa kept by her chair, pulling the table between them so Sita could see.

She leaned closer. "So that's what your research was? You were looking up winged people?"

"Sort of," he replied. "That's not all I was doing, but I can't tell you about the rest of it. Now, no more interruptions, I don't have that much time left before I have to get back." Sita nodded and kept quiet. Rob pointed down at the papers. "I found that in the magical plane—which, I know, I haven't told you about yet, I'll tell you later on—there used to be an entire clan of winged people. Well, not all of them were winged, only certain members, but they all lived together as a huge family." He nodded to the papers. "The details are in those papers. It should make for some interesting reading."

Sita reached eagerly for the papers. They were parchment rather than typical paper, and the unusual weight of the stack surprised her. She picked them up and studied each one as she carefully unfolded the stack. "Where did you find these?"

"It's called a library, Sita." He grinned when she gave him an exasperated glance. "I found them in an old book in a 1,000-year-old library. Trust me on this, the information is good. I checked with the Librarian. She wasn't very happy with me for bothering her, either."

Sita's eyes widened. "God, Rob, you didn't rip these out of a book, did you?"

A horribly offended expression decorated Rob's face and he brought one hand to his heart. "Sita! What kind of monster do you think I am?" She laughed, as he had intended her to, and he dropped his hand. "No, they're not ripped out. They were very carefully copied out."

The five pages sat in her hands, waiting for her to read them. She itched to dive into the material, but that wouldn't be very polite. "Fine, fine, you're not a monster. Thank you for this,

Robbie." With a soft smile, she stood and planted a kiss on Rob's cheek. He blushed furiously, but she said nothing about it. "Now go so I can start reading! You're distracting me."

Rob smiled. "OK, fine. See you again soon, Si." And he vanished before her eyes in a flash of blue.

Sita plopped back down in her chair and eagerly began to read.

Vanessa walked in hours later, long after the sun had set. She hummed to herself happily. *Why's the room dark? I thought Sita would be here* . . . She flicked on the lights and almost had a heart attack. *Oh, she is here.* Vanessa rolled her eyes and leaned on the door frame. "You know, Sita, you're supposed to read with the lights on, not off."

Sita looked up from her seat in the bucket-chair, her eyes bleary. "Hey, 'Nessa. What time is it?"

Vanessa glanced at her watch. "Um, nine-thirty." She looked her roommate over. *She looks like she's just been sitting there for hours. What the hell's she doing?* "Si, you OK? You look horrible."

"Oh, yeah, I'm fine. I've just been . . . thinking," replied Sita, rubbing her aching eyes.

"Well, if that's what you look after a thinking session, maybe you should do a little less of it." Vanessa laughed and grabbed Sita's hands to pull her from the chair. "I thought you were doing homework?"

Sita scratched her head and blushed. "I was. But then Rob showed up . . ."

"Rob! When? Why didn't he talk to the rest of us? What a prick!"

"Vanessa, shush! He wasn't here for more than five minutes. He was just telling me what he'd been researching. Remember, last month, he was off doing research?"

"Yeah, yeah, there's always something with him." She leaned back against her bed, fingering the green comforter. "So what did he say? What was he looking up?"

Sita hesitated a moment. "I think I should tell the others also. There was a little kernel of info in what he said that they might find interesting. Are they here?"

Vanessa tossed her hair and walked out of the room. She dropped onto the couch, shouting for the other two to join them. "Come on, Sita's got something to tell us."

Sita, meanwhile, hung back once Vanessa left. *I've made her mad, but how? All I said was the others should know, too. What's her problem?* Running her fingers through her hair to straighten it some, she grabbed the scattered papers off the table and walked out into the common room.

Roxie and Ariene joined Vanessa on the couch and chairs, their confusion plain. "What's up, Sita?" asked Roxie. "Vanessa said you have something to tell us?"

"First off," Sita began, "Rob was here."

Roxie looked shocked and scandalized. *"And he didn't even say hello to me?"* she screeched. Sita winced, the sound hurting her ears and increasing her already painful headache.

"He didn't stay more than five minutes, Roxie! He handed me some papers, talked a little, and left." Sita sat in the remaining chair, dropping the papers onto the table in the middle. "Now shut up and listen to what he told me." They did, and Sita related to them why Rob had stopped by. She emphasized the part where he had told her of the other plane. "He didn't say too much about it, but he made it seem like there's this whole other place where it's *just* magical people. He said he would tell us more later."

Roxie interrupted her. "He called it the 'other plane,' right? That makes it sound like some kind of alternate dimension or planes of existence, or something, doesn't it?"

"Kind of, yeah," answered Ariene. "And he still hasn't told us about his 'organization', you know. He keeps a lot of secrets." Ari rolled her eyes. "But that's normal for him. What do the papers say?"

Sita shuffled the papers as she searched for the first one and began to read Rob's notes. *"'The original, founding family was known as the House of Awle. But the clan didn't stay as one House. Instead, it split into three different groups: the House of Awle (page 2), the House of Ang (page 3), and the House of Loe (page 4). The three Houses split somewhere around what would be the third century in our time.*

'Somewhere around maybe the eleventh century, there was the Great War. The House of Ang had become a warrior clan, and so of course they fought in it. They were annihilated. There is no longer any trace of them having ever

existed in society except in the history books. And the House of Loe had decided on just the opposite, becoming pacifists. They ended up being wiped out as well. Only the original House of Awle survived the Great War.

'It is this House that Sita is descended from.'" Sita paused and squinted at the margins of the paper. "Here it says 'recent wandering ancestor.' I wonder what that means."

Ari snorted. "I'm more interested in why the Clan split and how they died and all. I mean, if they were important, the split would be a big deal, but the death of two-thirds of a Clan would be an even bigger deal!" She rifled through the papers, scanning the words for a clue. "Did Rob say anything about it, Si?"

Sita shook her head. "Nope, but there might be something about it in the papers that I missed. Does it say, Ari?"

Ari looked through the papers in the waiting silence, reading. Finally she stopped and had a closer look at one paper. She grinned in triumph. "Found it! Rob did write it down. Here, this is about the split: *'The House of Awle was headed by a man named Arvin, who had three sons. Their names were Josse, Mael, and Brayan. Brayan was the heir who would take over the stewardship of Awle once his father passed. Josse and Mael, however, were not content with their lot or with the way the House was run. Josse wished to have a more war-based house, while Mael preferred an extremely peaceful and isolationist one. Arvin finally passed on, and Josse and Mael began to fight with Brayan over the stewardship and the future of the House. When they could not agree, Josse and Mael decided to leave and found their own clans. They did, taking like-minded relatives with them, and thus creating the rift in the House of Awle. The House of Loe was Mael's branch, and the House of Ang was Josse's.'"*

Vanessa whistled. "Talk about your family problems, huh? That's taking it a bit far."

Sita played with her lower lip. "I'll say. So that's why they branched off. Does it say anything about the war, then? We know that Ang was killed off because they all fought back, but maybe they weren't really very good fighters. And we know that Loe was killed because they *didn't* fight. But does it say why the war was fought in the first place and why the Houses had to get involved?"

Ari returned to shuffling through the papers. After a while she shook her head. "No, I'm not really seeing anything on it here. Sorry, Si."

"Guess he didn't really think it was too important," said Roxie. "Geez, he doesn't say hello, he doesn't give us enough info . . . what's next?"

∞

Peace reined in the suite the next afternoon. Sita sat comfortably wrapped in a soft blanket at her desk with Rob's papers in front of her, reading them over and over as if another clue to her ancestors would suddenly appear if she just read it one more time.

The ever-fragile peace shattered when the door to the suite slammed shut as someone stomped inside. Sita put down her book and listened. "Vanessa!" shouted Ari. "*Vanessa*!"

Sita stared at her roommate. "What did you do?"

"Nothing!" But Vanessa looked nervous.

Ari came and pounded on their door. "Vanessa, get your skinny ass out here right now!"

"No!"

"What did you *do*?" said Sita. "Whatever it is, you'd better just get this over with before she breaks down the door!" When Vanessa refused to move from her bed, Sita rolled her eyes and put a hand on the door knob. "Ari, I'm opening the door. But you have to promise that you won't kill Vanessa."

A muffled growl came from the other side. "Ari . . ." Sita said in a warning tone. "Promise you won't draw blood."

"You take all the fun out of things."

"Yep." Sita decided that would do, and opened the door. Ari's red face greeted her, and she looked about ready to burst she was so angry. "Now, what's going on?"

But Ari had spotted Vanessa. "You! You selfish, rich daddy's girl!"

Roxie popped her head out of her room. "What's going on?"

"Oh, just trying to stop a bloodbath," said Sita. "Wanna help?" Roxie came up behind Ari and waited.

Meanwhile, Vanessa had scrunched herself up on the farthest corner of her bed. "I didn't do anything!"

"Bull!" Ari shoved her way past Sita. Though considering how much stronger Ari was compared to Sita, she didn't put up much resistance. "You were mean to Jack! You told him I didn't want him as a study buddy anymore! And you insulted him and called him a snow-pale computer nerd who couldn't get a girl if he tried!"

Vanessa squeaked. "It wasn't me! I swear!"

Ari placed both hands on Vanessa's bed and leaned in close, a snarl on her lips and fire in her eyes. Sita put a restraining hand on Ari's shoulder. "You are a selfish, two-faced bitch. I can't believe you're lying to my face! I know it was you because when he told me that one of my roommates treated him like a dog, he said it was the blond one who looks like she has indigestion all the time!" Vanessa gasped. Sita and Roxie bit their lips to smother laughter.

But Ari wasn't finished. "And since Sita doesn't have her nose in the air like she's better than the rest of us and doesn't insult people like that, I *know* it was you!" She grabbed Vanessa's wrist and pulled her close. "Now, you're going with me to Jack's dorm and you're going to apologize, or during our next session in the warehouse you and I are going to have a little one-on-one practice time." Her voice held a growl when she said, "And I know who is going to lose in that fight."

Protesting feebly, Vanessa tried to escape Ari's grasp, but the prick of claws against her wrist made her think twice. Sita stepped back and out of the way. Roxie did the same. Ari dragged Vanessa from the room and the suite, Vanessa coming to her wits enough to scream bloody murder at Ari by the time they reached the front door.

Finally, the pair was gone and silence returned to the suite. Sita glanced at Roxie and raised both eyebrows. "Well. That was interesting."

Roxie snorted. "Yeah, interesting how much of a rich girl your roommate is. I know one thing for sure though."

"What's that?"

"Vanessa isn't getting anywhere near a guy I like."

Sita laughed and returned to her reading.

Chapter Ten
Light at Night

Joe walked down the mostly deserted street, careful to avoid any of the people still outside. At midnight, most decent business people had already been home for hours in this district. These buildings were all offices of some kind.

He pulled up a mental map and turned right onto a larger street, trying to recall the directions given him by Mr. Knight. The building shouldn't be very far from here now. Joe clutched the briefcase he held, feeling a shiver run down his spine and the hairs on the back of his neck rise. Someone was following him.

The follower had been on him for almost a mile now, much longer than usual for a random stranger to follow another random stranger. Joe had been chased by enemies before, but something about this was different. This seemed too random, too happenstance, to have been planned.

He was gaining, but Joe tried not to show he had noticed—maybe he would go away, like animals that only ate live meat. If he pretended disinterest, perhaps the stranger would pass him by.

But he wasn't leaving. He kept coming.

Unable to pretend any longer, Joe looked over his shoulder, dropped the empty briefcase, and took off running down the street. His breath came in short bursts, much faster than he thought it would. He kept going, pushing himself on, hoping to reach safety and the chance to escape. He couldn't hear the man behind him anymore. The yellow streetlamps flashed past as he looked over his shoulder again.

It was only one man behind him, but something about the pursuer sent shivers down Joe's spine. He didn't run—didn't seem to move at all—but he kept pace behind Joe, following him as if he were gliding over the ground. This man looked familiar, like someone he should know but couldn't place. The man's graying hair glowed unnaturally bright. Shadows clung to the man, obscuring the light from the streetlamps as he passed, and there was something about the eyes . . .

Joe tripped and sprawled on the pavement. He cried out in fear when he saw that his shoelaces had been tied together while he ran, tripping him up. The stranger roared with laughter.

Joe fumbled with the laces and got them separated. He clambered to his feet and ran forward, running straight to where he knew he would find a busier street. The stranger suddenly appeared to his left, just when Joe would have turned there. Joe skidded to the right down another road, the stranger appearing again out of nowhere. Joe spun and pelted back the way he came.

The stranger stopped him a third time, laughing, herding him, staying out of sight until Joe thought escape was possible, then showing himself again to push the butler down another street. Joe emerged on a side road of the busy main street he had been aiming for earlier. Hoping he could make it, he put on another burst of speed and ran for the sickly yellow lights just ahead.

Joe cried out again when he saw the street magically disappear into a dead end, and now he could guess what he was dealing with. Joe's hands began to sweat—Mr. Knight forbade Joe to do any magic, had made him swear not to, and that vow was binding.

He put his back to the magical wall and held his hands out in front of him, hoping to be as threatening as possible and knowing he failed. The man chasing him followed Joe down the strange road and crept forward. Shadows deepened with every step he took, and Joe felt sweat trickle down his forehead. "Stay back!" he shouted. "Who are you?"

A low chuckle came from the front of the alley. "You know who I am, Joe, from pictures you have taken yourself. I know who you work for." He walked even closer, his movements slow and sure. Joe tried to disappear further back into the wall, but the wall remained solid at his back. "And I am going to send a message to your employer. He will know exactly what he's dealing with soon enough."

Joe's hand shook in violent spasms as he tried to raise it in front of him. "What do you want? I can't help you, and I won't betray my people!"

The strange man chuckled again, and that small laugh almost unhinged Joe completely. "Do you want to live, Joe? Do you want to see your friends again, your people? I might be able to help you."

Joe swallowed, his tongue sticking to the roof of his mouth. "I don't want any help you could give, you evil bastard. I am loyal to my people, and no one else."

Darkness closed in all around the two men. The stranger had a height advantage over his victim. He grabbed his victim's neck, arm muscles bulging. His grip was tight enough to cut off airflow, and Joe gasped and gurgled, his fingers scrabbling at the stranger's arms in terror and desperation. The stranger's lips turned up in a cruel smile, full of sharp and predatory white teeth.

With one hand holding Joe against the wall, the stranger reached into his pocket with his other hand. He pulled out a beautiful clear diamond, almost the size of his fist. It reflected very little light, since it too was engulfed in the shadows, so Joe barely recognized it for what it was.

The stranger brought the diamond up to his victim's eyes, turning it until one huge facet faced Joe. Patient and slow, the stranger began speaking in a strange guttural language, nothing Joe had ever heard before—or would ever hear again. As he spoke, the shadows lengthened, drawing closer and closer to the man pinned on the wall.

Shadows reached out to the victim, sneaking into his mouth and ears. Joe shrieked and writhed in pain, but the stranger continued speaking, increasing the ferocity until the words echoed in his victim's ears and permeated straight through to his brain. The shadows worked further and further in until they reached the center of his body.

Suddenly Joe felt something essential snap. Something very important was simply swallowed by shadow. A triumphant smile appeared on the stranger's now-silent lips as his victim went limp, arms falling down to his sides and head lolling on a loose neck.

If he had been alive to see the diamond, Joe would have been astonished, would have offered to buy the jewel then and there. For the instant Joe went limp, the diamond began to glow, illuminating the false street as clear as midday with clean white light. It sparkled and shone as the stranger turned it in his hands, examining it.

Once the stone had stopped brightening and held steady for ten minutes, the man let his dead victim drop to the ground, forgotten now that he had served his purpose.

The smile returned to the mouth of the man. He pocketed the stone and turned to the mouth of the alley, banishing the shadows.

"Perfect."

The man disappeared. The dead end vanished, leaving Joe's body now visible in the middle of the road.

∞

Robert sat in the padded chair in Alexander Knight's office. Nausea rose in his stomach, and he fought it back—the expenditure of power today had cost him a lot. He played with the edges of the papers he held, waiting for Mr. Knight to look up. Finally he did, and Rob slid the papers across the desk. "I have a hunch you already know this information, sir, about the Awle line. It seems like something you would research."

Knight smirked in good humor and glanced through Rob's report. Rob continued. "They have been working together to enhance their gifts, and build their fighting abilities. They're getting better at working in concert during practice sessions."

"And they have been getting stronger? Their practices have enhanced their abilities?"

A gleam lit Knight's eyes as he thumbed through the papers and found the sections about the magical practice sessions. Knight looked too eager for Robert's liking. His eyes narrowed. "Yes, sir, it's all there in my report. I left nothing out. They're all very gifted." Robert licked his lips. "Unusual, isn't it, how five such extraordinary young women end up in the same school? On the same floor. Four in the same suite."

Knight's smile faded and his lips curved downward. He threw the papers down on his desk and leaned back in his chair. "What are you suggesting, Robert?"

"Sir, meaning no disrespect, but I would not be surprised if you m—"

Robert never got to finish his sentence. A man opened the door and barged inside, a man who wasn't Joe. He looked hassled and dirty, out of breath from running. "Sir, emergency. Joe is dead."

Knight and Robert jumped up from their chairs. "What?" Robert said.

Allen James leaned on his knees, catching his breath. "I just recovered his body, brought him back here from D.C. He's dead, Mr. Knight, there's no question about it."

"Where did you put him?"

"Downstairs in the sitting room."

Knight hurried from his office, trailed by the two younger men. They ran down the stairs and into the sitting room, Allen just keeping to his feet. Rob paused and turned to help Allen, half-carrying him into the room. Allen nodded his thanks and collapsed on a couch, easing his dirty jacket off.

The body lay on another couch, stretched out in state, pale, stiff, and very clearly dead. Knight began to inspect him, looking for a wound. Robert watched, waiting. "What happened?" he asked Allen.

The other man shook his head. "I don't know. All I know is that when I found him, he was dead for hours. I couldn't find any wounds, no reason for his death at all." He sat up, looking better now. "I thought bringing him back here would be for the best." Alexander nodded to show he heard but continued looking over Joe, watching as his magic ran over every inch of the body.

At last he stood up from Joe's corpse. "He wasn't killed, precisely."

Knight paused for a long time. Rob and Allen waited. Allen's breathing slowed to a normal pace. Knight tapped his bottom lip in thought, absorbed in Joe's death, and clearly oblivious at the moment to Rob and Allen. "What was it then?" Robert asked.

The older man turned his back on the dead butler. "His life force was stolen."

Allen and Robert stared at each other, then at him. "Excuse me?" said Allen.

"His life force was stolen." He sighed when they continued to look at him with uncomprehending stares. "His soul, his heart, his life, whatever you would like to call it. That which makes us all live and breathe, makes us alive. That was stolen from Joe. That was what killed his body."

Robert could hardly believe his ears. He blinked hard. "Do we know how?"

Alexander Knight stroked his chin. The small hesitation before he spoke gave Robert pause. His eyes narrowed in suspicious thought. "No. Not yet. Allen, you will help Robert. Try to see if you can't find out how this happened." He looked back at both of them. "Be extremely careful. No mage alive today should know how to do something like this without risking the death of his own soul. This magic is dirty, perverted, and forbidden. Our enemy may be the ones using it, but we cannot be sure. Find out, and quickly, or the girls you love, Robert, are going to be in far greater danger than ever before."

Chapter Eleven
Romance and Family

The two professors met in the hidden room as they had just two months before, at the beginning of school. Instead of Sandara's seductive dress from the first meeting, she now had on warmer clothes, a brilliant suit that defined her figure. Alan merely added an indoor jacket in the November chill.

Sandara sat down in the same chair, crossing her arms across her chest to keep warm. "So what's the next plan? How long do we stay here teaching these idiotic children?"

The other professor poured them both glasses of red wine. He handed her the glass. She nodded curt thanks. "You will leave as soon as you prepare the attack for those girls, as we discussed." He sipped at the red liquid. It was a good flavor. "I, however, will leave within the next few days. I need to check on the manse, and get everything ready for the beginnings of my plans. That place needs to be cleaned before it can be lived in." He took another sip. "Luckily, I have plenty of mindless idiots in this organization who will gladly do the cleaning. At least get things dusted off and the bedrooms sleepable."

Sandara smiled and downed her wine in a single gulp. "So you get to skip out early. Do we care if they find our disappearances suspicious?"

"Not at all. Once your task is accomplished, leave immediately for the manse. I will leave you the Ripper to get there."

Sandara set her glass down on the table. "Thank you, professor. I appreciate it."

"Just do your job, Sandara, and remember who owns your life."

Her red lips curled into a cruel smile, making shivers climb up Alan's spine. "I never forget, sir. Have no fear of that."

Eric and Sita walked down the street to her building. Dinner was superb, and Sita felt way too full, and a bit sleepy. Eric had one arm wrapped around her waist over her light jacket, pulling her close to him while they walked.

He leaned over and kissed her hair, timing the kiss between steps. "How are classes going?"

Sita shrugged. "Not so bad. Most are interesting. I like my History class."

Eric pulled her closer. "So are you going home for Thanksgiving?"

"Yeah, I can't wait to get home. I miss my sister, believe it or not. You?" Sita replied.

"Yep, but I'm not really looking forward to break."

"Why not?"

"'Cause I'll be away from you."

Sita blushed and looked away, smiling. "Well, I'll miss you, too. But it's only a week, it's not that long."

He sighed theatrically. "But a whole week without your pretty eyes is torture to me!"

"You'll live," she said. He looked wounded, so she shut her mouth uncomfortably. After a few minutes of silence, Sita spoke up. "Look, Eric, I'm sorry, it's just . . . I'm not very good with this whole dating thing." She paused, thinking. "I usually only open up to my friends, and only my *good* friends. Trying to be open and fun and interesting and charming all at the same time is . . . well, it's hard." She stopped walking so she could look him in the eye, hoping he understood. "It's not that I don't like you, I'm just not good at this, and I really do like you, and . . ." she said in a rush.

Eric laid a finger on her lips to make her stop. Smiling, he laughed at her surprised expression. He held her hand and caressed it. "Sita, it's all right. I understand." He tucked her arm in his again and continued walking. "We'll take it slow."

She looked up at him, smiling again, her face radiant. "Yeah. We'll take it slow."

They walked the remaining distance in a comfortable silence, listening to each other's breathing, shivering a little in their jackets in the chilly breeze. Sita's heels click-clacked on the brick stairs as he opened the door for her. The dorms appeared empty.

Eric walked her up all three flights of stairs to her suite. Standing outside the door for a minute not saying a word, Sita decided to break the silence. "I had a good time. The restaurant was a good idea, it was great."

He laughed. "Sita, do you ever stop talking?" She smiled as he leaned in for a goodnight kiss.

∞

"Dad, come on, be reasonable, *please?*"

Roxie stalked around her room, the cell phone glued to her ear. What had begun as a phone call to her mother for emotional support had turned into a financial fight with her father. "Dad, I can't find a job right now."

"*You see! You see, I told you you would never find a job as an artist.*"

Roxie hit her forehead with the heel of her palm. A headache began to form behind her temples. "I'm not looking for a job as an artist!" She was beginning to sound hysterical. "I'm looking for something on-campus, part-time, and with a decent wage, though at this point, I've really widened the net to places off-campus and with horrible pay! *No one is hiring!*" Her father said nothing, merely growled from the other end. "Now, I need help, from my parents, because I can't find a job to buy clothes and groceries and gas. Please?"

The phone was silent on the other side. Roxie waited, her breath painful in her throat. "Dad, please. I swear I've done everything I can to find a job, any job. I can't get a job when no one is hiring. Maybe I can find one next semester, but for right now, I need the help."

Her father sighed. "*Fine. I'll send you a check this week.*"

Roxie squealed. "Thank you, Dad! Thank you, thank you, thank you!" She felt pathetically grateful. Her father grumbled and whined, and he got off the phone soon after, but Roxie didn't care. She got what she wanted.

Her desk chair caught her when she sat down, relieved. Something beige caught her eye on her desk, something that wasn't there before the phone call. She picked it up—it was a note from Robert, his messy handwriting on the outside.

Roxie unfolded the plain letter paper, reading through the sloppy scribble inside and wandering out into the common room. Sita waltzed in, her timing uncanny, and walked as if she were in a trance. Roxie hid a grin and stopped her just in time from running into the couch. "Sita, I need to show you something."

Sita nodded her head, hearing but not really comprehending what her friend said. "OK, Rox, sure . . . whatever you say." Roxie snorted in humor and pushed Sita onto the couch. She snapped her fingers in front of Sita's eyes. Sita jumped, focusing on the noise and then on Roxie. "Oh, sorry, Rox, um, what were you saying?" she asked, blushing.

Amused, Roxie sat down next to her. "I take it tonight was a good night?"

Blushing even redder, Sita could only nod. Roxie rolled her eyes. "Well, I'm glad, but I have some news from Rob."

Sita lost her day-dreamy look. "He's been gone a week since he last showed up. It's about time. What does he want?"

Rox held out the letter for her to read. She did, groaning in exasperation. "He wants me to meet some old guy? Is he serious?"

"Yep. Apparently he's a very skilled magician. One of the best, Rob says. I'm supposed to go with you, too. I don't know why Robbie wants me to meet him, I mean it's not like he can teach me, I'm not a mage. But I'm going anyway."

Sita sighed and rubbed her eyes. She perused the letter again and threw it on the table in annoyance. "I don't really want to meet some old, decrepit mage who thinks I don't know anything. Why does Rob want me to meet this guy?"

"He just wants you to learn more, Sita. He wants us all in top condition. He worries about us, you know that."

"Yeah, I know, but it's over Thanksgiving break, and he wants me to go see some strange mage on break. It's supposed to be down time, that's why it's called a *break*!" Sita leaned back into the couch and sighed. "Do we really have to do this, Rox?"

A knock on the door made both of them jump. Roxie checked to make sure there was no evidence of magic out before she rose and opened the door. Jack stood outside. He smiled shyly and made an awkward wave. "Hi Roxie, is Ari here?"

Roxie bit her lip to keep from smiling. He looked so eager and Roxie didn't want him to think she was laughing at him. "No, I thought she was studying tonight. But she's not in."

His face fell. "Oh." Reaching into his bookbag, Jack pulled out a bunch of papers and a textbook. "Well, could you give her this please? She let me borrow her notes from class and I wanted to make sure she has them for the test tomorrow."

Rox took the papers and book and set them on the couch. "Sure thing. Thanks Jack."

Jack rubbed his nose. Just as Roxie went to close the door, he said, "Hey, I thought I heard you guys talking about mages." Roxie's eyes widened, but he didn't seem to notice. "Were you talking about video games?"

"Um, yeah." Rox glanced over her shoulder at Sita, who simply shrugged. No help from that quarter apparently. "Yeah, we were talking about, um, a cool fantasy computer game we were playing."

"Oh, really, what was it?"

Roxie began to sweat. "Don't remember the name, sorry, I'll make sure Ari gets the papers! Thanks Jack, bye!" He looked about to say something more, but Roxie shut the door and leaned against it, listening for him to go away. After a moment she heard his shuffling steps moving back down the hall. Rox shook her head. "What a weird guy."

She grimaced and returned to the couch. Picking up the conversation, she nodded in a matter-of-fact way. "Yes, we have to do this. Rob told me about this guy. He's a dark blue mage, stronger than Rob, not a part of any group and is totally neutral. All kinds of organizations have been after him for years, trying to turn him to some side or other, but he hasn't budged. He's older, like in his sixties, I think, but he's still really powerful. You might actually learn something, Sita." She put a hand on Sita's shoulder. "All he wants you to do is meet him. If you guys think you'll get along, he'll train you. That's it."

Sita rubbed her hands on her thighs, thinking it over. A clock in the next room beeped seven o'clock. Her lips pursed as she came to a decision. "Fine, I'll meet him, as long as you go with me. You know how I am with strangers. Did Rob tell you this guy's name?"

Roxie grabbed the letter off the table and looked through it, finding the code Robert had encrypted the name in once she knew what to look for. "Yep, his name is—this is such a weird name—Ka'len Lera."

Silence met that pronouncement. Sita stared at Roxie, trying to decide if she was joking or not. "Are you serious?" she finally asked. "That's really his name?" Roxie nodded, her face stoic. Sita closed her eyes. "Great. The man's a nut-job. Just perfect."

Changing the subject, Roxie set the letter down and tucked her feet underneath the cushion to keep them warm. "So what do you think of Darci joining the practice sessions? You think it'll be all right? I mean, if she's going to get worse, then what would that mean for us?"

Outside the suite they heard Skylar and Estelle walk into their own room, their loud chatter fading as their door closed. Sita shook her head. "I don't really know. I think Rob was right when he said we should be her friend as much as possible, but as for the practices, I think we'll have to play that by ear. It might go well, it might not." They sat in silence again, each thinking their own grim thoughts. Sita looked up when she heard loud noises outside the door. "Hey, isn't tonight a movie night?"

Roxie nodded. "Yep. You coming?" she asked as the door opened, framing Estelle, Skylar, Darci, Vanessa, and Ariene in it.

Sita rose and ran to her room. "Just let me change!" she shouted over her shoulder.

The next morning, Sita sat in her history class, daydreaming and barely listening to the professor drone on about World War II. Vanessa poked her awake. "Sita!" she hissed. Professor Bryant obligingly kept talking. Vanessa pushed a folded paper at Sita, who took it with a surreptitious look at the professor.

Opening it, she read: *Hey, when's our first mission?* Grabbing a pen, Sita wrote back: *Don't know, I think it's after Thanksgiving. Ask Roxie.* She waited for the good professor to look at his notes before passing it back to Vanessa's waiting hand.

She doesn't know either.

Well I don't know!

How was the date last night? Get any action?

No! Not that it's any of your business anyway . . . well, he did kiss me good night.

Is he a good kisser?

Maybe . . .
Is Darci going to be practicing with us from now on?
I think so. Why?
She makes me nervous.

They both jumped when Professor Bryant stopped talking and the other students packed away their books. Vanessa grinned and picked up her notebook. "Did you hear any of the lecture?" she asked under her breath.

Sita chuckled, hoisted up her bag and shook her head. "Nope. You?"

"Not a word." They laughed and walked to the dining hall for lunch, meeting the others there. They all waited in line for their food, then congregated at their favorite table by the window. Darci showed up, quieter than usual. They talked about the mall and movies and classes for a while as they ate. Eric made an appearance, pulling up a chair next to Sita and kissing her hello, to the amusement of everyone else at the table.

Vanessa glared at Sita and Eric. Darci glanced around at the others, also glaring at Sita, but not in the same way as Vanessa. Vanessa's glance was calculating and cruel, and wandered more toward Eric than anyone else's eyes did at that meal. Sita saw. Darci's glance, which Sita never saw, held a different kind of calculation.

The group finished together and began to leave, migrating to the door and skillfully dodging other students. Eric had to leave for another class, but he promised Sita he would see her later. She smiled and kissed him good-bye. Skylar and Estelle left for their own classes, but the others made their way back to the suite—Sita and Vanessa both decided to skip their last class—and invited Darci to join them.

She declined and stalked into her own room, leaving the others to themselves. Vanessa turned on the radio and began putting clothes away. Roxie and Ariene claimed the chairs in the room, while Sita sat on her bed. Vanessa glanced at Ari. "I heard about Professor Alan being replaced. Does that class suck now?"

"How did you hear about that?" Ari said.

Vanessa shrugged. "There's a rumor going around campus that he's missing."

Sita cut in. "I heard two professors talking yesterday, they said that no one can find Alan anywhere. They think he left for good, but no one knows why." Roxie shrugged in reply. "We have Smith teaching for now until they get Alan back."

"If they do," Rox said.

Vanessa changed the subject. "Are you going home for break next week?"

Ari nodded. "Of course. You?"

"Yep, I'm going back home to my nice cold Vermont. I miss the snow," she said, her eyes clouding over. "Is everyone going home?" she asked, snapping out of her trance.

Nods all around. Roxie reclined in the chair, toying with a pen in her hand. The sun shining through the window hit her in the eyes, so she shifted a pinch to the right to avoid its glare. "Well, I guess we'll have to postpone the practices, then. We're all going to be busy packing and doing last-minute homework, so let's not have one this week. We can pick it up again when we get back. Everyone agree?"

Ariene shrugged, yawning and crossing her legs. Vanessa nodded, mouthing the words to a song on the radio. Sita nodded as well and said, "OK. Sounds good to me."

Roxie held up a piece of plain paper. "I've also gotten our first assignment from Robert." The others stilled and stared at her, looking like breathing statues. "It's after we get back from break, about two miles from here. We can make that easily." She folded the paper back up, shoving it in her pocket.

The other three waited impatiently for more information, but Roxie was silent, playing with them. Finally Vanessa could wait no longer. "Well? What are we doing?"

Roxie pursed her lips, laughter in her brown eyes. She looked down to study her fingernails. "We're going to be spying on a bunch of bad guys, who Robert's employer thinks are in league with the guys gunning for us. Rob says he thinks he can make it in time to go with us, but just in case he can't, he says to just spy. If we have an opportunity to capture them, we should. He told me where to take them if we do end up capturing them."

Sita grinned. "Yes!" she cried. "Our first mission! I can't wait!"

∞

Later that night, Vanessa lay awake in bed, Sita in a deep sleep across the room. Thoughts tumbled through her head, aggravating her and only making her angrier. *What does Eric see in Sita?* she thought. *I'm prettier, I'm better looking, I'm so much more desirable than she is. Why didn't he even look at me?* She tossed and turned, glaring at her stuffed rabbit and shoving it aside. It fell to the floor with a soft thump. Vanessa growled in annoyance, climbed down from the raised bed and grabbed the stuffed animal, then tossed it back into her bed.

Instead of climbing back up, she wrenched open her door and paced the common room. She prowled for almost an hour before a thought came to her. *I just have to show him how great I am. Then he'll leave Sita for me.* Clapping her hands in childish glee, she raced back to her room and looked at the clock—it wasn't even midnight. She dressed again in the dark, snatched her key, and ran from the suite.

She jogged down the stairs and into a building almost on the other side of campus. Taking the stairs two at a time, Vanessa ran to the second floor and found Eric's room, which he shared with Allen. Catching her breath, she saw that the light was still on and smiled. Arranging her hair and fixing her shirt, she knocked on the door.

Allen answered it, brow furrowing when he saw who it was. "Vanessa? What are you doing here?"

Vanessa simpered and flipped her hair. "Is Eric here?"

He looked behind him. "Yeah, he is, I'll get him." He closed the door a little while Eric pulled on a shirt.

Eric pulled open the door. Vanessa smiled wide—and pounced. She smothered him with a single kiss. Eric's eyes opened wide, and his hands braced on the door and wall, completely stunned and unable to react. Vanessa kissed him thoroughly, her hands running through his hair and pulling him closer. Eric, after a moment of shock, put his hands on her shoulders and shoved her away. Vanessa stared at him, confused.

Eric stared back at her, mouth agape. He took a slow, deep breath and then opened his mouth again. When he spoke it was very careful and slow. "Vanessa, what the hell are you doing?"

She placed a hand on his face. He pushed it away. She smiled. He frowned. She looked at him as prettily as she could and answered in her sweetest voice, "I want you, Eric. Don't you want me? I'm better than Sita, in every way. I'm smarter, and prettier, and skinnier, and I really like you, Eric."

Rubbing at his eyes with his right hand, Eric paused before he said anything more. "Vanessa, listen very carefully. I do *not* like you. You are a devious snake. Neither one of us will tell Sita about this, but if you ever try that shit with me again, I won't be responsible for what I do." He started to close the door, Allen visibly rolling on the floor in laughter, but thought of one more thing to say. "Oh, and, you can't compare to Sita. Not in a million years could you equal her. And I would never be interested in someone as shallow as you." He slammed the door in her face.

Vanessa stood outside the door, shaking in shock and confusion, unable to comprehend why Eric hadn't responded to her the way she thought he would. She touched her puffy lips, bruised from the kissing. One shaking hand came to her cheek and she could feel the confusion and humiliation making her face red with heat.

Then the confusion turned to exasperation, and finally to anger.

An idea sprang into her mind, a horrible, disgusting idea. "I know why you don't like me," she said to herself. Luckily, it was late enough at night that no one was in the hall with her to hear. "Sita put a spell on you. She turned you against me!" The hand against her cheek came down and turned into a clenched fist, nails digging into her palm. Her breathing quickened and her eyes narrowed, a feeling of outrage building in the pit of her stomach as she had another thought. "She's turned everyone against me with a spell! No wonder they all treat me the way they do! Ah!" With a flip of her long hair, she stalked down the hall.

Alone with her thoughts, Vanessa began the long walk back to her suite.

Chapter Twelve
New Meetings

Ka'len Lera bustled around his kitchen, making lunch for three. His long robe swirled around his ankles, and his long sleeves kept getting in the way of his sandwich-making. Exasperated, he finally resorted to magic to finish the sandwiches. The bread and turkey stacked in order and then the sandwiches arranged themselves on the silver tray, next to the small bowl of potato chips and the plate of carrots and dip. The kettle began to whistle as Ka'len moved the tray onto the living room table.

The old man grumbled to himself, his voice deep and grating. "I do not know why I agreed to meet Robert's girls. I have not taught in years." He poured out a cup of tea for himself, setting the kettle back onto the stove to keep it warm. "There are always powerful people out there in need of training, I do not know why he wants me to train this one . . ."

The doorbell rang, echoing through the house. Ka'len sighed and went to answer it. Straightening his tunic and finger-combing his short beard, he took a breath and opened the door.

Two young women stood outside his house. The tall one radiated power, while the shorter one looked to be Robert's friend Roxie. Raising his brow, he stepped back from the door. "Good afternoon. You must be Sita and Roxie. I am Ka'len Lera. Please come in." Greeting him politely, the young women walked inside, stopping in the foyer. Ka'len closed the door behind him and pointed to the living room. "Please have a seat. I have prepared some lunch for us and I will be with you in a moment." He left the young women to find their own way in a hurry. *Damn that boy, he knows I am not very good with younger people, why he wants me, of all people, to do this . . .* Ka'len grabbed his tea cup and walked out to see his guests.

The blond one, Sita, sat on the edge of the couch, looking uncomfortable and stiff. The other one relaxed into her cushioned chair, clearly at ease. Ka'len sat down in his own chair, studying the pair. "Please, have some lunch. The sandwiches are turkey and mayonnaise. I hope you like them." Sita reached forward and took one of the sandwich plates off the tray. Roxie copied her. "Would either of you like something to drink?" he asked.

Roxie nodded. "Just a water, please, Mr. Lera."

Ka'len laughed, taking a liking to the girl. "Oh, no, Roxie, please call me Ka'len. I have little use for formality among friends anymore." Roxie smiled and nodded. Ka'len conjured a glass of water from the kitchen and onto the table. Both looked very surprised, and Roxie tentatively touched the glass, as if she thought it an illusion. The old man smiled and turned to Sita. "And for you, Sita? What would you like?"

"What do you have to drink?" the girl asked.

His eyes narrowed. *She does not seem to want to be here at all. How unusual.* He watched her take a bite from her sandwich before answering. "I have water, milk, cranberry juice, wine, and that vile concoction of this time, Coca-Cola. The drink is poison, but I have taken a liking to it."

Sita considered her options. After what appeared to be a moment of thought, she blinked once and conjured a second glass of water as Ka'len had conjured the first. Smiling now, she picked it up and took a sip, her eyes meeting Ka'len's with a sparkle of laughter and challenge. "Your water is very good, Ka'len. Thank you."

Ka'len's eyes narrowed further. His stomach clenched and his heart fluttered as he considered her action. *She has cheek, this one. And a great deal of power.* The power she displayed in just that one act had shocked him to the core, more so than the rudeness she had shown in carpeting his home in her magic without his permission. That one display had opened a small window into the well of her power, and he had seen how deep it ran. A tremor swept through his hands.

Setting his tea cup down, he decided to skip right to business. "Well, Sita, Roxie, I assume Robert has told you why he requested you see me." Both young women nodded, their sandwiches finished now. "Good. You should know that I have not taken on a student in quite a long time. Can you tell me why I should teach you? What makes you worthy of my time and patience?"

Sita looked at Roxie, who shrugged her shoulders, confused. She looked back at Ka'len. "To be honest, sir, I don't know why you should teach me. All I know is that Robert seemed to think I need more instruction than he can give, and that you're the right person. That's the only reason I'm here. If you don't want to teach me, then I see no reason why we should take up more of your time." Glancing at Rox, she stood up.

The old man waved her back down. "Hold." He studied Sita for a moment, looking deep into her eyes. Sita held the eye contact. He broke first and rose to his feet. A small, old wooden cabinet leaned against the far wall. Ka'len beckoned them over and opened the two doors.

He gestured for Sita to move closer and pointed to the object inside. Sita peered at it. She peeked back up at Ka'len before looking again at it. Ka'len, grinning, spoke again, his voice quiet. "I would like for you to please take this box out. Open it, if you can, and then put on what is inside." She looked at him in surprise. He continued. "If you can do that, then I will teach you."

Folding his arms and standing back, he smirked, sure of himself. *No one who has come to me for teaching has been able to open that box, much less move it. It requires the right person, the right magic.* He leaned on the wall and prepared for the disappointment.

Sita, meanwhile, studied the box. It was an ancient rectangular creation, and its only adornment was the shield on its front. Curious, she leaned closer to see it better. The oak had been carved into a family shield, the kind usually associated with nobility. Unpainted, it was impossible to tell what the colors were supposed to have been, but the animals—a horse, a griffin, and a stag—were very clearly carved onto the surface. Ka'len watched her look at the rest of the box, trying to see what the catch of this test was.

She reached her right hand inside and extended a finger toward the box, moving slow to check for traps. Ka'len smirked, knowing what would happen next if she touched it. But the result he expected didn't happen. He peered at the girl. Her arm had stopped moving forward. Sita withdrew her hand. Closing her eyes, Ka'len saw her blanket the box in her magic, just touching the shield around the box before it flared crimson and collapsed.

Ka'len's eyes widened. *It seems I am in for more surprises today.* The thought unsettled him and sent a chill over his skin. *Will I really have to teach this child? I do not really want to teach again, despite what I promised Robert. There are so many complications with young people today.* He shushed himself and went back to watching.

Grinning now, Sita pulled the box out of the cabinet with her hands and set it on top of the fine oak wood. She continued to study it as she searched for the catch to open it. Purple magic extended from her again to probe the box's edges. She examined it once more before her index finger quested forward and touched the edge. Taking a breath, she used her magic and her finger to lift the lid, quickly turning off the blasting trap just inside.

Impressed, Ka'len reconsidered. *Maybe teaching her would not be so bad. She seems fairly capable already. Perhaps she just needs some fine-tuning.* He watched as she opened the box and saw what was inside. Her blue-green eyes darkened. "A ring?" asked Sita. "What's so important about a ring that it's behind all these shields?" She lifted it from the cushion and turned it over and over in the light to get a better look.

The ring looked ancient in its design. A softening of the metal along the rim showed the ring had been worn before, and for many years. Its only adornment was the same shield and crest from the front of the box. The deep gold color of its metal reminded her of real gold. "Is this *real?*" she asked Ka'len, handing him the ring.

Taking a deep breath, Ka'len took the ring from Sita, feeling the familiar weight of it in his fingers. "This ring is the signet ring of the House of Awle. Do you know anything about them?"

Sita and Roxie both seemed very surprised when he mentioned the name. His smile tinged with sorrow, he continued without their answer. "Ah, I see you both have heard the name. Well, this ring has been passed down through the centuries from heir to heir, until it came into my possession. You see, the true heir to the stewardship of the surviving House had disappeared." He walked back to his chair, indicating the silent girls should sit back down as well. "This was almost four hundred years or so ago, when I used to live in Corá. The heir had been my student and my good friend, and she was brilliant. Her name was Lena Koniet, of the House of Awle." Ka'len laid the ring on the table. "She decided to leave Corá to live elsewhere. Here, in fact, in Maryland.

"Lena was incredibly talented. The most promising mage I had ever had the privilege to teach. But when she left Corá, she left behind her signet ring as well. She asked that I keep it safe until the heir came back." He looked down at the ring and closed his eyes. "However, she never did come back. Lena was murdered ten years after she came here, after she and her two children had begun to build a new life. So I put it away, added the shields, and never opened that box again. From then on, I tested every student to see if they could open the box. None of them could, and then I started using the box as a test for taking on students. When no one could open it, I stopped teaching."

Sita and Roxie listened, silent and a little shocked. When Ka'len stopped talking, Sita took a turn. "Do you think that's why Rob asked us to come here? He only told us about the Houses this month, but it doesn't seem like an accident," she said, turning to Rox.

Roxie nodded. "It probably was. Rob knew what he was doing after he got his hands on that information." She turned to Ka'len now. "Ka'len, I was wondering . . . exactly how old are you?"

Ka'len opened his eyes and let a chuckle escape his lips. "Ah, caught that, did you? Well, I am just over four hundred and thirty years old. See, magic has a way of extending life. It grants an extra 25 to 30 years naturally. But sometimes, the more powerful mages can choose to extend their lives even further, as I have. Not all choose it, but some do."

"And what nationality are you? Your name is so . . . um, unusual," Sita asked, humor laced in her voice.

He tweaked the end of his snowy beard. "I am not a nationality of this plane. I am from Corá. We do things differently there." Seeing their bemusement, he smiled. "Dear Robert has not told you yet of Corá, has he?"

Roxie shook her head. "No, but he's mentioned an 'other plane' before, when he told us about the Houses. Are Corá and this 'plane' place the same thing?"

Ka'len nodded. "Yes, indeed. But I think Robert would enjoy telling you about Corá, so why not leave that to him, shall we?" He climbed to his old feet and floated the now-empty tray back into the kitchen. "But now, young ladies, I believe the hour is getting late, and you should be going home."

Taken by surprise, Sita and Roxie rose at once, grabbed their purses and followed Ka'len. He led them to the door, opened it, and smiled. "Ladies, please tell Robert I have agreed to teach. When you return to school, I will contact both you and him. And Sita . . ." She spun back around to face him as she was half out the door. Ka'len summoned the ancient ring to him from the table. "Please take this. It is yours. Wear it, but keep it safe. It could be useful one day."

Jaw slack as her mouth hung open, Sita held out a hand to take the ring, which he placed in her palm. Then she followed Roxie from the house, staring at the ring all the while, as Ka'len closed the door behind her.

The old man rested his forehead on the door, feeling all of his 400-plus years. *Lena, Lena, your heir is as amazing as you were.* He walked back to his chair and sat down, silent, contemplating. *Lena, I wish you could see her. She looks so much like you, she even has your eyes. She has your wings, too, if Robert is correct.* Ka'len watched the two young women walk to their car and drive away. *Lena, I miss you so, my darling. I wish you had never left Corá.* The tears he had never allowed himself to shed slipped down his leathery cheek in the lonely silence.

Roxie turned the car onto the road. "So, what do you think of him? He doesn't seem all that bad. And you even got a ring out of it!" Trees whizzed past as Sita stared out her window. Roxie glanced over. "Si? What is it?"

"Hmm?" Sita turned back to her friend. "Oh, nothing. I was just thinking . . . I'm sure I've heard that name before."

"What name? Ka'len's?"

"No. Lena Koniet. I'm sure I heard that name before. Something my mother once said . . . something about doing family history research but not being able to go any farther than someone named Lena." She tugged on her lower lip, troubled. "She said it was like the trail was demolished, like all our ancestors had dropped off the map. There was nothing."

Roxie turned out onto the highway and merged into the high-speed traffic. "Maybe it's the same person. Ka'len did mean you're the heir when he gave you the ring, right? It's got to be the same person." She smiled. "And now you know why your mom couldn't get any further in her family tree—you guys didn't exist here until four hundred years ago!"

Sita stared out the window again. "Lena Koniet . . . the name sounds so familiar. I feel like I've met her before."

Chapter Thirteen
Rings

Alexander Knight sat at his desk, twirling a pen between his fingers. A tentative knock came from the other side of the door.

"Come in, Robert."

Robert entered and closed the door. The young man bowed to his employer. "Hello again, sir."

"Have a seat, son. Tell me what news you have."

Knight was amused to see that the boy looked nervous. Sweat beaded on Robert's forehead, and his fingers never managed to stop fidgeting when in his presence. He was pleased to see that the boy could at least deliver a report through his nervousness.

He listened as Robert relayed everything he had learned in the past few weeks since his last visit. Knight nodded occasionally, encouraging him to continue. What Robert told him was indeed very interesting, and Knight allowed his eyes to go out of focus while he thought.

When Robert finished, Knight nodded at him again. "Very good, Robert. You have exceeded my expectations." He opened a drawer in his desk and pulled out a small palm-sized bag. It bulged to the brim. Knight slid it across the desk's top. "As promised, here is your next pay. Two hundred pieces of gold."

Robert grinned. "Thank you, sir. I was beginning to have some trouble paying the rents on my places. I may have to get rid of one if the market keeps on like this."

Knight frowned, returning from his murky thoughts. "You have the house in Torthal, and the two apartments on Earth, correct?"

"Yes, sir."

"Hmm." Knight stroked his chin for a moment. "As I recall, the Torthal house costs you twenty pieces of gold per month, the one apartment costs less than one thousand dollars, and the other costs almost two thousand?" Robert nodded. "Then I will allocate another one hundred and fifty gold for you. I want you to be comfortable in paying your bills while in my service."

Robert smiled and bowed his head. "Thank you, sir! I appreciate your generosity."

"You are a valued employee, Robert, and you have always done good work. I wish to show my appreciation and make sure you know how highly I value you and your service."

Alexander Knight was about to dismiss him when Robert leaned forward, his expression earnest. He paused, curious at what would make Robert light up in this way.

"Sir, I'd like permission to take them into Corá."

Knight's eyebrows shot into his hair. "Pardon?"

Robert's eagerness dimmed only a little. He gestured as he spoke, his enthusiasm obvious. "I want to take the girls into Corá, sir, but I need permission to get the rings for them to enter. I want permission to tell them more about Corá in the meantime. I don't feel right keeping them in the dark, especially since I think Sita, and maybe some of the others, are probably descended from people who came from here."

Knight reclined in his chair. "Tell them about Corá . . . this is something that could possibly be to our advantage." The more he thought about it, the more he liked the idea. "Yes. You may tell them about Corá. I will draft a letter with my support for the rings that you may take to the Council. I will deliver it to you through the usual means."

This time Robert heeded the dismissal. Clutching his bags of money, he rose and bowed deep. "Thank you, Mr. Knight. I appreciate this, sir, more than you know." Rob let himself out and closed the door.

Alexander Knight returned to fiddling with his pen. He reclined in his chair and stared at the cabinet across the room, the one that held his most prized possession. A slight glow made its way through the cracks of the cabinet, the pearlescent light pulsing in anger. "Yes, you heard her name, didn't you?" he asked the light. "You recognize her as one of your own." The pulse increased, the light illuminating lines and cracks on his dark wooden floor. "Well, my dear, you will have to wait for her to join you. She has yet to come to me."

The light would have been blinding had he been looking straight at it. "But she will be coming into Corá soon. And there I have more opportunity to influence her, persuade her. Make her mine. You would hate that, wouldn't you?"

If the cabinet were open, Knight would have been not only blinded, but overwhelmed by the strength and anger of the light. He could feel the outrage emanating from the object within, and it filled him with glee and a deep satisfaction. In a fine mood, Knight set about making plans.

∞

Sandara Cane walked down the hallway to her office in the English department wing. Her colleagues were all gone for the Thanksgiving holiday, so the office was mercifully quiet and lacking the normal sound of complaining students. Sandara breathed a quick sigh of relief as her bright red pumps beat a loud tune on the polished floor.

Her office door came up fast, its tanned front blending in to the rest of the wall. The professor pulled out her keys and unlocked the door, anxious to get inside and away from any remaining prying eyes that might still be around, however unlikely. She flicked on the lights and strode inside, enjoying the peacefulness.

A computer hummed on her desk, idle. Pushing the door closed, Sandara locked the door and pocketed the keys again, walking over to her desk. "I can't believe I forgot those files here," she mumbled to herself. Sitting down in the plush black chair, she fluffed her black hair and pulled herself closer to the desk. "Now, let's see what we have here . . ." she let the sentence trail as she opened the first student file.

The five files, stacked in a neat pile on one side of her desk, had been delivered just yesterday by an unwitting student, who handed them over with a sleepy look in his eyes. In the first one, a picture was clipped to the front of the folder. Sandara studied the photo. She had never seen these girls, since none were in her English classes, but she would need to see what they looked like in order to work her magic on them.

Satisfied with the picture, Sandara leafed through the papers, skimming here and there to get a sense of what the girl was like.

Her thin eyebrows rose a fraction—the girl was impressive in academic circles. "Well, I'm afraid all those book smarts aren't going to help you with what I have planned, darling." She smirked as she closed the file.

Setting that one aside, she picked up the next. Each one she went through caused her to smile with restrained glee. "Oh, none of these girls are a challenge!" she cried as she finished leafing through the last folder. "Why couldn't I have gotten a better assignment from the professor? These girls will be so easy to take down . . ."

Grinning like a cat, Sandara placed the folders back into a pile and shoved them into the center of her desk. One painted fingernail traced a wide circle around the files. She closed her eyes and held out both hands palm-up in a supplicant gesture, and concentrated only on the papers. Breathing in a slow, deep breath, she gathered her magic in her hands, which began to glow in the light from two transparent emerald globes nestled in her palms. Exhaling all at once, the light disappeared from her hands and the papers erupted in flames, contained by a ring of brilliant emerald light on the desk.

She smiled in satisfaction and brushed nonexistent dirt off her flawless black trousers, her red nails highlighted by the contrast of light and dark. Spinning on her heel, Sandara walked closer to the door and studied one of the two photographs she had saved from the fire. A dark-haired student stared back at her, barely smiling for the sake of the camera. Sandara grinned as she closed her eyes again and sent a shaft of emerald light through the photograph where the girl's head was. "Heighten the uncertainty . . . heighten the instability . . . use what is already there to my advantage," she whispered in a powerful command to the picture.

The professor closed her eyes and weighed the level of power still at her disposal. It was still high—this casting had barely cost her anything, so the insomnia that was the price of her magic would be next to nothing tonight. She pulled her keys from her coat pocket and opened the door. "Oh, this will be too easy."

A vibration in her pocket made Sandara pause. She pulled out the cell phone from her pocket and looked at the caller ID. Layla Cane. Sandara closed her eyes for a moment, the phone still buzzing in her fingers, before she flipped open the phone and held it to her ear. "Hi, Mom."

"Sandy, where are you? I thought you were coming home this year."

Sandara turned on her heel to softly close the office door and lean against it. Her darkened office felt comforting, cozy . . . but also lonely. Her mother waited on the other end of the line for an answer. Sandara had to give her mom credit—she never pushed, she just waited. "No, Mom, not this year."

"Again? You work too hard, dear."

"I know, Mom. I know."

A familiar feeling crept up on her heart. Her chest felt like it would pop if she didn't allow the emotion free rein. Uncomfortable, Sandara pushed off from the door to stumble to her chair, where she plopped down.

"Danny's here, you know, with the girls. With Amy gone, he didn't have anywhere else to go this year, so he brought the girls here."

Danny. Her brother. And the girls, Melissa and Karen. Both much too young to have lost their mother, but Amy had passed away last year from cancer. Danny was a wreck afterward. Sandara saw depths to him that she never would have guessed he had, and for many months, her brother walked around as a shadowed, desperate human being.

She had never felt closer with him.

Layla Cane sighed on the other end of the phone. *"Sandy, dear, please come home. Work can't be that important. It's Thanksgiving."*

Sandara felt a tear well in her eye. The drop of salty water slid down her cold cheek and landed on her arm. She paused before she said, "I can't, Mom. I'm sorry."

"So you're going back to your empty apartment?"

"It's not empty. I have Morgan."

"A cat."

"Yes, Mom."

"Honey . . ."

In a fit of emotion and a sense of foreboding, Sandara hung her head and said something she never expected to say. "Mom . . . in case something happens to me . . . will you take care of Morgan?"

Layla Cane paused for a full minute before her voice came through the phone, hesitant and laced with fear. The fear fed into

Sandara's mind and snapped the hold her heart had placed on her. She breathed deeply as her mother spoke. *"What are you talking about? What are you involved in?"*

Sandara's voice held steady this time. "Just promise me you'll take Morgan for me if something happens to me. OK?"

"OK. I promise." Her mother clucked her tongue. *"As long as you promise to come home for Christmas. I'm not mailing your presents to you again this year."*

The bargain and her mother's annoyed tone made Sandara smile. "I promise. I'll be there."

"Good. Do you want to talk to your father?"

Sandara's eyes darkened, and her free hand clenched hard enough her nails almost pierced the skin. "No."

"But . . ."

"No."

"Fine." Pause. *"He says hello and happy Thanksgiving. And come home next year."*

"Yes, Mom. Next year."

Layla Cane said a final good-bye and Sandara hung up the phone. She glanced to her desk, the walls, the door.

She was alone.

After a moment, she climbed to her feet, legs steady now, and smoothed her clothes. Then she opened the door and left to make her way home.

∞

Robert stood in front of the Council of Nine. He swallowed hard, hoping his nervousness didn't show. The page who had announced Robert closed the large doors behind as he left. Robert stood in front of a group of nine men and women, all senior to him in age and politics, and all chosen to represent their lands on the Council. This body kept peace between many of the nations of Corá, and governed with an iron fist who received rings for entry into Corá. Catherine, Queen of Gennaios, sat in the meeting as well as mediator, as was her right as ruler of the host country to the Council. Rob waited for Dagwood Shale, the First of Nine, to finish reading his request. Dagwood had always fascinated Robert. As one of the famous Sandmen from Namith, far to the south,

Dagwood could manipulate and control sand. He even had the ability to turn himself into sand. Robert never had the courage to ask Dagwood about those abilities though; the man was intimidating. The First looked up, his dark blue eyes emphasized by the white burnoose he wore, and studied Rob. "You want the Council to approve *five* rings? You do realize, Robert, how difficult it is to receive just one?" The First stroked his white beard as he set the papers aside on the table.

Khaden Whed, the Fifth of Nine, tapped a finger on the table. "If we admit five, why don't we simply fling open the borders and let everyone in?" she said, her powerful voice infiltrating every corner of the room. Khaden, also from a country to the south but not as far as the First, never failed to remind Rob of a serpent. The red color she favored in her dress only helped the impression.

The Seventh, Yuriyi Vasgel, glared at Khaden, who promptly shut her mouth. Smoothing his expression, the Seventh looked back to Rob. "Your employer has agreed to vouch for all five of these young women, yes?" he asked as he read his copy of the request. Rob simply nodded. The signature was on the paper, along with a glowing endorsement from Knight; the question was unnecessary. Of all the people on the Council, Rob wasn't to upset this one the least. Pale Yuriyi Vasgel with eyes like clear water was the most powerful earth-working mage on the planet. He could cause earthquakes if he chose, and never bat an eye. "Tell us, Robert, why we should let these women into Corá. What makes them worthy of crossing our borders?"

Rob clenched his fists and stared the members of the Council down. "What makes them *worthy* is that they are fighting for you. They fight and train and learn all they can to help *you*. And they have no idea this place even exists! They have no real idea of what they are fighting for, or why. All they know is that they've chosen the good side, and so far that has been enough." Some of the Council members had the grace to look a little ashamed, though the First and Seventh hid their feelings behind masks of polite interest, and the Fifth stared at the floor in obvious boredom. Robert forced himself to take a deep breath and forge forward.

"But it won't always be enough. They need and deserve to know the truth. And that means not only telling them about Corá, but *showing* them. Let them in, and they will fight even harder to keep this country, this *world*, safe. Keep them out, and soon they will lose their reason to keep going."

Rob steadied himself and worked hard to unclench his hands. He didn't want to push them too hard, but the Seventh's words had pushed *him* too hard.

None of the Council members spoke. The First looked to each member, and receiving nods—some reluctant, some enthusiastic—he returned to Rob and smiled.

"Approved."

Chapter Fourteen
Struggles

The common room of Suite 400 was quiet. The doors of both bedrooms stood open, but there was no sign of life inside. Only the sound of the small refrigerator in the equally small kitchenette could be heard, humming to its own electrical tune. The place was clean—trash had been taken out a week earlier, the floors had been swept and counters scrubbed off. Windows had been closed and locked, and the blinds or drapes drawn down to keep out light. Only a lone stuffed animal in the right-hand room was out of place, the brown horse lying forgotten on the floor.

A flash of bright blue light reflected in the window. A man appeared in the center of the common room, hair out of place and clothes rumpled. Robert attempted to smooth them before looking around and noticing the silence. "Huh. Looks like I just beat them back."

He barely finished the sentence when a key was inserted into the front door's lock, and the sound of feminine voices could be heard laughing on the other side. Robert grinned while he waited for the beige door to open. It finally did and raucous laughter erupted into the room, the girls following it inside.

Roxie stepped in first, taking her key from the lock and dragging a suitcase behind her. "So I said to him, I said, if you do that one more time . . ." She stopped when she turned away from Sita's smiling face and realized Robert was there, waiting for them like a statue. "Robbie!" she cried as she dropped everything and ran to hug him. "Where have you been, it's been so long, what's been going on . . ." Roxie inundated him with questions while he just smiled down at her.

Rolling her eyes, Sita hauled her suitcase over the floor and into her room. It looked exactly as she had left it, clean and neater than usual except for her stuffed animal lying on the floor. "Oh, sorry Ruffian, you must have fallen off the bed when I left!" She picked up the stuffed horse and replaced him to the perch on her pillow. "There, much better."

Robert and Roxie followed her, still laughing. "So how was break, Sita?" Robert asked. "I know you met with Ka'len. How did it go?" He dumped himself into one of the desk chairs, lounging with grace. Roxie climbed up onto Sita's platform bed and perched there, clearly intending to let Sita tell the story.

She shrugged. "It went fine. He seemed nice. He said he would teach me."

Impatient silence. "And . . . ? Was that all?" Robert asked.

"He gave me a ring." Robert's eyebrows rose so high he actually felt a twinge of protest in the muscles. He attempted a stoic expression—but judging from Sita's narrowed eyes, he failed. "He said it was mine, and I should hang on to it."

"May I see it please?"

Sita fished one hand around in her left pocket until it emerged with the heavy golden ring. Rob held out his hand and, after only a small hesitation, she dropped it into his palm. He nodded his thanks and pulled the ring closer to his eyes for a better look. Sita and Roxie waited in silence at least a full five minutes.

He knew this ring. He had seen it so many times in drawings. Ka'len had drawn him a picture once, perfect in every detail. Rob almost didn't believe that it sat in his hands, but the truth of its existence could not be denied. The gold felt warm against his palm.

Finally Rob looked up from his palm, amazement written all over his face. "This is the ancestral signet ring of the heir of the House of Awle. I know this ring was kept in Ka'len's protection for many years, and he would never just give it away. How did you get it?"

Sita raised an elegant eyebrow and shared a glance with Roxie, who shrugged. "I used magic. I didn't have to use that much, though, I don't understand how other people couldn't get in. The box pretty much opened by itself."

She had used magic. Robert closed his eyes, not bothering to keep the fading shock and resignation from his face. "OK. That's what I was afraid of." He held the ring out to her and Sita took it back, slipping it onto her right ring finger, where it fit best. "I guess it's time that I explain some things." He sighed in regret. "But I should tell you all at once, so I don't have to repeat myself. When do the others get back here?"

"They should all be back tonight, classes start again tomorrow," Roxie answered. "I think Darci is already back, though. I thought I saw her car in the parking lot."

"All right." Robert stood and stretched. "Then let's see if she wants to hang out until everyone is back and we can all chat. And let's get some food, I'm starving."

Darci was indeed back and unpacking in her room. Roxie invited her in and ordered pizzas while the others chose a movie and caught up on the events of their breaks. Sita told them about meeting Ka'len, leaving out any mention of magic due to Darci's presence. Darci chattered on about vacationing with her college-aged cousins. Sita smiled when she heard Darci actually talking comfortably with them all.

In the middle of their pizza comas and a movie marathon, Ariene walked through the door, looking tired but happy. "You got started without me?" she cried in mock annoyance. "That's not allowed!" She stowed her things and joined her friends in front of the television, where they finished off the last of the pizza.

Another hour passed before Vanessa waltzed in, her luggage matching her outfit. She took one look at the wreckage in the common room and huffed in annoyance. "You've been back, what, three hours, and already the place is a mess. Whatever are we going to do?" The group stared at her until she broke into a wide grin. "I guess we'll just have to make it worse, then, before the semester is completely over! No point in cleaning up now!" Vanessa joined the group, not even bothering to unpack before she came into the common room and took a seat by Rob. She ran a teasing finger down his bare forearm as she sat. Robert moved his arm away and barely hid his grimace.

He counted them all to make sure no one was missing. He got their attention by standing up. With a grin, he flicked off the movie and moved away from his chair. "Now that everyone's here, I'm calling a meeting. I have some things to tell you ladies, and I think you'll like the news. But first . . ." he circled to look each young woman in the eye. "I think it's time you told Darci. The semester has gone on long enough without her knowing the truth, and it's about time we explained that day to her completely."

They all stared at him, uncertainty and hesitation in each face. Darci glanced at her friends in turn. "Tell me what, guys? What's going on?" she asked.

Ariene spoke up first. "Remember that day before break, when you got that wedding card in the mail?" Darci's face closed over and the room became chillier, but she nodded and Ari plowed on. "I don't know how much you remember, but you went a little . . . crazy . . ." She paused and glared at Vanessa when the other girl snorted. Ari resumed once Vanessa shrugged an apology. "We were all there, we all remember it." She paused for a deep breath. "You're not the only one with magic, Darci. We all have it."

Darci sat in the common room of her friends' suite, mouth agape. Then she smiled so brightly she lit up the room and made each young woman smile in return. But almost immediately, her pupils shrank and she paled as if someone had struck her. Darci's smile faded and her face retreated into its mask again. She dropped her eyes to the floor and would no longer look at anyone.

Robert watched, concerned, but he kept his expression mild. He could see, with the aid of his own magic, that there was an internal struggle in Darci's mind, but he was unable to see clearly what it was, or why.

Sita walked over to Darci and sat on the floor near her chair. She touched her hand to Darci's. The contact made Darci jump, her dark brown eyes wide and scared. "Don't be scared, Darci. It's OK. We're here to help. You're one of us." Sita smiled at her, and the brightness of her smile compelled Darci to return the expression.

Taking a deep breath, Darci looked up at the others. "So what can you all do? Do you all have magic like mine, or are you different?"

Ariene only had to change into a tiger to show her powers off. Roxie walked over to the window of her room and called in a few squirrels lounging in a nearby tree, delighting them all for a minute with their antics before she sent them away again.

Vanessa stroked the leaves of a potted plant while she watched the others. Darci stared at her, and the blond flashed a grin. "It's hard to show you the full extent of my magic in here, where it's so small, but this'll do." She pointed to the leaves she had been stroking, two of which were now twice the size of the other normal leaves. "I can do more, but that's just a teaser. My powers are pretty badass, if I say so myself!" Her friends laughed and shook their heads.

Finally Darci twisted around to Sita, who still sat beside her. "So what do you do?"

With a smile, Sita stood up and turned her back to Darci. "Just watch for a sec," she said over her shoulder. "This won't take long." Darci sat in her chair and watched, fascinated, as two large slits appeared in the back of Sita's shirt and two *things* began to grow from her back. She soon realized what those things were when feathers emerged, and her eyes grew huge. Robert, watching from the other side of Sita, smirked at the girl's awed expression. In less than a minute, two enormous wings had sprouted from Sita's smooth back. She flapped them a little, rolling her shoulders. "Oh, that feels good. They were starting to get a little tight."

Darci reached out a shaking hand and ran her fingers over the white feathers. Startled, Sita jumped and craned her head back, but otherwise made no move to stop her. The feathers felt as glorious as they looked, smooth and soft and pristine. Darci ran her hands over the feathers, clearly stunned by the mere fact of their existence.

A single feather fell to the floor. Sita ruffled her wings in annoyance and sighed. "Damn, lost another one." She turned to pick it up. "Humph, at least it was small. The bigger ones hurt more when they fall off." Seeing Darci's still-stunned expression, she grinned and held the feather out to her. "Here. Take it."

Robert's jaw dropped. "Sita . . . do you know . . . " He let the sentence trail when she glared up at him to shut up.

Darci took the feather in a trembling hand, looking up into Sita's brilliant blue-green eyes. "Thank you." The other girl simply grinned and held out her hands, which began to glow purple. Darci stared down at them, fiddling with the feather as she watched and realized. "Your magic's like mine!" she cried. But her face fell when she made another connection. "But it's a different color."

Each face was solemn as every person but Darci reflected on what Robert had told them about the colors. Sita, however, let the glow fade from her hands and took both of Darci's into hers. "So? Mine's purple; yours is black. They're pretty damn close, if you ask me."

Darci looked up at her and smiled, and the internal battle that raged inside of her was at peace for this one moment.

Rob, on the other hand, could only see the surface, and decided it was time he reminded them of what he was there for. "Good. Now that that's out of the way, why don't I tell you about your first mission?" Vanessa squealed in excitement, causing Robert to wince. The young woman reminded him too much of an old girlfriend he never wanted to remember.

"We're actually going on a mission then? When?" Ariene asked.

"I hate to call them missions, because they aren't, really, they're more like practices and team-building. A chance for you all to build up your powers and stuff," he replied. He leaned back against the armrest of the sofa. "But I don't know what else to call them, and 'mission' seems like the best word for it."

Roxie jiggled her leg, clearly impatient. "Oh, would you get on with it? What are we doing? And who are we working for?"

Rolling his eyes in mock annoyance, Robert reached over and tapped her on the back of the head. "Don't interrupt." She stuck her tongue out at him. "You're not working for anyone. You're doing this for yourselves, and just doing my boss a favor. I had promised I would tell you more of who I work for . . . I guess now is a good time." Ariene threw her hands into the air, the expression on her face one of exasperation. Rob blocked the words he knew she was about to say by forging forward. "I work for a man known as Knight. It's his surname, but it's the most common name for him. The 'organization' I work for is his. You all know I do spy work—that's not all I do, but you don't really need or want to know the rest. Basically, I work for Knight. You don't work for him. If you did, then trust me, you would have met him. You're just doing us a favor by agreeing to these 'missions' I have in mind."

Sita frowned and crossed her arms. "That doesn't really tell us a whole lot."

He shrugged. "It's what I can tell you. I don't really work for an organization of any kind, I work for a person, and that's Knight. There is no group or organization or faction—there's just Knight and the people who work for him, and those people traffic in information, most of the time. Now, your first task is to spy on a couple of minions of this enemy group. They're going to be moving some boxes into trucks, I think, and we want to try to see what it is they're transporting so carefully.

"Do *not* get caught," he ordered. "Do not engage them unless they attack first. And don't purposely let yourselves be seen," he added when Ariene grinned too wolfishly. "We need this information, not a fight. Think of this as a test of your abilities to hide, to wait, and to watch. We need to know how many of them there are, roughly how many crates they're moving, and if possible, what's in those crates. Then you get yourselves back here to me, where I will be waiting for you to report."

Roxie nodded. "All right. We can handle that. When is this?"

Robert looked at his watch. "In four days. Next Monday, they'll be transferring their materials at exactly ten PM. I've got a map for you already drawn out, so you'll know exactly where to go," he said. He fished the folded papers out of his jacket pocket and lay them on the table. "Now, I have to go. But I'll be back in a week. Get some practicing in before then, if you can. Keep up with your studies too. I don't want any of you failing classes for this." Sheepish grins all around proved the necessity of his words. Shaking his head, he gave Roxie a quick hug and cast Sita a last lingering glance before he disappeared in a flash of blue.

∞

For the four days, the group managed to cram three practice sessions into their schedules. But now they often had to work late into the night to finish homework they had put off. Roxie and Ari both cursed their professors many times over for assigning essays on the first day back from Thanksgiving, and they were both the ones to tire first during practices. Skylar eventually noticed her friends' exhaustion and ordered them to sleep, coercing them with the reminder that they would be worthless students if they fell over from exhaustion. Ari gave in, though she grumbled and huffed about it.

Darci joined the group now for practice, taking part in honing her skills with an eagerness that gratified the others. Vanessa couldn't help but be nervous when Darci joined them. She constantly thought of Robert's description of her power, and shuddered when she thought of what would happen if the other girl lost control.

But their friends showed no signs of minding her presence, so Vanessa let it be. Sita felt Vanessa's unease, but let the issue be, unwilling to bring up trouble before it was absolutely necessary. Besides, Darci composed herself well in the practices, and Sita couldn't see any problems with the upcoming mission if she joined them.

Finally Monday night came. At six o'clock, Rob popped into the suite—literally—and called for all his girls to gather. They did, and he described their mission more fully, telling them in no uncertain terms that if they engaged the enemy when it was not necessary he would skin them alive. When the clocks showed eight o'clock, everyone dressed in the darkest clothes they owned and reconvened in the suite. Sita was the most impressive figure, her body outlined by the snug black robe she used when flying.

Robert stood at the door, hoping he wasn't sending them straight into harm. He looked each young woman in the eye, and saw that if they felt fear, they kept it under wraps. Nodding, he stepped aside. "Remember, work *together*. Be a team. If you work by yourselves, you'll come back in pieces and I will be out of a job. I'll follow you, but I don't want to interfere too much. This is your learning experience. I'm just there in case something goes horribly wrong." Watery, shaking smiles were flashed up at him and then the group filed out the door, one dark clad figure after another, until Sita's flowing robe disappeared around the corner. Rob shut the door and followed in silence.

The five young women managed to avoid the other students by taking the back stairwells, those only supposed to be used in emergencies. The campus was quiet, and few people were around to see the dark figures emerge from the dorms and begin to run north. Ariene, holding the map, led the way, the others trailing behind her in a pack. Sita watched from the rear, Darci running near her, while Rob paced himself thirty feet back.

Darci, panting, began to fall behind. "I guess . . . I need more . . . stamina training . . ." she gasped. Her friends grinned, their anxiety lifted.

Sita shortened her stride. "We can work on that when we get back, dear. For now, let's just try to do our best and get through tonight." They continued to run in silence, but Ariene slowed the pace.

Fifteen minutes later, the group emerged in the industrial part of town. Ariene slowed to a walk, breathing hard, the others following her lead. She stopped to look at the map and rest. Darci braced her arms on her knees. She glanced over at Sita, who also breathed harder, but not as hard as the others. "How is this so easy for you? You're not as tired as we are," Darci said.

Sita raised an eyebrow in amusement. "I can fly, Darci. I have to have more lung capacity and stamina than you guys just to keep myself in the air." She shrugged. "I'm used to it, I guess."

Vanessa heard them and shook her blond head, her own breathing slowing down to normal. "Why don't you just fly there, then? Why are you running with us?"

Sita looked offended at the question, her frown severe. "We're a team. If you're running, I'm running."

The blond opened her mouth to say something when Ariene interrupted. "We're almost there, guys. I think we just have to go down this street and it's a few buildings away."

Roxie checked her watch. "We made good time. It only took us half an hour to cross campus and get this far. We've got a lot of time until they're supposed to be there." She glanced behind and searched the shadows. "Rob's still with us."

Darci finally stopped wheezing to breathe normally. "Let's walk the rest of the way. It's not far, right?"

The others agreed and began to walk, checking all around them as they went. Ariene led them down the narrow streets, warehouses and dilapidated business buildings on all sides illuminated at intervals by sickly yellow streetlamps. The air smelled of metal and rubber and a hint of gasoline—definitely the industrial side of town. Scratching noises, very faint and always in the shadows, followed the group as they walked. They were probably from rats or raccoons, but small animals like those would never present a problem to this group. One snarl from Ari and they would all go scattering. A half-moon just over the horizon played peek-a-boo in between the buildings.

Ariene paused to read the map, checking out the building now in front of them. She waved back to the others. "I think this is the place."

Vanessa came up beside her and snatched the map from Ari's hands. "Are you sure? I don't think it is. We came up to it too quick."

Glowering, Ari snarled and grabbed the map back. "Yeah, I'm sure. The map is pretty clear, and I followed it exactly." Vanessa shrugged and smirked before backing off.

The gray building loomed in front of them, and while Ari and Vanessa squabbled, Sita approached the front door. She reached out a hand and touched the cold metal. It opened, silent and slow. She jumped back, expecting people inside. When no one appeared, Sita approached the door and peeked her head in.

A musty, dank smell assaulted her nose. Bright purple light gathered around Sita's hands. She walked inside one cautious step at a time, motioning for the others to follow. The light from her hands illuminated limited parts of the darkened building, and the young women saw the boxes and shelves and stacks of a typical warehouse. Rob caught them up and stayed in the doorway.

Roxie caught up to Sita, tugging her to a halt. "We should split up and try to find the boxes before they get here. It's easier that way."

Sita nodded in agreement. "OK. Vanessa and Ari, you guys go left. Darci, Roxie, and me will go right. Let's meet in the middle every twenty minutes to see if we've found anything." She put her hands on her hips and closed her eyes, exasperated. "Next time, we bring walkie-talkies. Rob, you stay at the door and be our lookout, OK?" He nodded in silence and turned his back on them. Rob closed the door most of the way and took up his position as lookout.

The group split into two units and began looking in the crates. Ari changed her eyes into owl eyes to see better, while Vanessa tried to see what was in the boxes without damaging them. So far they uncovered only empty crates.

The other three had an easier time of it, as both Darci and Sita could send their magic questing over the boxes, searching for any that were full. They worked their way down the rows, Roxie keeping an eye on the time. They had walked halfway through their row when Roxie called the twenty minute mark, and the group converged in the middle. Ari shook her head. "We haven't found them yet. Do we still have time to look before they're supposed to get here?"

Roxie checked her watch. "We're supposed to have another thirty minutes, but I don't think we should push our luck too much—let's try to hurry this up so we can hide before they come in, OK?"

Sita nodded. "Good idea. So let's change up the groups. Darci, you go with Ari, and Vanessa, you come with us. I think we'll get through these boxes much faster that way." Nods of agreement all around before the two teams split off again.

Ari worked quicker now that she had Darci. Sita, Roxie, and Vanessa went back to the right side of the warehouse, running now as Sita's magic swarmed in purple waves over stacks and mountains of crates, always passing each one by. Vanessa *tsked*. "There's nothing here! This was such a waste of time . . ." she cut herself off when Sita's magic glowed brighter when it hit a row of crates in the middle, stacked no more than two high in each column.

Roxie called the others over while Sita tried probing the crates further. All she could feel inside were what felt like hundreds of lumps of stones, adding up to thousands when she tallied the number of crates. "I can't really tell what's in them, but there're at least twenty boxes full of whatever it is. There's a lot of it in there."

Darci joined her, smiling with triumph. "We found a few boxes too when you guys called us over here. Not as many crates, only five, but I think they're all holding the same things."

Sita withdrew her magic from the other boxes and concentrated it in the air around them, making them all glow in violet light, but now they could see better. Roxie studied the crates before turning to Ari. "Ari, you're the strongest. Do you think you could pry the lids off without leaving so much damage we can't put them back on tight?"

Cracking her knuckles, Ari answered by walking up to the first crate and carefully wiggling the lid off. She set the lid on the ground. "It's easy enough to put back on. Just pound it back in and it's like it was never taken off."

Smiles reflected all around. Vanessa was the first to peer over the edge of the enormous wooden box, rooting through the cushioning for what was inside. Her delighted gasp startled them all. "Diamonds!" she cried as she picked one up. She cooed like a baby as she studied it, elated. It was the size of her fist, the largest diamond any of them had ever seen, and appearing absolutely flawless to their untrained eyes.

Roxie walked over then, looking inside the crate and realizing how many diamonds there were. "Where did they get them all? There're hundreds of them inside each crate! They have a fortune just sitting in here."

Curious, the young women crowded around the box, oohing and aahing over the wealth inside. Sita hung back, sending out her magic again into each crate. Now that she knew what she was looking for, she tested each sample of stone in each box. "Guys, it's not just diamonds," she cried. They all stopped and tore their eyes from the shiny gems to look at her. "There are emeralds in that box, sapphires in that one, rubies in there, and a whole lot more diamonds, too!" She nearly choked when her magic told her what was in the boxes on the other side of the warehouse. "Celestite and angelite? Those crystals are expensive, where did they find so many? I have to see them . . ." She ran to the other side of the building, calling for Ari to follow her to open the box.

Roxie glanced down at her watch and swore. "We have to find a place to hide. It's almost time for them to be showing up." The others winced but lifted the lid back into place and hammered on it with their fists until it was back on. "Sita, hurry up!" Roxie called.

Sita and Ari ran back over, Sita's face flushed. "I was right, those were whole crates of celestite and angelite. That could be a bad thing."

Ariene snorted. "The only bad thing right now is if we're caught. Can we please find a hiding place?" Sita blushed and followed them back up the aisles. They chose a spot behind crates that had an easier view of both ends of the warehouse. The young women crouched on the cold concrete floor with bated breath. Sita doused her magical light when she saw Rob duck into the shadows next to the door, out of sight of the oncoming targets.

They hid just in time. Light from the streetlamps outside poured in as the outer door opened, and five tall men slouched inside. Once the door closed behind them, they flicked on flashlights and hastened down the main aisle. The women tensed when the men approached and then passed, and breathed quiet sighs of relief when the men reached their crates without noticing them.

"Let's hurry up an' get this o'er with, Vitch. I dunna like bein' in this world. It feels too heavy," whispered one of the men. The girls looked at each other, perplexed. Vanessa almost opened her mouth to speak but Ariene sunk her now-long nails into the other girl's arm. Vanessa clamped her mouth shut to avoid the outraged squeal that would normally have erupted. Sita held a finger to her lips and went back to listening.

The leader was talking. "We have ta get these crates o'er there now, or *he'll* have our hides. So quit yer blabbering and get ta work." Silent now, the five men started lifting the crates onto a sled they pulled over from the other end of the building, setting the crates of precious gems on the metal.

Suddenly one man stepped back from the crates, looking around the warehouse's gloom. "This crate's been *opened!*" he cried in astonishment. The men looked at each other before they split up and began searching the aisles. The leader headed straight for the hiding place of Sita and her friends.

Sita held out a hand to the others, motioning them to be still. She already had a plan in mind. She turned to Ariene, motioning with her hands what she wanted her to do. With a nod, Ariene watched and waited, ready to spring.

When the leader was almost on them, Ariene changed into a large yellow Labrador and burst away from the crates, knocking a few over in her haste. The leader shouted to his comrades and pursued her, but he didn't get far. Sita leaned around the crate at her back and took careful aim, sending a bolt of purple fire into the man's back. Stunned, he stumbled and fell, shouting for his men to turn around.

Sita saw the moment she was waiting for. "Run!" she cried as she sprang to her feet. The others followed her lead and ran up the aisles, Ariene following them on four feet. The men pursued, gaining on the women. Sita realized why—she and her friends were already tired from the journey over. These men were fresh. *Maybe my plan wasn't so great after all . . .*

Ducking behind more crates, she hurried to revise her plan. "Split up!" she called, and ran off. Roxie, Ariene, and Vanessa continued straight. Darci followed Sita to the right. Cursing, the men also split up, sending two men after Roxie, and three after Sita.

Darci ran with all her strength, which wasn't much. She had to push herself to keep up with Sita, especially after the run they'd had just to get to the warehouse. Panting hard again, she followed Sita around a corner and almost ran into her.

The man continued to run past them. Sita sighed and braced against the crates. "Catch your breath for a minute, Darci," she whispered. "Then we have to find the others."

Both looked up when they heard a dog barking and masculine cries of pain. They winced when the sound of boxes crashing to the floor reverberated off the walls. A flash of blue reflected against the walls and metal. One of the men had stumbled into Rob. Sita looked over, silently asking if Darci was ready to run. Darci nodded and followed Sita back around the crates into the main aisle again.

Both teams converged on the same spot when from the corner of her eye Sita saw a small black orb hurtle through the air toward her. She skidded to a stop, her arm thrown out to halt Darci. In the darkness she couldn't tell what it was until it landed at her feet.

Time slowed. She looked up with wide eyes to the man thirty feet away—the leader had risen and thrown the object, his smile feral and brown eyes triumphant. "Grenade!" she cried, warning her friends to stop running toward them. She gathered her power.

The grenade burst, sending flames toward Darci and Sita. But the flames never touched them. A black dome placed itself over the bomb, and a dark purple shield covered the black one. The bomb erupted inside the dome, a conflagration of fire and pieces of concrete hitting the barriers and bouncing back in on itself. Sita and Darci were thrown back from the force of the detonation, landing hard on their backs, bruising their heads when the hard concrete caught them.

"Sita! Darci!" Roxie and Vanessa shouted as they rushed over to them, worried, keeping watchful eyes on the men. But the men had other ideas. They used the distraction of the grenade to finish loading the crates onto the enormous sled and began pulling that over to the leader. Sita, her eyes blurry from afterimages of the flames, tried to focus on what he was doing.

He sneered at her and held a golden ball in his hands the size of a small basketball. He held it up, pressed in two blue buttons on the top and twisted. The top half of the orb spun all the way around twice before the man held it out again. The young women watched, some seeing more clearly than others, as light beamed from a hole in the top of the orb. It coalesced into a large square door, electric red light dancing from one edge to the other.

The men hurried to pull the sled into the square. The women watched in shock while the four men and the sled disappeared, seeing nothing but the dancing red light as each one walked through. Finally, the leader leapt inside the square.

It convulsed, collapsing in on itself. The light disappeared, and the warehouse became dark again.

The breathless group sat on the cold concrete, huddled together, nursing injuries and sore muscles. "What the hell was that?" Vanessa said, shaking and clutching a bleeding arm where her pursuer had scratched her with a knife.

No one answered. No one had a satisfying answer. Rob limped over to them. A gash on his leg bled sluggishly, but otherwise he appeared unhurt. Unsteady and frightened, the young women rose to their feet and walked together from the building with Robert at their backs, into a terrifying, quiet, and cold night.

Chapter Fifteen
A Few Explanations

The door to the suite opened with a bang. The group made their way inside on unsteady, jelly-like legs. As the last to enter, Rob closed the door and leaned his forehead against the solid wood. "Is everyone OK?"

His girls sank onto the couch and chairs as a chorus of groans erupted from their throats. Roxie, lounging in the fluffy blue armchair nearest the door, brushed her dirty russet hair from her eyes. "Do we look like we're OK, Rob? Clearly not. But we're not dead, we're not dying, and whatever injuries we have are minor."

He watched them get comfortable as they shed their dark coats and jackets in the relative warmth of the dorm. When they finally settled, he grabbed water bottles for each, and brought over a bowl of water and towels to wash their wounds. He passed out the drinks and sank onto his heels near Vanessa, who cradled her left arm. "Tell me what happened," he said as he wet a towel and washed off Vanessa's cut. She hissed when the hot water hit her skin but let him continue. "From the door I couldn't see what you were doing in the warehouse, or how the fight began. Start from when we split up."

Roxie spoke up first, her voice thin. "There were a lot of empty crates, and we had to search almost the entire building before we found anything useful."

Vanessa sighed, her eyes unfocused. "So many diamonds . . ."

"Diamonds?" Rob asked, staring up at her. "Are you telling me there were diamonds in those crates?"

"Lots and lots of diamonds," interjected Ari. "Some as big as our hands. They were beautiful. But I don't know how many crates there were . . ." She trailed off and looked to Darci and Sita.

Sita picked it up there. "Ten crates of diamonds, three of sapphires, two full of rubies, two of emeralds, and three of opals.

Plus three crates of celestite and two of angelite." She counted off each kind of stone on her fingers as she recited.

Robert fell off his heels onto the floor. He noticed that his own gash still bled, and if he didn't move soon it would bleed onto the floor. "Are you serious?" They all nodded. "Oh, that's not good. How did they get so many . . ." He wrapped a bandage around Vanessa's arm. "All right. What happened next?"

They explained everything in as much detail as they could. He listened while he tended to their wounds and wrapped a bandage around his own scrape, but asked them to slow down when the story reached the middle of the fight.

"We all ran into the middle at the same time," Sita said. "But then something flew at me, and Darci and I stopped." She shivered, rubbing her bare arms. "The leader had recovered from my first attack. He threw a grenade at us." Robert stopped his ministrations and stared at her in shock. "I shouted at the others what it was, trying to get them to stop. And then I just . . . reacted. Darci, too."

They all looked at Darci, who wouldn't look at any of them. "Survival instinct, I guess," she muttered.

Sita's hand flopped into her lap. "Well, if she hadn't acted first, we might be a lot worse off. She put down a dome shield over the bomb, and I put down another shield just after hers right as it detonated. We were blown off our feet." She groaned and laid her head back in the chair, eyes closing. "No wonder my head hurts so much. I hit it, didn't I?" Darci only nodded and winced, her own head pounding. "Concrete is obviously not nice to heads."

"We all rushed over as soon as we could get around the bomb," Ari continued. "But it was weird. No flames got out of the domes, no pieces of concrete. No one else was hurt."

"And then we saw the men go back to loading up the sled with the last of the crates. And then they walked through an electric door and disappeared," Vanessa finished.

Robert stood up, shaken. His girls had come so close to being captured, or killed, that it terrified him. He tried to smooth the worry from his face as the young women rested and looked to him for answers. "They disappeared?" he asked quietly. "In an electric square." Nods all around. Rob closed his eyes and groaned. "Did one man have what looked like a golden glowing ball?" Nods again. "Damn it."

The girls stared at him, unnerved despite themselves. He got up and began to pace, hands running through his floppy brown hair. "How did they get their hands on one of those? How could they . . . where are they in Corá . . . oh, this is bad, so bad, so bad bad bad . . ." he trailed off as he walked back and forth, eyes cloudy.

One of the words sparked Roxie and Sita's interest. "Rob? What exactly is Corá?" Roxie asked.

"That's the second time we've heard it in two weeks. I think you owe us an explanation," Sita added.

Vanessa looked between them in confusion. Robert jerked to a stop and sat on the edge of the kitchenette counter. He fell silent, thinking, while his eyes stared off into space. Finally he swallowed hard and tugged on his right earlobe.

"So, I know I've mentioned this before, but there's another plane. Well, OK, there are many planes and worlds, but to make this simpler, we'll say there's only two. Earth is our home plane." He laid one hand on top of the other, so that the top hand was just off the mark of being directly on top. "And Corá," he wiggled the top hand, "Corá is another plane, existing parallel to Earth but not exactly the same." Then he moved his hands farther apart. "Corá and Earth are almost the same, but they're just far enough off to be different." He looked around at them. "Am I making sense?"

Ari grinned. "I think I get it. It's like two identical pieces of paper put right on top of the other. Only, one page is slightly off. They don't line up perfectly. Just a little bit off, but it's enough to make a difference. A kind of parallel world."

Robert nodded, relieved. "Exactly! That's pretty much it. Does everyone else understand?" Nods all around. "Great. Now, in Corá are all the people who are like us—the magic users, mythical creatures, etc. Pretty much any kind of fantastic creature you can think of is there, and some you can't think of, too."

"Are there dragons?" Vanessa squeaked.

"Not really, they have their own plane, actually," Rob answered thoughtfully. "They don't come out much. Anyway," he pulled a ring out of his pocket and held it up. "I got permission to take you all there, but I'm waiting on more of these. You can only get into Corá if you have permission, and if you're wearing one of these rings, which you can only get from the Council. Otherwise, you'd be killed just trying to get in."

Roxie shook her head. "I'm confused. If that's where those men went, how did they get in? They didn't actually have permission, right?"

"Absolutely not. That's why I was so worried when you told me about the device they had." Robert put the ring back into his pocket and sighed. "What they had is what we call a Ripper, because it does exactly that. It rips a hole through the borders of Corá to let anyone in as long as the device is active. Once it's inactive, the hole closes up." His eyes flickered in anger. "And now they're actually *inside* Corá. Which means we don't know as much about them as we thought we did. I need to tell my boss about this immediately."

Darci scrambled to sit up. "Wait, don't go yet!" she cried. "You have to tell us more about this place!"

"And what about my ring and Ka'len?" Sita added. "I thought you said there was something you had to tell us about that, too."

Robert halted, his face contorted in thought. "I really need to get this information to them." He studied their faces, noting the dark circles and weary expressions. "And you all have had a hard night. I think you should get some rest and I'll tell you about it when I return. Deal?"

Sita and Roxie, though reluctant, nodded their agreement. Robert grinned, taking a step forward before disappearing in a flash of bright blue.

Roxie frowned. "I hate when he does that."

"Why?" Vanessa asked. "I think it's pretty cool."

Rox held out her hands in exasperation. "And that's exactly why! I can't do it!"

They chuckled, too weary to truly laugh. One by one they trickled off and climbed into their beds, each falling into exhausted, dreamless sleep.

∞

Roxanne woke the next morning to the sunlight streaming through her windows and Ariene's grumbling. Ari groaned, her alarm clock whining, piercing the deep fog of dreams. "Oh, shut up," she mumbled at it. Roxie chuckled. Slapping at it, Ari somehow found the off button and rolled back over. "I'm taking the day off. Tuesdays suck anyway."

Early morning sunlight streamed through the window to land square on her face. Ari pried one eye open and glared at it. "You're not the alarm. Go away." Her voice sounded like gravel even at a mumble.

Roxie rolled over to stare at Ariene with bleary eyes. "Ari, you're loud. Shut up. I wanna sleep more." She yawned and groaned when her phone began to ring. Fumbling for it, she nearly flung it to the ground before getting a firm grasp of the device. She stared at the number displayed before flipping it open. "Allen? It's eight in the morning."

Ari sat up and sighed. "At this rate I'll never sleep again." She climbed down from the raised bed, wrapped a blanket around her shoulders, and walked out to the empty common room and vacant couch.

Rox flopped back onto her pillows, trying to wake up enough to hear what Allen was saying. "Oh, yeah, I forgot I asked you to wake me up this morning," she managed to say before yawning again. "But I'm just gonna sleep all day today. Classes would murder me right now." Pause. "Yes, I'm fine, I'm not sick. Just tired." Another pause and a sleepy grin. "Sure, come over later. See you then. Bye."

A loud knock on the front door caught Roxie's attention, and she chuckled when she heard Ariene's exhausted groan from the common room. Climbing slowly down from her bed, she joined her roommate, who stumbled up from the couch with a blanket still wrapped around her shoulders to open the door.

Ariene glowered at the man standing there. "Do you realize how early it is?" she growled.

Eric grinned and offered a small bow, clearly only half joking. "I'm sorry, Ari. I thought I was supposed to wake Sita up. Was I wrong?"

She relented and opened the door wider to let him in. "Well, come on in. It's about time that lazy ass woke up." Shoving the door closed, Ari shuffled back to her perch, now joined by an equally sore Roxie. "I figure if we're up, she has to be up, too. Last night was her idea."

"What was last night?" Eric asked, trying to keep his voice down out of respect for their obviously aching heads. "You girls doing some illegal drinking up here that you all didn't inform me of?"

Roxie attempted a laugh but cut it off when her head began to pound. "You could say it was something exciting, that's for sure." She massaged her temples and snuggled back into the cushions.

His eyes lit up in speculation. "So if it wasn't alcohol, does that mean it was . . . " And he wiggled his eyebrows and winked.

The two stared at him, too tired for what he said to register at once. Once it did, they roared with laughter, the aches in their bodies forgotten. Eric snickered and walked over to the closed door of Vanessa and Sita's room. He tapped on the worn wood. "Sita? You in there? You asked me to wake you up this morning."

Muffled curses in Vanessa's high pitched voice floated through the door. Thumps resounded on the floor as it sounded like both girls jumped down from their beds. Eric, Ari, and Roxie listened as Sita said something unintelligible to Vanessa and her roommate blasted a scathing retort.

The door was ripped open by Vanessa, her hair wild, her pajamas rumpled. "What the hell, Eric? It's eight AM. I *was* asleep. I would like to stay asleep for at least three more hours, but thanks to you, that won't be happening." Sita could be seen behind her in the room, frantically trying to untangle some clothes to wear. "Now go away and leave us to sleep!" She slammed the door and stomped away.

Eric stared at the door, crossed his arms and waited. He chuckled as he glanced at Ari and Roxie. "Three . . . two . . . one . . . ." The door was wrenched back open, this time by Sita.

Ariene looked aside at Roxie. "If I had known this morning would be this entertaining, I would have popped some popcorn for us." Roxie nodded in amusement.

"Sorry, Eric," Sita said with a smile as she pulled her shirt down. "Vanessa didn't wake up on the right side of the bed this morning." Loud cursing erupted from the room. Sita closed the door behind her with a grin. "Thank you for waking me up. I could use more sleep though."

Eric wrapped her in a giant hug and kissed her cheek. "You should have called me. If I'd known you ladies would be partying, I wouldn't have followed orders to wake you." He winked at her.

Roxie raised an eyebrow and glanced at Ari. "She is sickeningly awake for this early in the morning."

"And they are sickeningly sweet for any time of day," answered Ariene, shaking her head.

Eric ended up skipping classes with them that day to hang out in the room and watch movies with Sita and her roommates. Vanessa emerged sometime around lunch and glared at Eric. He waved a cheerful hello, Sita asleep on his chest. Vanessa glowered again and stalked away to find food. Smiling, Eric pulled the sleeping Sita closer and went back to the movie. Roxie laughed to herself as she watched the exchange. Later on, Skylar and Estelle came to join them.

Sita woke up and asked about Darci, but Skylar said when she had knocked on Darci's door, Darci had yelled that she was sick. Roxie settled down with the others to watch a full day of movies. Allen knocked on the door after lunch, and Roxie persuaded him to join them. Blankets were gathered and pulled out—the heaters of the suite had still not turned on, or if they had, they refused to actually work. Roxie stuck her tongue out at the heater and made hot chocolate for everyone.

"Hey, is Darci actually sick? Or is she just avoiding us?" Roxie asked over the clamor of Vanessa and Ariene trying to agree on the next movie.

Skylar shrugged and fluffed up the pillows behind her back. "I don't know. She seems tired. I think she needs to get more sleep."

Sita sat up from her seat next to Estelle on the couch. "Did anyone invite her to movie night tonight? Maybe she'd like to join us." She shivered and rubbed her arms. "Wow, it's cold in here! When will that stupid heater start working?" she cried. She nursed her mug of hot chocolate closer.

"I haven't seen Darci all day," Rox said, watching Allen attempt to settle the movie dispute. Loudly. "Are we sure she's even here?"

Sighing, Sita rose from Eric's embrace. "Well, I can settle this. I need another mug, though, and another packet of cocoa for my plan to work."

Roxie handed her both and Sita made her way out of the suite. But when she closed the door, she heard something in her mind. A strange voice, with strange whispers, saying strange things. Standing still and listening, she reached out to the Voice, curious and a little afraid. *Why are you even asking her?* the Voice said. *She's a loner, she's weird, just leave her alone. Why do you want someone like that around anyway?*

Sita huffed and stalked off down the hall toward Darci's room. *Screw you, Voice. Shut the hell up. She's my friend. I won't leave her as long as she wants me around.*

The Voice had nothing else to say. Satisfied, Sita shoved the strange matter from her mind and kept walking.

Darci sat in the chair, her favorite blue blanket pulled up over her knees and to her chin. She stared out the window at the inky sky, listening to the thunder roll over the school and watching the lightning brighten her room every few seconds.

A soft knock on the door, almost drowned by the sudden clap of thunder, made Darci turn her head. The person knocked again and Darci rose, draping the fleece blanket over her shoulders. She grabbed the handle and pulled the door open. "What is it?" Her voice rasped from her raw throat.

Sita stood in the hallway, wearing her purple star-decorated pajamas and holding a steaming mug of hot chocolate. She smiled. "Hi, Darci!"

Darci didn't answer. *What does she want?* She stared at the other girl until Sita held out the mug.

Kill her! Do it now!

No! Darci cried at the Voice in her mind. She blinked hard and looked back at Sita.

Sita's eyes grew sympathetic. "I thought you'd like some hot cocoa. The girls and I are in the suite, having kind of a rainy day party to recoup from last night. Lots of hot cocoa and marshmallows and candy. You're welcome to join us if you want. We're getting ready to put on a movie." Darci didn't say anything, she simply stood in the door and clutched the soft blue blanket closer to her. Sita's eyes unfocused for a second or two, and Darci caught the angry look in her eye. But then Sita shook her head violently and touched her temple with one hand, and the anger disappeared. Darci lowered her eyes before Sita caught her staring. Darci reached out and grabbed the mug, enjoying the warmth on her cold hands. Sita half-smiled and let her take it. Darci glanced up at Sita as she took a sip of the hot liquid. She managed a small watery grin. "Thank you," she squeaked out.

"You're welcome." Sita backed away a little. "Remember, you can join us any time. Just come on in!" She waved and walked back to the suite, leaving Darci to herself.

Darci shut her door and sipped again at the cocoa. *Why didn't you kill that disgustingly sweet girl while she was just standing there?* whispered the Voice. *Just imagine what your power would have done to her . . . how that pale skin would have burned with the lightning . . .*

"NO! SHUT UP!" she screamed—or tried to. Her throat was so raw from the screaming, it hadn't recovered and healed enough yet for her to talk without rasping. "I won't listen to you! Why should I hurt her? She's nice to me!" She took another sip of the soothing liquid.

She's the enemy! Everyone is! Destroy them all, and let everyone see your power, your strength! Destroy, destroy, DESTROY!

"No, no, no, no, no!" She said as she sunk back into her chair, the blanket tightly wrapped around her thin and shaking frame. "I won't do it. I won't. Whatever you are, you're horrible, and I don't want to be like you."

The skies burst at last and the rain poured down.

Chapter Sixteen
Leap of Faith

Professor Alan watched the men open the crates.

The thunder rolled outside the small manor house that was his secondary base. Rain lashed the windows, attacking the house furiously. The professor walked to the nearest window, inspecting the fine glasswork. It had stood for centuries, and was still in fine condition. Danoli craftsmen really were the finest in all the worlds. Alan refocused his vision outside the window, watching the rain.

It only rained in a two hundred yard radius around the house.

Beyond that rainy circle the sun shone golden. The lightning never struck a tree in the sun, the rain splashed no blades of grass not shadowed by storm clouds.

He frowned, the expression contorting his face into a grotesque visage reflected in the unflattering glass. This horrible weather brought back half-formed memories of a stormy night, of a woman screaming and two boys crying as they woke suddenly from sleep. And, of course, those memories led inevitably to the result of that stormy night, when Alan learned the truth.

The goddess of this world could not possibly know how deeply such storms affected Ray Alan. *No, it is impossible. She knows nothing of me. This is simply her displeasure, the bitch.*

Alan turned from the window and walked back over to inspect the opened crates.

The frown faded as he ran his hands over the diamonds, admired the sapphires, and regarded the rubies. But his face broke into a possessive grin when his eyes alighted on the shards of celestite and angelite. Picking up one of each, he held them close to his face, inspecting them with delight. "These are worth more than your lives, gentlemen. If even one is lost or damaged, your lives are forfeit." The workmen, still dressed in their drab clothes of the night before, glanced at each other and began to sweat.

Sandara appeared behind the professor. "I trust everything is to your satisfaction, Professor Alan?"

Alan turned around, the specimens still in each hand. He looked up at the woman, not bothering to hide his glee. "You have begun the task I assigned to you earlier, correct?"

The woman nodded. "I've already begun amplifying the girl's thoughts to our purposes. However, you were correct when you warned me the other one would be more of a . . . challenge." She frowned in displeasure. "I've not been able to break through her barriers yet."

Alan shrugged. "As long as you make progress, I don't care if the fair one is out of our reach. She is, in the end, nothing." He then held up the crystal shards, pleasure making his eyes sparkle like knife blades in sunlight. "Do you realize how much power these crystals will give us? What they will do?"

Sandara walked over to glance at the gems herself, unable to keep her eyes from lighting up when she saw the diamonds. "No, I do not," she replied, biting her lip. In a corner of his mind, he heard her thoughts: *Humph, that bastard just wants to make me admit I don't know.*

A knife tip pricked the skin at the back of Sandara's neck. She froze, her breathing immediately shallow, her muscles tensed. Professor Alan leaned in close, his breath tickling strands of her hair. He felt the enormous effort it cost her to make no move at all. He bared his teeth in a snarl. "Do not ever call me a bastard again, Sandara." Her eyes widened, and he felt her heart begin to beat just a little bit faster. "You have pledged yourself, by promise if not by formal induction, to my organization," he said. "You have pledged yourself to Imbri Mors. By this pledge, you give me access to you. Your mind is no longer off-limits. Your body could even be mine to control in any manner I choose."

Her knees grew weak when she realized his meaning. He saw the look in her eyes and smiled, cold and sharp. "You see now, don't you? You know. You are my creature now, and you always will be. Your very thoughts are no longer your own. And when you are inducted, I will not only be able to hear your thoughts, I can *control* them." Alan laughed and the workmen fled the room in terror. Slowly he moved a hand to her throat, tracing the outline of her collarbone. Sandara shuddered and closed her eyes.

"You are mine."

As suddenly as he had attacked her, he let her go. Surprised, Sandara opened her eyes and regained her composure. Gasping, she calmed herself down and forced herself back to the original topic. "What will these stones do for us, Professor Alan?" she asked in as respectful a tone as possible, endeavoring to keep the loathing she felt from her voice. Of course, he felt it anyway, and felt all of her efforts. It amused him to see her squirm.

Alan picked up the specimens he had dropped earlier and walked back to the crates to place them gently inside. "They will be our energy," he said, a triumphant light adorning his smile. "They will be our energy and the key to eventual victory."

∞

Sita lounged on her bed as she read a book. She sighed. For some reason, she couldn't get into the book. She smirked. *Huh. I can't stop thinking about Eric!* Putting the book down, she settled her head on her folded arms and stared out the window to enjoy the pleasant view. *I wish it weren't December and cold outside. It would be a nice day for playing.*

She rolled onto her back and closed her eyes, slipping into daydreams. A certain young man had just entered the current daydream when a disturbing thought popped into her mind. **You know you can't trust him. He'll turn against you someday.** Startled, Sita sat up, her breathing heavier. Once she calmed down, she lay back on her bed and drifted off again. "Only three days after the first mission, and I am already bored," she said to herself, her lips managing only a mumble. She was almost asleep once more when through the barrier of her closed lids she saw a flash of blue light. Sita sat up again and looked around.

Robert stood in the middle of her room. "Robert!" she cried. "What are you doing here? You never did come back and talk with us again, you know. You still owe us explanations."

He held up his hands to ward her off. "I know, I'm sorry. I had some things to report and explain to my boss, and then I got called into the Council to have a chat with them . . . " He frowned and his shoulders sagged. "The past few days have been hell for me. Are the others here?"

Sita shook her head. "Nope. They all abandoned me to classes." She shrugged. "My class was cancelled for today."

"How's the job search going?"

She slumped. "Oh, actually, I put it on hold. I wasn't really finding much. And I think between keeping up with school, dating, *and* working for you, I'll only get burnt out if I add a job to it all. Besides, I don't really need a job. My allowance is enough."

He took a seat in Sita's desk chair. "Si, why did you give a feather to Darci? Don't you know how dangerous it is, to give away things like that?"

Sita pursed her lips. "I'm not stupid, Rob. I'm a mage, of course I know the danger." She ran a hand through her hair, twirling the ends. "My feathers are a part of my wings. My wings are a part of me. By giving away a feather, I'm giving away a part of myself. I know all that."

"You gave a weapon to the enemy."

"To my friend. She will always be my friend."

Rob shook his head. "Don't you know what she could do with that? She could use your feather to trace you, wherever you are. Or summon you to her, or plant thoughts. She could even control your mind, if she knew the right techniques. If she knows any of that, you could have just put yourself and all of us in danger."

Sita's chin stuck out at a stubborn angle. "She's my friend, and always will be. She needs *someone* to believe in her. I do. And no matter what happens, she can rely on me to help her, as long as I'm not hurting anyone else by doing so."

"Are you sure about this?"

Now she grinned. "As sure as I am about anything else."

Robert said nothing in reply. Nodding as if he had decided something, he broke into a smile and lunged over to the door, slamming it closed. He pulled her off the bed and stood her up in the center of the room. "Well, that's settled, then. Now I have some incredible news for you," he said. He ran to the window to close the blinds all the way and pull the drapes closed.

Sita stared at him in the half-dark, confused and just a bit alarmed. "Rob, what's going on? What's so important?"

He grinned, almost dancing with excitement. "You're really going to like this. I finally got the rings from the Council. I can take you into Corá!" He grabbed her hand and pulled her to the side of the room, still grinning like a child with presents. Then he stepped in front of her, grabbed both her shoulders, and looked down into her eyes. "But this requires you to trust me. If you don't trust me, you'll never get there."

Sita stared back into his brown eyes and saw the eagerness, the excitement, he felt reflected there. Suddenly she was aware of how close they stood, and of the warmth of his hands on her shoulders. She licked her lips. "Um, why? Isn't this pretty simple? You know, put on the ring, get teleported, that sort of thing?" she asked, her face reflecting her uneasiness. She stepped away from him a little, unsure of where he was going with this. *He's acting a little crazy.* Rob continued to look at her, his face serious but his eyes sparkling.

He swept his arm out behind him. "You need to see this. I'm taking you there, now, because you need to know." His voice held a hint of desperation in it, and sadness. "Too many of us go crazy from loneliness because they never have anyone to show them how to get here. I'm not letting that happen to my girls." His mouth quirked up a little on the side. "Besides, these people need a reason to hope. That's you girls."

Sita, in her anxiousness, had let her wings slip out without thinking while he talked. She looked at the closed and shuttered windows, her wings fluttering behind her. "And how exactly are we getting there?"

Rob took a tense breath, holding his hand out to her. "This is where you have to trust me. I'm going to build a magical gate. And you have to go first." He pointed to the middle of the room. "I'll set up the gateway in a minute, and all you have to do is step through. Except you won't be able to really see the other side. You'll have to simply *believe* that it's there and trust me that it's there."

Sita stopped him. "Rob, stop." She swallowed hard, still unsure. But he waited, and shut his mouth, and let her think it all through. "All right. I'll try." She glared at him. "But I'm leaving my wings out." He smiled, relieved. Fishing around in his pocket, he pulled out a velvet bag. Opening the top, he selected a ring and passed it to her. She took the cool metal band and studied it while he put the bag away. It appeared to be a simple innocuous gold band, but she could see faint lettering around the whole, and on the inside as well.

Trying it on her fingers, it fit best on her right middle. She slipped it on.

Without another word, he held out his hands to the middle of the room, allowing his sparkling cerulean-blue power to unfold and stream from his hands, dancing in the air as if an artist were painting haphazardly in the sky. She watched, fascinated, as the power wove itself into a pattern, which then fitted itself into the shape of a tall, upright rectangle. The air around it looked distorted and made her a little queasy. Sita closed her eyes. Now that she couldn't see the tangible effects of his spell, she could still feel the patterns Rob had asked it to weave and study the framework. *It's the pattern for a door...*

He touched her elbow and her eyes snapped open. He gazed into her face, as if searching for something. Nodding to himself, he led her to the doorway he had created. Her heart felt like it would beat from her chest, and the butterflies in her stomach threatened to enter her throat. Inside the blue outline of the door, she could see so many shades of black and deepest blue, and little specks that looked like stars. A small, light breeze came through, and it felt like no wind she had ever felt before. As if it were alive, and could feel her gawking into the void. The rip in space stared back at Sita as if it knew she waited on its threshold.

Rob's hand on the small of her back and his mouth next to her ear brought her back to reality. "OK, now, you simply step through the doorway. The ring will let you pass the borders. Close your eyes, it's a little easier that way. And trust me. I'll be right behind you."

Sita nodded, her eyes closed. She felt a playful puff of wind caress her face and lift her hair, making it dance and stream. She grinned. The gentle caress, brief and light, was like a promise. *The wind will never let me fall.* Taking a breath, she stepped forward and into the black void...

And into an entirely different world. Instead of touching the empty air, her foot stepped onto sturdy stone. Her eyes, open now, could not comprehend what they saw. Robert appeared at her side, right behind her, just as he promised. He touched her shoulder again in understanding. "This is our world. Our true world, where others like us and our friends live. Its name is Corá." He looked around, his face alight. "Like I said before, think of it as a kind of parallel world. It parallels the world we usually live in, but it's different, and can only be accessed by certain people. So while you just left your college, you haven't really left. You're still in the same basic geographical area. But the people are different, and the buildings." He rubbed his head, blushing. "It's a little difficult to explain," he said.

Sita could only shake her head and gaze around her. Trees, taller than almost any tree found on Earth, greeted her eyes. A quaint town sat nestled within this forest, with hills behind to one side. Sita could feel her jaw dropping with each passing second that she and Rob stood outside the town. Like a drawing from a history book, most of the houses stood beneath thatched roofs, and the larger streets were paved with cobbled stone. A town square took up the entire middle of the town, and a large gray fountain bubbled at its center. "I don't understand. If this is a parallel world, then shouldn't it be more like ours?"

"Well . . . short answer, yes. Long answer, not exactly." Rob scratched the back of his head. "Like I said, it's kind of complicated to explain." He glanced at her wings. "I think it's probably a good idea to hide those now. Wings aren't common, even here."

Laughter and voices from the townspeople reached her ears, and while the accent sounded off, Sita found she could understand some of the words. His words sunk in and she retracted the wings into her skin. "Then start explaining. Long answer, please."

Robert rolled his eyes. "OK, I'll try. Remember my paper analogy?" He held one hand on top of the other, with the top hand only slightly overlapping the bottom hand. She nodded. "If this were a true parallel, then it would be more like home. But it's not overlapped far enough with our world to be a closer copy." He moved his hands to demonstrate, with the top hand now mostly overlapping the bottom. "The closer a world is to another, or the more they overlap, then the more alike they are. But the farther apart they are—" he slid his hands back to the starting position. "—the less alike they are. They share less with the original world, but they're still a copy of sorts. Got it?"

"Maybe. No. I don't know." Sita turned on him and slapped his shoulder. "Why didn't you tell us all about this before?" she demanded, only partly angry.

Rob rubbed his shoulder. "Ow!" He made a face at her. "I couldn't. I told you, I only just got the permission from my boss and the Council to not only tell you, but let you in."

She glanced at him, perplexed. "Why? Who could possibly find this place?"

He shook his head. "It's complicated. First off, I can only tell you girls. Normally, only mages can access this world. The rule only applies to humans. Anyway, only mages can enter, and only a mage can tell another mage, and only with the permission of a qualified foundation, organization, or order." He paused for breath before continuing. "You can bring over non-mages, but you have to have permission and you need a special ring that you can only get from a certified committee, namely, the Council. They are *very* hard to get. That's what these rings are. You have no idea how long I've been lobbying for these. The Council is very strict, after all. Without those rings, you can't get anyone else in. Technically, being a mage, you don't really need one, but you'll want it if you enter without me for a while."

Sita walked to a stone bench and sat down, a giant tree providing cool shade. A fountain nearby bubbled and splashed, and she let the noise calm her. "So, I have to keep this a secret." She looked up at him. "That actually shouldn't be too hard. Who outside our group would believe this?"

"I know," he said with a lopsided grin. "But you have to. If you tell someone who's unauthorized, they'll know and they will lock you *and* them out for good. You will never get another chance." He sat beside her, hoping she understood how important it was. She nodded, relieving his worry.

"What does the writing on the ring say?" she asked, holding her right hand up.

"It's a language very much like ancient Greek, actually. The Danoli speak it here. In English it says 'Come in peace if you be true.' And the inside says 'Death to all who betray Corá.'" He smiled without any real humor. "A subtle reminder to keep the secret."

Sita shivered. "Has anyone told the secret before?"

Rob's eyes grew shadowed and she regretted asking the question. But he answered. "Yes. Once. I saw it." He swallowed hard. "The ring consumed him. It was not a pleasant sight.

Afterwards, even the ring was destroyed. It left nothing behind to betray its existence except the ashes." Shocked, Sita sat silent for a long time, thinking.

Something small in the fountain caught Sita's eye. She looked at it and gasped, astonished. "Rob, what is that?" She pointed to the small thing in the water.

The small thing Sita spied was truly tiny, barely more than three inches tall. Its skin was a dark blue that seemed to shimmer, changing as it moved, and scaled. The little creature had two arms and legs, but the hands were more akin to fish fins, as were the feet. Somehow it had propped its small body on the lip of the fountain, half in the clear water, and was staring at them in its own apparent astonishment. Even though it was small, Sita's magic could study it clearly, and told her that the creature's eyes were huge and round, and a very aquamarine color. Its teeth were small, sharp fangs, and it had gills on the sides of its cheeks. The hair was stringy, and reminded Sita strongly of seaweed in color and texture. Her power told her this one was a female. The tiny fish-woman wore nothing at all, except for a belt of weeds with a very tiny knife in it.

Rob looked over at the creature and smiled. "Oh, that's an Elbi. They're very nice people. They live in the water practically all the time, but they have the option of using their noses and shutting down their gills if they want to come above the water, like this one has." He cocked his head in thought. "No one has ever been able to see how they switch from gills to breathing like we do, but I guess we don't really need to know. It's not like we can do it." He laughed. "They're nice, but they can be fierce. Even though they're small, they can fight!" He looked over at her, while she still sat in amazement. "Do you want to meet her?"

Sita nodded. Rob pulled her up and led her to the fountain. The Elbi grinned, revealing the sharp teeth Sita's magic had discovered a moment ago. The little woman held up her hand—or fin—in greeting. "*Oorbish yingam at grap!*" the Elbi said, her voice as fluid and strong, yet delicate, as the water she swam in. It was a pleasant voice, and Sita was strongly reminded of the fountain itself. She elbowed Rob. "What did she say?"

He grinned. "She said 'Hello to the great one.' That means you. She likes you." Sita stared at him, uncomprehending. She looked down at the tiny creature. Smiling, Sita bowed her head, nodding her thanks for the kind greeting. "Hello, Elbi. Do you have a name?" Sita crouched down to meet the little creature at her level.

The Elbi chittered a few words, which Rob deciphered as, "She says her name is Alashankara, but you can call her Alasha for short."

Sita laughed. "Alasha. It's a very pretty name. I'm Sita." She held out her pinky finger for the Elbi to shake. Alasha did so, grasping the giant human finger in both of her cold and slimy fin-hands. When she let go, Alasha chattered something and then vanished into the water, disappearing in a few seconds. Sita looked at Rob. "Where'd she go?"

Rob watched the Elbi swim away. "She said 'good to meet you' to you. But she said 'we are pleased' to me." His face became a mask, unwilling to reveal emotion. "She likes you, and will carry word of you to her people. She's a lake Elbi, living in Lake Grimin with her people. They have a small kingdom there called Grimindon. The Grimindon Elbi . . . " He fell silent. "If the Grimindon Elbi like you, it's really good. Humans haven't endeared themselves to the Grimindonites at all, and it is rare for any Elbi to like a human, but especially a Grimindonite." He grew silent again. "A very good thing," he muttered to himself.

He shook off the pensiveness and smiled. "Well, should we have a look around? There's a lot more to see, and we don't have to be back for a while in our world."

Sita beamed at him. "What kind of question is that? Of course I want to see."

"Then I know exactly where I want to take you." He rose and offered her a hand. She took it and they walked down the road, hand in hand, Sita studying the thatched houses around her. "This place is Thirka. It's a pretty small town, but they're prosperous because they sit at the crossroads of two trade roads. Every month there's a trading fair on the outskirts of town. Remind me to take you there sometime."

The cobbled street turned to dirt when they left the main square. Sita sighed, glad for the relief to her aching feet. The cobbled stones bit into her sneakers. Rob continued speaking. "I'm taking you to see a house. It's a long walk, but worth it. I think you'll really like it." He smirked. "It's the mansion of the House of Awle."

Chapter Seventeen
Awle Mansion

Hundreds of miles away from Thirka, Sandara felt an icy shiver run up her spine. Unnerved, she shook off the feeling and rose, walking over to her work desk. The room was large, but dark, like the rest of the manor house Professor Alan owned. She almost needed to squint in the half-dark to see. She set her hands down on the desk, searching for the cloth. Finding it, she grasped the silky fabric and pulled it away, revealing a shimmering golden liquid sitting inside an ebon basin.

Setting both hands on either side of the basin, she closed her eyes and concentrated on the shiver and what it portended. Once she had a firm grasp on the thoughts, she sent them into the gold liquid, projecting her thoughts into the basin to form a picture. The strange liquid began to glow and churn, lighting up the musty old room. Once it reached a swirling frenzy, Sandara stopped projecting her thoughts and said in a foreign tongue, *"Paue tó ugron."* The liquid stopped moving at once.

Sandara opened her eyes and inspected the contents of the basin. Gold light reflected back at her, but the liquid was as solid as a mirror, and showed her an image. A moving image. Her eyes widened with hunger and anticipation. The picture in the liquid was that of a young man walking with a young woman, who had long blond hair and blue-green eyes.

Her red-painted finger pressed a button on the edge of the desk. "I'm busy, Sandara," said the Professor's voice.

Sandara, her eyes still riveted on the image, replied without preamble or apology. "One of the girls you asked me about is in Corá. With a man I have never seen before. They're alone."

Silence. She heard the creak of his desk chair as he moved closer, and his voice became louder. "Alone? Would our agents be able to attack?"

"Yes, sir."

"Then arrange for a team to find this girl and take care of her, Sandara. And make sure you note who the other man is as well. I'm curious as to how she got across the borders, and why she is here."

"It will be done, Professor."

∞

A passing farmer offered the hiking pair a ride on the back of his wagon. Robert and Sita accepted, hopping up on the rickety wooden wagon to chat most of the way. The farmer pointed out various things for Sita, from the tops of the green Grenol Hills to the tiny Jat'il Creek. Robert asked the farmer for news about Corá, and he talked their ears off about the latest happenings and gossip. Sita had trouble understanding the man—his accent sounded to her like a very heavy Old German, like her great-grandmother on her father's side used to speak.

The wagon crested a hill and the farmer stopped, heaving on the reins of the tired draft horse. Robert and Sita clambered down and thanked the man. He waved and wished the pair a good day before moving his horse off down the other side of the hill.

Sita looked around, in awe at the sheer amount of forest around her. "I don't think I've ever seen so many trees."

Rob steered her down the road, taking her elbow in one hand. "There're lots of those around here. Come on, the house is this way."

Following behind him, Sita marveled at the landscape. She breathed deep—the air smelled sweet and fresh, like it does after a big rainstorm. Rob noticed and hid a smile. "It always smells like that here. There's no pollution." Blushing that her thoughts were so easily read, Sita calmed down and followed where Rob led her.

The wide dirt roadway spread before them with no end through the forest, and trees crowded along its banks. An unexpected break in the trees appeared on their right. The pair stopped, and Robert spread his hands before him. "There it is. The ancestral mansion of the House of Awle."

Sita stopped all at once, awestruck. Beyond a stone wall higher than her head stretched lush and unbroken grounds. Not even two hundred yards away, facing the fine iron gate, stood the mansion, enormous and imposing, so large it could be called a castle instead of a mansion. Beige stone gleamed in the sunlight, and the windows winked at them as clouds obscured light and then let it shine on the glass again. Sita counted three floors, with probably an attic, and even what appeared to be a tower on the back corner. Two wings flanked each side of the house, stretching back on diagonals. And it was very, very empty.

"No one has lived here for hundreds of years. I don't even know if it's possible to enter now," said Rob in an undertone beside her. His words permeated her surprise but she didn't really hear him—her eyes and mind were captivated by the picturesque scene, and she had the strangest sensation of coming home. So engrossed was she that the shadows behind her failed to register as enemies until they attacked.

Rob pulled out a hidden knife from under his shirt and blocked the first man's attack. Sita dove out of the way to back up against the wall. She watched as more masked men swarmed from the trees, rushing to them with murder in their eyes. She tried to raise her hands and realized they were shaking. *What?* Two men charged at her. *What's happening? Why can't I move?*

You froze because you know you're no good! The thought shook Sita to the core, unnerving her further. The thoughts danced through her head, cavorting around and around until she was trembling and confused. *Sita is nothing! Sita will die! The bad men will kill her because she is a coward! You are a coward, a coward, a coward . . .*

All the men wielded knives, long and curved sorts of weapons that Sita had never seen before. Robert looked over his shoulder, defending against the swarm, and realized what was happening. "Sita!" he cried as a blade nicked his arm. "Would you *please* wake up!" Snarling, he gathered magic in his hands and sent it blasting into the three men facing him. They tumbled twenty feet away and Rob turned to the attackers behind him.

Rob's voice broke the hypnotic spell of the Voice in her mind and she finally moved. Sita threw up her hands, still shaking, and formed a barrier in front of her. The two enemies stopped, wary of her dark magic. Their knives twitched in their hands. She noticed one of the men staring at her hands and she dropped them behind her back. Allowing herself to breathe, she forced herself to calm down. Inching to her left, Sita found the iron of the gate and pushed it open. "Rob!" she shouted. "Get over here!"

Another blast of blue shot into the men, giving Rob room to run. He sprinted for Sita, and when he was close enough she shoved her shield out and into the two men waiting for her. They reeled backward, stunned.

Rob and Sita hurried inside the gate and closed it behind them, Rob fumbling with the latches. Sita pushed his hands away and closed them herself, the locks eager to cooperate at her touch. "It's closed," she said, backing away. He tugged her sleeve and pulled her further back.

He looked behind him, judging the distance between house and gate. "I don't know if they can climb over that wall, but I think we should make for the house." Sita only nodded. He pushed her up the path. "You start. I'll make sure they don't try to throw anything at our backs."

They inched their way up to the house, the overgrown weeds tangling their feet and making the going rough. Rob walked backward to watch the men as they prowled on the other side of the gate. As suddenly as they had appeared, the ten men disappeared. Sita turned when Rob paused, one foot lifted off the ground, and both watched to make sure they were really gone. Uncertain, they continued the walk to the house.

Sita scrambled up the grand stone stairs, tripping over the first stone as the tall grass obscured the beginnings of the stair. She climbed to her feet and looked down—there was actually a stone path underneath the plants. Shaking her head, she tugged on Rob's shoulder. "We're at the stairs."

Turning, he followed her up. "I don't know how we got through that gate," he said. The giant mansion loomed over him, forcing his head back in order to get a good look. "I've tried to get in hundreds of times and it's never budged." He placed a hand on the front double doors and pushed hard, but neither door moved. "Maybe we just got lucky."

He stared at the carved doors, as if by staring at them he could make them move. A pair of stylized wings graced the center of each door, crowned by three stars. On the outside borders, trailing vines had been carved in intricate patterns so artistic they appeared to be real.

Sunlight wove in and out between the clouds, and the wind whispered over the tall grass, making waves of green ripple around the house. Sita lifted her hands to her hair to keep it from her eyes when the dappled sunshine made something glint from the corner of her eye. Startled, she lowered her hand and stared at the second ring there. A frown tugged at the corners of her mouth. *When did I put the Awle ring on?* She blinked. "Rob, I think we got in because of the ring," she said.

Curious, Sita walked over to the right-hand door and pushed on it. Bit by bit, and with a loud groan, the door creaked open. Robert watched, eyebrow cocked on one side, as the door swung entirely open. Sita slipped in, Rob following behind. Once inside, they both stopped in awe.

Wood paneling covered all the walls to absorb the soft light filtered through the windows. Plush carpets lined the floors, the dark reds complimenting the cherry wood paneling. Fine chairs, padded in red cushioning and made of the same wood as the walls, stood at attention on one side of the foyer, waiting hundreds of years for guests to arrive. A hallway ran along either side of an enormous staircase that reminded Sita of a ballroom, the stairs sweeping out to the sides at the top and bottom. The ceiling of the first floor was so high that only the edge of the second floor landing could be seen from Sita's view. On either side of the foyer were two sitting rooms.

Sita's eyes climbed upward and she caught her breath. A gorgeous crystal chandelier, unlit at the moment, hung from the ceiling above her, glinting madly as yellow sunshine coming through the upper windows played over the crystal shards.

The pair walked further in, the door sliding shut behind them of its own accord. Both tread softly, fearing to disturb the silence of the place. "This is beautiful," Sita whispered.

"This could take weeks to explore completely." Robert opened the door of a hall closet and peeked inside. "We'd have to come back, we can't see it all today." They walked on, gazing around in wonder and admiration.

Dust motes danced in the light, coalescing as fine golden mist. Sita sneezed hard. "And next time, let's bring tissues. My allergies can't take this." She ran to the staircase and began climbing the carpeted wooden stairs. Rob trotted after her.

The second floor was as fine as the first. Wide hallways led to opulent rooms. Sita walked to the first one and stepped inside, fingering the fine bedcovers and opening the closet. In the darkness she could see simple dresses hung on one side and gorgeous ball gowns arranged on dummies on the opposite wall. Her eyes widened in delight but Rob pulled her away. "Let's keep exploring," he said. Reluctant, she followed him back into the hallway.

Six more rooms on that side of the hall were bed chambers, as spacious and magnificent as the first. The last room was a music room, full of both strange and familiar instruments. Sita almost stayed, her eyes captivated by a violin, but Robert again pulled her away.

On the other side of the hall were more bedrooms, washrooms, and sitting rooms. It was the last door at the end of the hall that caught their attention. The door was carved in the same style as the front doors, vines tracing the frame and outer edges of the wood. In the middle were the two spread wings, but in the center of that was carved an open book. Robert tried the knob but it wouldn't turn. He pulled his hand away in shock, shaking it as if burned. "It zapped me!" he cried. "Stupid door."

Sita snickered and stepped closer to try the door herself. She felt a little tingle run up her fingers to her hand, fading when it stopped at her signet ring. The door slid open easily when she pushed.

Darkness met them inside—not even the glow from a window shone through. Confused, Sita stopped in the doorway to let the scant light from the hall drift in. All she could see were the edges of an enormous plush rug over a wooden floor and the leg of a chair.

Rob lit his hands and felt around along the walls, looking for candles. "There has to be something here, or how did they see?" Fumbling, he found a metal fixture and held his hand over it. A flame sprang to life, igniting the next candle near it, and the next, until a whole train of candles were being magically lit one after another around the room.

Sita and Robert stared once more, their jaws dropping open. The room was a giant library, thousands of books and even ancient scrolls sitting on finely carved shelves. It rose at least three floors high, which confused the pair who knew the house to be *only* three floors high, and there was no library on the first floor. The only door in was the one they had entered through. An empty and sorrowful fireplace gaped at them from the far side. Grand drapes hung from two windows, as tall as the room itself, and Sita ran to pull them open.

Golden sunlight filled the room and the colors came to life. Despite the obvious age of the place, the furnishings were as vibrant and beautiful as the day they had been brought in. The enormous rug covered more than half the floor. Sita could barely see all of it, but it seemed to show the scenes of great battles, ones with demons and dragons, whole nations at war, and the great heroes who reigned triumphant at the end.

However fine the room itself, it was the books that really captivated them. Once they could see, Sita and Robert lunged to the shelves, scanning spines and gently pulling out the interesting ones.

Rob climbed a spiraling staircase up to the second level, finding books on magic there. Sita stayed on the first, slowly going through the rows until a book caught her attention: *Battles of the Great War* by Lena Koniet. "I know that name," she whispered to herself, edging the cloth-bound book off the shelf and into her hands. She looked back up and realized there were more books by Lena: *A Brief History of Gennaios*, *The Clan Wars*, and *A Genealogy of the Ancient Winged Clans*. Stunned and excited, she pulled the other three down and added them to her pile.

Meanwhile, Rob scanned through the books on magical theory and practice. A few caught his eye and he took them down, but he continued to look through the stacks. Sita climbed up the stairs to show him what she had found. "Rob, look! Books about the clans!" she said. She held them out to him, grinning like a mad woman. "Think of how much we could learn from these! And Ka'len mentioned this woman, Lena, so these are bound to be helpful somehow!"

He gripped the books and read the spines, a smile tugging at his lips and his eyes lighting up more and more as he read each one. "These are great! They're just what we need." He looked out through the window, only to realize the sun was going down. "How long have we been in here?"

Sita shrugged. "No idea. Let's keep looking, there's gotta be more . . ." she trailed off as Rob grabbed her elbow.

"No, I think we should be getting back. The others will be missing you if you're not there by now, you didn't exactly leave a note . . ."

"I didn't exactly have much of a choice!"

"And besides, we haven't had much to eat today," he continued, smirking as her own stomach betrayed her by growling at the mention of food. Sita crossed her arms in a pout. He grinned and handed her back her books. "Come on, let's see if we can find a bag for those."

They clambered back down the spiral stairs, cradling the precious ancient books in their arms. As they passed the low table in the middle of the room, Rob paused and looked down. A carry-bag, just the right size for the number of their books, sat on the table. "There . . . there wasn't a bag here when we came in, was there?" he asked, his voice hushed.

Sita shook her head, hair flying. "Nope, but let's use it. These are getting heavy." She grabbed the bag and put all the books inside, slinging it over her shoulder.

Rob stared at the bag. "Well, I guess we know how this place is so well kept—the house is doing it," he muttered. "We need to get back. It'll take forever to get back to Thirka, we can just leave from here." He tugged her over to an open space in the middle of the floor. He sighed. "I hope the house doesn't get mad at me for doing this."

His hands began to glow with cerulean light, the magic stretching out and weaving together the door again. It looked almost exactly like the one he had formed in her dorm room, but it was smaller. "I had to use a little more energy this time," he said. "Since we aren't in the same place as where we're trying to get on Earth, I have to create a kind of tunnel that connects our location here to your dorm there on the other side. It's just a little more complicated than simply opening the window into the corresponding Corá area."

The glowing blue gateway was fully formed now and Rob bowed her forward. "Ladies first!"

Laughing, Sita hauled the bag a little higher on her shoulder and clung to the books, hoping they didn't fall while she was inter-plane. *Inter-plane. Is that even a word?* she wondered as she stepped into the darkness.

Chapter Eighteen
Frightening People

Noon could only ever be a busy time in the city. Restaurants were filled to capacity, offices nearly emptied, and traffic became hell to get through. This was the most important time of day for what was planned, the hour when the most people would be affected in the smallest radius.

The young man walked down Connecticut Avenue in Washington, D.C., watching for the perfect spot. He glanced every so often at his watch, speeding up his stride to find a better intersection.

A small square object bounced against his waist, deep in the pocket of his jacket. He reached a hand inside and fingered it, glancing at his watch again. Ten minutes until noon. His fingers curled around the cube, twitching in excitement. This cube was very important for his mission. It was only one of hundreds designed by Imbri Mors.

He crossed a street, deciding again that this intersection wasn't big enough. Imbri Mors depended on him for this first attack, the first public step in their new plan. But no one would know his name, not even the great Professor Alan. He was nameless. He was nothing but a pawn in the game. He was to be used as a tool—a valuable tool, but a tool nonetheless—and discarded, forgotten, once his task was done.

Five minutes to noon and he found the perfect intersection. The young man stepped aside and pressed up against the wall of a building, pretending to be waiting for someone. He glanced at his watch. Four minutes.

People walked all over the street, mindless drones ignoring everything around them until they arrived at wherever they were heading. The man smirked. It was too easy, with all of them reading newspapers, or talking into cell phones or headsets, or stuffing their faces, and a great many punching away at the buttons on their phones. Three minutes. None paid any attention to him. Like a good tool, he was invisible until needed.

Two minutes. He straightened, keeping an eye on the cop who just stepped out of his car, an enormous oversized cup of caffeine in hand. The young man pulled the small square object out of his pocket.

One minute. The streetlight turned red, on a stroke of luck. He held his finger over the trigger button.

Twenty seconds . . .

Beads of sweat trickled down his forehead in his anticipation.

Ten seconds . . .

He saw the cop stare at him and begin to head in his direction.

Five seconds . . .

The young man smirked.

One second . . .

He pressed the button.

A brilliant flash of light blinded him. It was the last thing he saw before he died, his body falling untouched to the ground.

All around him every person the light touched fell over and died, their souls captured by the light from the small square object carried by the Nameless.

It spread for miles.

Far away in Corá, one room at the top of the manse's tower lit up inside. Piles of gems lay on the floor. Some glowed now, to varying degrees. They were filling up with the light zooming in through the windows. Some filled up more than others as the lights found gems still containing room.

Professor Alan stood in the doorway, one hand on the small amulet that never left his neck. He watched the gems fill to capacity with the shining ephemeral lights until he was bathed in the glow of hundreds of stolen lives.

∞

Sita's room looked exactly as she had left it that morning. But Vanessa was now sitting on her bed with her mouth hanging open, a textbook forgotten in her hands. "Where did you come from . . . and that blue thing . . . what's going on?" Vanessa asked loudly.

Robert stepped through behind Sita and closed the glowing door, making the room significantly darker. "Hey, Vanessa! Have a good day?"

Vanessa crossed her arms and scowled. "Explain."

The sack of books was set carefully down on Sita's bed. Her face lit up in excitement. "Oh, wait until you hear this!" She told Vanessa the highlights, saving the details for later. "Are the others here?" she asked.

"Yeah, they're here, we all just got back from dinner," Vanessa said. "You could have taken us with you, you know."

Sita rolled her eyes. "Take that up with him." She pointed back at Robert. "He pulled me into it and he brought me back. I had no control over it." She grabbed the bag and opened the door. "Let's go tell the others, Rob."

Tossing his head to the open door, Rob looked at Vanessa. "You should come too, you know. You'll want to hear the rest of it."

Vanessa grumbled and jumped down off her bed, following Sita out into the common room. Rob watched her leave, his brow wrinkling. *What is her problem? Is she angry? About what?* He walked out to join his girls. *I wonder if she's jealous . . . that could be a problem if it's true.*

A knock on the door stopped Sita's animated retelling of her day to Roxie and Ari. Vanessa, the only one standing, reached over and yanked the door open. Eric stood there, surprised, one hand behind his back. He smiled at the five people staring at him and waved a hand. "Hey, guys. How's it going?"

Robert froze. Luckily, no one was looking at him. All of their attention was squarely on Eric. *Who is this?* he thought.

Sita jumped up from the couch and ran to Eric, smothering him in a tight hug. "I didn't expect you here!" she cried. "What's the occasion?"

He smiled down at her. "I tried calling you earlier, but you didn't answer your phone. So I thought I'd surprise you." He brought his hand from behind his back and held out a small bouquet of flowers to her. "Surprise!"

Sita squealed and took the flowers, all purple crocuses. "How'd you know these are my favorite?" she asked. He didn't answer, merely smiled as she held the blooms to her nose. "Have you eaten dinner yet?"

"Nope. Want to get something?"

"I'm starving." She spun around. "Rob, do you mind telling them the rest of the story? I really need to eat."

Rob nodded, unable to muster a smile. Now he remembered a little tiny fact that he knew he'd heard before, but which hadn't really registered at the time when Roxie had told him. This must be Sita's new boyfriend. "No problem. Just leave me here to die of starvation myself." Sita smiled and blew him a kiss before setting the flowers on the kitchen table and grabbing her jacket. Rob's heart felt like it had plummeted to the pit of his stomach and would stay there for eternity.

Once the door closed Roxie and Ariene turned on Rob. "*Why didn't you take us?*"

Eric led Sita down the street to a café, which he claimed had the best coffee and pancakes in town. A tired waitress handed them menus and brought them their drinks. She took their orders and went away again. Eric gazed at Sita, sipping on his soda. "Did your parents come down for parent's weekend? I can't remember you ever mentioning them."

She took a sip of her own drink, shaking her golden head. "No, they didn't. It's actually just me and my little sister. She's in high school still."

The waitress brought them refills, telling them their food wasn't ready yet. They thanked her and she shuffled away. "I'm sorry, Si. I didn't know. What happened to your parents?"

"They died, my mother only a few years ago. She was in an accident, but Dad was in the military. My sister doesn't really remember him all that well." She took another sip. "Do you have siblings?"

Eric's face clouded over, his eyes stormy. Sita regretted the question and wished she could take it back. Instead, she placed her hand on top of his. He held her hand as if it were a lifeline. His mouth curved downward, his eyes narrowed. "I did," he said. "I had a brother. But he means nothing to me now."

"I'm sorry," she said, squeezing his hand. Her eyes narrowed a fraction—she could feel something in her mind, something *slimy*, that threatened to rise once more. Growling at herself, she stuffed the insidious thoughts behind an imaginary door and locked it.

Eric didn't notice. "Not your fault. I just generally don't talk about *him*. He hurt me, hurt our parents, and I can't forgive him for it. I'll find him one day, and I'll make him apologize, I'll make him pay." He sighed, the tension leaving him. "But I'd be happier, really, if I never saw him again. Ever. As long as he stays out of my life, I'll be all right." Eric smiled softly at her then, and kissed the hand he held, making her stomach flutter and her heart race a little. She leaned forward and kissed him.

The moment was interrupted by the waitress, bearing their food. She set it on the table and walked away, glaring at the two of them as if they were being rude. Eric glanced at Sita and they dissolved into giggles.

They had just finished their meal when the television above the counter began flashing a red screen. Eric gaped up at it, startled. Sita followed his gaze. The red screen was part of a news channel's urgent update. The shot went from the flashing red screen to the anchorman, who referred the viewers to someone else in the field. Sita watched in concern. "Did something happen today that I missed?" she asked.

Eric shook his head, confused. "Not that I heard. Maybe this just happened?"

They could barely hear the newswoman with the volume so low, but they could make out some of her words: "*Noon today . . . Washington, D.C., blocking main roads . . . hundreds of people suddenly died for no apparent reason . . . police have no idea how so many people died or why . . . the FBI reports no terrorist activity recently . . .*"

Sita looked at Eric, her eyes wide. "What? In D.C.? My house is near there . . ."

They watched a while longer, the channel showing earlier footage of people lying dead, then panning the camera around the current scene. Dust floated everywhere in the evening light. The bodies lay immobile, men, women, and children passed out. They looked peaceful, as if they had just fallen asleep. After ten minutes, however, Sita and Eric were unable to stomach any more. They walked back to campus, subdued and weary.

Eric said goodnight to Sita at her building, waiting for her to get inside before walking away to his own. He shoved his hands into his pockets, deep in thought. Allen was in the room when he opened the door, watching the news broadcasts of the mysterious killings. "Did you see this?" Allen asked him. "I can't believe it. I'm from around there."

The newscaster said the same things over and over. Finally Eric got tired of listening. He put on his headphones and climbed into bed, blasting music into his ears so loudly it almost hurt. He turned to face the wall. *So they started phase two,* he thought.

Allen watched his roommate from the corner of his eye, thinking some of his own thoughts about the matter. *It had to be Imbri Mors.* He flicked from one news channel to another, with everyone saying the same things and showing the same photos again and again. *And Eric . . . he has something to do with this. I saw his face when he came in.* Allen turned off the television and the lights and hopped up into his own bed, wriggling under the covers to get comfortable. *After time with Sita, he should have been all smiles. Not all frowns. And his eyes. I've only seen him get that look when he talked about his brother.* Allen turned onto his side, to avoid looking at Eric. *I should let Robert know about this in the morning . . . he has to keep them safe. He has to, or we're all lost.*

∞

Allen sat in the same café where Eric and Sita had sat the night before. He blew on his hot coffee, taking a careful sip. The waitress ignored him, her eyes glued to the television, which was still showing clips of the murders from yesterday.

A flash of blue light diverted Allen's eye, and Robert walked into the restaurant. He glanced around until he spotted Allen. Sitting down, Robert ordered a coffee from the waitress, who brought it to him and left without a word. "Well, she's as snarky as ever, hey?" Robert said. He stirred the hot liquid around, not entirely interested in drinking it.

"You should be more careful about where you appear, you know," Allen said, his eyes hard. "If someone saw you . . ."

"But they won't, you know I take care of that." Allen harrumphed and crossed his arms. "Now, what did you want to talk to me about?"

"Eric."

"What about him?"

"I think something's up with him."

Robert shrugged. "Finals are coming up for them in two weeks. Maybe he's just feeling some academic pressure."

"Ha. He doesn't really care about school. This is something else."

"So ask Sita."

Allen leaned forward, his voice low. "You want me to ask her if her boyfriend is working for the enemy? I don't think so. I value my life a little too much."

The television flipped to another channel, the waitress' eyes still glued to it. The few other patrons of the little café ignored everything else but their own food. Robert leaned forward, lowering his voice as well. "You think Eric is working for Imbri Mors? Why?"

Allen took a sip of his coffee while mulling over what to say. "Last night, he should have been happy—he was with Sita, after all, he's always happy after he sees her. But he came back, and he had that *look* on his face that I've only seen once." The porcelain cup clinked as he set it down on the saucer. "He only looks that way when his brother is brought up."

"So maybe she asked him about family. That's not enough, Allen . . ."

"I know, but this is a gut feeling, Rob. I know we aren't exactly on the same team here, but you know I want those girls to win this. They have to. I have no desire to be turned into someone's slave, or be killed. I'm too young." They both smirked. They had both said and heard the litany many times before. "And Eric . . . there's something about him that isn't right. I don't have any magic, so I can't just ferret it out like you can. But he's hiding something from me, from all of us, and it's not a good thing. I can feel that much."

Robert drank more of his coffee, cringing when he found it was lukewarm. He set it down in distaste. "So you want me to check him out."

"Yes."

He eyed Allen. "You haven't told anyone else about this, have you?"

"No."

"Why not just ask your employers? Who are you working for this month? One of them should be able to tell you if Eric's been recruited by someone."

Allen raised an eyebrow. "You want me to ask if anyone's hired Eric? Sure. OK. I might as well paint a target on my back. I start asking questions like that and I'll end up dead for sure. You have no finesse for the spy game, Rob. Trust me to know my craft, OK?"

Rob sighed, eyes on the tabletop. "All right, I'll see what I can do. But remember, if he turns out to be bad, Sita will take care of it. That will make her mad, more than anything."

Allen ignored his comment, and they sat in silence for a while, thinking their own thoughts. Rob glanced up at the television. "Did you see about those deaths? Last count was at 462."

"Yeah, I saw," Allen answered. "You think Imbri Mors did it?"

"I don't know how, but I know it was them." Rob held up his hand to the waitress for a refill. She walked over and poured hot coffee in his cup, coming close to splashing him with it. The woman spun on her heel and went back to watching the news. Rob eyed her with distaste and returned to the conversation. "No one else can see it, but if you're attuned to magic, you can see the faint traces of magical residue all over those people. We've had no other reports of enemy groups operating on Earth. It has to be them."

Allen sighed this time. "But how?" He pushed away his coffee, finished with his caffeine burst for the day. "How could they kill that many people with no one noticing? I heard they just keeled over, whatever they were doing. Just stopped and died."

"I think . . ." Rob paused. His brow furrowed, and he continued. "I think it has something to do with those gems they were moving into Corá."

The name brought Allen's head up, but his mind was onto another topic now. "You took Sita into Corá the other day, didn't you?" he said.

Rob winced. "Yeah, I did. What about it?"

"That's dangerous. You shouldn't do it again. She could have been attacked, or lost, or kidnapped . . ." He stopped at the chagrined look on Rob's face, his face reddening in anger. "You *were* attacked, weren't you?" Rob pursed his lips and averted his eyes. "What were you thinking, taking her in there?"

"I was thinking that she needed to see. They all need to see what they're actually fighting for! I wanted her to understand." Allen opened his mouth to say something, but Rob forestalled him. "And I would have taken the others with me that day, too, but they were in classes. Sita was the only one there. Eventually, they'll all go to Corá. That's the way it will be."

Allen turned red, his hands beginning to shake. Rob glanced around at the other customers and the waiters before he let slip a little of his power. It twined around Allen's hands and mouth, keeping him from shouting. Allen glared at him over the invisible gag. No one else noticed. Rob sighed with relief before turning his attention back to Allen. "I know it's dangerous," he said. "But they all have to see it. They all have to know. And whether you like it or not, I am taking them there eventually." The bonds tightened a fraction, and Allen winced from the pain. "You will have no say in this. I am their caretaker, I am their mentor. You are their friend."

He released the gag and manacles. Allen gasped, still glaring at Rob, but he kept his temper under control. "You son of a bitch."

"Oh, don't insult the poor lady dogs. They have nothing to do with me."

"If I had power, I would challenge you."

Rob's eyes glinted and he frowned. "You wouldn't stand a chance, Allen, and you know it."

Allen clenched his fists and rose, throwing the money for his bill onto the table. "If they get hurt in Corá, I will hunt you down and murder you, power or no power." He stalked out of the café, hunched in his jacket. Rob sighed and watched him go.

∞

The ten men knelt on the ground, heads bowed. Sandara Cane stood in front of them beside Professor Alan. She smirked when she saw some of the men attempt to look at her covertly, fear in their eyes. *I'm not the real danger, you fools. Anger me and you will suffer. Anger the Professor . . . well, you'll soon wish you had made me angry instead.*

Professor Alan waved his hand in a bored manner. "Report."

172

The leader rose, a tall man with a strong figure that shadowed his men. He kept his eyes downcast. "Sir, we found th' man an' th' winged woman, as you tol' us to. We ambushed 'em, but didn't kill 'em. They were able to 'old us off an' escape into th' mansion. But we did find out 'ow th' woman got into Corá in th' first place."

"Tell me."

"She was wearin' an approved ring. The Council gave permission for her to be here. But we weren't able t' figure how she found out about Corá, or how she crossed th' barriers. She was wearin' another ring, an interestin' one with th' look of a signet ring."

Sandara's eyes sharpened. "Did you get a good look at it?" she interrupted. Professor Alan glared at her but let it pass.

The leader glanced up at her before looking away. "I did, ma'am. It was gold, an' bore the shield of th' mansion they 'scaped to. It had all three trademarks—th' horse, th' stag, an' th' griffin, ma'am."

Professor Alan and Sandara shared a look. "Thank you, men. You are dismissed for now," said the Professor. The men rose, saluted, and left in a hurry.

Both figures stood silent in the chill of the manse. It was raining again, the water raging at the windows, with sunshine visible beyond the circular border of the house. Lightning lit the room a second before Sandara spoke, her voice soft as velvet. "So that's how they got into the mansion. The Heir has returned."

Professor Alan's face was grave, anger flickering in the lines around his eyes and mouth. His eyes flashed, but Sandara was unable to see whether it was anger or fear that shone in them. "And I know exactly where she got that ring from. Ka'len Lera has joined the ranks once more. We will have to be especially careful now." He moved to the window, thunder growling overhead. "There's no telling when he will show up again."

"And the Aligerai?"

Professor Alan snorted. "How did those girls pick up that ridiculous name?"

She hid a smile. "I heard an Elbi using it. Word has spread far already. Soon it will be all over not only this country, but all of Corá."

"Well, keep doing what I have assigned you. We can reconfigure our plans, if necessary, later on."

"Yes, Professor."

"Oh, and Sandara?"

"Yes, Professor?"

"Let the underlings know to continue with phase two at once."

"At once, Professor."

∞

Allen and Robert met in Alexander Knight's office, where he waited for them. Knight hid a grin when he saw them, saw how uncomfortable they still were in working together. They each shifted from foot to foot, and tried not to glare at the other. "Gentlemen, please have a seat."

Both young men sat down in one of the chairs in front of Knight's desk, their backs stiff and straight. He noticed the strain around their eyes and mouths, the slight frowns each wore that he couldn't quite attribute only to their dislike of each other.

Allen was the first to speak. "Sir, about those murders two days ago . . ."

"Yes, the strange mass murders. They are the reason I called you both here." Alexander passed them both a paper. "Here is a summarization of everything I will tell you today. You may pass it on as you wish to the girls."

Robert scanned down the list on the paper. "How are we supposed to keep them safe when we don't really know anything about the attacks? We can't bar them from every city, that's impossible."

Knight leaned on his elbows on the desk. "That is exactly what you must do." Allen and Robert stilled, their shock plain. "We don't know what is going on, but we do know Imbri Mors is involved. They are behind the mass murders, and they are attacking cities. You have probably heard of the attacks in New York and Philadelphia as well?" The men nodded. Knight continued. "They have not attacked in Corá yet as far as we know, but there is no predictable pattern to the attacks, aside from the fact that all the cities have been in the east."

Allen blinked. "And we are supposed to keep them from any place bigger than their university."

"Yes. Without a pattern, we can't predict when or where they will strike next, and I don't want our girls near any place that could be struck."

"Do we know anything about their attack methods?"

Knight shook his head. "All we know is that whatever their weapon is, it kills everyone within a one mile radius. The victims have no wounds, no visible means of death. So their weapon kills them without leaving a trace on the body, and the police are baffled."

The two young men were silent. Knight watched them, almost seeing how all the pieces clicked into place in their brains. Folding his hands, he leaned back to wait and watch.

Robert looked up, his eyes round and worried. "What about the possibility of an enemy in the school? Could they attack there?"

Knight gave him an approving half-smile. "I thought of that, and I have asked some agents to watch the school. I will ask the both of you to be on the watch as well, but I know you already have your hands full as it is. Which is why I have placed the extra security until the threat is gone."

Both breathed small sighs of relief. Knight rose from his chair. "That is all, gentlemen. You may go."

Allen and Robert rose as well, giving him the courtesy of a slight bow. Then they walked from the room.

Knight sat back down in his chair, staring into the distance with a smile on his face.

Now he could only wait for events to play out. He hoped they would go as he planned.

Chapter Nineteen
Doses of Reality

"We have a problem."

The girls looked up from their study session to give Robert blank stares. He stared back, confused at their blandness. "Well?" he said. "Aren't you going to ask what about?"

Roxie crossed her arms and harrumphed. "Why? You're obviously going to tell us anyway, so just get on with it so we can get back to studying for finals, which, by the way, are in less than two weeks and thanks to your missions, none of us are up to speed on our homework."

He pressed a hand to his heart. "Ouch! Someone's touchy this morning." Grinning at her, he flopped down on the couch. "Now, our problem. Those crystals you saw those men take . . . we think that the crystals are linked to the mysterious mass murders."

Vanessa sparked up. "How? They're just rocks."

Rob wagged a finger at her. "Not in a mage's hands, and it's plausible to assume that Imbri Mors has a number of mages on their staff."

"How are they dangerous then?" asked Ari.

Sita cringed, wishing she had the power to appear invisible. Too late—Rob spotted her and turned to her. "Sita, have you ever used crystals along with your power before?" She was reluctant to answer but nodded. "What do you use them for?"

She touched her necklace, a clear quartz on a silver chain. "I use this one to store extra power. A reserve. I've never had to use it before, but I figure it's not a bad idea to have it, just in case. And I've used celestite to store power before, but I don't have that particular stone with me anymore." She flashed him a sardonic smile. "Celestite and angelite are my favorite stones to use, other than quartz. They're very . . . happy . . . to do what I ask."

Rob studied her expression. "You've used those two crystals before?" Another nod. "You didn't . . . at the warehouse . . ."

Shamefaced, Sita held out her hands and summoned two stones into them, violet light illuminating her face. In the left was a small sample of celestite, and in the other, a stone of angelite. "Yeah. I did," she said. The others looked at her, amazed.

Rob only crossed his arms and shook his head. "I can't believe you stole two crystals from the enemy. And no one noticed." He chuckled. "OK, then, where is the other celestite stone you mentioned? Why don't you have it? You should know how dangerous it is to just leave those things lying around."

"It's not just lying around! I left it at home! I put enough power into it to arm a shield around the house. It's keyed to my instructions, and no one else can use it."

"You left it there?" Rob ran a hand through his hair, incredulous. "How could you let a stone keyed to you out of your sight?"

"To protect my sister." Sita lowered her eyes. "She's living in that house all alone, and my aunt doesn't care to be around enough. So I keyed the stone to put up a shield around the house at all times, allowing only family or friends of my sister through the door. Then I told it that if my sister becomes distressed, that it would kick the person out and lock the shields up so they couldn't get back in. Next I told it that if she remains in high distress, it's to get a cop there immediately."

Rob stared at her. "It can do all that? One stone?"

"Yeah. I made sure it was in place before I left." She licked her lips and played with the hem of her jeans. "Marie doesn't know the shield is there. I hid the stone in my room, and never told her about it."

Vanessa interrupted. "That's nice and all, but what does protecting your sister have to do with Rob's mass murders?"

He raised his eyes to the ceiling, as if praying for patience. "Don't you get it? Those stones can be programmed with instructions. They can hold power. Any kind of power." They still stared at him blankly, except Sita. She understood what he was getting at. "Look, what we suspect Imbri Mors is doing with these murders is they want to collect more power for themselves. The easiest way of doing that is to steal it from someone else." He paused, waiting. No one else caught on. "They're killing these people by stealing their energy, their souls, their hearts, whatever you want to call it. Whatever it is that makes us live, that's what they're stealing. And they're storing this power in those crystals to use for themselves.

"The more crystals they have, the more power they can collect. The celestite and angelite are important stones because they're very willing to follow a mage's wishes. Plus, they can not only store a huge amount of power, but *augment* that power. They magnify the natural energy of their users, and they will do the same for whatever energy is placed inside of them. These stones also balance, or align, the natural energies so they can work to the best of their abilities. When these two stones are in the hands of a good mage, they can be very beneficial to him and others. But in the hands of a bad mage . . ." A shadow passed over his face. "Can you imagine what kind of power a mage could get if he had even one celestite, filled to capacity with the very potent power of human souls? He might come close to Sita, or Darci."

"But there were only a handful of boxes in that warehouse," Ari said. "That wasn't enough crystal to hold hundreds of peoples' souls."

He held up a finger. "That was only one warehouse. Imbri Mors is a worldwide operation. For all we know, they're stealing these crystals and gems from all over the world." His face became downcast. "The murders haven't only been in the U.S., guys. They're happening everywhere. England, France, Germany, Russia, Australia . . . anywhere there are people, Imbri Mors will target."

Roxie cut in, slamming her book closed. "Well, how do we stop them?"

"We can't."

The five girls gasped, incredulous. Sita felt a chill run over her body, and she saw her shock reflected on her friends' faces. "What do you mean we can't?" cried Ari. "We did it once before, we can try it again."

Robert held up his hands for silence. "For the record, you didn't stop them. They beat your asses and got you injured, *and* they got away with the crystals. Although, it's true you weren't there to stop them, just spy on them." He sighed and waved a hand. "We can try to stop them locally. But that won't make much of a dent in their operations. If we become too much of a nuisance here, they'll just relocate elsewhere. They have a world of mines and jewelry stores to choose from. Do you want to give up your collegiate hopes to go chasing them all over the world?"

No one answered. He didn't really expect them to.

He continued. "Now, I've brought this matter up with my boss, who has in turn brought this to the attention of the Council in Corá. They may ask you to fight with them, but I really don't know what they're going to say. When I know, you'll know." The girls nodded, looking morose and tired.

Standing up, Robert beckoned to Roxie. "Rox, can I talk to you for a sec?" Glaring at him, Rox sighed and set her book down to follow him. They went into her room and Rob closed the door behind them. Immediately the others began to argue. Sita leaned back into her chair, the two stones sill sitting in her hands. She closed her eyes and let their steadiness take her anxiety away.

Curious despite herself, Roxie leaned against her bedpost, eyeing Rob as he passed her. "All right, now, what's this about? You know I'll probably end up telling the others whatever you tell me." He cocked an eyebrow at her. "Unless you swear me to secrecy, of course," she said, rolling her eyes.

Robert grimaced and took a seat in Ariene's desk chair. "Rox, you might want to sit down. What I'm going to tell you might be a little bit of a shock." Roxie didn't move, but stood by her bed, waiting. He resumed. "Fine, have it your way. I'm just gonna come out and say it. Allen knows about Corá. Allen does work very much like my own." He rose and approached her, touching her shoulder softly. "Rox, Allen is a triple agent. One, he works for my boss to spy on Imbri Mors. Two, he works for Imbri Mors to spy on us. And three, he's part of a loose group of spies that work mostly independently and only ally for protection and information. His primary allegiance is to himself and no one else. But he's mostly a good guy," he hastened to add.

Roxie merely stared at him, unable to think of anything to say. She closed her eyes and swallowed hard. "Allen is a triple agent? He knows about me, about all of us?" she said. Her voice shook.

Now she remembered what Sita had said months ago—that Allen had attacked her in her own home. No one had really believed it could be Allen, especially Roxie. She had chalked it up to a case of mistaken identity and forgotten all about it.

But now . . .

"Yes. He knows about all of you. He knows what you all can do."

She fumbled to sit in her chair. "Why didn't he tell me? If he knows all about us, why didn't he say anything?"

Rob knelt down in front of her, taking her hands in his. He was surprised at how cold her fingers felt. "He couldn't tell you, Rox. Not when he's a triple, not when he's spying on so many people. I couldn't tell you before. I had to keep his job secret, for your protection and his. But now that you're so close with him . . . I thought you should know."

Her breathing quickened. "Was I . . . was I ever . . ."

"No!" he cried, understanding. "No, you were never on his list of jobs. Once he found out who you all were and what you could do, his assignment was over." He brushed a hand against her cheek. "He stayed here to protect you, and for no other reason."

Her eyes closed again and she took a deep breath. "I want to talk to him." Her voice hardened.

Robert nodded. "I thought you would. He's on an assignment now, but he'll be back in a few days. You can talk to him then."

A thought occurred to Roxie. "Eric? Is he in on it?"

"No, Eric is . . . something else altogether. A wildcard."

Roxie's brow furrowed. "What do you mean, a wildcard? You don't know what he is?"

He sat back on his heels and ran a hand over his mouth. "Allen and I are concerned that Eric is involved, but we can't figure out how. And we've both been in this game long enough that we know who most of the players are. So for now, he's a wildcard until we can figure out why Allen feels uneasy about him."

"Do we tell Sita?"

"No."

∞

Sandara sat behind her desk in the manse, rain still pounding on the windows. Thunder cracked overhead. She winced. *I'm tired of all this rain. Everything is so gray here. I thought Corá was supposed to be more colorful.* The woman glared at the wet glass, her lip curling in disgust.

180

A silver glow in front of her recaptured her attention. Instead of water in her bowl, today she used molten silver, liquefied by her magic. She could hardly stand over a hot burner all day and still do her work, after all, so she used a touch of magic to heat the metal and melt it down.

The molten silver swirled and churned in the bowl. Sandara passed her hand over it and concentrated. She extended a thin wisp of her power into the bowl, emerald mixing with the silver. An image of a young, dark-haired woman appeared. She was curled up in a chair and reading a textbook. Sandara's lips curled into a wolfish smile. *This is so easy now, I barely have to touch her mind and she's doing my work for me. I use so little of my own power in this that my insomnia has been almost nothing!* The image grew stronger, then faded. Sandara wasn't worried, however. She already knew the girl's mind would take to the magic sooner or later.

Darci hadn't slept in days.

Terrible dreams kept her up late into the night, making her toss and turn. She bit her lip until it bled to keep from screaming her fear. In these nightmares, all her friends and family died. And she killed them.

Last night had been one of the worst. She was drenched in sweat, tired, sore, and shaking. Her appetite was gone completely, so she didn't try to leave her room at all that day.

Her history book lay open on her lap. "I have to study, damn it, concentrate!" she mumbled to herself. "Finals are in two weeks, and you've got a lot of work to do." But she just wasn't interested in learning about the First World War. "Even though what Rob said two days ago was much more interesting, you have to stop thinking about it! Now study!" Thoughts of her dreams resurfaced.

You know you love these dreams.

Darci froze, her eyes wide. Pages slipped from nerveless fingers. "Who's there? Who are you?"

I'm you, and you are me. Don't you know me?

"Go away! I won't listen to you!"

The Voice chuckled in her mind. She shrunk back into her chair, sweat beading on her forehead, her breathing growing shorter. *You can't be rid of me. I am you. The true Darci, and you know it.*

"No!" Darci clamped her hands over her mouth, afraid someone would hear. Tears shone in her wide eyes. "Please go away," she whispered. "Leave me alone."

You are meant for greater things. You are a destroyer, a killer, you were meant for power. Kill!

Ebony power sparkled in her palms. Darci gasped—she hadn't called her power to her, had not asked for it to come. She fought to dissipate the sparks twining over her fingers but it refused to leave. Sobbing now, Darci knelt on the floor, tried again and again to make it stop. *Submit to your nature, Darci. Admit that you are meant to destroy, and you will be free!*

"No!"

Embrace me, Darci.

"No . . ."

A knock on the door startled Darci. "Darci?" said Skylar's voice. "Are you OK?" Darci swiped clumsy hands at her eyes and ran shaking fingers through her hair. Unsteady knees lifted her and she opened the door. Skylar looked her up and down, disturbed. "Are you OK? I thought I heard something . . ."

Darci nodded. "I'm fine, Sky. Thanks. It was just the TV." *Kill her! Hurt her, break her bones!* She closed her eyes and shuddered, but pushed the Voice away.

"Are you sure?" Skylar asked, reaching out to touch Darci's paler-than-usual cheek. "You don't look like you're getting enough sleep. Are you sick?"

"No, really, I'm fine. I didn't sleep all that great last night, is all." She took Skylar's hand away. "I'll see you guys later in the dining hall, OK?"

Still hesitating, Skylar moved back a step. "Well, all right, if you say so. But if you aren't feeling well, you should sleep. And you'd tell us if anything was wrong, right?"

"Right." Skylar went back to her room and Darci closed her door.

The Voice didn't bother her again until night fell.

∞

Sita doused her hair under the hot water once more before shutting the shower off. She reached for the towel, but it slipped through her fingers and landed on the floor. Picking it up, she wrapped it around her and grabbed another to dry her long hair.

Her thoughts, however, were far beyond the shower's four walls. *What was that dream?* Water trickled down her damp back as she pulled her hair up into a bun. *Who was that guy? He was handsome, whoever he was.*

She walked back into her room, towel wrapped around her. The door to the bathroom closed behind her once she entered her room and she leaned against the warm wood. *He looked familiar . . . like someone I've seen before . . . I know I've had that dream before but I feel like I've met him elsewhere.*

Sunlight glanced off a framed picture sitting on her desk. Sita walked to it and smiled, remembering the day she and Eric had taken that picture. She picked it up and studied it. *The man looked a little like Eric, but it definitely wasn't him.*

The picture slipped from her damp fingers and crashed to the floor. The glass broke.

"Oh!" Sita knelt down, the towel slipping free. She picked up the frame, little glass pieces falling out. Angry tears welled up, but she kept them at bay while she cleaned up the glass, the slivers nicking her fingers. "Damn it!"

She pulled out the picture and gathered all the glass, throwing it into her trashcan. She pulled out her first aid kit and wrapped small bandages around her cuts to stop the bleeding. "What was that about?" Sita looked back at the picture, a sense of foreboding settling into her gut.

Shivering in the coolness of her room, Sita aimed a black glare at the ineffective heater and picked the towel back up, rewrapping it around her naked body.

Vanessa chose that exact moment to walk through the door, startling Sita so much that she nearly dropped the towel. "Ahh, keep that towel on!" Vanessa cried, throwing her hands up to shield her eyes. "I don't wanna see you naked!"

"Then maybe you should knock," Sita retorted. She tied the towel around her and sat down on her bed, still bandaging her fingers.

Vanessa noticed. "What'd you do? Did you hurt yourself?" She dropped her books and clambered up onto her own bed, watching.

Sita shook her head. "I just cut myself on some glass, nothing serious." She waved the picture in the air. "I dropped the frame and it broke."

"Oh. Why'd you drop it? You love that picture."

"Well, I didn't mean to," Sita said, exasperated. Vanessa smirked. "My fingers were wet and it just slipped." She looked down at the picture, worrying at it. Her brows knit and a small frown creased her mouth. "But when I picked it up again, I got the strangest sense of . . . well, I don't really know what to call it. Foreboding? Doom?"

Vanessa snorted. "So now you can 'sense the future' or something?"

"Psh, of course not." Sita didn't see the dark look on Vanessa's face; she was too busy studying the picture, looking for a clue to her bleak feeling. "I'm pretty sure I haven't started seeing the future or anything. I'll leave that to the seers, thanks very much."

Vanessa shrugged and put on her headphones, turning up her music. Sita peered at her before shaking her head and curling up on her bed, damp hair sticking to her dry skin. *I don't understand. What could be bad about Eric?*

Chapter Twenty
Visions of Darkness

Roxie stalked down the hall to Allen's room. She ignored the looks from the other guys on the men's floor, not in the mood to flirt with anyone. Allen's door came up on her right and she rapped on it hard. "Allen!" She knocked again. "Allen, open up!" A thump and a curse resounded from the other side of the door while Roxie fidgeted. Footsteps pounded on the floor and the door was flung open. Allen stood there, disheveled, dressed in boxers and nothing else. "Roxie!" he cried, his face brightening. "Come in, Rox, I'm glad you're here."

She stomped inside with a scowl on her face and waited until he closed the door. He smiled at her and kissed her on the cheek, his eyes uneasy. "Is something wrong, Rox?"

"Yeah." She crossed her arms and backed up a step. "Robert told me something very interesting a few days ago."

Allen froze, eyes narrowing. "Did he? And what might that have been?"

"You know about me. You know about my friends."

He threw up his hands, exasperated. "Well, of course I know about them! You live with three of them, I've met them all!"

Roxie snorted. "Not what I meant and you know it." She came closer, her face an inch from his. "You know about Corá. You've probably even been there." She circled him while she talked. "You know about my powers. You know about all of our powers. You're a triple agent. You broke in to Sita's home before we even met and attacked her."

Allen stood still, fighting to keep a bland face. "Me? How do you figure I know all this information, hmm? And do I attack people?"

"I trust Rob. He wouldn't lie to me."

"Hmm." Allen escaped from her circling to walk around her now. "So you think I'm a triple agent. But for who?" He ran a hand over her russet hair. "Do you think you were part of my assignments?"

"Was I?"

He stopped in front of her to gaze deep into her eyes. Roxie stared back, challenging, her jaw set. Allen touched her face with a gentle finger. "You weren't an assignment. You never will be." He stepped closer. "Everything Rob told you was true. I couldn't tell you, please understand. As a spy, I have to keep secrets."

Roxie stepped nearer, their faces again almost touching. "You couldn't even tell me something? You couldn't trust me with that?"

"This is not about trusting you," he snapped. Allen wrapped his hands around her upper arms, holding her close. "I trust you with my life. But telling you could have gotten more people in danger, betrayed identities and the trust *they* placed in *me*!" He pulled her as close as he could. "I love you, Roxie. I love you. Never doubt that."

Her eyes widened. "You love me?" she said, her mouth dry.

"I do."

She stood with him, unmoving, her mind blank. Then she beamed and closed the remaining distance between their lips. He returned her kiss, wrapping his arms around her and holding her tight. Roxie came up for air. "I love you, too," she whispered.

He chuckled and returned to kissing her.

In turn, Roxie let go of all her anger at him, all her arguments, and decided to enjoy his sweet kisses.

∞

At the same time Roxie met with Allen, Sita and Eric enjoyed a night out on the town. Eric was more than happy to follow her anywhere, but tonight she seemed distracted. All throughout the movie she had stared at the screen, and only at the screen. No kissing, no touching, nothing. All in all, a sadly empty and disappointing movie-going experience.

An idea came into his head. Sita continued to walk down the mostly-deserted road, her coat wrapped around her tight to ward off the cold. Smiling to himself, Eric shortened his stride to come up behind her. Sita walked past a secluded doorway and Eric seized the opportunity. He grabbed her arm, whirled her around, and pulled her into the little alcove, hidden from sight on the street.

She gasped. Eric leaned down to kiss her, holding her close to him, feeling her heart faintly beat through the fabric of their coats. Their breath steamed in the cold winter night, curling in wisps of thin fog around their heads.

Sita pulled away, her hands on his chest. "Don't, Eric."

Eric turned away from her, running one hand through his tousled hair. "Why won't you let me kiss you, Sita? Why won't you let me even touch you? You haven't let me do anything all night. I'm not going to hurt you, damn it!"

She winced and tried to think, but her mind felt foggy, messy, as if tumbleweeds blew through her brain nonstop. "I don't want to be hurt. I don't want . . ."

"I want to hold you in my arms, I want to hold your hand when we're in public, I want to cuddle with you when we watch a movie together and hold you. I want to kiss you and show you how much I care about you. But you won't let me! If it's too fast, then say so, but stop doing that pulling away thing that you do every time I've tried to touch you tonight. I won't hurt you, Sita, I love you!" Eric said.

She glared at him and backed up even further, almost leaning against the opposing wall. "Don't you dare say that. Don't throw that around with me. That might get you into other girls' beds, but it won't work with me." Her face shuttered as she looked over her shoulder at him. "I don't want this."

He sighed. "You do, Sita, I know you do. I can see it in your eyes. You want someone to love you, to hold you, to whisper sweet things in your ear as you fall asleep. You want someone who will be there for you and do nice things for you for no reason at all except to see you smile. You want someone to say 'I love you' and really mean it." He walked behind her and wrapped his arms around her waist. Whispering in her ear, he said, "I just said it. And I mean it. I won't hurt you, Sita. I won't."

A tear leaked down her cheek. He brushed it away. She began to cry, her hands grip the doorsill. She gasped through her sobs, "Don't you dare hurt me, Eric. Don't you dare hurt me." She moved her hands to where his were now settled on her abdomen, turning her head to the side to see his behind her. "Truth is, I think I love you, too," she said in a murmur.

He beamed and squeezed her, then lifted and twirled her in circles. She squealed, still crying, and turned in his arms to face him when he set her down. Taking a chance, he leaned down and kissed her.

She kissed him back, a tear on her lips.

∞

A few days later, Ariene lay passed out on the couch. A pen slipped through her fingers and tapped onto the floor. Roxie sat next to her, Ari's legs propped up on Roxie's lap. A pillow cushioned Roxie's head, her eyes closed from exhaustion. Vanessa fanned herself with a study sheet, curled up in the chair next to the couch and sipping on a soda. The television was silent.

Sita strolled through the door, letting her bookbag slide off her shoulder and down to the floor. She leaned against the wooden doorframe and slid down it herself. "Is it break yet?" she said. Her voice was tired.

"Sadly, no," said Vanessa. She watched Sita pull herself up onto her feet and collapse in the last chair. "The last day of finals is tomorrow. *Then* we can be free. A whole month of freedom!"

Roxie opened a sleepy eye. "Can you two shut it, please? I'm trying to sleep."

Sita swiveled her head toward her. "Shouldn't you be studying?"

"Nah." Rox shifted, moving Ari's feet to the right. "I figure it's better if I sleep than if I study. Sleep is important, you know."

"Yeah, so is studying," said Skylar, walking through the door just in time to comment. She tossed each of them a bag of snacks, Ariene's landing on her stomach. Sky plopped down on the floor next to Sita, her curls bouncing. "But we've only got one more day. Where are you all going for break?"

Roxie sighed and opened her eyes in resignation. She wiggled out from under Ari's heavy legs and headed for the refrigerator. "I am going home. Goodie. *So* looking forward to that."

"Sarcasm much?" Vanessa asked. Roxie scowled at her and opened her soda. "I'm going home, too, but I plan on enjoying it,"

Vanessa continued. "Lots of snow means lots of skiing. I can't wait."

Sita leaned her head on her hand, eyes drooping. "I'm going home for a while. But after that, I don't know."

A knock on the door proved to be Estelle and Darci. Sita and Sky moved to chairs to get away from the door. A chorus of weary hellos greeted the newcomers as they walked inside and took seats on the floor, dropping their bags next to Sita's. Both of them looked as tired as the rest, with dark circles under their eyes and shoulders sagging. "What's up guys?" asked Estelle.

"Eh, just talking about plans for break. Where are you going?" Roxie said, much more awake now than she had been a few minutes ago.

Estelle shrugged. "Just going home. Nowhere special."

"Darci?"

"Home, too," Darci replied, her voice soft and sleepy. She got to her feet with a groan. "Actually, I should go pack. I'm leaving right after my final tomorrow night. I have to get all my clothes ready." She grabbed her bag and marched out the door to the surprise of the others.

Ariene woke up as the door shut. She peeked around, blinking owlish eyes. "Hey. What's goin' on, guys?"

A pillow thrown by Sita bounced off Ari's arm, making everyone laugh. "Sleepyhead's awake, finally," said Vanessa. "We're just talking about break, Ari, are you awake enough to join us now?"

"No." Ari sat up, shaking her head to clear it of cobwebs. "Are finals over yet?"

Laughter erupted. Surprised, Ariene watched the others, a smile creeping onto her face. "Well, I'm going home for break," she shouted over the noise. "Anyone wanna join me? I'm gonna be bored out of my mind."

After a while longer, the young women decided to put away their books and pack their things. No one had even begun putting bags together, and the result was chaos. Clothes flew everywhere, trash was gathered and thrown out, shouts of glee and pillow-fights ensued, lasting long into the night.

The next morning, while Sita and Roxie slept in, Vanessa and Ariene woke up early for their last final. Skylar, Estelle, and Darci joined them, sleep-filled eyes barely open enough to read the test. Sita woke up and stretched, relishing the fact that she could go home tomorrow. She went out into the common room and put on a movie, waiting for Roxie to wake up.

Sita was staring blankly at the television when a flash of blue light interrupted her line-of-sight. She squeaked and scrambled to sit up, the blanket twisted around her legs. Robert stood there, blocking her view of the movie, smiling like a fool. "Robert! Geez, no matter how many times you do that, you still scare me!" Sita cried.

"Sorry," he said with a grin. He collapsed down on the couch beside her, putting his feet up on the coffee table. "But I have a surprise for my girls. Guess where we're going."

Roxie's door opened. She pounced on Robert, hugging him. "Are we going into Corá?" she cried, excited.

He laughed and pulled her onto the couch with him and Sita. "Yes, yes, I'm taking you all to Corá. I thought you would like an after-finals present before you all left for winter break. You like it?"

Both girls squealed and hugged him, laughing. "All right, but we have to wait for the others. I'm taking you *all* there," he said.

One by one the others trickled in, relieved their tests were over. Vanessa arrived first, followed by Ariene and then Darci. As each one came in, Robert told them the news and handed them their ring. Each girl took it, studied it, then slipped it onto her right middle finger, the ring molding itself to fit.

Once Darci had put her ring on, Robert shooed them to one side while he turned around and opened the gate, blue light filtering throughout the room. "Is the door locked?" he asked. Darci, who was closest to the door, nodded and he finished erecting the gate.

Awed despite themselves, all of the girls except Sita stared at the gate in fascination. Ari approached it, reaching out her hand to touch the blue edges. The magic played around her fingers and she grinned. "I feel better about going through, now. It seems safe enough." Robert hid a smile.

He motioned Sita forward. "Sita will go first. The rest of you should watch her and follow. I'll come through last, to make sure there're no problems on this end."

Sita glanced back at him. "What if there are problems on the other end?" she asked under her breath. "Like another ambush?"

Rob touched her shoulder. "Set up a shield so the others can come through safely. Then we can face them together."

Nodding, she stepped forward and through. Roxie was next, not even hesitating as the magic brushed over her skin. Ari disappeared, then Vanessa. Darci was last. She stopped, unsure, staring up at the gate. Robert came up behind her and settled a hand on her back. "Darci, it's OK. It won't hurt you."

She looked up at him, her dark eyes worried. But she nodded. "If you say so." She stepped up to the edge and disappeared. Robert followed her.

His girls waited for him on the other side, each one looking around in wonder. Smiling, Robert closed the gateway behind him and threw an arm over Roxie's shoulders. "Well? What do you think?"

Vanessa circled around, her eyes wide, taking it all in. "This is amazing," she said. "I can't believe it's actually real, you were telling the truth."

"I do that a lot, actually," Robert said with a laugh.

A warm breeze whirled around the eight of them, lifting the edges of jackets and sweaters. Ari took her coat off. "It's warmer here than at home."

Robert spread his arms out wide. "So, what do you want to see first? We have all of today to explore!"

Cheering and laughing, the young women followed him around town, touring until sunset.

Chapter Twenty-One
Homecoming

Eric hated going home.

It was more than being under his parents' thumb once more. It was more than the absence of freedom. He hated going home because of his brother.

His brother's room was closed off, kept exactly the way it was when he left. Eric knew his mother went in there sometimes, always coming out with tears streaking her face and her eyes dead. He tried to avoid her when she came out from his brother's room. Eric couldn't stand seeing her so broken.

His father never went into his oldest son's room anymore. He avoided it at all costs, in fact. Eric knew how his brother's condition had hurt him, how much it had cost his father. It had hurt even more when his brother suddenly disappeared. One night he was there; in the morning, his bed was empty and cold, only his journal missing.

Eric dragged his bags into his room, not bothering to unpack them yet. His parents were still off at work, and wouldn't return until late. That was fine with him. Eric wasn't thrilled about being home for the next month, and would be happiest seeing as little of his broken parents as possible. They only ever made him remember that which he would rather forget, anyway.

Steeling himself, he crossed the narrow hallway and stood in front of his brother's closed door. He breathed deep, grasped the doorknob, twisted it, and pushed the creaky door open.

Of course, the room looked exactly as it had that day, nearly eight years ago. Only an imprint of his mother's weight on the bedspread was different, the only change in what his brother had left behind. He skulked inside, studying the familiar walls and furniture. His fingers played over the dusty wood, remembering. The curtains over the window filtered the sunlight, keeping the room shadowed and cool.

"Why did you have to tell us your secret, brother?" he asked the silent room. "If you had said nothing, you could've stayed. If you had said nothing, we'd still be a family." His face twisted into a frown. "But you had to leave, didn't you? You couldn't stay after you told us. You just had to kill our family."

Disgusted, Eric stalked back to his own room, slamming his brother's door. He pulled out a mirror from his bags, a small polished thing made of black glass and an ebony frame. Eric had never seen anything else like it, and had paid a hefty price for the object. The black glass reflected as well as a normal mirror would, but it had more depth to it than a regular, silver mirror.

Concentrating, he held the mirror in front of his face. He called up the image of his brother in his mind, sending that thought into the mirror. The mirror's surface wavered, flickering with a dark light. Eric concentrated harder, until the picture in the mirror firmed.

In the mirror was his brother, a man with dark eyes and dark hair, as opposite Eric in coloring as it was possible to be. Only their facial structure linked them as brothers. Eric stared unblinking into the mirror. "Show me where he is," he whispered. "Tell me where my brother is."

The mirror dissolved the image of his brother, colors swirling in violent waves. It brought up a picture of gray, nothing but grayness in the background, and the image of his brother's face. Eric sighed. "As usual. Why can't you tell me where he is?" He heaved a sigh and flopped down on his bed. "I should have bargained for a talking mirror instead," he muttered.

The front door downstairs opened and closed. "Eric!" called his mother. "Eric, are you here?"

Eric swore to himself. He swung out of bed. *What's she doing here so early?* "Coming, Mom!" He set the mirror on his bed and ran from his room, slamming the door behind him.

The sun's light shone on the mirror's ebon back, highlighting the two initials engraved there:

I. M.

∞

The clock in the living room chimed noon, and still there was no sign of her. Marie sat on the couch, arms wrapped around her knees. She stared at the clock and counted minutes, waiting. "Come on, Si, you said you'd be here at twelve," Marie said to herself.

A knock on the front door prompted Marie to rise and look through the peephole. She squealed and opened the door. Sita waited, laden with bags but grinning. "Sita," Marie cried. Sita dropped her bags and swept her sister up in a huge embrace. "You're late!"

Sita extricated herself from her sister's chokehold and laughed. "I'm sorry! But it's a long way. I can only move so fast." They toddled inside the house and Marie shut the door. "How are you, Marie?"

The younger girl shrugged, the gesture elegant by teenage standards. "Oh, you know. High school drama, graduation next semester, so of course the teachers are piling on the pressure, tons of homework and they're pushing college applications. Same-old, same-old."

The bags were heavy, stuffed full of clothes. After trying and failing to move them, Sita gave up and used her magic to waft them upstairs. "So have you decided on college yet?"

Marie shook her head, following Sita up the stairs into her room. "Nope. I don't know if I even want to go to school, Si. I haven't figured out what I want to do after all this." The bags thudded down on Sita's floor. Marie stared at them. "Think you packed enough?"

Both of them chuckled. "Well, most of my clothes are at school! I had to bring them all back here so I'd have something to wear!" Sita sat on her bed, the familiar softness comforting. "Now, we need to talk about you." She fixed her gaze on Marie, who shuffled her feet and looked at the ground. "You know you can't keep being so indecisive about your future."

"But . . ." Marie began. "But I don't know what I want. I'm not really good at any one thing, you know?"

Sita rolled her eyes. "Of course you're good at something. You just have to sit down and think of what you're good at, what you're passionate about." She pulled Marie down onto the bed with her. "You'll think of something, I'm sure."

Marie sighed. "Yeah. Sure." She shrugged again, getting up from the bed. "Let's go get some food, I'm hungry." Sita rolled her eyes, but followed.

The next morning, Sita woke to the tune of traffic whizzing past her house and the beeping of the garbage truck just outside. She rolled over and glared at the clock. *Can't I sleep in for just one day?* She sat up slowly, her head pounding. *Ugh, and I've got a massive headache.* Groaning, she stumbled downstairs for breakfast.

All day Sita lounged around the house, enjoying the quiet and solitude. Marie was still in school for another week, so during the days Sita had the house to herself. And the car. Sita grinned, realizing she could go for a relaxing drive if she wanted to. *Ah, the possibilities.*

She picked up a book and settled in on the couch in the den, propping the novel up on her knees. She didn't get very far before something caught her eye. Sita looked over at the side table, curious. Sitting there was a piece of paper with intricate, loopy writing on it.

The paper felt thin in her hands. She picked it up with care, squinting to read the archaic handwriting. "Meet me in Corá in three days. I'll be waiting at the gates of your mansion. Ka'len." Sita growled. "Can't I get a break? Geez." Her headache grew worse. She massaged her temples, waiting until the pounding abated a little before picking up the book again. "I guess he wants me to figure out how to open the gates to Corá by myself. Though now I have to figure out how to explain my absence to Marie. That's gonna be tough . . ." She set the book down again to think, wondering what Ka'len wanted after all this time of silence.

Marie came home late in the afternoon, and Sita still had not thought of an excuse to leave. They ate dinner, which Sita cooked, and then Marie settled down to do some homework. While Marie was busy, Sita fiddled with an idea she had thought of a few weeks earlier. She pulled out sheets of paper, drawing and redrawing until she finally came up with a design she liked. Marie looked over her shoulder. "What's that supposed to be?"

Sita jumped. She hadn't heard Marie come up behind her. "It's an idea for a present. But I haven't finished it yet." She rolled up the papers and stuffed them into her bag. "I still have to figure out how to make it."

"It looked nice. Will you make one for me?"

Sita swiveled in her seat to look at her sister. She smirked and took Marie's hands in her own. "Tell you what. I'll make a special one just for you. It can be your Christmas present this year, OK?"

Marie nodded in delight. "Deal." She went back to her homework. Once Marie finished and went to bed, Sita took over the couch, unable to sleep. She lifted the note from Ka'len out of her jeans pocket and smoothed it out. *What does he want? I guess I'm supposed to go for training. That's just great.*

Two days passed and Sita was supposed to leave. She still had not thought of an excuse to tell Marie. *Though I guess it's too late now. She's at school and I'm leaving for Corá in an hour.*

Sita pursed her lips, thinking. Finally she fetched a sheet of paper and wrote out a note to Marie, explaining that she had gone on a short impulse trip to visit a friend for a few days. She shook her head. *She'll give me hell for it when I come back, but it's the best I've got right now.* The stairs creaked as she climbed up them into Marie's room, setting the note on her sister's bed.

She went back downstairs, hoisting her bag onto her shoulder. "I have no idea how I'm going to get there, but let's give this a shot." Sita closed her eyes and folded her hands in front of her, concentrating. She called up her magic, her hands glowing.

Sita traced the outline of a large rectangle in the air as she had seen Rob do. She asked it to open in front of the gates of the Awle mansion, visualizing in her mind the way it looked the last time she was there. Another burst of power and she felt a kind of buzzing in the air that tickled her skin.

The door was there, and through it she could see a tiny segment of the vast universe, stars and planets winking back at her through the void. Sita studied her handiwork closely, walking around the rectangle and seeing how the magic worked. From behind, the magical door disappeared entirely. When she walked around to the front again and peered through the door, she noticed a tiny spark much brighter than the others, and while the other sparks moved ever so slightly and sometimes twinkled, this light did no such thing. It beckoned to her, directly ahead, and Sita knew that was the connection point to Corá. She grinned and stepped through, holding tight onto her pack. The door felt as Rob's doors felt, the same tingle on her arms and the same second of darkness before coming out into the light again. Gasping, Sita emerged into Corá whole and exhilarated.

Ka'len stood in front of the gates smoking a pipe and relaxing. His tanned face was amused. "Good afternoon, Sita. I am glad to see you received my message." He emptied his pipe and put it away in a tunic pocket. "Are you ready for training?"

"You pulled me away from my vacation, Ka'len!" Sita said. She stalked up to him, annoyed. "I could be spending time with my sister right now, and instead I have to be here." She held out her hands, placating. "Don't get me wrong, I don't mind being here. Just on my own terms. Add into that the fact that I had to lie to Marie, and I am not a very happy sorceress."

He said nothing, merely observed her while she marched to the fence. The black metal gates opened at Sita's touch. Ka'len stepped behind her and rapped Sita on the head with his knuckles. "Ow!" she cried, spinning around. "What was that for?"

"You have not earned the right to use the title of Sorceress, Enchantress, Witch, or any other magical title." Ka'len stared hard into her eyes, making Sita freeze as a deer caught by a predator. "You will not name yourself as such again, especially not in my presence, until you have earned the right to do so." His voice softened and he backed off, his glare less intense. "However, I can guarantee you, Sita, that by the time I have finished training you, the most powerful of those titles will be within your reach."

Sita sobered. "Oh." Thinking of nothing else to say, she pushed through the gates, Ka'len following behind. The gates closed by themselves once they were both through. Sita's brow furrowed. "Do I need a wand? I don't think I do, but all the stories I've heard of witches, sorceresses, and enchantresses and such say they have wands."

Loud laughter erupted from Ka'len, his short beard quivering. "A wand? You mean one of those long sticks you swish around in the air and magic bursts from their ends?" He continued to chuckle. "No, you do not need a wand. An utterly useless piece of equipment, something only a child or a pompous popinjay of a magician would use."

The doors of the mansion opened as the pair neared, inviting them inside. Sita relaxed when the doors closed behind her, feeling more at home than she could have imagined. Ka'len beckoned to her and led her into the kitchen, where food awaited. He sat at the table and pulled a grape away from the bunch in the middle of the table. Sita's jaw dropped. "How did . . . where . . . how did that get there? It wasn't here when Rob and I came."

Ka'len's eyes twinkled at her in humor. "Did you ask for food? No. However, I asked for food to be here when we walked in, and here it is. I have not had lunch yet, and I am hungry. Sit down, eat for a while, replenish your energy."

Sita sat, a little unnerved, but she plucked a grape as well and picked at a piece of chicken. "Did the house conjure this stuff here?"

A nod was the only response for the moment—Ka'len's mouth was full of grapes. He swallowed and pulled out more. "Have you truly not realized this yet? Your mansion is a highly magical place in and of itself." Sita's eyes widened. "Even when there is no one to live here, the house dusts, washes, and does everything else that is necessary to keep itself clean. It even has a fully stocked larder, as well as cows and sheep outside, well away from the house."

"So . . . magic is what does all of this?"

"Yes."

"OK." Sita grabbed more of the food and piled it up on her plate. "Then I don't feel so bad eating more. I felt like I was imposing before."

Ka'len guffawed. "Sita, my dear, if anyone is imposing on this house, it is me. I am not the owner, after all."

"Well, no one owns it, right?"

"Wrong." The old man leaned forward, arms resting on the table, his eyes more serious. "You are the owner now. This is your mansion. No one may be here who does not have your permission to be here."

Sita nearly choked. "What?" she managed around a mouthful of chicken. "What . . . do you mean . . . it's mine?" She coughed until she could breathe again.

He talked over her coughing fit. "The signet ring recognized you that day, Sita. It recognized you as the Heir to the House of Awle. When Robert, bright and dear boy that he is, brought you

here, even he did not quite realize what having that ring means."
Ka'len popped another grape into his mouth, reclining back in his
chair again. The wind on the windows was the only sound as Sita
waited for him to continue. "I am not sure how to explain this
adequately. The ring gives you a status in this world to all who
recognize it. You cannot give the ring away, trade it, sell it, or lose
it. It will be with you for life. The Heir was the Heir until either
they became the rightful leader, or they died. That ring would allow
no one to pretend to the rulership of Awle."

She stared at the ring in silence, losing all interest in the food.
"So . . . this is my home? I can come and go whenever I want?"
Ka'len nodded. Taking a deep breath, Sita made an impulse
decision. "I want to bring my sister here, Ka'len. I want to give her
a better home. Can I?"

Now it was Ka'len's turn to sit in silence. He thought for a long
time, so long that Sita finished her lunch and sent the food away.
Finally he refocused on this world and studied Sita instead. "I . . .
do not know, Sita. This Council is a new invention since the time I
lived here. I do not understand fully how it operates. It may be that
you will have to petition the Council for permission. Be prepared,
however, for the Council may not grant it. Your sister has no
magic, does she?" Sita shook her head. "Nor wings?" Another head
shake. He sighed. "I do not believe they will let her live here. But
you should try. Always try, no matter what you think the outcome
will really be. Life may surprise you, after all."

Sita smiled. She saw Ka'len's eyes reflect a sudden pain, saw his
face close over. He gave her no chance to question him, however.
Ka'len clambered to his feet and scooted his chair back under the
table. Sita rose as well, copying him. "You should explore, rest, do
what you want," he told her. Her face reflected her surprise. "Why
not have dinner together tonight, and then we will start training
tomorrow?"

"We aren't starting today?"

He shook his head. "No. It is too late in the day to begin. We
start tomorrow, right after breakfast. The sun will wake you, so no
need to worry about alarms or sleeping in too late. I believe you
found the library when you were last here. That would be a good
place for you to explore." With that, he walked out of the kitchen
and disappeared out onto the grounds.

Sita shrugged and found her way back up to the library, hauling her bag with her. She had remembered to pack the books she and Rob found last time. Once inside the enormous book-filled room, Sita sat down in the armchair and pulled the first one out. Pausing, she looked at the empty fireplace, a thought occurring to her. "Um . . . fire, please?" she asked. She jumped when a fire sprang to life and began to heat the chill room immediately.

Content, she opened *A Genealogy of the Ancient Winged Clans* and settled down to a night of reading.

Ka'len was waiting for Sita after breakfast the next morning, as he promised. She found him meditating outside on the front steps. Sita tiptoed closer and sat down facing him. She wrapped her jacket tighter and settled in to wait.

She didn't have to wait long. "Today you are only showing me everything you know about your magic," he said. His voice was soft and carried by the chill wind, but she heard every word. "Everything. How you call it, how you dispel it, how you ground and center yourself, and what you can do with it. I anticipate this to take all day, so I hope you ate plenty of breakfast."

For the next four hours, Ka'len pushed Sita to her limits. She showed him how she meditated (or as he called it, grounding and centering), how she brought her magic out and then turned it off. He corrected her on almost all she did, making her wince every time she heard him inhale to speak. But the truly hard part came next.

Sita worked through lunch and all the way until sunset, showing Ka'len all she could think of that she could do with her power. He observed while she worked, his eyes missing nothing. As she began running out of ideas, he started calling out things for her to do or try, until she truly began to loathe the sound of his voice.

Finally, sunset came, the disappearing light turning the sky brilliant scarlets and golds. Sita shuffled to the front steps and collapsed onto them, spent. Panting, she looked up at Ka'len. "So how'd I do?" Already she was beginning to shiver in the cool winter air, her drying sweat making her even colder.

Ka'len sat down beside her, conjuring up a platter of fruits and sweets. However, when he looked over, he found Sita passed out, her head resting on the stone of the stairs. He waited five minutes, then ten, then raised an eyebrow as her eyelids fluttered and she slowly sat up. "I passed out, didn't I?"

"Indeed."

She swiped a hand over her damp face and rested her forehead on her knees. "It's getting better, then. I wasn't out for that long, right?" Ka'len nodded. "The practice with my friends must be helping with that."

He handed the platter to her and she dug in, ravenous. "Indeed. You did well for one so young. You already know a great deal. However, there is much you still must learn if you are to reach your full potential. Some of your techniques are sloppy at best. And, you tire much too quickly." He stood and offered her his hand, which she took with good grace. Ka'len pulled her to her feet and they walked inside the mansion. "If you are to be of any help to anyone, I will teach you how to fight and use your power to its fullest. This way, during conflicts which may last many days or even weeks, you will not be so tired and useless after only day one."

Sita was too tired to help carry a full conversation. "How?"

"How will I teach you to fight?" She nodded. "First, we must raise your stamina level, both physical and magical. Then I will teach you the proper ways of grounding and centering your magic, followed by a review of the basics. Next, after I can see you have mastered the basics, I will show you how to fight on the ground and from the air."

"And just how long will this take?" They stopped at the top of the stairs, Sita itching to go take a bath in that huge bathtub in her suite.

Ka'len ran a hand through his short beard and considered. "Hmm. If we are lucky, your basic training should only take two weeks. No more, though unfortunately I will only be teaching you this in theory. I cannot manufacture a full-scale battle by myself, just for you to get some practice. Your full training will take much longer than two weeks—years, in fact. To be a good mage, you must never stop learning."

Sita slumped against the wall. "Two weeks? My sister will kill me when I get back!"

"Did you not tell her you would be away?" he asked, bemused.

"Yes, I did, but she thinks I'm at a friend's house on an impulse trip," Sita cried, her arms flailing. "I thought I'd only be away a few days. Not two *weeks!*"

Ka'len shrugged. "I apologize, Sita, but your training is more important right now than your relationship with your sister. She will forgive you in time." He turned on his heel and stalked down the hall to his room.

"Yeah, but you don't have to live with her until she does," Sita grumbled. She stumbled into the bathroom of her suite and began undressing, anticipating the soothing warm water. "I guess I'll just have to bring her here after all."

Chapter Twenty-Two
Unexpected Visitors

Roxie and Ariene dropped their bags, surrounded on all sides by Roxie's brothers. The boys pulled the both of them into the family room and besieged them with chatter. Roxie's mother stood in the doorway, wiping her hands on a kitchen towel and grinning. Roxie's father was nowhere to be seen.

The welcome-home party continued late into the night, including a dinner that could easily be called a feast, and a huge cake Mrs. Dalton had spent all day baking. When Rox and Ari were allowed to go to sleep at last, they were exhausted.

They slept in Roxie's room, with Ari on the air bed. Nothing was said until they were sure the others of the Dalton family were all asleep, hours later. Then Roxie rolled over to stare in Ari's direction in the darkness. "Well, we're home."

"Yeah," Ari replied. She tucked her arms under her head and lay on her back. "You know, I miss Corá. I want to see it again."

"Me too."

"Do you think we could get there ourselves?" Ari sat up. "We have the rings now. Think we could get there on our own?"

Roxie fingered her ring, which hadn't left her hand since Rob gave it to her. It glinted in the moonlight. "I don't know." She put her hand down. "We might need a mage like Rob to open the gate. We don't have that kind of power."

"Couldn't we try? Don't you miss it?"

"We were only there for a day, Ari. You can't possibly miss it *that* much." Roxie fiddled with her ring again.

Ari flopped back down on the bed. "Humph. Didn't you feel it, too?" she asked. "Didn't you feel that connection with the place? The sense of really being *home* for once?"

There was no answer from Roxie's side of the room. Rox could feel Ari's glare burning into her back until Ari began to get tired. She heard Ari yawn and turn to face the wall when she replied.

"We can try tomorrow."

∞

Sita sat for hours.

Ka'len watched in silence. He knew what would be going through her mind. She would try not to think of anything. She would try thinking of nothing, of emptying her mind. The longest she could manage was an hour before her face would contort and Ka'len could tell when her thoughts began to stray from meditation. Every time she lost her focus, he tapped her hard on the head with a stick. And every time he caught her, she would purse her lips and try again. He knew it was hard to concentrate once the cold began trickling through her thin t-shirt and jeans, her skin, and into her bones.

Ka'len whittled a stick with a knife and watched his student, seeing the change in her facial features when she began to think again. He reached over and thwacked her on the head. With a frown, she sighed and tried again. "Do not think," he said, his voice melodic and hypnotizing. "Think of nothingness. Concentrate on emptying your mind completely."

"I *am* trying," she grumbled. "This is hard to keep up for more than an hour. What's the point of this anyway?"

He sat down next to her, apparently ignorant of the chill in the air. Sita frowned at him. "Hmm. I believe it is safe to say your concentration is broken for the day." He threw the stick out into the grass. "The point is to make your mind and your magic listen to you. If you tell your mind to empty itself, it must obey. Control, that is what this exercise helps teach you. Control over your mind, control over your body, control over your magic."

"I already have control."

Ka'len raised an eyebrow. "Really?" he said. "Have you never noticed that when you use your power, you tire quickly?" She blinked at him, at a loss for words. "I am not talking about the normal side-effects of using magic. I am talking about the effect of your magic being used inefficiently. In addition, when you use your magic, you inadvertently absorb the magic and the exhaustion of your friends." Sita lowered her eyes. "If your magic were in control that day in the warehouse, you and Darci would not have been injured, all of you could have escaped notice, and most importantly, *you would not have tired as quickly* because your magic absorbed a part of your friends' exhaustion."

"Oh."

"Yes, 'oh.' This is what I am trying to teach you," he said. He opened his mouth to lecture further when a loud popping noise startled both of them. A doorway opened in front of the house gates, the square-shaped door distorting the air inside it like a mirage. Sita and Ka'len stood up, wary. No one came through for several minutes, but soon baggage was being thrown through from the other side, bags that Sita thought she recognized. After another minute, a woman stepped through.

Sita shot down the house path, Ka'len ambling behind. She ran to the gates and opened them in time to see Ari come through the door and have it close behind her. Ari and Roxie both looked stunned but elated. Sita swept them into a huge hug. "How did you get here?" she cried.

Both girls held up their rings. "We figured out a way to use our magic to open a gate, with the rings!" Roxie said. "We both wanted to come back here, so we just decided why not pack some bags and spend a few days? If we could open the gate, of course." Ari nodded behind her.

Ka'len appeared just inside the black gates, where he stood and stared. "Neither one of you are color mages, though. You should not be able to use the rings in that way." The three young women looked at each other and shrugged. He closed his eyes. "Now, I must ask, if you could not get into the mansion—and I assure you, without Sita here, you would not be able to enter—what were you planning to do?"

"I remembered seeing an inn in Thirka. Town isn't that far of a walk, right?" Ari said.

"And how would you pay for your stay? They do not accept Earth money here," he countered. Roxie and Ari had nothing to say to that. Ka'len rubbed his forehead. "You need to think before you act. If you do something as impulsive as this in battle, you could get yourselves and others killed." All three had the grace to blush and look shamefaced. "But you are here now, and you are safe. Come inside. We were just about to have some lunch."

Sita helped the other two carry the baggage and they followed the old man up to the house, where the mansion took away the abandoned bags and served them a magnificent lunch of fresh fish and chicken. After lunch, Sita took her friends on a tour of the house, showing them the music room and the library first. When she ran out of things to show them around mid-afternoon, Ka'len called them all downstairs.

They assembled on the grand staircase, still looking a bit abashed in his presence. Ka'len chuckled to himself. *They remind me of puppies with their tails between their legs after a reprimand. As they should!* He turned and beckoned them into one of the sitting rooms, a red and pink affair that Sita was not overly fond of. "More training Sita, and this will be good for both of you as well, Roxie and Ari. Please get comfortable, but not so comfortable that you will be distracted or fall asleep."

Each did as requested, setting themselves up on the couches and chairs. Ka'len remained standing in the middle of the room with his hands clasped behind his back. Once they settled, he began the lesson. "Control is the key to your powers. This is true of any power, but takes on a whole other meaning when applied to the mage-gifts. If the slightest lapse of control occurs, countless numbers of people could end up dead." His kind smile reflected in their wide and frightened eyes. "Roxie, Ari, you will not have this problem as such. Lack of control on your parts will, in general, have consequences only for you. However, Sita, lack of control for you means the lives of other people are in your hands. You already know this, I think." She hesitated, but nodded. He continued. "This is what today's lesson is about. Controlling your powers so that you are in absolute control. We will practice this until all three of you can use your gifts with nothing escaping your grasp."

"How?" Ari asked.

"The grounding and centering training—or, as Sita likes to call it, meditation—is crucial. I will teach both you and Roxie this after today, Ariene. However, since you arrived late, we will continue. It is possible to do this stage of training without the first stage, and you may well pick it up as we go today. First," he now brought both hands around in front of him, cupping them with right hand on top of left, palms up, "you must bring all your magic inside your body."

The three young women glanced at each other in confusion. "Uh . . . isn't it already inside our bodies?" Roxie asked.

Ka'len chuckled. "Of course. But not all of it. Have you heard of auras?" Each nodded. "This is a similar concept. Your magic has cast a magical aura, or halo, around you that others can pick up on and even feed off of. You must pull this 'halo' inside you, control this small bit of extraneous power." He paused. "Can any of you tell me why this is necessary?"

They were quiet while they thought. Roxie answered first. "Is it because others can see and take that magic from us? And if it's always there, then doesn't that mean that even if they feed off the 'halo' one day, there'll be a new one around us the next day?"

"Excellent," Ka'len said with a grin. Roxie blushed. "That is exactly right. This halo over your body is natural to all who possess magic, no matter their talent. The extra magic affects those around you, and evil-natured beings could siphon off your magic day after day with you none the wiser until you fell from sheer exhaustion, unable to replenish your stores of magic adequately." All three nodded in understanding. "Now, here is how you do this . . ."

He showed them how to pull the power inside their skin, teaching them how the grounding and centering exercises not only allowed them to calm their minds, but consciously control the halo of their magic. The first try was pathetically abysmal, but after the first attempt, each of them seemed to understand what he was trying to say, and they improved from there.

Ka'len watched them with his physical and magical sight, since Roxie and Ariene's magics didn't show up in physical sight. Roxie was the best at it, able to pull and extend her power with ease. Ariene picked it up fairly quickly as well, but she wasn't as adept at extending the halo around her. Sita followed the both of them, requiring more of her concentration to even pull all of her halo into her skin. He watched her pause, her breathing heavy, sweat beginning to bead on her forehead. She lost control over the halo and it extended back to its previous state. He peered closer, comparing her halo to the other two.

Ariene's was much smaller than Sita's, about half the size. Roxie's halo was larger than Ariene's, but not by much, extending almost a forearm's length out from her body. Sita's, on the other hand, extended almost a full arm's length on all sides. He frowned.

Her halo is enormous. Even mine was much smaller than hers when I was learning. He tugged on his beard, thinking. *Perhaps she is not progressing as fast because there is more for her to pull in.*

Sita leaned back in her chair, gasping. "Is it working?" she asked. "I think it is, but I can't really tell. I feel like I'm pulling in *something,* but I keep feeling like there's more to grab."

Her friends looked at her in confusion. "Didn't you get it, Si?" asked Ari, incredulous. "I could tell you were doing something, so I thought you'd gotten it. I know I did." She grinned. "It felt great, like I was finally at home in my own skin, with nothing missing."

"That is how it is supposed to feel," Ka'len interrupted. "You and Roxie did very well. I am very pleased with you both. Now, Sita, you have a bit more work to do." She looked down, disappointed. "It is not because you are doing something wrong. In fact, you are also doing quite well. You understood the technique and applied it correctly." Sita looked back up at him in confusion. "You are having problems because you were correct; there is more there to be pulled inside. Your halo is twice the size of Ari's or Roxie's. It will simply take a little more time for you to master how to pull all that extra power in at one time. But I have every confidence that you will achieve this with no problems."

Sita grinned, her smile tired. "Thanks, I think. Should we keep going, or are we done for today?"

Ka'len raised an eyebrow. "Sita, you are tired. You need food and rest. We are done for the day. Go eat and sleep, and we will resume tomorrow. Very good work from all of you!"

Elated, all three of his pupils trekked out to the dining hall for food. He followed them with his magical sight and waited for them to begin eating. Then he slunk to the front door and snuck outside, the doors opening and closing without a sound. Thanking the house for its discretion, he loped down to the pond just inside the forest edge with a speed that belied his long years.

The pond—really more of a small lake—was a favorite place of his in his younger years to spend hours reading a book or simply lay in the grass and cloud-watch. He sat near the edge now, the dead winter grass still providing a soft enough cushion that he was not uncomfortable. Trees loomed above him, their branches bare and creaking in the embrace of the constant breeze. That was one thing he dearly loved about this place—the wind never stopped blowing.

He reached out his right hand, hovering just above the level of the water, not quite touching. Concentrating, Ka'len sent out a call into the water, his magic turning the water bright blue. Then his call was finished and his magic retreated. He was left to wait, and to admire the glassy water of the pond.

Barely more than twenty minutes later, a splash in the center of the pond caught his attention. A small creature watched him. He did nothing, only waited and watched. It would not to do rush his contact; he desperately needed information. The creature must have decided he was safe, as it dove under the water and emerged again at his feet a moment later.

Ka'len smiled. "*Oorbish yingam*, Alashankara," he said.

The Elbi grinned up at him, pleased. "*Oorbish yingam*, Ka'len Lera," she said in her watery voice. "*Haefalil toguanti et nobim tae.*" (– *What kind of information do you need?*–)

"I need to know about the Aligerai," he answered, still speaking in the Elbish tongue. "What has been said of them?"

Alasha pushed herself out of the water, making herself comfortable on his shoe. When he didn't protest, she continued. – *The Aligerai are five young women, who are of Corá but not of Corá. They will be our saviors in the coming war.*–

"And the name for this group means . . ."

–*Winged Ones.*–

"Why are they called that?" he asked, becoming more agitated the more he uncovered. If word of the girls had spread far, it could be very bad for them, but an advantage to their enemies.

–*Because of who their leader is. And because of what they will accomplish.*– Alasha regarded him, her aquamarine eyes mournful. – *Not all is as beautiful as it seems here, Ka'len. Many things have changed since you left for Gaia. Many who are power-hungry have achieved leadership in many countries, aided by Imbri Mors.*– She saw his eyes narrow at the name. –*Oh yes, they operate here as well. They have a base in each country, even here. My people have been lucky so far; these disgusting creatures cannot breathe underwater. But we are not so foolish to believe we will be safe forever.*–

He nodded in agreement. "I have seen how ruthless these people can be on Earth. They are only attacking humans for now, though I see no reason for them to stop there. What else has been happening in Corá? Who rules here?"

Alasha grinned. *–Gennaios has been lucky as well. Queen Catherine still sits her throne, and she has managed to keep Imbri Mors at bay when she can. I have heard rumors of kings in other lands, even so far across the seas, who are cutting down whole forests, even killing the tree-people, the Trints. I heard the Nanta went even deeper into hiding in those areas, but the Danoli seem to be faring well still.–* She lowered her voice, even though both knew there was no one listening. The little Elbi shook with rage and fear. *–And I suspect not a few of the Council members are more of these Imbri Mors creatures. How else could their minions come into our world?–*

Ka'len bowed his head, his mouth quivering. "I fear you may be right, Alasha. It is more than time I made my presence known in Corá again. Perhaps that will help." Alasha nodded sagely. "But I need to know how far these rumors of the Aligerai have spread, and what kind of information is carried in them. Please, will you tell me?"

She laughed, and even her laughter sounded like rushing water. Elbis were some of Ka'len's favorite creatures. *–Of course! They are your students after all, you know all of this anyway. When I met the first one, Sita, I was so surprised to see one of the Aligerai, I went straight home and told my people! We are all terribly excited, and we spread the news. We watched and waited until they all came back, and we told others that there are five of them, and all have that touch of power around their heads that tells me they will all be great in the coming war. They will all have parts to play, very important parts, and Sita will be so important.–* Her voice lowered again and her eyes opened wide. *–She is like the great goddesses of old, the Sorceresses, with so much power and grace. I knew when I looked in her eyes. She must survive, Ka'len.–* she said, touching her fin-hands to his shoe in urgency. *–She must! We all will need her in the end. I know not how or why, but we will need her. She carries too much power, and too much love, for us to lose her. –*

"How far have these rumors spread?"

–All the Elbi know. We told the Danoli traders, who spread to the Trint, who spoke to the Nanta. Beyond that, I do not know. But I would say that they have spread very far indeed. Surely even Queen Catherine has heard the news.–

"Yes, yes, Catherine . . ." Ka'len's voice trailed into the night. The Elbi scrutinized him as if she memorized every detail for later. He came back to himself and leaned down to her. "Thank you, Alasha. Thank you for coming all this way. I do appreciate it."

Alasha shrugged. She slid off his shoe and back into the water. *—It is always an honor to talk to the great Ka'len Lera, legend of Gennaios. I did not mind answering your summons.—* She was about to dive away when Ka'len stopped her, a last question on his mind. "Wait! Alasha, you did not give to me a satisfactory answer on the naming! Why 'Aligerai'?" The Elbi was floating further out into the water now. *—I came up with that name for them, because when I touched Sita's hand, I saw a part of what she could become.—* Alasha smiled in ecstasy, and even with her so far away, Ka'len could see it. *—The Winged One, if she succeeds, will raise her friends with her to great heights, swift and true. And she will take all of Corá with her into the heavens, a goddess among mortals.—* With that last bit of information, Alasha dove back into the black waters of the pond and disappeared.

Ka'len sat beside the water for a very long time, the wind whistling around him, but no real comfort at all.

Chapter Twenty-Three
Sparring Matches

Sita ran around the bushes, peeking behind her shoulder and through the branches as she went. Her wings were tucked close to her back, but they still stood out against the brown of dead trees. Cursing, she ducked down behind the bare bushes and watched the field in front of her, looking for any sign of Ka'len.

She didn't see him, so she tiptoed further along the forest, carpeting the wooded floor around her with magic as she went. Her nerves were on fire, expecting attack at any moment. The dead field in front of her was blown apart in places, deep holes marking the points where her attacks or Ka'len's had struck. Faint smoke wafted up from the tiny craters to burn her nose.

Light from the left caught her eye and she rolled out of the way, snapping her shields up when she hit the ground. Ka'len's dark blue magic crashed into her shield, causing shockwaves and rippling blue rings to roll over her. Sita swallowed. *I barely saw it in time! Better keep the shields up.* She crouched again, scanning the area for her opponent. *The attack came from the left, but he's not stupid enough to stay over there. He's moved, but which way?* Tree branches rustled behind her, but she ignored them, figuring it was the wind.

She was wrong.

Ka'len's hand landed on her shoulder, sending a tiny shockwave through her that was just powerful enough to immobilize. He walked around and crouched down in front of her, a wide grin on his face. "Remember to watch your back, Sita. The enemy is not always in front of you." He stood and released the magic.

Sita sagged on the ground, crossing her arms. "How do you move that fast? You're too old to be this good."

"Oh, well, thank you. But might I remind you that I did in fact defeat you?"

She half-smiled and climbed to her feet. The effects of using her power were starting to kick in, and she felt as if she had run for a week. This time, at least, she wouldn't pass out—her endurance had grown enough that now the comas would only come on after using an enormous amount of magic. She sheathed her wings. Roxie and Ari were heading in their direction, so Ka'len and Sita began walking over the field toward them. "We really tore this place up, didn't we?"

Her teacher scratched the back of his head and chuckled. "This is what happens when two mages duel, even in practice. This is why I asked your friends to stay far away and watch from a distance. I did not want them to get caught in crossfire." Sita nodded in agreement. She wiped sweat off her face. "Now, tell me what you learned from today's practice."

"Always keep an eye behind me."

"You have been training with me for four days, and that is the best you can do?" He scoffed and frowned at her. "Try again."

They walked in silence while Sita thought. She replayed the whole exchange in her mind, walking through it attack by attack. "Ah . . . attacks can . . . get through my shields?"

"Closer."

"People can get through my shields?" she hazarded. "Wait, how did you get so close to me without my carpet warning me you were there?"

Ka'len held up his finger. "There is more to magic than simple layers and shields. This is what I am trying to teach you. You are still thinking with this–" he jabbed his finger into her forehead, "–instead of this!" His finger dug into her chest just above her heart. "Your brain tells you all the drawbacks and advantages of an attack, tells you if one move will work better over another. But it slows you down."

Sita's brow furrowed, her mouth quirked into a frown. "So . . . you're saying I should use instinct over thought?"

He threw his hands up in exasperation. "At last! She understands!" Roxie and Ari were almost close enough to hear them now.

"But I thought . . ."

"Exactly, you thought," he cried. "Thinking will get you nowhere in this kind of battle, with your kind of magic. You must learn to use your instincts over your mind, or you could be killed. Your instincts are the only thing that will save you at the last minute." The other two women had joined them now, and they hung behind to listen, letting Sita and Ka'len lead the way back to the mansion. "If you had been using your instincts, instead of your mind, you would have known I was right behind you. You could have gotten away or defeated me with that knowledge."

Sita hung her head. "Oh."

Roxie shoved her from behind. "You say that a lot lately," she said, laughing. "Harder than it looks, is it?"

"Yes," Sita said. Her voice was quiet. "Yes, it is." Suddenly, she unsheathed her wings and ran ahead, gaining enough speed to labor into take off. Ka'len and her friends watched her fly away into the fading light.

Sita flew all the way back to the mansion, tears leaking from her eyes. She pumped her wings hard, strong wing beats propelling her up and forward in a rocking motion. "I don't understand," she said, her words ripped from her lips by the wind. It was cold this high up, her body slicing through the chilly air. Her sweater, which had seemed stifling while she fought, was barely enough to keep her warm now.

She used a touch of magic to warm herself up, spreading a layer of power over her body. "I don't get how Rox and Ari figured all this out so fast, and I'm still not getting it." Tears and the cutting air blurred her eyes. "How am I going to get better in just over a week?"

The mansion was growing larger in her view, and she put on a burst of speed. "What am I missing? How did those two do it? Magic has always been easy for me, so why am I not getting this now?"

Finally, the forest line broke and the fields of her new home appeared. She slowed her flight and dove for the tower roof, backwinging when the weathered stone started to get uncomfortably close. Her muscles screamed at her and she winced, knowing she would pay for the wild landing later.

She curled up against the crenellated wall, the stone like ice against her back. Sita pulled her sweater closer and increased the heat of her magical layer until she was comfortable enough to lean against the wall again. She smirked, her face wan. "Even after fighting Ka'len for most of the day, I still have power to spare." Her necklace bit into the nape of her neck. She pulled it out from under her sweater and held it tight. "At least I'm smart enough to create reserves." The crystal glinted in the declining sunlight, beginning to pick up reflections from faint stars. The quartz, warm from her skin, felt like home in her bare fingers.

Sita gazed up at the sky, fiddling with the crystal. The stars were comforting, even in this strange world with none of the constellations she saw from Earth. Darkness began to take over, and for a while, Sita watched night slowly embrace day, until day was hidden in the folds of a starry robe. Tears still leaked from her eyes and stained her cheeks.

Hours later, Ka'len came looking for her. He cracked open the trapdoor and looked around, spotting her off to one side. Shaking his head, he opened the door and walked up the last few stairs. The old man approached Sita, noting the tears and the layer of power over her sleeping body. "She still, even now, has power to spare for such trivialities," he murmured in wonder. The effects of using his own power for that small amount of time still lingered, leaving him with a feeling of slight nausea. "But why is she crying?"

With as much care as he could muster, Ka'len crouched down and lifted Sita into his arms. She didn't wake, but stirred enough to wrap her arms around his neck and hold on. Ka'len carried the young woman down the three flights of stairs of the tower, opening and closing doors with magic.

He was almost to her room when he heard Sita murmur into his shirt, "Why can't I get this right?" Ka'len paused to glance down at her and really look at her face. Her features were twisted into a mask of pain and confusion, her brows knit close together, her eyes shut tight. Holding her closer, he resumed the walk to her suite, feeling paternal. "Why is this so hard?" she whispered, the words fading into his tunic again.

The doors of her suite opened when he asked, and he carried the sleeping Sita to her bed. Ka'len set her down on the sheets. He pulled off her shoes to place them on the floor by her closet. Sita rolled over, hugging her pillow in a death grip. Ka'len watched her for another moment, his face softening. "I am sorry, Sita," he said softly. "I am sorry to push this on you so fast. You will understand before we are through." He untwisted and tugged the comforter up to her shoulders, and after a moment her body dropped the magical heat layer. "I promise."

∞

In the middle of the night, Sita woke, her eyes snapping open of a sudden. She bolted upright, sweat rolling down her face. "It was a dream . . ." her voice said in a whisper. "It was just a dream . . ."

She sat on the edge of her bed after untangling herself from her sheets, hanging her head as she caught her breath. "But it felt so real . . . who was the man? It wasn't Eric . . ." The whisper was absorbed into the walls and tapestries of her room. She looked up and out the window at the bright moon—it couldn't be much past two or three o'clock in the morning. Sita bit her lip in frustration. "That's the third time I've had that dream. What could it mean?"

A candle lit itself at a wave of her hand. The light burned away the last of her uncertainty. She began shedding the clothes from yesterday, the sweater and jeans uncomfortable now. Leaving the dirty clothes on the floor, Sita reached a hand into her bag for fresh clothing. Her hand hit empty air. "Damn," she said. "Well, despite how magical you are, house, I don't think you can clean my dirty clothes in just two minutes. So let's check out the closet," she said aloud to the house.

The closet was huge, and held dozens of clothes that Sita would never have been able to afford on Earth. She walked inside and reached for the candles overhead. They lit and she stared around her, looking for something that she could get dirty in without ruining too much. Her hand ran over each dress, each outfit, but found nothing suitable. Either it was too ornate, or not suitable for magic.

One dress caught her eye, a simple blue design. She pulled it off the hanger and tried it on, grinning when it fit. She twirled around, enjoying the feel of the skirt against her ankles. Sleeveless, it was perfect for working magic since it allowed her to actually use her hands freely, and the sloping neckline meant she couldn't choke if the dress was pulled or stepped on. Satisfied, she walked back out into her rooms, closing the door behind her.

A thought occurred to her, making her pause. "It was a dream . . . but it was actually real?" she mumbled. Her brows knit together in confusion, trying to puzzle out the feeling of instinct about the reality of the dream. "If it was real, then there's a man out there looking for me?" she squeaked. Then she shook her head and pulled her black robe off the back of her chair, throwing it over her shoulders. "Well, if that's the case, let's let the dreams go on. Maybe he'll tell me what the hell he wants, then I can send him away. Besides, I wanna know what he looks like."

She began to open the door of her suite but she stopped before the knob had even turned. Her mind felt a little numb and cobwebby. "What am I doing? It's the middle of the night! Where am I going?" Closing her eyes, she took a deep breath and tried to settle her mind. But it wasn't her mind that needed settling—that was still mostly asleep. No, something else was urging her to go outside, urging her to practice. Something was telling her she was running out of time.

Her eyes cracked open again, clarity coming to her. "Oh! This is what he meant by instincts." Sita grinned, overjoyed to have figured it out. "This is what it feels like. My brain isn't thinking all that well, but I'm listening to my instincts now." Humming to herself, she gathered her skirts and robe around her and walked down to the kitchen. Grabbing some fruit, she left a note for Ka'len and hurried out to the fields, eating breakfast on the run.

The sound of Ka'len's slippered feet padding down the stairs and through the halls was the only noise in the house. With the sun barely risen over the horizon, the old man didn't expect the girls to be awake for at least another three hours. The tile of the kitchen was chill, even through the soles of his slippers. He shivered and sat down at the table.

A piece of paper caught his attention just as the food appeared. He snatched it out of the way of the materializing bowls and read it. Surprise stole over his features. "Sita is already outside? At this hour?" He popped a piece of sticky doughnut into his mouth. "This is interesting. Perhaps I should hurry then." Ka'len ate as fast as he could without making himself sick, then jogged back upstairs to change from his robe into a more suitable dark green tunic and beige trousers. His pipe went into his pocket and then he hiked down the stairs and out to the fields.

Sita sat cross-legged in the chill of early morning. Through her closed eyes she could see the sun just beginning to rise, giving the fields a foggy, ethereal quality. She sat and meditated, sinking further into the wellspring of her power. The concept had finally clicked in her head, after Ka'len trying for five days to show her what he meant. She floated, her magic feeling warm and comfortable, like a second skin. She was centered—her magic was inside her now—and grounded—her magic had a steady base to pull from.

Sita sank deeper and deeper into her power, glad now that Ka'len had taught her how to do this with the grounding and centering training. Her power appeared to her mind like a glowing sphere of violet, taking up her entire middle, compact and powerful. Her "mind-self" floated in and all around it, enjoying the feeling of home and warmth. She sank into the violet sphere even further, her mind looking deep inside while her instincts kept track of her surroundings. The ghost of her "mind-self" looked into the center of the sphere and noticed for the first time the hint of something silver even deeper inside, nearer the core. She was about to fly toward it, curious, when her instincts sounded alarms.

Her mind-self rushed to the surface, and while her mind was still foggy from the meditation, her reflexes and her instincts were not. Shooting to her feet, Sita turned around to face the forest, where the mansion lay. She could see nothing that threatened her, so instead she took a deep breath and closed her eyes. The rising sun on her skin felt good. *Focus, damn it! This is no time to be distracted!* Sita closed off her mind as well, letting her instincts have full rein.

Suddenly there was an alarm in her mind—her instincts told her there was a presence just in front of her, not five feet away. Sita gathered her power, moving her arms in a sweep, first curved out to the sides, then swinging them stretched out in front of her, pushing her palms and her magic outward. The presence leapt backward and to the side, avoiding her attack.

Ka'len stood there, no longer invisible. Sita smirked, her blood pounding through her veins. "Shall we have a rematch, Ka'len?" she called, her voice excited. Ka'len merely smiled at her and threw off his short cloak. Sita gathered her power and decided to take the offense.

Her hands were in motion long before her mind made a decision to move. Her hands glowed violet a few seconds before she attacked again, pushing her hands forward and "pushing" out with her power. A bolt of purple shot at Ka'len, aiming for the ground at his feet. He jumped up in the air and out of the way just as it hit, the grass and dirt exploding in a furious shower of debris.

He was silent, but Sita kept her eyes closed, seeing with her power and trusting to her instincts to tell her where he was. She already knew, from the mock-battles they had fought in previous days, that he was a silent fighter. He liked to creep up on his enemies and take them by surprise. So all she had to do was keep him on the defensive and not let him get behind her, or so far away that she couldn't sense him.

Sita unsheathed her wings and took to the air. The view was better from above, and perhaps Ka'len wouldn't expect her to use this tactic since they had not yet talked about it in practice. It was good she had her eyes closed when the blinding sun fully rose over the treetops, tinting her white feathers with gold.

From below Ka'len looked up, following his pupil as she rose into the air, the sun behind her. He squinted and shielded his eyes with magic. Now he could see without the glare, so he ran to the left, heading into the trees for cover. She would see him, but the trees would impede her attacks from the air.

Another bolt of magic seared the ground just behind him. Sita could see he was just inside the forest line and aimed her attack with care. The bolt was just close enough that if he had not kept his momentum he could have been hit, and actually doing injury was not the point of their training exercises.

Two more presences caught her attention. Roxie and Ari were sprinting down to the fields to watch the mock battle. Sita shrugged them off, putting them in the back of her mind. She turned her attention back to the fight at hand. Ka'len was entrenched in the trees now, his green and beige clothing helping to hide him. *But I can still sense him with magic!* Sita crowded to herself. She took careful aim and sent another bolt into the trees, knocking one or two down in the vicinity of Ka'len.

Sita flapped her wings to gain more altitude and waited for her quarry. She could feel a pressure building just behind her eyes, a slightly uncomfortable feeling. Confused, she gained more altitude and waited. Blue fire shot from the bare trees up into the air, aiming straight for her. Surprised, Sita dove and rolled in midair, straining her muscles. Turning off her mind, she flung wide her instincts and sent her magic questing, searching for the next hint of an attack.

It came after the first bolt. This time, Ka'len sent into the air an attack holding the shape of a giant eagle, designed to attack and grapple with her in the air. Impressed but not fooled, Sita sent her own magic into the transparent construction, forcing it to explode. She used the explosion to cloak her movements as she dove down to the ground, hovering just above the treetops.

Ka'len lurked below and ahead, further along the forest than she had thought. Grinning with triumph, Sita hurled another attack at him, a huge magical ball that would gain power while it rolled toward him, sending it twisting around in an arc to come at him from his back.

Screams of shock and surprise startled Sita from her trance. She looked down and saw who was screaming: Roxie and Ariene, watching the battle from inside the forest, were straight in her line of fire. *Oh shit!* Frantic, Sita dove from the treetops, her hands out in front of her. She had to time it perfectly, or her friends would be incinerated. *I can't pull back the attack now, it's too late!*

Roxie and Ari turned to run, but Sita could see they wouldn't get out of range in time. Cursing her instincts, Sita strained even harder and shoved her power with all her might up and out through her outstretched arms. The power streamed from her arms in a giant river, shocking her body with the drain. Sita forced the power into an enormous, foot-thick shield between her attack and her friends.

The giant ball of magic slammed into the shield, bursting into a fireball of violet before it evaporated. Her shield held, and instead of taking it down, Sita left it up. *Better to leave it up, as long as they stay behind it. And since they can see it, they should have enough sense to stay put!* Sita banked to her left and skimmed up the wall, gathering enough power for one last attack.

Lightning bolts of blue shot at her from the woods, hundreds of them. Sita's shields strained to hold, absorbing the attacks as she plummeted from the heights, heading straight for Ka'len's position. Her own power broke through the blue bolts as she got closer and closer, and she pulled up all her power to the fore. Closing her eyes, she breathed deep one final time. Then, right as she would have impaled herself on the trees, Sita broke upward just when she loosed her final assault.

A cage descended on Ka'len, trapping him in place. The bars locked around him, and once he touched them, Sita's magic fit itself around his, negating it so he couldn't break her spell. He crossed his arms and nodded in approval even as the top and bottom slid into place above and beneath him.

Sita landed gracefully next to the cage, sheathing her wings once she landed. Her face lit up and her eyes glowed a brilliant blue-green. Ka'len watched her approach, his arms still crossed but a pleased twinkle to his eye that Sita liked. "Very good, Sita. You learn quickly." She flushed with pride. Ka'len held up a cautionary finger and wagged it at her. "But next time, you must do it with your mind working and your eyes open."

She looked at him in confusion. "But I thought . . ."

"I know what you thought, young lady, and you learned the lesson. However, you nearly killed your friends." She wilted a little bit, but her stubborn chin jutted out. "If you had found the balance between instinct and mind, you would not have made what could have been a very costly mistake. How would you have explained it to their parents if you had killed them? How could you have lived with yourself, hmm?" Sita looked down, ashamed. "You understand." Ka'len waved his hand at her. "Now you know better, so tomorrow, do not make the same mistake. Find the balance. That is when you will be ready, and your training with me complete for now."

Sita bobbed her head in acquiescence, her face pale from exertion. She crooked a finger at the cage and it disappeared, the power flowing back into her and revitalizing her so that she regained a more normal color. Ka'len stretched, his tunic and trousers still impeccable, even after the exertion of the morning. He put an arm over her shoulders and walked with her to where Ariene and Roxie sat. The poor girls were flopped down onto the forest floor, stunned and not a little frightened.

Ka'len fought to hide his smile. "Why not gather your friends and we will go back to the mansion for something more substantial to eat then our slight breakfasts, hmm? We will both be very hungry soon." Sita shook her head at him in amusement but followed him to help her two friends toddle back to the manse.

Ka'len sat in a chair by the fire in the huge library. His book rested in his fingers—he only pretended to read, his thoughts far away.

A soft knock on the door caught his attention. Sita stepped inside. She still wore the blue dress that once belonged to Lena, even in the winter chill, with a house robe draped over top. Ka'len bit his cheek—she looked so much like Lena at that age the resemblance was astonishing. "Sita?" he asked. "I thought you had gone to bed, my girl."

"No, not yet. I have something I want to ask you, if you don't mind?"

He set his book down on the side table and beckoned her inside. "Not at all, not at all! I like my pupils to ask questions. It usually means they are thinking."

Sita grinned. She handed him a drawing and pulled the other armchair over next to him. "I had this idea after our mission, because we had all been separated and it could have turned out much worse than it did. But I didn't start designing it until I got home on break. I thought I could make one for all of us."

He studied the design, seeing through the simple sketches to the idea beneath. *Impressive that she would think up something like this.* On the paper was the layout of a ring, a simple band of either gold or silver. Each band held stones embedded in the metal in a line on top, one stone for each of the friends. Ka'len glanced up at her. "A ring would be easy enough to make with some practice, and as long as you had all the materials at hand. You can probably find all of this in the Vault downstairs."

Sita perked up. "Vault?" she said. "I didn't see a Vault."

"You did not go underground, did you?" She shook her head, excitement flickering like firelight in her blue-green eyes. "This house holds more secrets than you know, Sita. You may never discover them all. Even I do not know everything of this place." He set the paper aside, the reflections of firelight highlighting his face in orange. "Are these rings decorative, or do they serve a purpose?"

Sita twirled a lock of her long hair around one finger. "I thought they would do something. Like, I know none of us wanted to be separated for even winter break, so I thought, if I could get all our respective stones attuned to each of us and then put one in each ring, we would be able to keep track of each other. Kind of like a huge web."

Ka'len nodded in interest, bushy eyebrows bunching together as something occurred to him. "But what if an enemy got hold of one of these rings? Would they not be able to tell where each of you are?"

"I thought of that," Sita said, holding up her hand. "I figured I could program the rings so that they can't be taken off. Well, I could take them off, but if I don't, those bands would stay on until death. No one but me would be able to just slip them off their finger."

He fell silent then, his thoughts racing as he considered the paper. Sita sat in her chair and stared into the fire. Finally, Ka'len squinted up at her and she whirled back to face him. "I think tomorrow we will have a different kind of training," he said. His lips twitched upward at the corners as Sita's eyes lit up with glee. "After breakfast I will take you and Roxie and Ariene down to the door of the Vault, and once you have your materials, come straight back up here. We will begin shaping these rings and hopefully be done in one day."

Sita, grinning and squealing, jumped out of her chair to hug him. He caught her and was glad she couldn't see how surprised, and gratified, he was. "Thank you, thank you, thank you!" She pulled away. "All right, I'll let you get back to your reading now!" The fire snapped once, as if agreeing with her. She capered out of the library, humming under her breath.

Ka'len chuckled. He picked up his book and watched her go. "Young ones are so strange sometimes . . ."

Chapter Twenty-Four
Rules Meant to be Broken

Sita showed Roxie and Ari the designs over breakfast in the morning, her voice animated and excited, hands gesturing wildly while she spoke. Rox and Ari ate their breakfast and listened, glancing down at the papers while Sita jabbered on. Ka'len watched from his side of the table with great amusement, having never seen Sita in such a mood. At last she ran out of things to say. "So, what do you think?" she said, breathless.

Her two friends glanced at each other and then at the designs. "So . . . these rings will be able to tell us where everyone else is?" Roxie asked. Sita nodded, her mouth full of food at last. "And we can't take them off."

"Righ', cush we don' wan' tuh enemy gettin' 'em," Sita replied around a bulging mouthful of cantaloupe. She swallowed. "I'll have them keyed so that only I can take them off. When you slip it on your finger, it'll fit itself to your exact size, and continue molding itself to you so that if you gain or lose weight—or shapeshift—it'll still stay with you." Comprehension dawned on their faces, but both still looked hesitant. Sita turned to Ka'len instead. "So where's this Vault?"

Ka'len rose from the table. "Follow me." His three students did so, trailing him down a flight of stairs they had never noticed hidden behind the pantry door. They walked down the wide stone stairs until they hit a landing, where they stopped.

Roxie craned her head around the corner of the stairwell, tugging on Sita's dark green dress. "It looks like it keeps going, doesn't it?"

Sita was about to reply when Ka'len interrupted. "It does," he replied, his tone short and clipped. "But we are here now, and this is the Vault."

A metal door set into the rough yellow stone stood guard in front of them, with no hinges or knobs that they could see. The dull gray metal reflected almost no light, and no reflections of the people standing in front of it either. Ka'len waved a hand at it. "Go inside, find your metals and your gems, then come back upstairs. I will wait for you in the front workroom." And then he left, brushing past them and climbing back up the stairs.

The girls watched him leave, dumbfounded. "But there're no knobs!" said Ari. "How are we supposed to get inside if there're no knobs?"

Roxie stepped closer to the door, reaching out a curious hand. One finger touched the cold metal, but she drew it back in a hurry with a yelp. "It shocked me," she cried. She stuck her finger in her mouth and turned to Sita. "It'll probably only let family inside, if it shocks strangers like that."

"I hate little things like this," Sita grumbled. "Why can't he just come out and tell you not to touch the door or you'll be shocked? It's so easy, takes no time at all . . ." she continued to harangue their teacher while she stepped closer to the door and held her palm up against it.

Instead of a shock, the door warmed beneath her touch, and a handle formed further down the metal's smooth surface. Hinges melted out from the metal. Sita stared at it in surprise. "Wow. Cool trick. Wonder if we could get my door at home to do this." She grasped the cold metal handle and pushed, the heavy door opening on silent hinges.

Roxie and Ariene followed her inside, but they didn't go very far. Sita stopped just inside, jaw wide open, hands limp at her sides. "Oh . . ." Ari said, her eyes bulging at the sight. "That's a lot of money." Roxie and Sita could only stare in wonder.

If the crates of gemstones stolen by Imbri Mors had been impressive, what the Vault held outshone those stones hundreds of times over. The room was a cavern, made of the same dull metal as the door, and lit by curious globes of light along the walls and tables. On the left side were piles and boxes of precious gems, more than any jewelry store the girls had ever been in could hold. In the center aisle were the semi-precious stones, sitting right next to piles of coins, gold and silver and bronze currency in neat stacks on long tables. And on the far right side were the metals, everything ranging from gold to iron, lain out in sheets or bricks or any other form imaginable.

They stared at the wealth only a moment longer before diving in, cooing like children over the shiny baubles. If not for their task, they could have spent hours in the cavern, playing among the expensive stones. But eventually they remembered what they were there for and got down to business.

"What kinds of stones do we need?" Roxie asked. "I think we could pick any kind of stone and it would be here."

"Something to be said for variety," Ari commented.

Sita pulled out her papers and consulted them in the dim light. "I need four each of amethyst, emerald, ruby, opal, and topaz." They split up and dove into the boxes of gems, pulling out what they needed and wistfully admiring the rest. "They don't have to be big," Sita called to them down the aisle. Their heads popped up over the edges of crates. "I'm putting them into rings, after all, so the smaller they are, the better." Rox and Ari nodded in reply and went back to their searching.

The girls piled their findings in the middle of the room, clearing off space on a table. The heap of small gems was a fortune on Earth, and they all knew it. Sita looked at her papers again. "What do you think, gold or silver?" she asked them.

Ari answered first. "Gold, duh. Why would anyone want silver?"

"I want silver," Sita and Roxie replied in unison. Roxie continued the argument. "Silver looks better on me than gold does. Can we make mine silver?" she pleaded.

Sita held up her hands. "OK, OK, calm down! We can figure out who wants a gold one and who wants silver. I want silver, and you want silver, but Ari wants gold. Think Vanessa would want gold?"

"Probably," Ari said. "I've seen her wear it before. But Darci would probably look better with silver."

"All right, that's three silver, two gold. And my sister's ring, which is silver. So let's figure out what that equals in those metals over there," Sita said. She led them over to the metal tables, where they had fun trying to equate the mass of six rings into an adequate amount of metal. Finally they just grabbed two bars of gold and three of silver and hauled them all over to the pile of stones on the table. Sita pushed her hair from her eyes, panting from moving the heavy metal. "Oh, yeah, my sister's ring. I need another amethyst and moonstones for hers." Heaving herself away from the table, she hurried to go find the stones while Roxie and Ari waited and rested their sore arm muscles.

Sita came back bearing the two stones, and she gathered them all up into her skirt. Rox and Ari both frowned. "Hey, now, how come you get to carry the light load and we have to carry the heavy stuff?" Ari said. "That's not fair."

Frowning herself, Sita glared at the metal. It levitated off the table and floated out in front of them. Sita turned to her friends, smirking. "Coming? Or are you going to sleep down here tonight?" Rox and Ari laughed and followed her out, the Vault closing itself behind them. The gold and silver bars floated in front of Sita all the way up the stairs, with Roxie and Ariene following close behind. They emerged at last inside the pantry and Ari closed the door behind her. It folded seamlessly back into the wall, only a small nick at the top right corner to betray its presence.

The trio trooped over to the workroom where Ka'len waited. He sat at the table, watching the door for their approach. Sita came in first, guiding the metals over to the table and setting them down. Ari and Rox came in a step behind her. "Will this be enough metal, do you think?"

Ka'len's bushy eyebrows shot into the air and his lips twitched in humor. "I think multiple bars are more than enough. You really only needed one of each, you know."

Sita blushed. "But I thought . . . for six rings . . ."

He waved her words into silence. "We will make these with magic, which uses much less of the metal than normal jewelry-smithing does." The jewels and metals slid over to his side of the table as his three students took seats around it to watch. "Now, we should start with the gold rings. Gold is softer, more pliable, and more willing to follow instructions." He pulled out one of the gold bars, setting it in the center of the table on top of a rough cloth. "First, center yourself, Sita. Roxie, Ari, you do not have the right magic for this, as you know, but you are welcome to stay and watch if you wish."

Sita took a deep breath and closed her eyes, sinking down into the well of her power. When she was far enough in, she opened her eyes again and stared at Ka'len. "Next, pull out a strand of magic. Just a strand, mind! You only want enough to take off a piece of gold, not enough to crush it." Blinking, Sita did as he asked, using her mind-self to pull out a shimmering strand of violet power and send it into the gold bar.

A piece of metal sloughed off, dropping onto the cloth underneath the gold brick. It was about the size of one of the eyepieces of Ka'len's reading glasses. Sita reached out and picked it up gingerly, expecting it to be hot. But it was cool to the touch, and she looked back at Ka'len. "What next?" she asked.

Ka'len summoned her drawings from her pocket and spread them out on the table. "Next you will concentrate with a slightly larger force of magic on the metal in your hand. Ask it to make this shape—" He pointed down at the ring design. "—and if it refuses, *tell* it to make this shape. Once it agrees and molds itself into a ring, use your magic to harden it."

"But what about the gems?" Ari blurted in surprise. "If it's hard, then how . . ."

"I will get to that," Ka'len interrupted. He scowled at her and Ariene shut her mouth with a snap. Still scowling, Ka'len waved at Sita to continue.

And so she did. Violet power wrapped itself around the glob of gold in her fingers, first asking, then insisting, that it take *this* shape, and take it *now*. After a few moments when nothing happened and Sita began to worry that something was wrong, the gold writhed in her hand. She almost dropped it, but managed to hold on as it twisted and turned, pieces dropping off as the gold reduced itself into a single, finely wrought golden band.

Ka'len reached for it and Sita handed it over. The ring kept its shape after she passed it to him. He turned it over in his hands before giving it back. "Excellent. Now to set the spells that will allow it to mold to and stay on its bearer's finger. This will take a little more power. Set the ring on the table."

Confused, Sita did as he told her, setting it down on the mahogany wood in front of her. Ka'len continued. "Then I want you to think, clearly and strongly, of what you want it to do—that is to say, how you want it to stay on. The other spells will be tied in to the gems themselves, so do not worry about those right now. Concentrate only on this spell." She swallowed hard. "Once you have your orders in mind, set them into the ring itself, and use your power to embed these orders into the very nature of the ring. Do you understand?"

Sita tucked an errant strand of hair out of her way, green eyes cloudy. She glanced up from the ring to him and back again. "Yeah, I think so." Closing her eyes, she concentrated as hard as she could on making the ring obey her. Once she felt she had the orders exactly right, she gathered her power, transferred her concentration to the ring, and *pushed* the spell outward and down into the ring itself. She felt the leakage, like a stream stemming from a river, as the magic spun around the ring, sinking into the metal as if it were transparent and not gold at all. The ring could only hold so much, however. As soon as she began to feel resistance, she shut down the spell and recalled the unused magic.

The old man watched her work with care, noting everything she did. He saw when the ring was full to capacity and nodded in satisfaction when Sita pulled back at that exact moment. She opened her eyes and peered at him. "Wonderful job. Now, make the other five rings." With a pained expression on her face, Sita did as he said, creating one more gold ring and all of the silver ones, with the spells included, in less than a half-hour. Roxie and Ariene watched in silence, intrigued, but a bit bored after a while. They both woke up when Ka'len pushed the jewels forward.

He had sorted the gems out on the table by type, but otherwise in no particular order. When Sita had finished setting the last spell on the final ring, he gestured to the stones. "Pick which one you want to start with."

Sita chose the moonstone. "This one. This ring will only have two stones in it, so let's start with that."

Ka'len agreed and took hold of a silver ring. "Watch carefully," he said. Grasping the moonstone between two fingers, he concentrated on the silver band, narrowing his eyes and pursing his mouth. This was harder for him than it was for Sita—his magic had been set in paths over the centuries that hers was not. But Sita watched his movements, both magical and physical, and saw what he did.

Blue magic enveloped the ring, making one spot in the center softer than the rest. Ka'len allowed his magic to grasp the stone as well, allowing him a much finer setting than using his fingers would give him. First he duplicated what Sita achieved with the metals: he shaped the larger stone down into a smaller one more suited to fit in a ring, the excess plunking down on the table in white chunks and pieces. Once it was pared down to his satisfaction, he lowered the tiny stone into the softened spot, pushing it in until it could go no further without being swallowed by the molten metal. Then he forced the metal to harden and released the magic.

The ring looked perfect, a single moonstone gleaming in the sunlight. Sita reached out and touched it, running her finger over the stone. "And do I set the connection to the person with the same spell I used on the metal?" she asked.

"A slightly different spell, but of the same variant," Ka'len said. He handed her one of the amethysts. "Duplicate what I just did, and set this in with the moonstone."

Sita did as he told her, but it took her much longer than it had taken him. It wasn't incredibly fine work, exactly, but more because it was troublesome, having to do the work in slow steps to avoid mistakes. But she soon got it right, and the amethyst sat in the silver band alongside the moonstone. She looked up at Ka'len. "And to set the connection?" she prompted.

"This time, instead of concentrating on the idea of molding to one's finger, think of the person each gemstone is connected to. With the moonstone, think of your sister and tell the stone with your magic that *this* is the person it belongs to, and *this* is the person it will remember. Think as hard as you can—the more memories you can dredge up about the person, the better, for a stronger connection will be established."

Sita closed her eyes and concentrated on the moonstone, thinking of her sister. When she had all the memories she could hold in the front of her mind, she engaged her magic and shoved those memories at the stone; the stone absorbed them all and held them. She thought her memories at the stone until it could hold no more. Then she broke the connection and moved to the amethyst, putting as much of herself into the stone as she could.

Once that one was full, she broke the spell, and was surprised to discover she could actually *feel* the connection of the stone. It was like a thick piece of silk thread, running from the center of her body to the amethyst of the ring. She sighed. *This will take some getting used to, but at least it won't be uncomfortable.*

Ka'len saw she was finished and feeling the effects of the connection. He pushed all of the rings and the gems to her side of the table in a wordless command. Reminding herself that this was her idea, Sita got to work. She set four stones in the rest of the rings, but five in her own, with the moonstone for her sister. With each stone, she repeated the process of softening, sculpting, setting, and hardening. Once all the stones were set, she focused in on each one, thinking hard about all of her friends in turn. The amethysts, of course, were her own stones, and she hardly had to think about those. Emeralds matched with Vanessa, and Sita attempted to think of the most charitable memories she had. There weren't many, but there were enough—apparently emeralds were shallow and could hold few memories. Rubies belonged to Roxie, and topaz to Ariene. The last stones she aligned were the opals, for Darci.

Once the last stone was connected, Sita slumped back into her chair, mentally exhausted, if not magically. Roxie began to reach for a ring. "Can I?" she asked. Sita pointed out which one was hers, the only ring without a ruby in it. Roxie picked it up and examined it. Then, with trepidation and excitement warring on her face, she slipped the ring over her left middle finger.

The ring did nothing for a moment, and Sita feared the magic hadn't held. But her fears disappeared when, to Roxie's surprise, the ring tightened itself around her finger, to the point of comfortable snugness. Amazed, Roxie tried to take it off and found she couldn't. "It worked!" she cried. "It's amazing! I can even feel the others! You, Si, are so tired you're about to fall over. And Ari, you're . . . hungry?" Ari blushed while the others laughed. "This is amazing," Roxie cried. "Here, Ari, put yours on."

Ari picked up her ring, the only gold one without a topaz set in it, and slipped it on the same finger Roxie had put her ring on. It behaved the same as Roxie's had, tightening until it fit. Once it finished moving, Ari's eyes widened as she, too, felt the connections to the other rings. "Wow."

Sita reached for her ring, knowing what she would find when she put it on. Hers behaved as the others had, and she was comforted with the knowledge that not only had her magic worked, but once the others had their rings they would all know where the other members of their group were at all times. And they would know at once if there was any danger to any member. She fingered the moonstone in her ring, feeling that her sister was safe, but annoyed. She winced. *I really need to go see her. Maybe I should do that tonight. And I can bring her the ring as an apology present.*

∞

Storm clouds rolled over the little manor house. It had been raining nonstop for months, and Sandara was heartily sick of rain, gray, and thunder. She liked the lightning, though.

Her search for the winged girl had gone well. Sandara knew the girl wasn't on Earth—she was in the Awle mansion, along with three other people. What frustrated her, however, was the fact that she could see nothing past the gates of the mansion. A great blue shield hovered over the entire property, concealing everything to her magical sight, looking like a giant bowl upended over about 100 acres of field and forest.

She ground her teeth in frustration. Ka'len Lera was a crafty old geezer, finding a way to hide his precious little underlings from *her* sight. Sandara tapped a finger to her cheek, pacing while she thought. *How long could they stay cooped up on that property? Granted, it is a huge place, but surely they have to get bored sometime!*

Humming to herself, she set the problem aside for the moment, certain that she would think of something to break the shield. Instead, Sandara sat down at her desk again and picked up a glowing gemstone. It was a diamond, its brilliant glow bright enough to hurt her eyes in the darkened room. She held the stone in both hands and breathed in deep, savoring the feel of power trapped inside the angles and facets of the stone.

Its brilliance dimmed a trifle. Sandara set the stone down in a hurry, not wanting to waste the power inside. Nor did she wish to alarm Professor Alan. He would not be pleased to discover that power had been siphoned off, whether it had been intentional or not. But she continued to admire the diamond, the light trapped inside twisting and turning, undulating in seductive waves. "I wonder why he wants all these stones?"

Sandara leaned back in her chair, her cat-like grace apparent even when no one was around to see. "And why is he stealing the life of all those people?" Her scarlet lips smirked. "Not that I object," she said, continuing to talk to herself and the empty room. "The fewer disgusting humans around, the better, in my opinion."

"Be careful, Sandara."

The woman straightened, shivers running down her spine at the iciness of her master's voice. She held her head down, not daring to look up.

Professor Alan continued. "I am one of those 'disgusting humans,' as are you. But I don't care if you insult yourself. Only if you insult me."

She still did not look up. "Yes, Professor. I apologize. I meant no offense." Sandara shivered again. It was a good thing Ray Alan couldn't see the fire, the anger, in her eyes, or he would strike at her again. Once was more than enough for Sandara.

"Good. Perhaps you have learned your lesson," he said. The professor stalked into the room, negating her wards and shields with his own. Dark blue lightning sparked at his fingertips. The storm finally broke overhead. Thunder crashed down on the mansion, the sky emptying itself in a violent fit of rage. "Now, as to your thoughts of why I have these stones and the human lives . . . it is currently none of your concern."

He fixed her with a beady glare, his power forcing her head up. Sandara just managed to get her anger in check before he saw her eyes. "I will tell you when you need to know, and no sooner. You see only the tip of the iceberg, so to speak. My plans are much more involved than you know."

Lightning ignited the sky behind him, reflecting in Sandara's eyes. The blue fire at his fingertips was still there, and Sandara knew that if she angered him now, she would regret it. "As you wish, Professor. I will do as you bid me."

Professor Alan snorted. "You will do whatever I wish you to, Sandara. Never forget that I owned your soul from the moment you joined Imbri Mors. I own you." With a flick of his wrist and a movement of finger, he called the diamond to him. It landed in his palm, the facets digging into his skin. "I believe I will take this with me. You don't deserve to have one anymore. You are nothing, now and always."

He spun on his heel and strode from the room, slamming the door behind him. Sandara resettled herself in her chair. Her teeth bared in a snarl. "I left Earth because of people like you, Ray," she said in a whisper. Her eyes could have ignited a fire. "My father was like you. He called me nothing, too." Sandara curled her fingers into claws. "But I am not nothing. I will never be nothing again. That's why I'm here." The reminder calmed her immediate anger, but nothing could quench the burning rage she always felt inside. Sandara thought on how best to get her revenge. A plan involving a certain winged magician came to mind.

∞

Sita woke, all of a sudden, in the pre-dawn hours of early morning. Stretching like a cat, she tossed off her bedding and hurried to change into something presentable. She checked on the others while she slipped into a black sleeveless dress with intricate embroidery on the hem. Ka'len was still asleep, as were Roxie and Ari.

Her friends were sure to be asleep for hours more, but she could only bank on maybe two or three hours until Ka'len rose. *More than enough time!* Grinning, Sita tucked her sister's ring into a wrist-bag and threw her black flying robe on over the dress—while winters were evidently mild in Corá, the winters in Maryland were generally not as nice.

The furniture pieces were far enough away from each other that there was plenty of room in the middle for her to set up a gate. She did so, elated at how much faster she had become with the complicated working.

In front of her were the edges of the magical door, glowing and distorting the space around it. Just inside, Sita could see the darkness of her old room. She frowned. "I wonder why Rob's gates never show what's on the other side?" she muttered. Shaking off the thought for a better time, she gathered her skirts and stepped through.

The gate shut behind her, taking all light with it. Sita paused to allow her eyes to adjust. Her room was very dark, except for the faint glow of yellow light coming from the hall. Sita recognized it as the night-lights in the bathroom and kitchen, and she was glad to have some light.

A soft noise echoed from her sister's room across the hall. Sita shook her head and smiled. "Crazy girl still gets up at the crack of dawn . . ." she said to herself. The light came on in Marie's room, and once Sita was certain her sister was awake, she eased out of her own room and over to her sister's.

She was just in time for Marie to open the door, standing there in nothing but her bra and underwear. Marie squealed and jumped backward, eyes wide. Sita held up her hands. "Hey Mar! It's just me!"

Marie blinked at her owlishly for a moment before anger contorted her features. Sita cringed inside, knowing that anger would explode in three . . . two . . . one . . . "Don't you 'hey Mar' me! You've been gone for seven days! *Seven days*! And all I got was a note, not even a phone call, nothing! Just up and left . . ." Sita let Marie rant on, her ears and cheeks turning pink. But once Marie began to repeat herself she decided to cut in.

She fished the ring out of its bag and held it up to the light. Marie stopped in mid-sentence, surprised. Sita held it out to her, her cheeks still scarlet red. "It was supposed to be a Christmas gift, but . . . since you're so mad at me . . ." Marie took the ring to study it with widened eyes.

"It's beautiful," she said, her voice much muted. Most of the anger was gone now, leaving only annoyance. "Where did you get it?"

Sita watched her slip it on to her left middle finger, and saw her jump a little when the metal warmed to fit her digit. "From my mansion. In Corá."

"You don't have a mansion," Marie said. She ran a finger over the ring, admiring it still, oblivious to the fact that she was still half-naked. "And where's Corá? Is that in Maryland?"

Sita chuckled. She strode past Marie into her sister's room to pick up the sweater and jeans Marie planned to wear. Once the clothing was shoved into Marie's hands, she stopped gazing at the ring and started slipping the clothes on. "Get dressed, goose, and I'll show you what—and where—Corá is."

Marie obeyed and followed Sita back into her room. Sita stood in the middle of the floor, her hands held out in front of her. She beckoned Marie to stand behind her. "You won't believe me if I told you. So I'm just going to show you."

The redhead was used to her sister's magic, but this display went beyond what she was used to seeing. Power flowed from Sita's palms and wove itself into a door, large enough to fit them both side by side. Marie's mouth dropped open. Through the "door" she didn't see the dresser and closet—she saw the interior of a large room, dominated by an enormous bed. "Is that . . . that's one of those wormhole gate things, like in the movies."

The ring on Marie's hand pulsed once, startling her from her trance, and pulsed again, prompting her to move closer. Sita grabbed her sister's hand. "Yeah, it's a gate into Corá. Now come on!" And Sita pulled her in.

When Sita grabbed her hand, Marie felt the tingle of magic. Then she was being pulled into the glowing doorway that led to who-knew-where. Marie would have screamed, or balked, or held her breath, or done *something*, but there was no time. One step forward and in, the floor disappeared, she felt as if a bucket of cold water had been dumped on her head, and then she was through the gate.

Sita removed her outer robe, revealing the simple black gown underneath. Marie could only look around in wonder. This room, which appeared to be her sister's, was full of luxury. A gigantic but simply carved mahogany bed. A walk-in closet big enough to fit Marie's entire bedroom inside, with room to spare, filled with fine clothes. A vanity stood near the closet, and on one side of the bed was set a small table.

She felt, for an instant, the most intense jealousy she had ever felt in her life. "This is *your* room?" said Marie. "How . . ."

Sita held her arms out wide to either side of her body. "This is the mansion of the House of Awle. My mansion. But, if you want to live here too, it'll be *our* mansion." She twirled in girlish glee, skirts swirling around her. "It's amazing, isn't it?"

"I . . . well, sure . . ."

Sita lunged forward and grabbed Marie's hands. Her bright blue-green eyes kindled a fire of excitement in Marie that banished the jealousy. "Come on, I want to show you everything! The house, the grounds, the *Vault*, Thirka . . ."

But before they even made it to the door, there was a brief knock and it opened from outside. An old bearded man walked in, his face furious, frightening Marie to no end. "Sita, what the devil are you doing opening a gate this early? You should be . . ." he began.

Ka'len never finished that sentence. His eyes lighted on the second, unknown younger woman in the room and he froze in mid-stride, his hands falling limp to his sides. He looked back at Sita. Blue-green eyes stared back at him in challenge, though she had the grace to blush.

"What. Did. You. *Do.*"

Chapter Twenty-Five
Midnight Deeds

The Jitari Mountains, in the very far west of Gennaios, were never visited by anyone, human or animal. Each end of the range looked normal: grasses grew, animals bedded down there, humans hunted. But the further in a person walked, the more desolate the mountains became. As the center neared, the grasses died. Animals did not peek out of hiding holes. And no traces of humans could be found.

A small valley lay in the center of this bitter range, protected on all sides by the snow-topped crags of the tallest peaks. The earth was frozen, here where nothing grew, where only a pattern of stones lain out in front of a closed-off cave marked the site's significance.

Even the sun's rays couldn't warm the place. As the sunshine faded, the valley grew colder.

People began to appear.

In groups of two or three, alone or in larger groups, members of Imbri Mors ripped through the fabric between worlds, or transported themselves from around Corá and into the valley. They arranged themselves in a loose mob around the stone design, lighting torches as the sunlight faded.

Professors Alan and Sandara appeared in the middle of the members, just outside the edge of one stone spiral's arm. Torchlight flashed against their faces, highlighting Alan's cool, confident expression and Sandara's trepidation.

Members continued to trickle in while the others waited in almost complete silence. Stars began to peek out of the night sky's dark robe. Sandara bit her lip hard, her hands curling into tight fists. "Are you sure we should be doing this *tonight*? I mean, this is a night of power for . . ."

"Sandara, this is the *only* night for this to happen."

"But . . ."

"The longest night is indeed a night of power for Corá," he said. He grasped her wrist and pulled her closer to the edge of one stone. She shivered in her thin black dress. "But this means she will be distracted. She won't be looking to this place since She will be too busy completing the rebirthing rites in preparation for spring in three months. And tonight is very important for us, as well." Alan positioned her so she was facing the start of the stone arc design. Four arcs of alternating black and white paving stones emanated out from the corners of a square, also lain in an alternating black-and-white design.

"As a night of power, the Veil will be thin tonight. It makes our task that much easier."

Alan walked away, leaving Sandara alone in the middle of the crowd. The last of the members trickled in. Torches flickered in the dead air, burning bright enough that the valley appeared lit by pinpricks of fire. An hour passed. Sandara stood in silence and watched for Alan's cue.

She licked her lips and closed her eyes. *My insomnia is going to be terrible tonight, after this.* The cold air in this shadowed valley wormed its way to her skin through the folds of her dress. She mentally kicked herself for choosing this dress—sleeveless and thin, made of the finest satin she could find, it was no protection against the elements. Sandara tried not to shiver, tried to use her magic to warm herself, but at the end of the second hour, her magic succumbed to the cold as well. She trembled, her breath fogging in the air.

All of the members now stood around her. Five hundred men and women, some gifted, many not, arranged themselves into ranks around the valley. Alan stood opposite Sandara, watching the moon move across the sky and waiting.

A third and fourth hour passed, the night coming closer to mid-point. Alan finally moved. He began walking in a wide circle around the stone design. "Tonight we formally admit a new member into our ranks. Professor Sandara Cane," he pointed his hand at her as he neared, "step onto the first stone, please."

Sandara took a deep breath, still shivering, but the excitement of the moment began to creep in and warm her bones. She stepped forward onto the first white stone of the arc.

Alan stood behind her now. "Remember, you are only allowed to speak when saying your vows. Aside from that, you must let no sound pass, understood?" She nodded. Alan smirked and moved on, addressing the crowd again. "As is tradition for this rite, the final act of the ceremony will take place at midnight, on this night of power. You will all either be silent, or speak on my signal.

"Obey only my signal. Anything else will get you killed."

A few men swallowed their nerves in the front row. Alan moved around the circle as he spoke until he stood at his starting position on the fourth arc. He caught Sandara's eye and held the contact. When he took one step forward onto the second stone, she stepped forward as well.

"Sandara Kerianne Cane, do you pledge yourself to Imbri Mors?" said Alan, his voice loud and clear, ringing through the valley to reach every person.

The pair took another step forward onto the third stone.

"I do," Sandara replied.

Step forward. Fourth stone.

"Do you offer yourself freely and with no prior claims on you?"

Fifth stone.

"I do."

Sixth stone.

"Do you swear to use your power for Imbri Mors alone?"

Seventh stone.

"I swear."

Eighth stone.

"Sandara Cane, will you serve your masters without question, without hesitation, until the end of your service?"

Ninth stone.

"I will."

Tenth stone.

"Do you give your soul to Imbri Mors?"

Eleventh stone.

"I give my soul freely to Imbri Mors."

Twelfth and final stone. The pair now stood on the black stone ends of their arcs, at opposite corners of a great stone square. Inside the square was a large circle, black stones marking four points on the circle that aligned with black stones on each side of the square. And inside the circle lay a triangle of three white stones alternating with three black ones, the points touching the insides of the circle.

Alan held a finger to his cruel lips. Sandara continued to match his movements. He traced the outline of the square, Sandara tracing it in opposition to him. They entered the circle and followed the design until Alan stood at the apex of the triangle, and Sandara stood on the black stone of the triangle's opposite side.

The woman continued to shiver in the cruel wind. The white stones of the design began to glow a sickening yellow.

A blue light sprung to life in Alan's cupped hands. The glow of the stones intensified, hungry for the touch of magic. The watchers felt a collective shiver run through their bodies, five hundred heartbeats attuning to that pulse in the stones. All eyes of Imbri Mors took on the same yellow glow, increasing the brightness in the valley.

Blue light surrounded Sandara, encasing her from head to toe. It stung, its touch invasive, and she had to fight to keep her mouth shut. No sound could escape her, or the ritual would be ruined and she would be dead. Alan's magic manipulated her arms around behind her back and tied them there.

Alan studied the moon's position before returning his gaze to his hands. "I make this offer on behalf of one who may not speak in this circle." Alan held his hands over the center of the triangle, holding them steady in front of Sandara's heart. "I offer this woman's soul. The soul of Sandara Kerianne Cane, who has pledged herself to Imbri Mors—" the stones glowed brighter, "—for all eternity."

A roar erupted from the direction of the cave, loud and animalistic, shaking the mountain crags around the valley. The white stones of the design burned bright, exploding with sickly yellow illumination. The eyes of the members shone like suns.

Sandara's mouth opened in a silent scream. Her back arched with the excruciating pain, but Alan's magic held her upright. Brilliant white light spilled from her every orifice, her eyes, even from her skin.

Alan's hands, wreathed in blue, waited for the whiteness emerging from Sandara's chest. The light was reluctant to leave, but Alan gave it no choice—he pulled his hands back toward him in a slow gesture. The light followed the insistent command of his hands. Sandara's body went rigid, held up now only by Alan's power. She couldn't say anything even if she wanted to.

At last, the light within Sandara was entirely without—her body went limp once her soul fell into Alan's waiting hands. He held the soul up in the air, and the waiting members could see something unusual in the whiteness—although her soul was indeed mostly white, streaks of black and gray ran through it, the white trying to evade the touch of those befouled pieces in vain.

The professor smiled in triumph and satisfaction. "Perfect," he said in a whisper. The stones, if possible, burned even brighter at his acceptance. "Sandara, you are now bound to me. You must do my bidding without question. I hold your soul, your life, in my very hands."

He lowered the soul down almost to the ground, letting it rest inches above the dirt. Her soul began to pulsate in time with the stones, turning blacker with each second. Alan glanced at her barely-alive body. He didn't have much time before the connection would be severed for good.

While the soul was still aligned with the dark powers in the stones, he said, "By my acceptance of your oath, so you are also sworn to my masters. Upon your death, your soul is theirs to keep."

Alan rose, guiding the darkened soul back to chest-level. Sandara's limp body stiffened again, the tiny ball of her soul reaching out for her, wanting to go home. Alan let it, releasing it from his hold. The soul sank back into Sandara's chest, her body glowing gray until it settled. She breathed again.

The blue magic holding her up faded. Sandara collapsed onto the cold stones and dirt, gasping. Alan watched her. "You may speak now, Sandara. The ritual is over." He held out his hand, offering to help her rise. "Welcome to the ranks of Imbri Mors."

Sandara fought to grin. She ignored his hand, climbing to her feet by herself. Quivering hands smoothed down the rumpled black dress. "Thank you, Professor Alan. I am glad to be here."

Cheers erupted from the crowd as the yellow glow from the stones faded into nothing. All eyes lost the yellow tinge—all but Alan's and Sandara's. Their eyes still held a hint of yellow long after the stones died.

As the rank and file of Imbri began to trickle away, a pressure built inside the cave next to the stones. No one noticed. No one felt it. But Corá's attention snapped back into focus on the valley, diverted from her rites for a precious few moments. She realized what had happened and began to weep, rain dropping from the empty skies around the world.

Sandara and Alan smiled at each other. They felt Corá's pain underneath their feet. Outside the barrier of the mountain range, a fierce snowstorm raged—Corá trying to break through. Alan held his hand out to Sandara again. This time she took it. "Come, my dear. I believe now is a good time to go."

She followed him through the door he created and the last of Imbri left the valley, leaving behind only the faint glow of yellow stones.

Behind the walled-off cave, hundreds of thousands of beings flew in a frenzy around their prison. Their eyes burned yellow. The largest one paused in the center, savoring the small taste of the soul Alan had granted him. It tasted good. He felt stronger. Strong enough that trying the walls of his prison again felt like a good idea. When he was stronger.

Chapter Twenty-Six
Enemies

The small manse was quiet inside, but outside the thick stone walls, the storms never ceased. Allen whistled to himself. The ability of Corá itself to so lash out impressed him every time he set foot in these walls.

He shook his head and cursed himself under his breath. Now was not the time to slip off into daydream and speculation.

Footsteps echoed behind him and Allen ducked into an alcove, hidden from sight. It was times like these that he cursed his lack of magic—it would have made sneaking around so much easier. A man passed the alcove without even glancing into it, and Allen breathed easier before moving off again.

Professor Alan's office was, of course, on the top floor. And, of course, Allen had to get in there. He grumbled as he walked down the halls. *Why can't they send someone magical to do this sort of work?*

Once he reached the office, however, he ceased his mutterings and got to work. He examined the lock—its magical locks may protect it, but to his surprise the door had no other defenses. Grinning, Allen pulled his lock picks from his pocket and set to, opening the door and slipping inside in a matter of seconds. He smirked. *Either Professor Ray is getting overconfident, lazy, forgetful, or even arrogant, but he's sure helping me out!*

The office was as dark and gloomy as the rest of the house. One large window facing the desk dripped rainwater on the northern wall. Bookcases lingered along the back wall, standing silent guard. A large rug, the colors dulled from years of sun exposure and dust accumulation, lay in the middle of the wooden floor. Allen looked around, noting everything, even the dust patterns. He crept over to the desk, alert for sounds from outside.

Papers were piled on the desk. A single candle-lamp sat nearby, guarding the pens underneath it. With one eye on the door, Allen began leafing through the papers, scanning each one before setting it down again. Long lists of supplies, encoded reports, names of agents here and there—but not what Allen was looking for this time.

He pulled open the drawers. In most, he found unimportant junk and papers he had already decoded. One small trick drawer held only a slim black book. Curious, Allen slipped it into his jacket pocket and kept searching. At last he found more papers. These were more like what he needed, even if they were in code. Allen sneered and started reading them. He had broken Professor Alan's simple mathematical code months ago.

The first page was nothing, as was the second. But Allen paused at the third, reading more carefully. He found the name and cursed again, running a hand through his rumpled hair. His brown eyes flashed in anger. "Damn you, Eric." Furious now, he was about to shove the paper away when a name on the fourth sheet caught his eye.

Allen read the page and his brow furrowed in confusion. "That's Eric's brother's name . . ."

Suddenly, the door of the office opened. Allen's head snapped up. He dropped the papers and met the eyes of Sandara Cane. The woman paused for the briefest second—but it was just long enough. Allen plunged his hand into his pocket and pulled out a small box half the size of his palm. He fumbled with the mechanism, and just as Sandara raised her hands to strike, he pushed the button.

And vanished.

∞

Sandara walked up the stairwell, glad she had chosen the dark trousers and fitted tunic for today. Skirts always got in the way on stairs. She actually hummed to herself as she approached her master's office. Today had been a great day—two of the men had needed to be disciplined for attempted theft of the gems. Idiots.

The underlings scurried out of her way in the halls, never meeting her eyes in their fear. The sight of them cringing away only made Sandara happier.

Professor Alan's office was in front of her now, and she transferred the papers from her right hand to her left. Her empty hand rose into the air and sketched out a complicated rune just in front of the door. Sandara felt the magic recognize the symbol and allow her through. She smiled and turned the doorknob.

Immediately she felt something wrong. The papers dropped from her hand onto the floor. She looked around the office and met the light brown eyes of a young man crouched down behind the desk. Snarling, Sandara raised her hands and began gathering her power.

The young man vanished. Confused, Sandara snarled again and blanketed her power over the entire room, filling it with green light. Nothing. There was no presence of the man. "Who the hell was that?" Sandara said to herself. She hurried over to the desk and picked up the papers the man had dropped. Leafing through them, she began to smile again. "Oh, maybe this won't be so bad. Perhaps we can turn this little mishap to our advantage . . ."

Just at that moment, Professor Alan appeared in the office. He looked unkempt, as if the disturbance had been a surprise. Sandara filed that away for future reference and held out the papers. "Professor. There was a young man here spying."

"I know that," he snapped. The older man snatched the papers from her hands and looked them over. His eyes narrowed. "So. This young spy probably knows the Aligerai, or is also watching them." He paced over to his desk, still studying the leaves of paper. "Did you see who he was? Did he look familiar?"

Sandara shook her head, her black hair falling to cover her eyes. "No, sir. I've never seen him before. But I agree with you—I think he has something to do with the girls." Her lips curved upward in a cruel smile. "And I think I can use this to our advantage."

"How?" he asked. The papers slid to the desk surface, arranging themselves when he let them go. His hand rested on a small drawer Sandara had never noticed before, a drawer which now stood empty. Alan's eyes widened just slightly, and Sandara took note of his unease while she listened to him continue speaking. "This young man saw quite a bit of important information. If he were to let it slip, it could be hazardous."

"Not if I inform the right girl before he does."

Professor Alan was silent. His eyes glazed over as he thought, until he finally nodded. "Yes, yes. I see what you mean. You have my approval to go ahead with this."

The woman gathered up the papers she had dropped earlier, calling them to her hands and then dropping them on the desk. She prowled closer to the door. "Do I have your permission to leave here and enter Thirka?" He glared at her until she realized why. "*Sir?*"

A curt nod was her only answer, but it was all she needed. Her red nails became like claws and her smile became feral as she stalked from the office.

∞

Ka'len glowered at his student, his eyebrows knit in a ferocious scowl.

Sita and Marie sat at the dining table, their heads bowed and eyes downcast. Roxie and Ariene were nowhere nearby, which was probably a good thing. With Ka'len this angry, he probably would have frightened them anyway.

He stood in front of the two young women, arms crossed, his face set. "Have you any idea what you did, what could have happened? The ring you accepted to enter this world should have killed you the second you told your sister about its existence. And even if it did not kill you then, it should absolutely have killed you when you brought her here."

Sita dared to glance up. "But it didn't," she said in a soft voice.

Ka'len scowled. "I realize that, Sita. I am not blind. However, you committed a very serious offense when you brought her here without permission." He began to pace around the table, circling the two girls like a vulture. "In fact, I am surprised that no one from the Council has shown up here to investigate this. What were you thinking?"

Marie shook beside Sita, her hands trembling. Sita reached over and took one of her hands. "Don't worry, he won't hurt you, Mar. He's just a little angry." Ka'len shot her a murderous look, which Sita ignored to answer his question. "I was thinking that I wanted to be with my sister, who you took me from. I was thinking that my sister would be lonely, and I didn't want to leave her there all by herself. I was thinking that I wanted to be with someone who wouldn't nag at me all the time like you do."

The old man went very still. Sita swallowed, realizing that he was even angrier. Ka'len stared at her until she dropped her eyes. A bright shade of pink stole over her cheeks. He walked closer until he could reach out and grasp her chin. He jerked Sita's face upward.

Her teacher shook her face until she looked him in the eyes. "All I heard in that drivel was 'me, me, me.' Do you still not understand that this is bigger than *you* and what *you* want? Your power is not your own, it does not belong to only you." He shook her face again for emphasis. "Right now, you are behaving more like a spoiled brat than the young, sophisticated lady I had thought you to be." He leaned in even closer, almost close enough for their noses to touch. "Get over yourself. Only when you have finished growing up will I complete your training."

Ka'len released her bruised jaw and stalked from the dining room, anger billowing behind him like a cloak of shadows.

Sita and Marie sat in silence for another ten minutes. Marie shifted in her chair and turned to look at Sita. "Was he right? Did bringing me here get you in trouble?"

Her sister shook her golden head. "Don't listen to him. He's just mad. I'm not in trouble. If I were in trouble, I'd be dead, or someone from the Council would be here on our doorstep." But she couldn't help but toy with the Council's ring, twisting it around and around on her finger. There was a small piece of doubt in the back of her mind that wouldn't rest, saying that Ka'len was right and she was wrong.

She thrust the thought back into her brain and stood up. She took Marie's hand and pulled her out of her chair. "Come on. I'm taking you down into Thirka and showing you around."

Marie followed her through the hall and out the door. "Where's Thirka?"

An hour later, Sita and Marie walked through the cobbled streets of Thirka. Marie couldn't get over how . . . well, *adorable* . . . the whole town looked. The thatched roofs, the fountains at crossroads and the town squares, even the people seemed like something straight from a history book. She trailed behind Sita, mouth agape, taking everything in.

Sita, on the other hand, listened instead of watched. She had already seen the town, but she had barely listened to what the people said. She glanced behind her to make sure Marie was still there. A smile worked its way onto Sita's lips and she chuckled at her little sister's wide-eyed expression.

One of the shops caught Marie's eye and she pulled Sita over to it. It was full of women's clothing, mostly dresses, but there were a few trousers and tunics cut for women. Sita was surprised—she had thought these people would be much like medieval villagers of Earth, and respectable women in that time never wore pants. She went to examine those while Marie cooed over the gowns, chatting with the shopkeeper. Sita joined her only to pull Marie out of the store with one dress before she bought the entire shop. Those coins in the Vault were useful at last.

The two sisters exited the store and ran straight into Roxie and Ariene. Roxie waved. "Hey! We thought we'd join you."

Sita laughed. "Oh, you just thought, huh? And you didn't want to get away from Ka'len's foul mood?"

Ariene blushed. "Well, maybe a little. He's still really mad at you, and he's been brooding around the house all morning. We finally got tired of it and followed you guys down here."

Rox studied Marie with interest. "Is this your sister?" Sita's head bobbed up and down. "Hi, I'm Roxie," Rox said. She reached out to shake Marie's hand. Marie returned the gesture, smiling as well. "It's nice to meet you, Sita's sister."

"Oh, my name's Marie," she said. Marie transferred her hand to Ariene, who also shook it and introduced herself. "And no matter what that old coot says, I'm glad Si brought me here," Marie said, her stubborn chin set.

A warning buzzed in the back of Sita's mind. She whirled around, searching the square. Something bright glistened from the corner of her eye and she flung herself at Marie beside her. "Get down!" she shouted at Roxie and Ari.

They all ducked just in time as a hailstorm of emerald daggers flew through the air. Roxie covered her head with her heads after one of the daggers sheared off a few hairs. Ari transformed into a mouse and crawled into Roxie's pocket.

The wave of green stopped. Sita raised her head. She noticed as she stood up that all the townspeople had fled behind closed doors. *Just as well*, she thought. *I don't think they'd be much help in this anyway.* Sita brushed off her skirt, which Roxie was tugging on to try and get her down again. "Would you get down and put up a shield please?" Roxie hissed. Ari meeped in agreement from her pocket.

Sita rolled her eyes and reached down to help Marie up, her pretty new dress in its plain packaging squished underneath her body. "The enemy's gone, I don't sense them anymore. Let's get back to the mansion, all right?"

Two green daggers shot out from the other end of the square. They hooked into Sita's dress and threw her back against the wall of a shop with a sickening thud. Marie screamed. Sita struggled against the daggers, her head woozy from the impact, but the blades were stuck in the wood—and she couldn't raise her power.

Her wide eyes met those of a tall woman coming toward her. The woman smiled, her crimson lips looking like the lips of a vampire. Sita forced herself to breathe, to calm down, to *think*. "Who are you?" she asked.

The woman paced closer. "You should really fix that arrogant streak, Sita. It's hardly becoming in such a pretty young woman." She laughed. "And look where it got you!" She chuckled deep in her throat, sounding like a feline purr. "My name is Sandara Cane. And I work for Imbri Mors."

Sita fought against the daggers. "What do you want?" Her mind raced frantically—if she couldn't raise her magic, even the weakest mage could kill her. And Ka'len was now too far away to sense her danger and help.

Sandara laughed again, sending chills down the girls' spines. "Oh, I'm not here to *kill* you! Not today, at least." Sita's eyes narrowed. "No, I'm using you as guinea pigs to test out these daggers—and pass along some information."

Behind Sandara, Ari crept out of Roxie's pocket. She transformed from a mouse into a white tiger, making Marie squeak in shock. Roxie reached out and gripped Marie's arm. Sita knew Roxie was telling Marie to stay still and quiet.

Sita's eyes flickered to the daggers. Her dress was beginning to cut painfully into her skin in places. "And these daggers do what, exactly?"

"Why, they negate the magic of any mage they touch, my dear. Except for the magic of their creator, of course." Sandara studied her red nails, taking her time. "I could keep you here indefinitely if

I wanted to. But don't worry, I won't take much longer." Grinning in sadistic delight, Sandara held her right hand out, palm toward Sita, and jerked her hand in a tight circle.

The daggers twisted a quarter turn to the left, making Sita cry out in pain as her dress tightened further into her skin. She cried out again when she felt something else—the daggers pulled a little bit at a time, but this time, she could feel her power draining away.

Sandara watched the violet power get sucked into the daggers, and through the daggers, absorbed into her. She inhaled deeply. "Hmm . . . maybe this will take a bit longer than I thought!"

A streak of white fur flew through the air to grab one of the daggers and rip it free. Before Sandara could act, Marie tackled her from behind, pinning her to the ground. Roxie ran to pull out the last dagger, helping Sita work it out from the wood while Ari snarled at Sandara.

Sandara threw Marie off and turned on the girl, her hands curling into claws. "You little brat!" she shouted. "I'll make you regret that!" She raised her hands and gathered her power.

Violet light interposed itself between Sandara and Marie. The woman screamed and tried to break through the shield. She failed, her emerald attacks negated. Sita pulled Roxie and tiger-Ari over to Marie and behind the shield, expanding it in a sphere around the four of them.

Snarling, Sandara stopped attacking the barrier, brushing her black hair out of her face. "Fine. You beat me for now. But Imbri Mors will win in the end." Backing away slowly, Sandara smiled in triumph. She paused halfway across the square. Her eyes lit up in cruel happiness. "Oh, and Sita . . . say hello to Eric for me. We've missed having him around." With a cackle, Sandara disappeared.

The square delved into silence. The four young women could see the villagers peeking out of windows and cracks in doors, checking to see if it was safe. One door opened and a portly man popped his head out, sweat beading on his brow. "Are ye all safe?" he called to them.

Roxie held up a feeble, shaking hand and waved it a bit. "Fine," she said. Her voice wavered and sounded thin. "We're all fine." The man nodded and stepped outside, returning to his business.

Sita stood trembling in front of them. Her hands clenched at her sides. She whirled around, her eyes wide and wild. Marie stood up, wincing, and took her sister's hand. "Come on, Si. Let's get back now, OK?" Sita only nodded and followed Marie. Ariene and Rox took the rear.

The journey back to the mansion took almost twice as long as the morning's walk into town. Sita shook with shock and refused to speak for almost half an hour. Once the quartet was inside the gates, however, Sita seemed to come out of her reverie. "What did she mean? About Eric, what did she mean?"

Roxie crept closer and took Sita's free hand. "I don't know, Si, but we'll find out. Maybe she was just trying to rile you—you know, make you upset so you won't fight back."

Sita shook her head, blond hair flying. "No, she was telling the truth, I could hear it in her voice. She knows something about Eric . . . and Eric's connected to them somehow?"

The doors of the mansion blew open. The four girls froze. Ka'len strode from the house in a black fury, his face ferocious. But then he caught sight of Sita's near-panic and deflated. Rox, Ari, and Marie breathed sighs of relief and coaxed Sita to walk forward a bit more.

"What happened?" asked Ka'len. He reached out and touched Sita's face. Even in her haze she knew, from the sudden alarm in his eyes, that he could feel the drain on her power through his fingers. "Sita, speak to me. Wake up." He patted her face but she did not respond. In silence Ka'len led the small party back to the house, casting anxious glances at them over his shoulder along the way.

The mansion seemed to feel their distress as well. It slammed the front doors behind them, dropped platters of food and pitchers onto the table, allowed shutters to rattle and floorboards to creak. Marie jumped in her seat every time something banged, expecting the house to come down around them.

Sita exhaled and came back out of her trance a second time. Her eyes focused on Ka'len. "I owe you an apology, Ka'len."

The old man's bushy gray eyebrows rose a fraction. "How so, my dear?"

"You were right." The young woman bowed her head, unable to look him in the eye. "I was selfish and disrespectful in bringing my sister here. I had no right to ignore the customs and practices of this world." She paused, her hands still trembling. "And I was wrong in thinking myself prepared to face our enemies. Please accept my apology."

Ka'len studied her and his face softened. "I accept your apology, Sita. I am not the only one you should be apologizing to, however."

She nodded. "I know." Sita turned to Roxie and Ari, their faces reflecting only confusion. "Rox, Ari, I'm sorry. We're a team, and I had no right to go haring off by myself like I did, or to act by myself. My selfish desires could have gotten all of us hurt or killed, and by violating the rules of Corá, I could have even gotten us all separated or disciplined. I'm sorry for putting you in that situation."

Roxie blinked. "Except for when you stood up and wouldn't sit back down in Thirka, I didn't think there was anything wrong in what you did. So you wanted to bring your sister here—big deal. You just did it in the wrong way. Your desires were otherwise bringing no harm to any of us, in my opinion." She crossed her arms across her chest and flashed a half-smile.

"I agree," said Ari. "You just need to work on your battle strategy a little more, hey?"

Sita laughed, the sound erasing the tension in the room and returning her face to its former playfulness. Eye still reflecting amusement, she shook her head at them and turned to Marie. "And I owe you an apology, Mar. I shouldn't have brought you here and put you in danger. I know better than that. Now was not the time to show you this place, and especially without the Council's permission. I'm sorry."

Marie stared back at her in astonishment. "Sorry?" she squeaked. "Sorry for what? That was the most excitement I've had in *weeks!*" The teenager turned on Ka'len. "And you, Ka'len, shouldn't be telling her not to bring me here. I'm her sister! Where she goes, I go. We're a package deal."

The old man straightened a bit, surprised. His eyes narrowed. Sita thought he was assessing her sister, as if something important were just beyond his reach, but assessing for what, or why, she couldn't tell. "That may be. But Sita is still bound by the rules of Corá. She accepted those rules when she accepted the ring. It is no longer her decision whether or not to bring you here." Ka'len stood up, sighing as he did so. His muscles protested and his joints creaked. "However, since you are here, you may stay for as long as Sita is here this time. But *only* this time. Agreed?"

Marie and Sita nodded, grinning at each other.

"What I don't understand is why the Council's ring didn't work," Roxie spoke up. The others turned to her. "I mean, wasn't it supposed to kill us if we told anyone without permission? Sita told her sister but she's definitely still here."

Ka'len stroked his beard and leaned back into his chair. The blue eyes unfocused in thought. "Yes, that is true. There should also be one of the Council members here personally to investigate the disturbance." He paused. "Perhaps I should look in on the Council. They should know that their rings are flawed."

"Ah . . ." Sita's cheeks flushed pink. "I don't think the rings are flawed." Ka'len raised an eyebrow. "When I told Mar about Corá, I felt a little tingle in the ring, but it wasn't even painful, so I ignored it. Nothing else happened."

The old man turned to Marie, who stared back at him. "Marie, what did you feel when you crossed into Corá? Did you feel any resistance of any kind?"

She shook her head, sending red hair flying. "No. Just that weightless feeling, and wind, and . . . this'll sound weird, but I thought I felt welcome. It felt comfortable. No hostility or resistance, definitely not."

Ka'len clapped his hands together, making the girls jump at the sudden noise. "Ha! That solves it. Corá herself allowed Marie inside the borders!"

The girls stared back at him, all eyes reflecting bemusement. "It can do that?" Ari asked.

"Yes. Of course *she* can. Corá is a living entity in and of itself, much like Earth once was. Corá can express pleasure or displeasure at our actions, can react to threats without our intervention, and so on. She even has a voice, though a certain type of magician is normally required to hear it."

Sita blinked. "Oh. Cool."

Ka'len laughed, his beard quivering. "Yes, 'cool.' Now, why not find a room for Marie to sleep in—I recommend the room nearest the tower on the second floor, it has an excellent view—and then we should have a bite to eat."

Laughing, the girls did as he suggested, the worry and strain of the afternoon completely sliding off every face but Sita's.

That night, Sita tossed and turned in her bed. She had hidden the worry from the others over dinner, and had pled a headache to go to bed early. The silence of her room enveloped her in a sweet embrace, allowing her to think without interruption. She had been thinking nonstop since Thirka.

"What did she mean?" Sita whispered into the dark. She hadn't even bothered to light a night-candle tonight, wanting the comfort of complete darkness. Sandara's words played over and over in her mind: *Say hello to Eric for me . . . Say hello to Eric for me . . .*

Sita rolled over, banishing the litany. "How is Eric tied to them? Or was she just tormenting me? Oh, I don't know!" A tear leaked from her closed eye, trailing down her nose and onto the pillow. "What if he *is* one of them? What'll I do then?" Her lip trembled. "Could I give him up if I had to?"

Her heartbeat pounded in her ears, drowning out the words. A sob escaped from her throat and she buried her face in the pillow, crying herself into an exhausted sleep.

Sita sat on the ground of a large empty space, stretching into the horizon indefinitely. Her mind knew this was a dream, but she really didn't care if it was real or not. Thin silver wisps of clouds floated around her, thickening until the white mist obscured the horizon.

She rose to her feet, surprised to find herself clothed in a fine sapphire dress. It was simple in design, with no adornments, but the gown fit her to perfection, reflecting a master seamstress's work. Her bare feet rested on the warm gray floor. Her mind laughed at the idea that she was dressed in a sleeveless dress and barefoot in the middle of winter, but Sita shrugged the thought away, enjoying this dream so far.

A dark spot in the clouds appeared, catching Sita's eye. She moved her hair away from her face and looked closer. The shape resolved itself into a man, tall and broad-shouldered. Sita smiled and waved. "Hello!" she called. "Who are you?"

The man didn't respond, he only moved closer and closer. Soon she could see that he wore nothing but a pair of black trousers. He had shoulder-length hair that Sita thought could have been brown or black at this distance—wisps of clouds were still in the way between them.

She began to walk forward, the silence unnerving her. "Is that you, Eric?" she said. "Hey, answer me! Who are you?"

All of a sudden, great white wings flowed out from the man's shoulders, and Sita could see his hair was not Eric's dark brown, but shining ebony. She paused, uncertain now, slipping her own wings out of their sheaths and fluttering them around her. "I don't know you."

The clouds began to thicken again, hiding the man's form. Sita could see him begin to run to her, his hand outstretched, mouth open to call out to her, but she could hear no sound, nor see his face at all. Soon the silver clouds swallowed him up, and Sita was falling, falling . . .

Sita sat up in bed with a strangled yell stuck in her throat. Her breath came fast and painful, as if she couldn't get enough air. She put a hand to her heart to calm down and shook her head. Her breathing slowed and she pulled in deep breaths of cool air, her heart beating slower. "That dream . . . I've had it before . . . but it's changed. I saw more of him . . . ."

Unnerved, Sita counted to fifty before she lay back in bed. She curled up on her side and frowned. She tried to remember what Eric's face looked like before she slipped away into a dreamless sleep.

∞

Three days later, Sita and Marie stepped back through the gate into their house in Maryland. Roxie and Ariene had also left Corá that day, heading back to Roxie's house elsewhere in Maryland. Marie walked into her own room and flopped onto the bed. "I think I like the bed at the mansion better, Si," she called. "It's softer."

Sita walked into her sister's room and sat on the bed with her. Late afternoon sunshine shone through the window, highlighting both girls' hair in gold. "Sorry," she said. "I can't exactly lift a mattress and carry it over here for you."

"Then let me live there," Marie replied, sitting up on her elbows. "Once I'm out of school in the spring. Let me live in Corá."

Her sister looked down at her hands. "Mar, I don't know. What would you do there? It's not like here, with a mall down the street and a restaurant around every corner."

Marie hugged her knees to her chest. "At least think about it? I know what it's like, I was just there! And what I know is that I felt more comfortable there than I ever have here."

Sita reached out to take Marie's hand. "I'll think about it, I promise. But if I say yes, then I want you to promise me one thing: you will stay out of Corá until after whatever war that's coming up is over. Agreed?" Marie nodded, auburn tresses bouncing. Sita smiled at her. "Good."

The fan whirled overhead, providing a rhythmic and soothing beat to the conversation. "So Ka'len said you were done training?" Marie asked.

"Yeah, that's what he said. Told me that all I had to do now was keep working by myself, with the grounding and centering exercises, and just let it take its own course." She lay back on the comforter, searching for heat in the chilly winter air. "And he said that my war training is adequate, but we could work on that more if the time comes that we actually get involved in this war or whatever."

"Cool."

"Yeah."

Marie looked uncomfortable, her eyes cloudy. "Si, do you think there will really be fighting?"

"I don't know, Mar. We've already had some run-ins with Imbri Mors, and they seem to keep getting stronger. Ari was telling me before we left about some strange dreams she had, but she wasn't quite sure what they meant."

"Will you die?"

"Of course not. I'll always be here. No matter what."

∞

Sandara found Professor Alan overseeing the delivery of another stolen gemstone shipment.

The rooms of the mansion were near full to bursting with gems, each stone divided by type and carted off to separate rooms. Three entire rooms held crates of diamonds, which were the more sought after of Ray Alan's operations. She picked her way around the workers, great brawny men that unloaded each shipment and carried the crates up and down all the flights of stairs into each room.

Ray turned when he felt her approach, but he kept one eye on the workers. "How was the trip into Thirka?" he asked. His blue eyes grew cold. "Any luck with wreaking havoc?"

Her white teeth flashed in the light. "Oh, yes. I dropped that tidbit of information to Sita about her beloved boyfriend. I expect she's crying her eyes out right now, incapacitated and bawling in a heap on her floor. Pathetic, but she is only a child." The professor nodded agreement, his smirk the only reaction to her news. He kept most of his attention on the workers while Sandara continued. "And I tested out the daggers I mentioned to you before."

His head whipped around and she found herself the object of Ray's full attention, his cobalt eyes narrowing to slits. "And?"

"They performed better than I ever expected, professor. These daggers can do as I promised: drain a mage of power and give it to the wielder of the dagger."

Ray exhaled, the sound of his breath like a heavy wind. He turned back to the workers, commanding one to stop in front of him. "Sandara, you have done extremely well." The woman smiled. "If those daggers work as you say they do, it will be much easier to obtain full gems."

Her brow furrowed. "Full gems, sir? Are some of them damaged?"

He glared at her in annoyance. "No, you idiot, I would never accept a damaged stone. Not for this." Ray opened the crate and pulled out a single diamond. It reflected the scant light in the room, sending rays of white dancing over the walls. "A full gem means it has been used, filled up. When it is full it is ready for my masters."

Sandara nodded, though her brow remained puzzled. "Of course, sir. My mistake."

The professor glanced up at her, amusement written in his eyes. "You have no idea what I'm telling you, Sandara. As it should be. Suffice to say that these gems, when they are filled with the souls of all those people, are called 'full' stones, and are then ready to be stored until my masters call for them."

This time Sandara understood. "I see. If I may ask, sir, who are your masters? I had thought you to be the leader of Imbri Mors."

All movement in the room stopped. Ray's face twisted into an ugly mask. The workers held their breath, waiting for the axe to fall and praying the professor wouldn't take his anger out on them. When he turned to Sandara, however, they breathed again and went back to work, leaving wide corridors around the two mages in their midst.

Ray bared his teeth and snarled at her. "I *am* the leader of Imbri Mors, and you will never forget that!" Sandara tried and failed to keep her eyes from showing her fear. She cringed, angering Ray even more. "You are a pathetic excuse for an agent, Sandara. Look at you! You were never one to cringe away from any man, yet you can't even meet my eyes now. What happened to you? How did you get to be this disgusting?" He raised a hand to slap her but clearly thought better of it and straightened his shirt instead. "And my masters are my own business. They have nothing to do with the operations of Imbri Mors. That is my own creation, which you would do well to remember."

The tall man returned his gaze to the diamond in his hand. "I intend to rule the world, Sandara. Not just one world, but many. These stones are crucial to that desire. And my desires will always be fulfilled. Anything and anyone is expendable in the pursuit of that goal." His cold blue eyes flicked to Sandara's pale face. "Even you. Don't forget it again."

He tossed the diamond to her and stalked out of the room, trailing anger in a cloak behind him.

Sandara stood in the middle of the floor, the huge clear diamond in her hands. Her entire body shook, and she was aware of the feel of her heartbeat against her chest. His words cut her to the bone. He was right—what had happened to her? She reached up and touched her temple, the beginnings of a throbbing headache starting to form. Even just a month ago if he had dared speak to her like that she would have lashed out at him to put him in his place. Yet now she had let him humiliate and intimidate her in front of other people.

The diamond slipped through her fingers. It landed on the floor with a loud thud. She looked up at the bustling men, who averted their eyes and cringed away from her as much as possible. Sneering at them in disgust, Sandara straightened her shoulders and followed in her master's wake.

∞

A world away, a dark-haired girl lay on her bed in her quiet home. Her skin was pale as marble, her eyes as wide as the moon. The morning sunlight peeked through her shuttered window, but the pale yellow light did nothing to improve the ivory of her complexion.

Darci rose with a groan. If any of her friends from school could see her, they would be shocked at her appearance. Her skin looked not only pale, but sickly. Her eyes, wide and unblinking, held desperation and fear, and just a hint of something more evil. The brown eyes looked almost black now. Her short hair, which before had been shining and lovely to look at, was now dull and tattered.

Unpacked bags stood at the ready in front of her dresser. Darci stood and fell to her knees beside them, too weak to try to stand. "I can't . . . I can't . . ." she whispered. Her dehydrated lips scratched against each other. "I can't let them see me like this." A single tear welled up in her eyes.

You can't let them see you at all.

Sobs broke through her dry lips, her throat scratching as she cried. "No, no, not again, leave me alone, please . . ."

You can't go back there. They don't want you. They always look at you strangely, they always fear you. As they should. You are Darkness incarnate. Stay away from them . . . or destroy them!

Darci curled in on herself. She wheezed, unable to get enough air. Only one or two tears trickled from her parched body. She couldn't even cry anymore. "I don't want to believe you!"

But you know I'm right.

A vision of Vanessa's green eyes broke into her mind. Those haughty eyes held traces of fear, glaring at her. Estelle's small brown eyes replaced that vision, laced with fear and loathing as well. Darci bent over even further, her head touching the bottom of her suitcase. "No, no, they love me, they're like my family, you're a liar!"

I am not.

Darci immediately tried to call up memories of her friends, the ones who only looked at her with love and caring. Only Sita's smiling face came to her mind. Even the eyes of Roxie and Ari seemed withdrawn, reserved. As if she could never touch them. She raised her head from the suitcase, sniffling and wheezing. "I'm going back. And you can shut up about it!" she said, her voice harsh and grating. "As long as there's one person who wants me around, I'm going back!"

The Voice fell silent, but seemed to regroup just when Darci thought she had won. *You will never be loved by them. They only want to use you, tap your power to defeat us, to defeat the better order. You will never be a part of them.*

Her knees shook as she rose, but Darci managed to pull herself upright and straightened her back with new purpose. She looked into her mirror and saw how disheveled and ill she had become, and she began trying to fix the damage. "You're wrong, and I'm going back to them to prove it."

Chapter Twenty-Seven
Seeing Green

Vanessa felt a strange sort of déjà vu overtake her as she walked into her open suite, lugging her bags and trunks with her. She panted while struggling to lift the last trunk without dropping the two duffel bags in her hands or the second trunk gripped in her other hand. Both trunks hit the doorframe with a resounding crack and Vanessa pulled up short, her blond hair flying around her face. "Oof!" She lost her grip on the trunks and they fell with loud thuds onto carpeted floors.

A brunette head popped out of the second bedroom. Roxie grinned at her. "Hey, Vanessa's here!" she shouted. Two more heads popped from her room as Ariene and Sita looked outside. Roxie hurried out to help Vanessa. "Geez, 'Nessa, did you really need to take all of that home with you? And bring it all back? Winter break wasn't *that* long."

Ariene lifted the second trunk while Roxie dragged the first. Ari laughed. "Yeah, and what happened to all your movers, hmm?"

Vanessa scowled, her face scrunching up. "Daddy said no this time. He said I should learn to do things by myself. He only hired movers the first time because he said if I didn't have help it would have taken me a week." Her three roommates laughed, which only soured Vanessa's mood further. Grumbling, she trudged into the room she shared with Sita and dumped her duffel bags on her bed while Rox and Ari scooted the trunks to her side of the room.

She stayed grouchy for the rest of the night, doing her best to ruin the others' moods. An impromptu party began in the suite once Skylar, Estelle, and Darci joined them after unpacking their own belongings. Vanessa did her best not to join in, sitting by herself in the faded blue corner armchair and throwing black looks in Sita's direction. The others were talking about their winter break exploits but Vanessa only listened with half her attention; besides, she had heard enough already. Soon, Skylar and Estelle both excused themselves to turn in early. Their trips back to school had been long and tiring, and the other five let them leave.

Once Skylar and Estelle had left, Ari, Sita, and Roxie discussed their trip to Corá in loud and excited voices, holding Darci enthralled with their story. Vanessa sneered. *What's so special about Corá anyway? It didn't seem all that great to me.* She shot another dark look at Sita, who sat in the middle of things for once and was saying something about her training. *And what's so special about her that she gets extra training?* Her lip quivered just a bit, and her green eyes darkened in anger. *What about me? Don't they care about my break?* Sita laughed and Vanessa shrank further back in her chair. *It's always Sita, Sita, Sita. How great Sita is, how powerful Sita is, how smart, how pretty, how awesome. I'm as good as she is, better, even! Why don't they care about me?*

As if the thoughts called her attention, Sita finished that part of her story and stood up, beckoning to Vanessa. "Come here, Vee, I have something for everyone. You guys'll love this!" She fished something out of the pocket of her blue jeans, wrapped in a small bag. Vanessa climbed out of her chair and took a seat on the floor. Darci sat on her other side and Vanessa inched closer to the couch.

A pair of glistening rings slid from the bag into Sita's palm. At once Vanessa's attention was captured by the shining metal and the gems embedded into each one. Sita held up a silver ring to peer at it. "Here, Darci, this one looks like yours, it's missing the opal." She tossed the ring to Darci, who fumbled but caught it, her face surprised but delighted. Sita handed Vanessa the remaining ring, prompting them both to put the rings on their left middle fingers. She grinned at Darci's obvious enjoyment.

The only person who didn't look excited was Vanessa, whose face remained a stoic mask. She had caught her ring with the air of someone only half-listening. "I guess I should explain these things now," Sita said, running a hand through her long hair. "I made the rings over break, as part of my training. They connect us all together! There's enough magic in them that each type of gemstone is connected to its respective person: rubies are Roxie's, the opals are for Darci, topaz is Ari's, and mine is amethyst."

Darci held her hand up to the light, admiring how the silver shone. "Are all these real?" she asked.

Sita nodded. "Yep, everything's real. You should all be able, with a little concentration, to feel the emotions of any other person connected to your ring. Like, right now, I can feel that Roxie is laughing at something and Ari is happy. See how it works?" She wedged herself back into her seat between Roxie and Ari, laughing as the others cooed over the rings.

Vanessa looked down at her own gold ring, the four stones winking back at her. She frowned. *This thing can feel my emotions, and tell the others how I'm feeling? I don't think I like that.* The ring continued to gleam in the lamplight, and with a sneer of disgust she tried to take it off. It stuck to her skin, not budging an inch. Her eyes widened and she tried again. Nothing; it remained on her finger, almost as if it were fused to her flesh. "S-Sita . . ."

Her friends turned to her, feeling her anguish through their rings. Vanessa's normally pale face had turned even paler, and her hands began to shake. Sita rose and hastened to her side. She took Vanessa's hands into her own. "What is it? What's wrong?"

Vanessa held up her hand. "I-It won't come off!" she wailed. "It's stuck!"

Sita relaxed, but there was a wary look in her eyes. "Vanessa, weren't you listening when I said that once you put the ring on, it would never come off unless I removed it myself?" Vanessa's eyes widened. "You didn't hear me?" Sita asked. Vanessa shook her head, her lip trembling.

"No, I didn't hear you. If I had, I probably wouldn't have taken the ring." Vanessa climbed to her feet, her face pained and drawn, and stumbled into her room. The door slammed behind her as Vanessa flung it shut.

She leaned against the door. The ring glittered against her finger. She sneered down at it and tried to take it off again. It stuck fast to her skin and tugged a bit when she tried pulling on it. She could feel the emotions of her friends through the connection—they were angry, shocked, and surprised.

Vanessa couldn't deny the usefulness of the connection. But she still didn't like it. "Damn it, Sita," she said in a whisper. It was the usefulness of the damned ring that galled her the most.

Sita sighed and dropped down to the floor, holding her head in her hands. "You all heard me, right?" she asked, her voice quiet even in the silence of the group. She looked up as the others all nodded, their own eyes reflecting either puzzlement or pity for Vanessa. "Well, I guess it's her own fault, then. I did tell her." Sita rested her chin on her knees, locking her arms around her legs. "Well, me and Rox and Ari have told you about our break—how was yours, Darci?"

They chatted long into the night, taking a quick break for dinner, where Jack joined them. Luckily Ari managed to shake him when he tried to invite himself back to the suite with the group by telling him she would hang out with him soon. Vanessa stayed in her room, even when the others came back to the suite and called to her. Ari suggested aloud that she might have gone to bed early. A whisper of doubt wriggled in the back of Sita's mind, trying to catch her attention. *You know there's something wrong . . . you know you hate Vanessa as much as she hates you . . .* She thrust the thought away, disturbed that it had even occurred to her. A coolness settled onto the back of her neck that could not be attributed to the mid-January cold. The thought didn't sound like her own. Sita shivered, returned her focus to her friends, and did her best to bury the strange voice in her mind.

∞

Robert knew he was late and winced. Allen would be angry. He picked up his step, the door of the room within sight at the end of the hall. Soft yellow light of desk lamps threw a man's pacing shadow onto the wall.

The sound of his footsteps echoed on the marble of the giant library. Allen stopped pacing and crouched behind a chair. Rob stopped in the doorway to the room. "Allen?" called Rob. "Allen, are you in here?" The whisper bounced off the walls and magnified, dying slow.

Allen stood, holding a slender knife in his hand. "You're late."

The other man held his hands out in a gesture meant to placate. "I know. I apologize. I got caught up with some things in my house."

"Are we shielded?" Allen's voice was harsh and guttural.

Rob studied him closer. Allen looked as if he hadn't shaved in a week. Dark circles under his eyes lent him an air of dementia, and his clothes looked as if he hadn't washed them for a few days. He was glad to note that Allen didn't stink—yet.

He moved closer, keeping his movements slow and non-threatening. "Of course we're shielded, I did that the minute I saw you here." In response, Allen stowed his knife and resumed his pacing. "I take it you discovered something, then?"

"Eric is Imbri."

Nothing else could have shocked Rob more. His mouth dropped open. "You're sure?"

Allen snarled at him, making Rob jump. He had never seen Allen this unhinged. "Of course I'm sure!"

Rob pulled out a chair and dropped himself into it. His hands trembled but his face betrayed none of his anxiety. "How do you know?" When Allen turned to growl at him again, Robert glared him into silence. "I believe you, Al, but I need proof before I can act, damn it!"

The pacing stopped and Allen sat down at the table across from Rob. He pulled a wrapped bundle out from underneath his jacket and threw the thing onto the table before Rob. Light flickered, as if counting the number of breaths they took. Robert reached for the package and picked it up. He almost dropped it—the weight was heftier than he expected.

With trepidation and utmost care, Robert unwrapped the object. His breath caught in his lungs once the brown paper fell away. "A scrying mirror?" he asked.

Allen didn't even blink. "Turn it over." Rob did so. His eyes grew wide, his breath grew heavier. "I found that in Eric's room over break. And while in Imbri headquarters, I found papers that listed his name, underneath the heading of Covert Operators."

"How did you get the mirror? Does he know?"

"Well, I'm sure he knows it's missing, but he doesn't know it's me that took it. The fool wasn't home when I snuck in, but that *thing* was sitting on his desk, plain as day. It was all the proof I needed, so I took it and got out of there."

Robert leaned back in his chair, the shadows of the lamps chasing across his face. He tapped his chin with one finger while he thought. "OK, we need a plan, then. I want him as far away from my girls as possible."

"Do I get to kill him?"

Rob snorted. "With that? That measly little knife you hide in your belt? You couldn't kill anyone with that."

"I'll have you know that most of my kills have been with this knife." Allen pulled it from his belt, the five-inch blade gleaming in the yellow glow.

The new information made Rob pause for a moment, but he shook off his amazement and continued. "Much as I would love to see you kill this lying bastard, I don't think that's quite the way to go."

Allen crossed his arms, his voice testy when he spoke. "Then what's the fun of being a spy and an assassin if you don't at least get to hurt someone?"

"I didn't say you couldn't bloody him up a bit. I said you couldn't kill him. Big difference." Allen rolled his eyes and groaned. Rob ignored it. "I think we should just scare him off. If he becomes a bigger problem, *then* you can kill him. Though, honestly, if Sita finds out, you may not have to. She'd probably do the job herself."

"That would be effective. Death by pretty purple magic."

Rob chuckled. He began rewrapping the mirror, not touching the sides with skin or magic. "I think we should wait a week—" Allen opened his mouth to protest but Rob overrode him. "—only *one* week. It would look suspicious if he left right when he got back from break, wouldn't you think?"

Allen nodded in reluctant assent. "Fine. We'll wait a week. Let me know when you're ready." He hesitated, but only a moment. "I found something else in the Imbri headquarters. It was with the papers I saw."

"Oh?"

"I think I've found, and read, Ray Alan's diary."

The news stunned Robert. He almost didn't know what to say. Just the concept of Ray Alan keeping a record of his thoughts and feelings, his motives for all the killings, confused and thrilled him. "You've read it? Do you have it?"

Allen reached into his pocket and pulled out the slim black book. He slid it to Rob. "There's some very interesting stuff in there."

"Like what?" Rob gingerly picked up the book, hoping it wasn't hexed in some way, and leafed through it.

Nothing came from Allen for a few moments, long enough that Rob began to think he wouldn't answer the question. "I think," said Allen, voice low and dark, "I think Professor Alan might actually be insane."

Whatever else he had been expecting, it wasn't that. Rob cocked an eyebrow and looked up from the journal. "Excuse me?"

Allen sighed deep. "It's all in there, so you can read it and decide for yourself, but I think he's insane. It says that his wife and two sons were killed, and apparently he caused the accident that killed them." He shrugged. "It was a little hard to tell with all the rambling, but I think it was a car accident and he was driving in a storm."

"I don't believe it. An insane enemy. Can things get any worse?"

Allen nodded. "Oh, yeah. Much." Robert closed his eyes, unsettled. "Read it, Rob. It has everything in there—what happened to his wife, his kids; how he thinks he hears their voices in the stones of his wife's engagement ring, which she was wearing when she and the boys died; how he started trying to get their souls back from the stones." His face drooped into a mournful frown. "The only thing it doesn't say is the rest of Alan's current plans. It stops after some research on stones. It's like he wrote in the journal until a big breakthrough, and then nothing." He rose to leave, pulling his jacked closer around his body when Rob stopped him.

"Have you ever killed anyone important, Al?"

The other man laughed, the sound harsh. "Of course I have. If I hadn't, I'd be nothing more than a common murderer-for-hire, unworthy of the title 'assassin'. Only assassins take out the important people."

He left Rob sitting in the half-darkness, staring down at the black mirror with veiled eyes.

Chapter Twenty-Eight
Truth and Lies

Sita lay on her bed, staring at the ceiling. Thin winter sunlight filtered in through the drapes on her window and the wind whistled past outside. The suite was empty except for her. Her full bookbag lay next to the door, waiting for her to pick it up and go to class.

The door of the suite banged open. "Hello!" shouted Vanessa. "Anyone home?"

"In here, Vanessa," Sita called.

Vanessa walked into their room, backpack slung over her shoulder. "Hey, Si," she said. Her long hair fell over her shoulder as she set her bag down by her desk. She looked back over to Sita, her face confused. "I thought you had class this morning. Aren't you going?"

"No," Sita replied. Her voice was light and dreamy. She continued to stare at the ceiling.

Her roommate sat down in one of the chairs. "Ah . . . why not? It's the first day of class. I mean, if you didn't go this week I'm sure you could explain it away as still being on break, but still, you should go to class, Si."

Sita rolled onto her side and glared at Vanessa. "This coming from the princess who never cared about classes before?"

Vanessa turned bright red and rubbed a hand in her hair. "Heh, yeah, well, Daddy kind of ripped into me over break when he saw my grades for last semester."

"Ah."

"You're really not gonna go?"

"Nope."

"Why not?"

Sita sighed. "Because classes just really don't matter to me so much anymore."

The other woman tucked a loose lock of hair behind her ear. "OK, I'm lost. You love school. What changed?"

"I did." Sita growled in frustration and swiped at her face with both hands, rubbing at nonexistent worry lines. "I still love school. That's not the part that changed. I just . . . I just think I can do more outside of school than I can inside it."

Vanessa listened but no comprehension dawned. "I still don't get it."

"I feel lost here. Like I no longer belong. Does that make any sense?"

"Yeah, I can understand that," Vanessa said. She looked away from Sita, fidgeting and worrying at the seam of her jeans. "But do you know where you do belong?"

"I don't know."

Vanessa scratched at her arm. "You don't know? How can you not know?"

Sita sighed again, growing more despondent with each moment of this conversation that passed. "I don't know. Let's talk about something else, 'kay?" Sita hesitated as Vanessa nodded and turned to her desk. "Vanessa, I was wondering . . . could I ask you something? It's guy related."

Her roommate whirled around, brightening at the subject. "Absolutely! Ask me *anything* about guys, I usually have an answer."

Sita grinned. She twirled a strand of her long hair around one finger. "Do you think I should tell Eric about my wings and my magic?"

"How long have you two been dating again?"

"Two months, three weeks, and three days."

Vanessa chewed on the end of her pen while she thought. Her eyes gleamed, and Sita wondered if she thought this was funny. "Hmm, tough one. Why do you want to tell him? You've kept it a secret from him for this long. Is there any reason to tell him?"

"That's just it. I've kept a pretty big secret from him, don't you think? I value honesty, and I think if this dating thing is gonna get any heavier, he deserves to know. And after what Sandara said in Thirka . . . I still don't know if she was goading me or actually telling the truth." Sita hesitated. "You're good with guys, you know a lot about them. Do you think he would be . . . I don't know, intimidated? Frightened?"

Vanessa shook her head. "Eric seems like a pretty decent guy. If you think you can trust him, I think you should tell him. And you can solve the Sandara problem by asking him if he's ever heard of Imbri Mors." The grin on her lips held an edge Sita didn't understand. "I think he'd be able to handle it."

She breathed a sigh of relief. "Thanks, Vanessa." Another thought occurred to her. "Can I have the room tonight? I want to try some magic, but I need to be alone."

"Sure," Vanessa said with a shrug. "No problem. I'm going to the movies tonight with Sarah and Megan anyway. Can I borrow your phone real fast? Mine's dead and I want to text Megan."

Sita handed her the phone without comment, her thoughts already far away.

Eric whistled as he let himself into Sita's suite. He checked his phone and reread the text. It said to let himself in, and the door had been open. Eric shrugged to himself and entered the empty common room. Her roommates must have vacated into Roxie's room for a while. He stepped up to Sita's open door and paused to adjust to the darkness. "Sita? Why is it so dark in here?" He wandered forward slow, waiting for his eyes to become accustomed to the shadows. A tall shape that looked like Sita stood in front of the window—but it couldn't be Sita. Two huge shadows connected to the shape's back. The moonlight from the window lit her hair in silver, and she shone in ethereal light.

The figure stiffened and swore in a voice he recognized. That made Eric freeze in his tracks, his breath caught in his chest. Memories swirled in his mind, memories of a winged figure from his past . . . memories he never wanted to remember.

Moonlight allowed his eyes to adjust much faster as the figure spun around. Eric's eyes widened and his mouth dropped open as he took in the sight of two huge white wings sprouting from Sita's back.

He ignored the look of shock on Sita's face. She held out one hand to him but he stepped back, holding out his own hands as if to ward her off. Sita stopped moving, tears in her eyes. "What . . . what are . . . *what are you?*" he said. His voice shook, but carried a heat in his tone that clearly scorched Sita. She flinched.

"Eric, you said you love me. This isn't how I wanted you to find out, but . . . since you're here . . . this is the truth." Sita looked up at him with her wide blue-green eyes. But Eric's mind babbled nonsense at him, and the sight of her with those things coming from her back sent Eric's soul screaming into the furthest recesses of his mind, trying to escape the horror of what he witnessed. He backed up, his eyes wide and frightened. *What the hell . . . no! No, this can't be happening! Not again!* That was when he noticed her hands glowed purple—that, combined with the moonlight, was what had made her appear to glow when he had walked in.

Eric couldn't speak. Sita wrapped her wings around herself and faced him down, waiting for a reply as she shook. "I have wings, Eric, but I'm not a monster." Her voice shook as much as her body, and she spoke very softly, as if to a frightened animal. "And I can do magic, but that doesn't mean I'm going to hurt you." She fell silent and waited again. Eric continued to say nothing. He shuffled and stumbled his way backward to the door, not daring to turn his back on the creature. He felt for the door handle and turned it, running through the door and rushing from the suite. "Eric, wait!" he heard Sita shout behind him. People in the halls cursed him and scrambled to get out of the way of his mad dash from the building.

He reached his dorm in uncommon haste, sweating from the fear and rage and despair enveloping his mind. Eric fumbled with his keys before he finally managed to fit the right one in the lock and turn it. The door didn't resist him as it always did, his anger forcing it nearly off its hinges. Allen looked up in surprise from the couch, a book now forgotten in his hands.

Eric didn't even glance at his roommate. He climbed up onto his bed and lay there, fuming. Allen, however, was now much more interested in his roommate's life than Eric wanted him to be. He saved his place in his book and set it down on the couch. "What's up, Eric?"

Silence. Allen stood up and walked to Eric's bed. "Eric?"

Eric threw a pillow at Allen's head.

Allen caught it with a grimace. He shook Eric's shoulder. "Talk to me, man. What's up?"

"Leave me the hell alone, Allen!" Eric turned over to face the wall.

Allen frowned in irritation. That was enough to encourage Eric, and he started babbling about his night. "I thought maybe I'd get lucky tonight, and the room was dark, and it looked really romantic, but then I saw the wings, big huge freakin' *wings* and they were huge and were real, they had feathers and everything! Then I looked down and her hands were glowing, they were *purple*, and I couldn't think, she was looking at me like she was confused, and I thought she might attack me, I didn't know what to think . . . "

He continued, talking softer, as if he were talking to himself. "It was disgusting, the way those wings just sprouted out, just *sprouted*, and she just stood there, expecting me to come touch her, to still love her, even when she was clearly a, a, a . . . *mutant!* That's the word, mutant, she's a mutant, she couldn't be anything else! With her wings, and her hands *purple*, actually *purple.*" He shuddered. "And she just held them out, as if she wouldn't infect me with her disease the second she touched me!"

Eric stilled, talking himself into an exhausted sleep. Allen grabbed his jacket and keys and left the room.

Ariene came out of her room, heading for the refrigerator. A soft sob from the left made her pause. She changed tracks when she noticed the open door of Sita's dark room. Ari walked closer and her body soon blocked the light coming in from the common room, her shadow thrown in with the rest of the darkness of Sita's room. "Sita?" she called. "Sita, what happened? Are you OK?" Ari tip-toed inside, watching for any sign of acknowledgement from Sita.

It didn't come. Sita stared in front of her, rivulets of tears streaming. Silver tears stained her skirt. She looked pale and sick to her stomach in the scant light. Her eyes stared straight ahead at the floor, and she shivered in her light dress. Ari sank to her knees in front of Sita and waited.

They sat like that for half an hour before Sita focused on her friend. "He ran from me, Ari," her voice croaked out, painful and harsh. "He ran from me, like I was a disease or something. He ran . . ." And she collapsed, falling into Ari's waiting arms gratefully, violent sobs shaking her body.

Allen pounded on the door of the suite. The noise roused Roxie and Vanessa from the other room. He heard them rush to let him inside. "How is she?" he asked, but all he got were uncomprehending stares from the two of them. "Don't you two pay *any* attention to what's going on?" He pushed his way over to Sita's room and paused at the doorframe. Sita and Ari sat on the floor, Ari stroking Sita's hair while she cried.

Allen bowed his head and backed out to where Roxie and Vanessa waited. "I think Ari has it under control." He pulled the door closed to give them some privacy and walked to the sofa, where he dropped down into the cushions with a heartfelt sigh. After a minute of silence, Rox and Vanessa joined him.

Roxie spoke first. "What's going on? Last thing I knew, Sita was planning to do some magic practice alone tonight." Her fingers danced themselves around each other in her anxiety. "Eric showed up, didn't he? I guess it didn't go well?"

Allen's derisive laughter was answer enough. He crossed his arms over his chest. "I saw the idiot when he came in, that's how I knew something was wrong. Once I got his side of it, I came right over here. For all I care, that bastard Eric can be alone tonight and for the rest of his life." He paused for a minute, collecting himself before beginning again. "He did see her wings. And her hands glowed, apparently. But Eric, being the moron he is, ran away from her when he saw all this. He ran . . . and when he was telling me this he actually called her disgusting, a mutant! He actually thought she would attack him, like some kind of vampire or something!" He surged to his feet and began to pace.

The door opened and Ariene stepped out, her face downcast and worried. "Guys, I don't think she's going to pull out of this any time soon. It might take a while." She plopped down on the remaining chair. "I think, somewhere between 'he ran' and her sobs, I heard that he said 'I love you' to her." Her head leaned back on the chair's cushion, her eyes tired. "He told her 'I love you' at some point. This is definitely going to take a while."

The door creaked open and Sita came out of the room. She looked tired and worn, and as if her carefully constructed façade would crack at the first hint of real pressure. The others looked at each other, uneasy. They watched her as prey would watch a possible predator. She trudged to the refrigerator and grabbed a bottle of water, draining half of it in a matter of seconds.

Vanessa stood up and walked to her roommate, her shoulders obviously tense and body ready to spring away. She reached out to touch Sita's arm. "Si? Do you want to talk about it? We're here if you do, you know."

Sita paused before she walked to the couch and sat down next to Roxie. Vanessa followed her back to her own seat. "I've decided that Eric isn't worth it," Sita declared in a soft voice. "I can guess what he thought of me. I saw his eyes. I still want answers, but if he can't accept me for who I am, then I deserve something better. And I won't lie to anyone I date." She sighed, wilting. "So maybe I should be a little more careful about who I date from now on."

Allen spoke up. "So what are you going to do next? I doubt, judging from what I heard when he showed up at the room, that he'll be changing his mind any time soon. No offense!" he added when Sita glared at him, holding up his hands. "It's just that I heard what he said, and you were right about what he was thinking, and I know how stubborn he is, so . . ." he trailed off, actually quailed by the look in her eyes. *Stop babbling man!* So he stopped talking, for once frightened by the power of Sita's eyes.

He swallowed in relief when she dropped her eyes. "No, Allen, I know. I shouldn't be angry with you, I'm angry with him. I'm sorry."

"So . . . what are you going to do?" he asked again.

"I'm going to get answers," she said, her voice dangerous. "And then I'm going to break up with him and get him out of my life for good." She stood up, her movements wooden and walked back into her room, shutting her door with loud finality.

Her friends watched her in silence, wincing as the door slam echoed in their ears. Allen glanced at Roxie. "Um, Rox, would you mind if I slept on the couch here? I have a feeling I don't want to be in my room tonight. Sita might take offense."

Roxie nodded, her face paler, but she kept herself composed. "Sure, Allen. In fact, why don't you sleep in my room tonight? We have an air mattress. That way, Sita won't take it out on the first male she sees in the morning."

"Good idea."

A week later, Sita still shook from Eric's refusal. She walked around in a daze, on edge and snappy at everyone, regardless of friend or foe. Vanessa took to sleeping on the couch for a few nights, just to avoid feeling the chill coming from Sita's side of the room.

Eric avoided Sita and her friends all week. They saw neither hide nor hair from him at all, making Sita even more edgy when she realized she couldn't find him in order to get her answers. Finally, after a week of searching, she saw him after her English class.

She ran after him, managing to follow him through the crowd of exiting students. "Eric!" she cried, tripping over her skirt. He didn't stop walking—if anything, he walked faster. "Eric!" she called again.

Sita shoved her way between two people and caught up to him. She grabbed his arm and dug in her heels to force him to turn around. "Eric, will you please *talk* to me? I want answers, damn it!"

Eric shot her a cold look and shook off her hand. "Why would I talk to you? I don't know you."

She stared at him, floored. "You don't *know* me? What are you talking about? I was your girlfriend, and you haven't talked to me since . . . uh, that night." Sita peeked around for eavesdroppers, keeping her voice low. "Why not, Eric? I know you were freaked out, but come on, I deserve some answers!"

His lip curled, and the contempt in his eyes sealed it for Sita. "You really expect me to date a freak? No way."

Sita's heart felt like it had been ripped into a thousand pieces for the second time in two weeks. "Wh- what?"

He snorted. "Think about it. I couldn't date *you*. How would I explain it to my family?"

"They'd never have to know . . ."

"And how would I explain it to my friends?"

"Why should *they* know?"

"And how do I know you wouldn't use your magic on me if you got angry?"

Sita put her hands on her hips. She felt outrage and immeasurable pain make her stomach churn and her chest contract. "I would *never* do something like that! I love you! You said you loved me! Did you mean any of it?" The anger kept the tears at bay for a while longer.

"I did, then." He looked at his feet, unable to meet her eyes any longer. "But how can I love a freak that has wings growing from her back and could kill me on a whim with her purple hands?" Eric

276

glanced back at her, disgust replacing the contempt in his eyes. "Besides, I know you've been dreaming of someone else, thinking about some other guy." Shock and surprise warred on her face, and she saw triumph gleam in his eyes. "How can I be with someone who's constantly thinking about someone else? I can't be with you, Sita. It would never work." He began to walk away, but her next words made him pause.

"It was working just fine until you barged in. I respected you enough that I tried to explain, tried to tell you the truth. And I would never cheat on you, and I wasn't 'constantly thinking' about anyone but you." She turned to face his cold back. "So which are you really running from? Me? Or the fact that I'm different and you can't handle it? Me, or your *fear*?" She stared at him, studying his fine chiseled features before turning her back on him. "I want you to leave. Now. And if I ever see you in my life again," she looked back over her shoulder, her voice hard and wintry, "I won't hesitate to kill you." His eyes widened a fraction in astonishment and not a little fear. "One more thing. Have you ever heard of Imbri Mors?"

Eric's face reflected complete shock as his jaw dropped and his skin paled. Sita's stomach clenched and her chest constricted to the point that it felt like her heart hammered against her ribs. That was all the answer she needed. He didn't say a word, but stared at her as if he couldn't believe what she had said. "Go away, Eric. Get out of my life."

Silence met her, and he hastily walked away, never once looking back.

∞

Robert knocked on the door of Allen and Eric's room. Even from out in the hall he could feel the chill emanating from inside. Allen opened the door. His friend looked significantly into Rob's eyes before opening the door wider to allow him in. Rob nodded in greeting and understanding.

Eric was busy pulling out a suitcase from under his raised bed. Rob watched him struggle with the bulky rectangle to make sure Eric wouldn't see him. When he was sure Eric was too busy with the suitcase, Rob pulled out the wrapped mirror and began taking off the paper. When it was unveiled, Robert called out to Eric.

The other man turned around, annoyed, but froze when he saw what Rob held. Eric's eyes widened upon sight of the mirror. He looked up at Rob. "What's that?"

"Oh, you don't recognize it?" Rob asked. He held out the mirror, which pulsed as it came closer to its owner.

Eric stood his ground but drops of sweat beaded on his forehead. "I've never seen that thing before. Where did you get it?"

"Your room," Allen said. He crossed his arms and glared at his roommate. "What were you, of all people, who is possessed of no magical power whatsoever, doing with a highly magical object of questionable nature?"

The silence in the room thickened. Eric began to sweat harder. He glanced between his two accusers. "So it's mine." He went back to pulling out his suitcase, heaving it up onto his bed. "Now how did you get it? Last I saw it, that mirror was in my room, which means in order to get it, you would've been trespassing."

Allen's lips lifted in a cold smile. "Be glad I didn't kill you then and there when I found that disgusting thing. We know where that mirror came from, and we know you're involved with Imbri Mors. We want to know why."

Eric laughed, the sound harsh and strained. "It's none of your business. And I want my mirror back, thank you very much."

A knifepoint jammed at the base of his skull pulled him up short. Allen rammed his roommate into the bed frame. "You will tell us now or I'll stuff my knife into your spine and paralyze you for life. It won't kill you, but you will be useless until you either die of old age or you take your own life." The steel point slipped into Eric's skin, spilling a single drop of blood. "Now, which one is it?"

Robert lounged against the wall. He held the mirror still, keeping it away from his skin. There was no telling what the black magic imbued in the object would do if it touched him.

The embattled young man across the room struggled to breathe at a normal pace. He failed, settling for great gulps of air while Allen pushed a little bit harder with each second that passed. "All right, all right!" Eric cried. Sweat drenched his shirt and his entire body trembled. "I'm looking for my brother. Imbri Mors promised me a way to find him. That's what the mirror was for."

"Did you ever have any intention of hurting any of my girls?" Rob called to him. Allen shoved Eric even harder into the wooden bed frame, cutting off all but the barest of air.

"No, no!" Eric said. "No, I didn't know anything about them, I have no idea what you're talking about! I just wanted to find my brother! They promised me that the mirror would lead me to him!"

Allen's eyes narrowed. "In exchange for what? Imbri gives nothing away without a price, and it's always an enormous one."

Eric managed to swallow. He closed his eyes. "In exchange . . . for the mirror . . . I promised . . . them . . . my soul . . . when I die."

Robert swore. "Then you're already taken. There's no saving you now, you idiot."

"We could kill him now and save them the trouble of doing it themselves, or of waiting for him to die," Allen said.

"Please don't kill me," Eric cried. Tears mingled with the sweat and he struggled against Allen's hold.

Allen sneered and let him go. His roommate crumpled to the floor and began to sob. Allen shook his head in disgust. "He's not worth killing." He leaned down and grabbed the neck of Eric's shirt to heave him upright. Eric tried not to look too terrified. "You miserable piece of filth. Sita deserves better than an ass like you." Eric's eyes went wide at the sound of Sita's name. Allen continued, waving the knife in front of Eric's face for emphasis. "So here's what you're going to do. You're going to pack your bags and get out of town. Transfer to a different college, drop out, whatever— but you are to be gone and off this campus by nine in the morning tomorrow."

Robert smirked while Allen let go and Eric dropped to the floor once more. Turning on his heel, Allen nodded at Rob and stalked from the room. Without even a backward glance, Rob rewrapped the mirror and followed his friend out.

From outside, Rob heard a frantic Eric begin to pack.

∞

Sandara and Professor Alan stood in his shadowed office, staring down at the picture on his desk. A bowl of liquefied silver sat next to the photo, steaming and churning in silence. Sandara thumbed the rim of the bowl. "It has been acting like this for hours, since I returned from another gem-retrieval mission. I believe it is time, sir."

Professor Alan picked up the photo, studying the dark-haired girl shown there. A transparent thick gray miasma hung over her head and turned her eyes black. He nodded. "Yes. Yes, it is time. But just to make certain . . ." The picture flew from his fingers and into the silver, disappearing in the violent waves. The silver began to swirl and roil harder, almost rising out of the bowl. It turned black.

The two professors nodded and grinned. "Go retrieve our newest member, Sandara. It's time she joined us."

"Gladly, Professor." Sandara disappeared in swirling green light.

Darci was working on an English paper late that night. It was due in the morning, and she was nearly done. She suspected nothing, and so the onslaught took her by complete surprise.

DARCI

The force of the Voice knocked her head back. Her neck creaked in pain. Stars floated in front of her eyes and tears began to flow. "Go away, damn you, get out!"

Darci, the time is now. Leave here and join your true family.

Darci began to beat at her temples, not caring now who heard her shrieks. "I said *get out!*" She felt her power rise and struggled to keep it in check. It fought her. Every command she gave it went unnoticed. "What's . . . happening . . . to me?"

"You are becoming who you truly are."

The new voice, low and feminine and sensual, chilled Darci to the core. But her power leapt in joy and surged to the fore. Darci beat it back down and turned in her chair to face this new voice.

Sandara stood there, her red gown floating in a magic-created breeze. Darci had never seen the woman, but she remembered Sita's descriptions of her from Thirka. The red nails, the gown, the black but graying hair, the cruel eyes . . . it must be her. "S-Sandara?" Darci whispered. Her eyes began to blur. "What do you want?"

Why, to take you home, of course.

Darci's eyes widened and she felt the bile rise in her throat. "It was you!" she shouted. "It was you making me go crazy all along!"

Tears flowed thick and fast down her cheeks. Her magic made another surge at her barriers. She gasped for breath. The desk lamp flickered, throwing eerie shadows over the walls. "Help me, help . . ." Her body seized up, then relaxed, then froze again.

The barriers crashed.

Ebony black power poured from Darci, filling her to overflowing before cascading outward. Darci's eyes rolled up into her head and she fell off her chair, the rolling tide of magic too strong for her to bear. Wild tendrils snaked around her body to claim her as its own.

Sandara watched in fascination. She had never seen anything to equal this, the complete and magnificent surrender to such great power. The girl twitched a bit, but her unconscious mind felt nothing. Soon the inky black power began pulling back into Darci's skin. The dim lights began to return to the room. Sandara hadn't even realized the light had gone, and she shielded her eyes as the brightness surged.

Darci lay on the ground, frozen, the shadows of dark power rippling over her body. Her arm rose, then her leg moved to the side, and soon she pushed herself up off the floor. Sandara watched the girl stand up in front of her, eyes still closed, face stoic.

Those eyes opened, and Sandara's hands began to tremble.

Darci's eyes held nothing but blackness.

Those black orbs focused on Sandara, who swallowed hard.

"Why are you here?" Darci's voice asked. It was her voice, but in quadruple and deeper, shadowed. "What do you want?"

Sandara stood straighter. "I was sent to take you home, if you wish it."

"And where is home, Sandara?"

"At Imbri Mors headquarters."

The being that was once Darci seemed to pause to think this over. Sandara waited in silence and was rewarded with Darci's cruel smile. The younger woman took a long white feather off her desk and ran it through her fingers before tucking it into her hair to bring along.

"Let's go home."

Sita sat straight up in bed. A scream tore from her lips and chest. Vanessa nearly fell from her own bed, but managed to push herself back against the wall just in time. Sita tumbled out from underneath her sheets. She hurried to pull on a sweater and jeans. Her roommate stared at her. "What's wrong? It's after midnight!"

She threw slippers onto her feet. "I had a dream. It was full of darkness and death." She paused and stared up at Vanessa's wide eyes. "It had something to do with Darci. I'm afraid . . ." But she couldn't finish the sentence. Sita lunged out the door, Vanessa stumbling behind.

The door to Darci's room was shut tight. Sita knocked. "Darci? Darci!" she called. There was no answer. She pounded harder. "Darci!"

Vanessa watched and eventually shook her head. "I don't think she's there."

Sita snarled at the aggravating door. Vanessa jumped. Sita closed her eyes and placed her left hand on the door. "I don't know if this will work, but let's give it a shot," she said. Vanessa only watched as Sita tensed and soon went rigid. She recognized the violet magic as it poured from Sita's hand into the door.

A moment later Sita slumped against the door. She kept her face hidden, her breathing harsh. A tear leaked down her cheek. Vanessa came closer, finally reaching out a hand to steady her. "What's wrong?" she asked. "What did you see?"

Sita numbly shook her head as Roxie and Ari finally tumbled out of the suite and into the hall behind them.

"Darci's gone."

Chapter Twenty-Nine
Shock

Darci ran.

She ran as hard as she could, aware that she wasn't really running. Not in the physical sense, at least.

The darkness drew closer, threatening to consume her. She ran harder, dredging up the last reserves of strength she possessed and putting on a new burst of speed. The darkness fell back, ebony clouds roiling behind her in angry waves. Golden rays that looked like sunshine pierced the fog just ahead.

Darci burst through the gray miasma, panting and gasping for air. Tears leaked down her ashen face. She sank to her knees onto grass and began to sob. She glanced behind her to see the dark clouds hit the fog surrounding her new haven, unable to breach the barrier they formed. Shaking, she dissolved into tears. "I'm sorry, I'm sorry, I'm so sorry . . ." she whispered through the crying. "Sita . . . please help me, please, oh please, oh please . . ."

The sunshine drifted over her, warming her back. Her thin hair veiled her eyes when finally the tears abated and she could stand up again. She sniffled. The sweet air here tasted good, the plains of green meadows vast and beautiful. Darci looked around in awe. "Where am I?" she whispered.

At peace for the first time in months, Darci forgot what had driven her to the meadows and instead began to explore her new home.

The Imbri Mors headquarters stood silent. No sound could be heard. None of the workmen dared to so much as cough or sneeze while still within range of the professor. Every one of them lined up outside the small manse, in their cleanest shirts and pants, all of them scrubbed to within an inch of their lives.

At least the storms had abated for the moment.

As if even Corá waited to see what Sandara brought home.

Green light flared in the open space just in front of the manse's steps. Sandara stepped out first, her crimson gown held high to keep it off the wet grass. She signaled her triumph to her master and turned back to the open gate behind her. All the men breathed a sigh of profound relief—none of them would be subject to the master's temper today.

Another woman stepped from the gate. Short black hair hung just to her shoulders, and pale skin shone in the reflection of the gate's green light. The gate flared behind her and winked out of existence again, emitting a noise akin to a scream as it faded away and closed.

The second young woman followed Sandara up to the manse, keeping her eyes on the men. She grinned at them and they all held their breath, certain they were about to die. A few of the men found they had wet themselves.

Professor Alan stepped forward with a smile for Sandara. "My dear Sandara, this must be the young lady you have been telling me about. I'm pleased your mission went so well."

Sandara curtsied to him, flushing at the praise. "I brought her home, Professor, as requested. She agreed of her own free will."

"Excellent, excellent. Well, let's welcome her home, shall we?" Professor Alan brushed past his second-in-command and walked to the young woman. "Darci?" he said. Darci's eyes flicked toward him but she made no move to speak. "My name is Professor Alan. I used to work at your school. Do you remember me?"

Darci remained silent. A white feather fluttered behind her ear in the wind. She stared at the man, her black eyes emanating power. The strength of what she radiated grew in force until the workmen and Sandara almost collapsed from the pressure. It kept growing and strengthening until even Alan felt it and was forced to look away.

The young woman smiled, but it was an empty expression that never reached her eyes. "Of course I remember you, Professor," said Darci. Her voice was multi-toned, reflecting not only Darci's natural speech but the power laying over it now. It was enough to make Professor Alan's mind scream in fear. "I would thank you not to treat me as an imbecile." Darci glared down her nose at him, giving the impression that she was taller despite the fact that Alan stood at least a good twelve inches higher than she.

Professor Alan swallowed hard. "Of course, I did not mean to imply that you are an imbecile, my dear. I was only curious as to if you remembered me at all."

"I am not your 'dear.' I belong to no one and nothing."

The silence of the field was deep and long. Alan stood there in the wet grass, unable to speak or move. This little slip of a girl had, in a span of five minutes, torn him apart and left him to hang. His authority hung by a thread now.

He chose the subservient route, bowing low at the waist, as deep an obeisance as he had ever given anyone—which is to say, his only obeisance. "My apologies, Darci. I meant no offense. How may we make you comfortable here?"

The being called Darci walked past him, black power trailing behind her like a cloak. She stepped up on the stairs, a smirk of satisfaction on her lips when the workers scrambled out of her way. The clouds began to groan in the sky and drop little raindrops on their heads. Darci turned to Alan and Sandara. "You can make me comfortable by making sure you do not forget how powerful I am. You can not kill me, and in fact, I could destroy this entire area in a fifty mile radius in the blink of an eye—and sleep very well afterward."

Alan felt Sandara tremble beside him. *Fifty miles?* They had never heard of such an attack radius that wide. Alan stood straight but kept his eyes down, his fists clenched at his sides.

Darci continued. "Just remember, Alan, Sandara—you wanted me here. You want me on your side. I can do a great deal of damage on my own. I do not need you. But you certainly need me. Do not forget it." She walked inside the wide open double doors just as the rain began to fall in earnest.

The workmen rushed indoors, hurrying to be out of the wet, with Alan and Sandara following at a slower pace behind.

Because they were looking indoors, they missed the fact that the rain was no longer contained in a circle around their manse. It spread for miles, as far as the eye could see, covering everything in fat ovals of water and mournful gray clouds.

Corá herself was weeping.

∞

The bleak mood on the fourth floor of East Hall permeated everything.

Sita had woken the others with her scream, and half the hall as well. While their other hall-mates grumbled and slouched back to bed, the four huddled in the suite to wait for Robert.

Sita was the quietest. She sat tense and straight-backed in her chair. Her face looked pale, more so than usual, and her eyes were red from too much crying.

Only Vanessa seemed at all unperturbed about the change in events. She hadn't shed a single tear, and now sat calm in her chair by the kitchenette. She twiddled her thumbs in boredom. *Who cares if Darci left?* she thought. *She always gave me the creeps anyway.*

A knock echoed from the door. The girls looked up while Vanessa, the only clear-minded one of the lot at the moment, went to open the door. Robert and Allen stood there, somber faces matching those of the group. Roxie ran to Allen, who enveloped her in a giant hug. Rob pushed them inside with a shadowed half-smile and shut the door behind him. "Does anyone know what happened?"

Each one of them shook their heads. "No," Sita spoke up. "We only realized she was gone when I woke up from a dream and knocked on her door."

"What was your dream?" Rob asked. He took a seat near Ari after giving her shoulder a comforting squeeze.

"I dreamt that there was death. Darci was in my dream, but this is where it gets confusing: in the first part, she's willingly going with Sandara, covered in her own black power. But in the second half, she was running from black waves of magic. She was terrified." Sita's voice trailed off, her eyes haunted.

She shook it off and returned to her story. "It was the second half of the dream that really scared me. I've never seen someone so afraid in my life. I woke up in a sweat, and I think screaming—" Vanessa nodded emphatically. "—and so I rolled out of bed and went to Darci's room. There was no answer." Her voice began to shake, and her hands trembled. Ari reached over and took one of her trembling, cold hands. Vanessa's mouth twitched in a frown. "When she didn't answer my calls, I put my hand on the door and called on my gift. It told me what happened. It showed me that

Darci's power has taken complete control of her, and that Darci is with Imbri Mors now. She's gone."

Robert and Allen listened in silence. Even Vanessa shivered at the end. Robert shook his head. "I knew they would come for her eventually. I just didn't think it would be this soon." He looked to Allen. "I wonder how they got her. She was too powerful for them to just come and pack her away to their headquarters."

The question roused Sita from her reverie. "They attacked her mind," she said. Everyone turned to her. "They tried to get at us both."

"What do you mean?" Allen asked. His arms wrapped tighter around Roxie.

"I mean they literally attacked her mind. They inserted thoughts. I don't know how, but they did, and they were the kinds of things that fed off of what was already there to begin with. Even if it was just a simple passing thought, they could read it and use it later against us, they were in our minds from the beginning . . ." Sita trailed off, tears rolling down her face. She held one hand to her face, the other still holding Ari's hand. "They were in my mind, but they were after Darci all along."

Robert waved his hands at her, his eyes wide and furious. "You mean to tell me that all this time they've been controlling your own thoughts and you didn't think to *tell anyone about it?*" Sita shrank back into her chair. The rage on Robert's face was new, a side to him they had never seen before, and it terrified them all. "What the hell were you doing?" he shouted. "You could have been taken when they came for Darci! Hell, if we had known about this sooner, we could even have stopped it! I know a hundred ways to shield the mind from enemies, but no, you didn't think to ask for help did you, you didn't think to *tell* anyone that another *voice* was in your *mind!* Damn your pride, Sita, sometimes you *have to ask for help.*"

The whimper from Sita's chair startled him into silence. Sita stared at him as if she had never seen him before. Wide blue-green eyes overflowed with tears. Rob's face fell into pale shock. "Oh, geez, Sita, I'm sorry." He walked over to her, intending to hug her, but she squirmed out of her chair and ran to her room. Sobs escaped just as she closed the door. Vanessa rolled her eyes at her roommate's lack of spine.

Ari slapped his leg hard from her seat on the floor. Rob focused on her, even more shocked than he had been at the sight of Sita's tears. "You shouldn't have yelled at her!" Ari said. "Don't you think she's beating herself up enough as it is?"

Robert slipped into Sita's vacant chair with a drawn-out sigh. He rested his head in one hand. "I know, I know. I apologize to all of you, as well. I let my fear get the best of me." Vanessa admired his profile as he leaned back against the chair and imagined what it would be like to run her hands through his hair. "The question now is, where do we go from here? The enemy now has a very powerful weapon in their hands, a weapon that may or may not have free will."

"What happens if she does have free will?" Roxie asked.

"That could be either good for us, or very bad," said a disembodied voice. They all looked around the room, confusion and fear rampant across every face, until a body began taking shape off to one side of the common room. The shape formed an outline, then firmed, then took on mass and flesh. In a moment, Ka'len stood before them, calm and serene as usual.

The young women gaped at him in shock. "How did you . . . what did . . . ." Roxie stuttered.

Ka'len grinned at her. "I am quite adept at getting around, young lady, and you should never underestimate a master, no matter how old he may appear to be." He paced over to the group and sat in the chair Robert vacated for him. "Now, if Darci still has free will, that could be good and it could be bad," he continued. "Good in that she could remember you and remember your kindness. Bad in that she may be the tool of her own power now, and she will not care who you are and what you have done for her. If the latter, then there is little hope of turning her back to us." The women frowned or studied the floor. "If she has no free will, it is entirely to our disadvantage. Imbri Mors will use her mercilessly to further their own ends, and they will undoubtedly set her against us."

Roxie scowled. "OK, so what do we do now? We just let her go?"

Ka'len's face fell. "I am afraid so, for the moment. You can hardly get her back now—unless you plan to invade Imbri Mors headquarters. I am certain you know who is behind all the killings of those poor people in the cities. Running straight into their grasp would be foolhardy."

"True," Robert said. "I think we need to let Darci go. I can't see any way of bringing her back right now."

Vanessa let out a very loud, theatrical sigh from the other side of the room. The others turned to see her lounging in her chair, completely unconcerned. She didn't have to pretend to look bored. "Great. So now we have that settled, where are we going for spring break?"

The others stared at her. Ka'len shook his head in disbelief.

Ari rose and stalked over to the suite door. She stopped just in front of it, her hand on the knob, when she turned around to glare at Vanessa. Ari's cheeks were bright pink and her normally kind eyes turned to smoldering fire. "Vanessa, you disgust me. Darci was just taken from us and all you can think about is spring break? We just got back from winter break! Haven't you had enough?" With that, she wrenched open the door and left the suite.

Vanessa's face reflected her surprise. *It's just Darci, what are they getting so huffy about?* Roxie's lip curled as Vanessa turned to her for backup. Rox shook her head and held up her hands. "Oh, don't look at me, Vanessa. I know you haven't always liked Darci, but how could you be happy that she's in their hands?" Rox rose from the couch, tugging Allen up with her. "Why don't you join them and see how it feels? Then you'll know why we didn't want Darci there in the first place." Roxie and Allen escaped into her room. They shut the door on Vanessa and the two men.

Vanessa fought to hide her anger and confusion. Instead, she hung her head. "I'm sorry," she said, her voice low. Robert and Ka'len stared at her, but said nothing. Vanessa looked up through the curtain of her hair and saw their unwavering gazes on her. She scowled and dropped the penitent act. So she jumped to her feet, grabbed a coat, and left the suite. If they were going to treat her like the deserter instead of a friend, then she would go to her other friends. And maybe track down Eric while she was at it.

That would really piss Sita off.

The two men sighed when she left. Ka'len rubbed his temples. "I do not know what to do with that Vanessa. She is too haughty and self-centered for her own good."

Rob dropped onto the couch. "I know. She's been causing tension for a while now, mostly because of the way she treated Darci. And by that I mean she completely ignored the girl. In fact, I think she went out of her way to avoid her. Barely talked to her, and if she did talk to her, she was condescending and just on the right side of politeness." He grimaced. His next topic left a bad taste in his mouth. "And I think she's jealous of Sita."

"How do you mean?" Ka'len asked. "I can understand the rest of what you have said, but why do you believe her to be jealous of Sita? I have seen no evidence of this."

"It's mostly instinct, I guess. But it's there, if you watch Vanessa. When she thinks no one's looking, she glares at Sita. And if looks could kill, Sita would be dead hundreds of times over."

Ka'len shook his head, his mouth set in a frown. "I am afraid that is not enough evidence. I trust your instincts, Robert, but we need more than simple glances in order to act. There must be more there."

Just then Sita's door cracked open and her head popped out. Her face was tear-streaked and red. "I thought I heard your voice, Ka'len." She opened the door wider and came out to join them. She took the armchair across from Ka'len's and next to the sofa.

Robert reached over and offered her his hand. "I'm really sorry about what I said, Si. I let fear get the better of me. Please accept my apology for yelling at you."

Sita smiled at him and squeezed his hand, her eyes clear and shining now. "Of course I accept. It was a very depressing moment, and I don't blame you for being human." Her features grew cloudy again and her eyes downcast. "And on top of losing Eric, this just pushed me over the edge and I let it get to me, as well."

Ka'len leaned forward, his eyes narrowed. "What do you mean you lost Eric? I am confused. Was he not in love with you and it was going well?"

"Yeah, that's what he said." Sita leaned back into the cushions, crossing her arms in a sad pout. "I guess he lied. I broke up with him."

"Why?"

"Because he's a jerk."

Ka'len scowled. "I am asking for an explanation, Sita, not excuses. Whether you like it or not, your welfare is my concern, and I need to know."

She groaned and averted her eyes from the both of them. "He ran from me, Ka'len. I broke up with him because he ran from me when . . . when he saw my wings. And my magic."

There was silence from his corner of the room. Rob took one look at his mentor's face and tried to make himself as inconspicuous as possible. Ka'len's face turned a dangerous shade of red. "He saw WHAT?"

Sita winced and bit her lip. "He saw my wings and magic," she said. Her voice was tiny in the overwhelming silence.

Ka'len scowled at her and put his hands on his hips. She swallowed hard. "Why did you do that? You were not planning to wed him, as far as I can recall, and so he did not need to know."

"I didn't plan it. I trusted him, and I wanted to tell him, but I wasn't really ready to show him either one." Sita sat straighter, a little indignant. "He walked in unexpectedly when I was doing some magic in my room. I had asked Vanessa to clear out for a few hours and told them what I was doing so I could work in peace, and he just walked in as if I were expecting him. I was in the middle of a spell . . . of course he saw my magic. And I had my wings out as well, since I was alone for a few hours, and my back was itchy. So he saw those too."

Her teacher paced around the room, his temper igniting the very air. "That was far too careless of you, but also far too coincidental . . ." Ka'len trailed off and stopped in his tracks, which startled Robert and Sita. His eyes narrowed again and the muscles of his face relaxed. "Sita, did you talk to someone else in advance about what you had planned for that night?"

Sita licked her lips and took a deep breath. "I'd thought about telling him for a while, but I'm not really very good with guys, and so I asked Vanessa what she thought, since she's really good with guys, and she said I should tell him, that it was a good idea to go through with it. I listened, though I didn't take her advice just then, and I asked if she would leave the room for me that night for a while . . ."

Ka'len slapped his forehead and groaned. "Of course she would tell you that. Of course." He sighed and rested his hands on

Sita's shoulders. "I realize you had good intentions, Sita, but from now on, please talk to me before you think of telling someone outside the group about your powers. You are endangering not only yourself but also your friends when you do."

"I know," she said. Sita gave him a melancholy smile and patted his hands. "I know I am. That's why I thought to ask Vanessa first, if it was a good idea. Are you telling me she lied to me? That she set me up?"

"Yes."

She nodded. "I thought so, too, afterward. And honestly, I thought he would react better to finding out, back when I was thinking of telling him. I guess I didn't know him very well after all. Though that's not the only reason it ended—he thought I was dreaming and thinking about someone else." The yellowed light of the suite lent an eerie glow to Sita's face and highlighted the dark circles under her eyes. She removed Ka'len's hands and regained her seat in the armchair.

Robert breathed easier for staying out of this fight. He knew it was probably unwise to inquire on that topic, but since she had brought it up herself, he couldn't see how he could resist. "Well, were you?" he asked.

Sita glared at him, and he winced inside, but she answered. "In a way, yes. But not because I really wanted to. Some vision of a man kept invading my dreams. That doesn't change the fact that I love—loved—and was devoted to Eric."

Ka'len looked thoughtful. He pulled at his short beard. "I wonder why he ran. This concerns me. While it would be a plausible reaction for anyone else, I should think him familiar enough with you to know that you would not hurt him in any way."

Sita tried not to look mournful at his words. "I don't know, Ka'len. Honest."

A cough from Rob's seat on the couch made them look at him. Robert knew he was beet red and he rubbed the back of his head. "I don't think you'll like hearing this, Si, but . . . Allen and I kind of found out something about Eric that might give us a clue to his reaction."

They waited for him to continue, but he stopped, unable to think of any way around telling her. Finally Sita became impatient. "Would you hurry up and say it, Rob?"

He jumped and quirked his lips in a small, guilty smile. "Sorry. I just really don't want to say this." He took a deep breath. "All right, here goes . . . just don't kill the messenger . . . Allen found out that Eric is part of Imbri Mors." Rob winced and threw his arms up to block whatever rage would come at him.

None came, and after a moment he lowered his arms enough to peek through. "Sita?" he asked. He looked toward her with a side glance at Ka'len's stunned expression. "Sita, are you OK?"

Sita sat in her chair, hands folded, eyes wide and staring into space at nothing. Her breathing was labored, as if she held off sobs by force of will alone. Her mouth flapped open and closed, but no sound came out. Tears rolled down her face.

Rob jumped up from the couch and grasped her face in both hands. "Sita, I'm sorry, I didn't want to tell you this so soon after the breakup, but I guess there's never really a good time to hear this sort of thing, is there? I'm sorry, I know how this must hurt." He paused, studying her face. "Please say something."

Her expression never wavered, but he could feel her skin getting colder and colder. She looked up at him, her eyes half wild. "I'm fine," she whispered. "I'll be OK."

Ka'len wheezed, his own breath harsh. "Well, I suppose that does indeed explain his reaction. Even if he is one of the enemy, he likely did not know about the girls. I doubt he was very highly placed. Seeing a human sprout wings and have glowing hands would remind him of his enemies. No wonder he thought you would hurt him—they have been training him to be wary of just such people."

Sita trembled now. "I put us all in even bigger danger than I knew." She rose from her chair, needing to hold on to the armrests for balance. "I can't believe he was one of them. I had no idea." Sita circled around toward her room. "I think I'll try to sleep now. I'm very tired." Her voice was strained and tense, and very soft.

The men could only nod their good-nights. Sita turned back to Rob, hugging her arms tight around her body. "Any more missions lined up?"

He blinked twice in surprise. "No. They seem to be operating far away from here, and I don't want any of you going near a city. We don't know when the next killing spree will be, or where." The bitterness in his voice stung.

"They're still killing all those people, then?"

"Sadly, yes. They've spread to every major city across the U.S. At best count, three thousand people have died at their hands."

She looked away. Her lip began to quiver. "And we do nothing. We should be out there stopping it, not fighting among ourselves or talking it through." The despair in her voice cut into Rob's very core.

But that weakness only made him harsh. "And what would you do? Join the thousands who have already died? I won't let that happen, Sita."

She glared at him. "How can I sit here and do nothing?" she cried. "We should be doing *something* other than talking!" The look in her eyes, so full of despair, cut into Rob's heart. He tried to wall away the feeling, to numb himself as he knew he must.

Ka'len reached out once more and patted her arm. "I know how you feel, my dear, but until we know how they are killing them, it is best to stay back and observe. We have to hope we will find a clue soon."

"The other groups have people on this, right?"

Rob hesitated for only a second. "Right."

With a tight nod, Sita said good-night and strode into her room. Rob waited until the door shut tight before he spoke again. "I agree with her, but we really don't know how they're killing all those people, do we?"

Ka'len shook his head. "No, we do not. I have talked with many other people who are aware of the deaths, and no one has been able to propose a satisfying explanation."

Rob slumped back into the couch. He rubbed at his hair, frustrated. "It has to have something to do with the stones!" he said, trying to keep his voice down. "Why else would they steal the stones? I know they're using them to store the victims' life energy, but why? For what purpose? What could possibly need that much pure human soul?"

The old man sat up straighter. "Wait a moment, Robert. Did you say they are using the stones to store human souls?"

"Yeah, or whatever else you want to call a soul. Heart, spirit, soul, it's all the same. But I think that's why they have so many of the crystals that are good for exactly that kind of thing. Every single one of the gems they steal is big enough to contain one soul, many are big enough for multiple. Alan is obsessed with souls—in his journal that Allen found, the professor thought he heard the voices of his dead wife and sons in the stones of his wife's engagement ring."

Ka'len held up his hand to halt conversation while he stared off into space. "Robert . . . can you think of anything that would feed off of human souls? Any creature that would require something so pure as a soul in order to even survive?"

Rob thought about the question but eventually shook his head. "No. I can't."

"Well, I can." Ka'len tugged at his beard again. "There are legends about ancient creatures, commonly called 'demons,' that require pure souls to eat." Robert's eyes widened in alarm. "Oh, 'demons' is not precisely the correct term for them, but it is the most adequate word to describe them that anyone has been able to concoct. I would say they are creatures of Darkness, consumed by their greed and their hate. They are the essence of evil in a human soul." He paused, brows furrowed in thought. "I cannot remember anything else about them, however, nor can I remember what they are called. I will look through the libraries in Corá and do some research. Perhaps the answer lies with those demons."

Robert struggled to breathe as the enormity of Ka'len's statement caught up with him. "So you think that Imbri Mors is helping these demon creatures? That they're killing these people to get them *food?*"

Ka'len shrugged. "It is a possible theory. But lacking any more solid evidence, I would say it is only a theory." His eyes twinkled. "Do keep in mind that while I am ancient and very wise, not even I hold all the answers." He winked at Robert. "Though I do not mind if people think I know everything."

The feeble joke made Rob laugh and broke his fear into tiny pieces. "You're right, as usual. I'll let some of the others in Knight's group know and see what they can come up with for your theory." He summoned a bottle of water out of the refrigerator and gulped some down. "Now, back to the problem of Vanessa. What do we do about her?"

"Hmmm . . ." Ka'len summoned his own bottle of water and took more moderate sips while he thought. "Perhaps she should leave the Aligerai."

The water in Rob's throat nearly went down his air pipe instead. He coughed. "Are you . . . sure about that? At least . . . while she's in . . . the group we can . . . keep an eye on her," he rasped. Swallowing another mouthful of water down the correct tube helped. "Besides, Sita gave them all those rings. We can't take hers back . . ." A new thought occurred to them both at the same time and they both groaned. "Darci still has her ring."

Ka'len downed the rest of his water as if it were sweet alcohol soothing his headache. "She will know where the girls are every minute of every day." He took aim and threw the bottle into the garbage can. "Though this could also work in our favor. Sita and the others will know where *Darci* is every minute of every day as well."

"True." Robert finished his own water and tried to get it into the garbage, but his shot went wide and the bottle banged against the wall. "Damn, why couldn't she have made those rings over spring break, instead of winter? It would cause me a lot less stress. I swear, these girls will make me go gray-haired and bald."

Ka'len chuckled. "Oh, I doubt that. But they certainly are exciting."

"Too exciting." Ka'len laughed again. "Now, if we kicked Vanessa out, she could join the enemy and give them all the information about us. Or she could go rogue, and join no one." He cocked an eyebrow at Ka'len. "I doubt that if she were to join no group that she would continue being involved in the fight we're all about to be involved in."

"I agree."

"But if she stays with us and we don't kick her out . . ."

"She could cause many more problems than we want to deal with."

"And she could force a division in the group just by being contrary and disobeying orders," Rob said. "I know she's never been that keen on the training, but she likes using her magic well enough."

Ka'len snorted. "I have seen that type before. All show and no work to support the show. They almost never last very long in any real conflict. They have not the practice to support their power for any length of time."

Rob nodded. "And that worries me. The girls will be depending on her as another teammate, and if she decides she's not going to practice, they won't realize that they can't depend on her in a real fight."

The two men remained silent for a few minutes, thinking their own thoughts and listening to the quiet suite. Everyone appeared to have gone to bed. Ka'len broke their quiet reflection. "Regardless of the risks of allowing Vanessa to stay in the group, I believe we should wait."

"Yeah, I came to that conclusion, too. We can't kick her out without more proof." He smirked. "Besides, if we let this continue, she'll either do something stupid and get herself kicked out, or the others will get tired of her and do the deed themselves. Sita can remove the rings if she wants to. She could take Vanessa's away."

Ka'len nodded in agreement. "Yes. It sounds like a good strategy." He stood up. "I believe we have caught up on everything now. Shall we call it a night?"

Robert stood up as well to gather his coat from where he had dropped it beside the door. "I think that's a great idea. I'm tired now." As if to prove this, he yawned. "Have a good night, Ka'len."

"Good night, Robert." In twin flashes of blue, the two men disappeared from the suite.

Sita's dreams that night were haunted not only by her discussion with Ka'len and Robert, but also by her desire to throttle Eric and her general heartache. But finally her dreams turned to something a little more pleasant.

She sat on the ground of an enormous, empty space. No walls could be seen, and no ceiling. There were no lights, only a mysterious, clean gray haze that floated around her. Outside of the haze there was only inky black.

She smoothed the panels of her cerulean dress as she stood, staring into the darkness. Her long hair she left to trail freely behind her for once, and her bare feet rested on cool ground. Sita looked out again to notice a shape coming closer. "Hello?" she called, her voice clear and soft. "Who's out there?"

No reply. The shape grew closer and resolved into a man's body. As the person walked closer through the grayness surrounding her, Sita took the opportunity to study him. This person resembled the vague shapes she had seen in previous dreams, but now she had more detail. It was clearly male, for he had the bare upper torso of a muscular and solid man. He walked with confidence, almost arrogance, and with power. But he also appeared to approach slow and soft, as if he did not want to frighten her. She grinned when she saw that he, too, had wings, glorious, huge white wings like her own. He dressed in only a pair of ripped and faded blue jeans and a black belt, his feet and chest bare.

At last his face came into the hazy light. He was close enough now that Sita could see every detail of him. She studied his face, the fine, soft mouth, the slightly-too-large nose, the strong cheekbones. There was something a little bit familiar in the sculpted lines of his face. His black hair nearly reached his shoulders and was tousled as if he had just risen from bed. But Sita especially noticed the eyes. Strong gray eyes that pulled her in and saw everything around him in an instant. She loved those kinds of eyes.

He stopped just inside the glowing grayness. Sita gazed up at him, for he was at least a head taller than she. "Hello," Sita said soft. "Who are you?" She didn't know if it was possible to be harmed in a dream—she drew her hands behind her back and gathered magic, just in case.

The man smiled, his gray eyes warm and soft. "My name is Owen. Who are you?"

Sita relaxed. He didn't seem very dangerous. "Sita. I'm Sita. Why are you here?" She sat down on the edge of a plush gilt chair that materialized behind her. Nothing seemed strange or unusual in this odd landscape.

Owen sat down in his own chair. "I'm looking for you. I've been looking for someone like you for a long time." In an instant he was on his feet behind her, his hands resting on her shoulders. "You have wings, too, don't you?"

Sita tilted her head to the left, watching him from the corner of her eye. She cut slits in her silky dress and drew her wings out. White feathers gleamed in the haze on both sides of her. The muscles in her back stretched and relaxed.

Owen grinned in triumph. Sita's breath caught when he smiled, and her heart began to pound louder in her ears. "I knew it," he breathed, his voice melodic and velvety. "Do you know anyone else with wings?" He returned to his own chair, but scooted it closer to Sita.

"No. I'm the only one."

"Not anymore." His wings fluttered behind him.

She grinned. "No, not anymore."

Owen glanced behind him before he refocused on her. "I believe it's time for me to go, Sita." He rose. She followed him as he began to walk away from the gray light. The chairs vanished with a puff of gray cloud when they both rose. "But don't worry," he said over his shoulder, "now that I've found you, I'll never lose you. Unless you want me to."

Sita stopped walking, not wanting him to leave. "When will I see you again?"

He turned around to face her, the movement reminding Sita of a cat as he stalked back to her. Owen reached out with tentative and gentle fingers to run them along her cheek. Instead of a kiss, he pulled her right hand up to his face. "Soon," he murmured, and kissed her palm. He smiled when her breath caught in her throat. "Remember me, Sita. Don't forget me."

"Do you have to leave? I have so many questions . . ." Sita asked.

"Soon," Owen promised again. He vanished as he stepped backward into the inky blackness, a smile just for her on his lips.

Sita stood and stared at her right hand. Then the seething cloud of black drowned the grayness and consumed Sita with it.

She woke with a gasp and the comforter pulled up to her chin. Tears rippled down her cheeks. "Owen," she murmured. "Owen. Please don't be just a dream."

∞

The next morning happened to be a Saturday. The girls would have slept in, but Robert and Ka'len had other plans for them.

At precisely nine in the morning, Robert and Ka'len popped into the suite. Without even looking at each other, Robert began to bang on Roxie's door while Ka'len knocked hard on Sita's. Loud cursing erupted from both rooms and thumps on the floor echoed as the girls jumped down from their tall beds.

Roxie jerked her door open. "What the hell?" she said. She still had sleep-fogged eyes.

Vanessa opened the door just after that. Rob watched from the corner of his eye in amusement as Vanessa opened her mouth to say something, thought better of it when she saw it was Ka'len, and shut her mouth again with an audible click. Robert held out his hands to Rox with a grin. "Come on, Roxie, get dressed. I have something to teach you."

Roxie slammed the door in his face. He struggled not to laugh when he heard Ariene's curses when Rox related the message.

Ka'len fared no better. He also had the door shut before him, but he hadn't said a word. Now he sat on the couch, waiting with infinite patience. Robert joined him. "Think they're annoyed with me?" he asked Ka'len with a laugh.

The old man smirked. His beard quivered in suppressed laughter. "Clearly. Perhaps I should impart the lesson. They may take it amiss if you attempt it, and try to teach you a lesson of their own, hmm?"

Robert laughed. "Of course, of course. You're a better teacher than I am anyway."

"Oh, come now, my boy, you have done a fine job so far."

The girls stumbled out of their rooms one by one, first Ari, then Vanessa, followed by Roxie and Allen, and finally Sita—who looked as if she had barely slept at all. They each took a seat on the couch or the chairs, flopping like ragdolls into the cushions. Ka'len stood up. "We have something very important we want to teach you," he said. The girls looked bleary-eyed up at him. Allen stood behind Roxie's chair. "This is something you have seen us do, and if you can learn how to use it with proficiency, it can even save your life." Ka'len waved them to take seats and nodded in satisfaction. He strode into the middle of the room and pushed the coffee table aside. "Now, watch closely. Try to see if you can see what I do."

He took a few deep breaths. Closing his eyes, he gathered his power and . . .

. . . popped out of sight and then back again on the other side of the couch.

Roxie sat up straighter, excited. "You're going to teach us how to do that?" she said.

"Yes. Now, could anyone see what I did?" Ka'len asked.

Sita leaned her head back against the chair head. "You gathered your magic as a kind of base, but you didn't actually use it. You used something else to make yourself move. I couldn't see what that was, though."

The old man smiled. "Exactly! I did *not* use my magic. This is very important. Allen, you should pay attention, boy!" Allen, who had been nodding off on his feet, jerked himself awake and stared at Ka'len. "This does not use magical power, and this lesson may very well be useful to you. Stay awake!" Ka'len commanded. Allen only grimaced at him.

He returned to his narration. "As I said, I did not use power. I used the magic as a base, to help focus myself, but it is not required. So if I did not use magic, what did I use?"

Roxie was the first to catch on. She glanced over at Robert. He saw the notion in her eyes and nodded to encourage her. She spoke up. "Is it *boulesis*?"

Ka'len brightened, eyes alighting on her. "Yes, that is it precisely! Wonderful job, Roxie! How did you come to that conclusion?"

She shrugged. "It was something Robbie said, a while back. He said I had a lot of *boulesis*, and that because I had this, I could do more than just my magic alone would let me do."

"Well, I am glad you listened to him. He is absolutely right. *Boulesis*, or will power, for those of you who do not know, can accomplish almost anything. It is the reason Ariene can change forms, the reason for Sita's flight, the reason behind any decision you follow through with," Ka'len said. "And we will be using *boulesis* to do what I just showed you."

Vanessa frowned, her brows coming together. "How? It sounds complicated to me."

The old man shook his head. "It is not as complicated as it sounds, I promise, though it may take some practice and time before you get it exactly right. Now, watch again." Ka'len repeated the exercise, crossing from one side of the couch back to his original starting point. Some of the girls nodded and watched his actions carefully. He flapped his hands at them. "Come now, everyone on your feet, on your feet. I want to see some real progress with this before breakfast."

Just then Ari's stomach growled. "Oh, breakfast . . ."

Robert watched them with a smile. Soon Ka'len had them all meditating and finding their own *boulesis*. Then once they were all awake but calm, he had them stand up and one by one went down the line. Each woman only had to cross the room, using *boulesis* to get her there. The first try was a dismal failure, but Ka'len said he expected that. Allen tried with the rest, but the technique didn't seem to click with him. Robert promised to work on it with him more later. Vanessa worked everyone's nerves by simply refusing to try during the first round. Exasperated, Ka'len moved on. Robert watched Vanessa from the corner of his eye while the lesson continued. Unfortunately, she caught him staring. She flipped her hair over her shoulder and flashed him an inviting smile. Rob just frowned and watched Sita instead.

On the second round, things improved. Roxie went first, and managed to make it halfway across the common room before her *boulesis* failed and dropped her unceremoniously on her bottom in the middle of the floor. She rubbed her aching muscles and rejoined the group amid her friends' snickers.

Ariene came next, but she didn't quite get the trick of it. Sita had her turn, and managed a little further than Roxie, but also failed to reach other side—though she landed on her feet, not her rump. Vanessa struggled as well, and did not make it on her turn.

Finally, and in less time than Ka'len and Robert thought possible, Sita made it across the room. Then Roxie succeeded, and then Ari and Vanessa. Robert glanced down at his watch; they had begun this exercise less than an hour ago, and every one of the women had learned to cross the room with *boulesis* alone. Impressed, he showed the time to Ka'len, who only smiled back at him.

Vanessa stamped her foot. "What's so important about this anyway? How can this save our lives, like you said?"

The two men turned toward her, surprise etched on their faces. Robert sighed. "Can you really not figure it out for yourself, Vanessa?" Ka'len asked. Judging from her scowling face, he would get no answer. He gestured to Robert. "Watch, all of you."

Robert held out his right arm, muscles tense as he prepared himself. Ka'len, in a lightning-fast movement, grabbed Rob's arm and held on tight. A flash of blue light blinded them all for a moment, but when the spots cleared, Robert stood next to Ari and Ka'len held nothing but air. Ka'len turned to Vanessa. "Did you see?" She nodded reluctantly. "If an attacker had you in his grip and you could not escape physically, the best thing to do would be to disappear. If he is stronger than you, he could kill you, but only if he can hold you."

The girls' mouths rounded into O's, as the implications of the demonstration sunk in. Ari spoke up. "Both you and Robert have a flash of blue light when you move, and you're both blue mages. Sita's a purple mage, but she doesn't light up in purple when she disappears. Why?"

Ka'len shrugged. "I honestly do not know. Sita?"

Sita shook her head. "Don't look at me. I just did like you told me to: don't use the power except as a base, and use your *boulesis* to move. I did." Now she also shrugged. "Maybe I just used less of a base than you have to."

Robert considered it, amazed at the implications of such strong power and *boulesis*. "Maybe. We'll have to think about it later, though." He grinned at them all. "If I hear one more stomach growl, I think I'll go crazy. Go get breakfast!"

In a rush, the girls stampeded through the door, leaving Rob and Ka'len far behind. On their way out, the two men could hear Ari's muttered exclamation: "I can't wait until these three weeks are gone and we can get into spring break! Their training will starve me!"

Chapter Thirty
Taking Action

A cloudless blue sky hung over the mansion. Wide meadows of grass spread out on all sides, the front meadow now bisected by the newly resurrected stone footpath leading down to the front gates. Sita walked beside the path, dressed in one of her favorite gowns, a simple long blue affair decorated with a flowered border along the bottom hem. The grass felt cool and slick under her bare feet, and she reveled in the sensation.

Someone came running up behind her. Roxie jumped onto Sita's back and tackled her to the ground. High-pitched giggles and laughter erupted from them both. "This was a great idea!" Rox cried. She sat up next to Sita on the ground. Sita laughed and brushed off her skirt. "It's the perfect place to spend spring break! Who needs a beach? It's overdone. But this! Who can say they've been here?"

Sita lay on her back and gazed up at the sky with her head pillowed on an arm. "True. I'm just glad you all decided to come with me. I needed to get away for a while, but I need my friends, too!"

Roxie's face fell. "I know Darci's here, too. Somewhere in Corá, I mean." She held up the hand that wore the ring Sita had made. Sunlight bounced off the metal and made them both squint.

"Yeah, I felt that also. So she knows we're here."

"Do you think she'll try anything?"

Sita lay silent. She squinted in the sunshine. A light breeze blew around them that tousled their hair and played with the hems of clothing. Sita brushed her hair back from her face. "No. I don't think she'll come after us right now. She's probably working on getting Imbri under control instead of thinking about us."

Roxie sighed. "Yeah." She picked at the edge of her jeans until she jumped to her feet again. "I nearly forgot the whole reason I came out here! Lunch is ready, Ari sent me out to get you."

The blond smiled. "Cool. I'm kind of hungry anyway. Let's get inside." Roxie and Sita walked back up to the mansion, content with companionship and pleasant scenery until they walked through the front doors.

Inside the mansion, pandemonium ensued. Ariene screamed at Vanessa, Vanessa screamed at Ari, and Ari screamed right back. The shouts echoed around the foyer in dizzying waves.

Sita took one look around and ordered the heavy front doors to slam. They did, which made a loud humming tone that set everyone's teeth on edge and stopped the screaming ones in their tracks. "What is going on?" Sita said, her voice soft.

Ari pushed Vanessa forward. "Vanessa didn't like hearing that she's a traitor." Vanessa pushed Ari's hands away and jutted her stubborn chin out, holding herself straight-backed and tense.

"I just woke up from a nap," Ari said into the thick silence, "And I had a dream. I swear, on my life, that it's not an ordinary dream." Now that the fighting was over, she sat down on the stairs and rested her arms on her knees. "I had a dream, but it was different from any other dream I've ever had." Sita nodded her understanding, and for her to continue. "In the dream, I saw a blond woman attacking you, Sita, and then I saw her running to Darci. She ran straight to Imbri Mors. Until then, I wasn't sure who the blond was—she could have been Vanessa, or she could have been someone from the enemy. All I knew for sure was that it wasn't you.

"But then, after the blond joined Imbri, she turned around and looked straight at me. And I saw Vanessa's face staring back at me."

"She's lying!" shouted Vanessa. Her eyes smoldered in anger and not a little fear. "She's lying, I would never join them!"

Ari interrupted her. "I woke up, came downstairs, and ran into Vanessa. I confronted her about it. That's how this started." She spread her hands out wide and pursed her lips. "I freely admit that I started the fight."

Vanessa growled, the words grating out through clenched teeth. "I wouldn't attack you, Sita, and I wouldn't run to Imbri! Why don't you believe me?"

"Why should she?" Ari asked from behind her. Vanessa whirled around to see Ari's scowl and crossed arms. "Why should she believe you, Vanessa? You've always been jealous of her, we all know that. And you showed so much indifference to Darci's kidnapping that it's disgusting. I can barely stand to be around you, I don't know how Sita manages to *room* with you at school . . ." Vanessa opened her mouth to retort when Sita interrupted them both.

"Enough!" She laced just enough power into the command to make sure it would be obeyed. "Enough." Sita turned to Vanessa. "I also believe you, Vanessa. What we don't know is the timeframe of when this will happen—or even if it will. So I believe you, too." She then turned to Ari. "And Ari, don't antagonize her. It's been a rough few weeks for all of us, I'm sure we're all on edge. We need this break, so let's try to make the most of it, all right?"

The others all nodded in agreement, some eager, some reluctant. Vanessa's nod was curt and terse, and once Sita stopped speaking she turned on her heel and climbed up the stairs in a huff.

Roxie sighed. "Well, it *was* going well. Maybe this wasn't such a great idea after all." She glanced at Sita sidelong. "First you dream about Darci. Now Ari dreams about Vanessa. Maybe there's something to these dreams."

Sita's shoulders slumped. The implications of that were a little frightening. "Maybe. Anyway, let's go eat. I'm starving."

Vanessa paced around her room, muttering under her breath. Her hands balled into fists. Fingernails dug into the soft flesh of her palms. "Who does she think she is?" she fumed. "Who is she to come in here and tell me what to do?" She swiped at the top of her dresser and knocked off all of her cosmetics and jewelry. The pieces fell in a glittering spray to crash onto the floor.

Another swipe at the painting on the far wall dislodged it, and it fell with a loud bang onto the hard wood. Vanessa continued pacing, her face contorted into angry sneers and snarls. "Precious Sita. Everyone loves Sita, everyone admires Sita. Sita this, Sita that." The suitcase toppled over and disgorged its contents. "Oh, Sita's so *powerful*, she's so *special*, Sita, Sita, *Sita!*"

A picture from inside the suitcase caught her eye. It fell out of her picture box, where she kept all the favorite pictures of friends

306

and family. Vanessa leaned over and yanked the photograph out, holding it up to the light. It was a picture taken months ago, when Darci was still around. Everyone sat on the couch during a movie night, and Allen had taken it for them. Sita was at the very back, sitting next to Vanessa, smiling.

Vanessa growled at the picture. She ripped as much of it as she could into confetti and left the bits lying on the floor. "I'm tired of everything Sita."

Grabbing a jacket, Vanessa strode down the stairs and out into the grounds. She stayed out long past dark and avoided the others for a very long time.

∞

Darci smiled. The map on Ray Alan's desk was quite perfect. A slim pale finger pointed to the town of Thirka. "Thirka is near the Awle mansion, yes?"

The professor nodded. "Yes, it's just below the hill. There's a trade road from the town that goes up the hill and past the house. But Thirka is still almost an hour's walk away from the mansion."

She waved at him to shut up. "Yes, I can see the road, thank you." Darci stalked to the window. Gray sky every day could be so boring. Her fingers drummed a beat on her arm. "I have something for you to do."

"Yes?"

"Send out whatever troops you have—oh, don't look so surprised, of course I know you have troops—and attack Thirka."

Alan studied the map. "What is our objective there?"

Darci looked over her shoulder. "Draw the Aligerai out. If they act the way I think they will, then they'll do everything they can to help that meaningless town." She went back to watching the rain. "And if they don't, your troops have lost nothing. They might even gain something."

A slow smile crept over Alan's face. "It will be done, my queen. I'll start immediately."

Only the window saw Darci's eyes turn a darker shade of ebony and the feral grin that turned her lips. "Good."

∞

Dark clouds slunk over the horizon just as the sun began to set. The sky, tinged with crimson from the sun's dying waves, gave over its domain to the darkness. The townspeople of Thirka watched from their unprotected village while an army of some one thousand men marched closer.

The people gathered in the square, bickering and fighting over what to do. Nimiander stayed out of the press and dragged her brother with her. She fought her way out of the crowd toward the side of the square. Glints of steel and weaponry shone between the houses as she passed. She cursed. "This was the worst timing ever," she said to her brother.

The younger man leaned against the shop at his back. "You know we can't disobey Mother's orders. Imagine the thrashing we'd get back home if we did. She said the mage would be here now, and so here we are." He sniffed. "Deal with it."

Nimiander cuffed him over the head. "Don't talk back to your big sister." She saw the mayor of the town get up on the fountain's steps and begin to speak. "Now shut up and listen."

Finally the people decided a runner should go to the Awle house in the hope that help could be found there. In the meantime, as many people barricaded themselves inside homes and basements as they could. Clearly they hoped the army was only passing through.

Their hopes came to ruin when fire arrows rained down on the first houses.

Sita sat at the kitchen table, but she was barely awake. Her head slumped against her chest, and a dream captured her mind.

She was in the gray mist again, sitting in the same chair as before. Her dress this time was just as simple, just as elegant, but white instead of blue. Her wings curved around behind her over her shoulders.

A man stood before her, clearer than she had ever seen him. "Owen," she said. Sita stood. He held out his arms and she walked into his embrace. He felt warm and comfortable and sturdy. It felt like home. "Owen. You aren't just a dream."

"No, Sita. No. I'm real. I swear."

She raised her head. His wings stretched to wrap around her, and she shivered at the feeling of foreign feathers on her skin. "Where are you? You're clearer than before. You're more real in the dream than ever."

His gray eyes pulled her in deeper. She felt herself getting lost in those eyes, but she didn't care. "I'm almost to you. I'm coming. Then we can be together."

Sita smiled, and he smiled in return. The warmth, and promise, of his smile made her stomach flip. An instinct ran through her head. "You aren't just looking for me, are you?"

His smile faded. "No. I'm looking for someone else, too. But please don't ask me anything more about it right now."

She nodded. "All right." A question popped into her mind. "Owen, do you have any family?"

The air of her dream crackled with tension. Owen's face froze. "Why do you ask?"

"I was just curious."

He pursed his lips. "Please don't ask me that. Not now. Let's talk about something else."

Confused, she nodded and smiled again. "Fine. Then as long as you're coming to me soon, I know what I want to talk about."

Sita stretched up on her toes to reach his mouth. He leaned down and touched his lips to hers. She sank into the kiss, sank deeper into the feeling. His kiss deepened until she felt her knees begin to shake with the effort of holding herself upright. She broke off the kiss and gasped for air. Owen's fingers ran down her cheek, through her hair, and he kissed her again.

The house buzzed an alarm in her mind. It yanked Sita from the pleasures of the dream. She grumbled but hurried to the front doors and flung them open. She dimly registered the alarm of her friends, who ran down the stairs behind her. Sita could see a young man beating on the gate, and she hiked up her skirts to sprint down the path. Half-way there she could see his fists were bloody with the effort. "Help!" he rasped, his voice all but gone. "Please, open!"

Sita waved her hand and opened the gates. The bloodied boy fell inside, caught in Sita's arms. "What's happening? What's wrong?" she asked.

The boy coughed. "Soldiers . . . attacking Thirka . . . need help . . ."

Sita turned to see her friends behind her. Their wide eyes reflected their unease. Sita turned back to the boy. "Do you know how many soldiers?"

He shrugged. "Thousands? Maybe more . . ."

With a groan, Sita helped the boy to his feet. "All right, it's going to be OK. We'll go down and help. Can you make it up to the house?" The boy looked up at the mansion and nodded. "Good. Get yourself up there. Food is on the table in the kitchen, help yourself to it, and then I want you to rest. When I come back I expect to find you sleeping on a couch, all right?" The boy nodded again and stumbled up the path. Sita watched him go to be sure he wouldn't pass out half way, but once he began walking, the momentum carried him forward.

Satisfied, Sita then turned to her friends. "Think of this as a mission. We can't leave those people to defend themselves against an army that size. They're completely unprotected. We need to even the odds a little bit." All nodded, even Vanessa. Sita watched Vanessa a moment longer than she did the others, noted the angry fire in her eyes. All she could feel through the ring on her finger was anger, but not the focus of Vanessa's emotion. So Sita shrugged to herself and led the way down to the village.

Ari took the rear. She shook her head mournfully. "Even on vacation, we never get a real break." She sighed and ran after the others.

The small army had already worked its way through half the village. Roofs burned and the soldiers lit anything flammable on fire. A few houses went up in flames. The people who had barricaded themselves inside earlier in the day now fought to escape a fiery death. Children and animals ran everywhere. Their screams and shrill cries added to the confusion. The adults choked in the thickening smoke, unable to see. Many ran straight into the enemy to be impaled on swords and pikes.

Roxie was near tears when they stopped on the hill above the town and saw the devastation. Even from that distance the sounds of strife were clear. Black smoke wafted into their faces to sting their nostrils and make their eyes burn. Sita swiped at her watery eyes. She didn't want to think about the smells—it was possible people burned below.

Sita stood in front of them, a general studying the field of battle. She watched only a few minutes before she turned her back to the chaos. "Roxie, call as many of the animals as you can. Send them against the soldiers still outside town. Ari, fly first over the army and see how many there are. Stay out of range of arrows. Come tell me and then go help Roxie."

Sita angled toward Vanessa. "Vanessa, get up as many plants as you can. Make them big and wild. Tell them to go after any person wearing an army uniform in or outside the village."

"What will you be doing, then?" Vanessa asked. Her chin jutted out in a mulish way.

Sita ignored the look and turned back to town. "I'll be looking for the leader of this mess and try to get some information. Then I'm taking out the officers. Hopefully this will all be enough to make them leave." Her friends nodded. Sita unfurled her wings and stretched them to the dark sky. "OK, go!"

They split up. Sita and Ari took to the air while Roxie and Vanessa headed into the woods. Sita flew with Ari for a time, then flew off to look for the commander. Ari came back soon enough to meet Sita in mid-air. "It's bigger than we thought!" she shouted. "There's got to be almost three thousand men!"

The two women hovered in the air and watched the massacre progress. The townspeople had picked up any weapon they could find and fought back, but they were no match for trained soldiers. Roxie's animals accomplished some sabotage, but Vanessa's plants did very little against the men. Sita snarled at the feeble attempt Vanessa made but set the anger aside for the moment. "Why are that many men coming against one town? They can't possibly expect to gain much from this."

Ari shook her feathered head. "I don't know. I just tried to count them. About half are mounted, which I think is weird, but that's just me. I'll see if Roxie can get control of their horses." Ari flapped away to the right to search out Roxie.

Sita looked for the leader, but he kept himself notably absent. In frustration, Sita took aim for any officer she could find. Purple streams of magic poured from the sky like lightning with each attack she offered. She didn't know if the men died or were merely disabled, but at least they were unconscious, and that was what mattered.

She was about to aim again when Ari came flapping back. "The soldiers almost found Vanessa and Roxie! They've both pulled back up to the hill. I can't do very much without Roxie to back me up, so I'm going to join them."

Cursing, Sita flew behind Ari's falcon form back up to the hills, trying not to breathe in any of the acrid smoke. The others were just getting to the top, their clothes singed and dirt all over. Sita landed and looked them over. "Everyone OK?" Silent nods all around.

The four young women stood on the hill, tired and bruised, and watched the soldiers swarm the town. Vanessa walked over to Sita, who stood in front of them all, shaking, her hands clenched. "Come on, Si. Let's go home. We can't help them now, there are too many soldiers for us to take on." She laid a hand on Sita's shoulder. "Come on. You can't help them. We have to leave." She let her hand slide off Sita's back as she turned toward the distant hills behind them, turning her back on the town. The others sighed and began to follow.

Sita gathered every last bit of nerve and courage she possessed. She stood her ground, hands clenched, as the others turned to leave. "I'm going back down there."

Vanessa whirled around. "What! You can't!" She shoved back through her friends until she reached Sita's side and shoved the other girl around to face her. "Are you crazy? You can't help them now! Let's just go home before one of us gets killed!"

"I'm going back." Sita shrugged off Vanessa's grip. "I will not leave those people to die when I can help them."

"But you can't! You don't have that kind of power! You can't help them, Sita!"

Frustrated, Sita turned to face Vanessa again. Vanessa took an involuntary step back, then another.

Sita's eyes began to glow a deep violet. Her hair whipped in a wind that didn't exist, and her lips curled back in a feral snarl. "Wanna bet on that?" she growled. Vanessa took another few steps back. The other two stood their ground but a tinge of fear laced their eyes and they fought to keep their expressions neutral.

Vanessa swallowed. "No."

"Good." The snarl disappeared but the power remained. "I will *never* abandon people who need me." The eyes focused on Vanessa again. "Unlike you."

"Wh-what do you mean?"

Sita growled deep in her throat. "I know what you're capable of, Vanessa. That meager attempt of raising the plants to help those people was disgraceful, and far below what you're capable of." She reached out and grasped Vanessa's neck in both hands. Vanessa squeaked. Her own hands scratched and scrabbled at Sita's grasp. The others only watched in painful silence. Sita leaned closer. "We rely on each other. That half-assed attempt at an attack was like feeding us to the enemy. If you ever betray us like that again, I'll kill you myself."

She unfurled her wings and sped down to the town. Her friends waited on the hilltop for whatever would happen next.

Down below the hills, the townspeople scurried everywhere and tried to fend off the second and then the third waves of soldiers that charged through town. Swords flashed in the firelight, and the townspeople screamed over and over again.

Nimiander crouched against a wall, hidden from common sight. Her brother lay beside her, bloodied at the hip. "You'll live, brother. Just don't get hurt again, OK?" He nodded with a grimace set on his face. She raised her sword and looked out from their hiding place. "You know, we picked a really bad time to visit this town," she said sidelong to her brother. "We should have waited a few more days near home, started our journey later. We'll never find this girl." Frustrated, she banged her hand on the wall. "I told Mother she didn't exist. What a waste of time."

But then Nimiander heard the swoosh of wings in the air above her. She peeked outside and gasped. "Brother! Brother, it's her! We found her!" she cried.

Outside her hiding place stood Sita, wings extended, sheathed from head to toe in her violet power. Nimiander tried to look closer, but without success. The young woman stood in the middle of the road with her hands limp and an almost serene expression on her face as she stood still. The chaos flowed and ebbed around her as if shunted off to the sides by her gift. Sita turned her head, and Nim froze. A gasp escaped her lips. *Her eyes . . . her eyes glow! They're purple! How is that possible?*

Sita never saw Nimiander or her brother. She never saw any of the townspeople around her. Never heard the chaos, never smelled the smoke. Her focus dwindled to one thing. She glared around her and spread her magic out to carpet the ground. She waited and let the people run past, not even registering their cries of fear when they saw her. Her wings fluttered in rage.

A small voice in the back of her head echoed through her mind. It almost broke her concentration when she finally heard its words. *You and Darci are cut from the same cloth. Her power kills. You can not escape this fact. You are just like her. Your power is just like hers. Let it consume you, let it kill . . . * But Sita brushed it back. *I will* never *listen to you! I am not like Darci! I am protecting these people from those soldiers, who will rape and pillage and murder. I am not like Darci.*

The violet power intensified as the enemy came further inside the town. When they were in a prime position, Sita lifted her head. Her lips parted, and she grinned.

Nim shivered. *I've never seen anyone look so wild.*

A harsh wind buffeted Nim, causing her to cry out. She saw Sita stiffen at the sound. "Listen to me!" the mage shouted, her voice magnified by hundreds to boom into the ears of all the townsmen. "Listen! I will erase this enemy from your land, but you must trust me not to harm any of you. Stay in your homes. Stay with your families. Do not fear."

The wind returned, stronger than before, but it didn't touch Nim. Amazed, she watched as the wind played with Sita's hair and feathers and twisted her clothing around her slim frame. Sita smiled again. The light in her eyes shone brighter. As the enemy drew closer, so her power grew.

Up on the hilltop, Sita's friends heard her voice. They shivered and shrank back further toward the safety of the hills, climbing onto a taller rise for a better view. Roxie squinted. "What's that?" she asked, pointing to the center of town.

Ariene followed her finger. "I'm not sure. It looks like a mini sun, though, doesn't it?"

Vanessa felt a chill run up and down her spine. Dizziness swamped her, and she fought it back enough that the pounding in her head retreated some. Annoyed with her magic, she snapped at her friends. "She'd better hurry up. I'm getting cold out here. And those soldiers are gaining on the town."

The edge of Sita's magic stopped just outside the town's walls. She gathered her power and waited for the moment to strike. Many of the soldiers, at least a full thousand, were already inside the walls, but she wanted to get all of them, even the ones outside.

Finally, she felt the first line of soldiers outside touch the edge of her magic.

For a single, solitary moment, there was absolute quiet—and then Sita screamed and let loose her rage.

From above in the hills, the detonation of Sita's anger looked like the eruption of a huge land mine. A great plume of purple rose from the center of town and sent shockwaves outward. After the initial shock, Sita's power began to swirl around the center, like a miniature violet typhoon.

The soldiers fell to their knees, weeping for mercy. Sita's power grew and spread through the town. Enemy soldiers slammed into walls and wells to slump to the ground dead. City fountains became graves, walls cracked with the force of the bodies' impacts.

Outside the walls, violet magic goaded the animals into a stampede. Men were tossed off their panicked horses and fell to the mercy of stampeding hooves. Their screams echoed around the town and up into the hills. The noise could be heard for miles around, with the people in neighboring towns roused from their beds to quake in unexplainable fear. But Sita showed no mercy to the soldiers. A wave of her hand sent a second wave of power out beyond the walls. Any soldier that still lived succumbed to that wave, overwhelmed by the onslaught of magic.

A single finger flick brought the captain straight to her. The captain fell to his knees. "Please, mistress, goddess, lady, do not kill me!"

Sita looked down on him, her violet eyes cold. "Do you deny these people would have been murdered?"

The captain shook at the sound of her midnight voice. "No, lady."

"Then why should I spare you?"

The captain only bowed his head and wept.

Sita growled. "However, today is not your day to die, captain. I want you to carry word back to the people you serve. Tell them to leave the innocent alone. If they want a fight, they know where to find me. But leave the bystanders and the innocent victims of this fight out of their schemes, or they will answer to me!"

The captain swallowed and crawled backward from her. When she showed no signs of stopping him, he scrambled to his heels and ran as fast as he could. She followed him with her power as far as the outskirts of town, where she saw him catch a horse and ride away.

Satisfied, she allowed the power around town to fade. Sita allowed the magic in her to dwindle until it was all captured inside again, and she retreated back to the hills.

Nim would later tell her mother it was like being in the center of the famous hurricanes on the coast, or at the middle of a swirling sun. None of the magic or the wind touched Nim, but she could see it, and feel its tingle on her skin when it identified her as a friend. She watched the mage talk to the soldier and then send him on his way. Then the mage took to the air.

Nimiander watched her go, awed despite herself. "I can't believe . . ." she whispered to herself. "I can't believe it . . ." The woman watched as Sita flew back into the hills. Then she gathered herself together and shook her brother to his feet. "Come, brother, it's safe now. We have to go back home. We have some news to tell Mother."

Sita labored back to the hill, her body limp. She felt the coma threatening to overtake her, and she fought to reach the hill before it did. When she finally reached the hilltop, she set down one slow wing beat at a time, and collapsed.

Ari caught her before she hit the ground. Sita's eyes fluttered open. "Ari?" she said. Ari strained to hear the weary voice and leaned closer. "Can you take me home?"

"Of course." Ari picked Sita up carefully and began to make a slow retreat.

Roxie stood another moment, watching the town. The army was gone now, but their bodies would be a problem. What would a town that small do with all those bodies? Roxie tugged on Vanessa's sleeve. "Hey, do you think you could get rid of the soldiers' bodies?"

The other woman turned back to the town as well and studied it with a critical eye. Then she reached out with her power and sent a command into the ground and surrounding plants. She turned away. Roxie waited, making sure all of the soldiers' bodies were swallowed up by the plants and earth before the townspeople even saw them decay. Then she followed the others back to the mansion, her head lowered and shoulders slumped. She just missed Vanessa, who waited by the side of the trail, hidden by the foreign branches a tree.

Vanessa watched them go, her lip curling. She looked back at the town. It was calmer now, though wailing drifted up on the wind and made her shiver. The dizziness of using her power earlier made her angry, made her hate the others, who looked so strong and unfazed even after this fight. She turned and walked back to the mansion, her fists curled into claws.

Chapter Thirty-One
The Pain of Heartbreak

The group spent the next two days resting, healing the injuries to their bodies and their souls. Sita stayed in bed and slept most of the time. She fell so deep into the coma that she never heard the doors slam when Ka'len and Robert walked in the day after the incident, both demanding to know what happened.

Robert sat on Sita's bed. His fingers rested on her wrist while he checked her pulse and her breathing. Physically, he could find nothing wrong with her except a few minor scrapes and bruises. He looked deeper inside to see how low the wellspring of her power had ebbed. But even as he studied it, he could see that the well was filling back up. He came out of trance and smiled at Roxie and Ari, who hovered nearby. "She'll be fine," he said. "She just needs to rest."

"But what's wrong with her?" Ari asked, her forehead creasing in concern.

Robert shrugged. "Nothing, really. She just used up a lot of power in a very short amount of time."

The girls' mouths became giant Os. "That can really happen?" said Roxie. "I thought that was just a myth. That's never happened to me."

Rob wagged a finger at her. "Now, now, Roxie, lying hardly becomes you. It has definitely happened to you, just not on this scale. Think back to your training sessions. Weren't you tired and hungry afterward?"

"Ye-e-e-s," she replied, remembering. "I always felt drained. But nothing so bad that would make me pass out."

"Exactly." Robert stood up and ushered them out the door. "It's all about degree. You were only using a small amount of power during training, so you were only a little tired. The fatigue is proportional to the amount of power used." He nodded his head in the direction of Sita's door. "She almost depleted her power during the fight, so she's of course going to be very, very tired. None of you can function very well if your magic is drained. It supports your own normal physical strength." He paused. "Does that make sense?"

Both smiled. "As if you ever make sense?" Ari said.

Rob chuckled and headed down the stairs. "Come on, then. All this talk of fatigue is making me hungry. Let's get some lunch."

Sita woke three days after the Thirka incident. She opened her eyes to see Roxie sitting beside her bed, face down in the blankets and weeping hard. With effort Sita raised her left hand and set it on Roxie's head. "Rox? What's wrong?"

Roxie's head bounced up. "Si! I didn't hear you wake up!" She swiped at her tear-streaked face. "How are you feeling?"

"Don't change the subject," Sita said. She winced when she heard her scratchy voice. "What's wrong?"

The redhead bowed her head. "I was just thinking . . . why us? Why can't we be normal? We can't even live in our homes without being attacked or ridiculed or ostracized."

"Ooh, big S.A.T. word."

"Seriously, Sita. I'm kind of tired of being forced to hide."

Sita struggled to sit up. Roxie lifted her and stuffed a lumpy pillow behind her back. "We don't have to hide, you know. We could walk around like this all the time."

"Do you know how many doctors and scientists and people like that would love to study us if we did that? I don't think so. I value my freedom, and becoming a lab rat is not my idea of freedom, thank you."

Sita chuckled. "Well, then we could give it all up. Or keep hiding. There really aren't too many choices in this, though." She began to sound stronger, her speech no longer as labored.

"So . . . so what are we supposed to do? Just stop using our powers? We just, we just sit on the couch, go to parties, be 'normal' college kids?" Roxie's hands flailed in the air. "Are you kidding me? Are you fucking kidding me?" Sita remained silent. "And you know we can't just stop using our gifts. They're a part of who we are. Not using them is like drowning."

Tangible pain seeped through in Roxie's voice. "Why us? Why not someone else? Look at you, Sita, you've been lying here in bed for three days, and for *what*? Saving people is great and all, but why do *we* have to be the ones to do it? Why us, when it costs us so much?" Another tear managed to slip from Roxie's wide eyes. "Why do *we* have to do this, have these responsibilities. Why can't we be normal?"

Sita touched Roxie's wet face. "Sweetie, we're *never* going to be normal. Even if we didn't have our magic. We'd still be freaks." Both of them smiled. "And I'd rather have my powers, thank you. Makes self-defense so much easier if some sleazy guy decides to get a little too handsy." Roxie laughed and swiped at her eyes. "Now, help me get out of this bed. I'm tired of lying around doing nothing."

Roxie laughed again and helped Sita up, both of their moods brighter than before. They toddled down the great stairs to find Sita her breakfast.

As the week-and-a-half of spring break progressed, tensions cooled, tempers calmed, and the girls finally appeared to take a real break. Ka'len and Robert barely made an appearance after that third day, except for an occasional hello at a meal when they stopped by the house. Roxie and Ariene decided to practice on their disappearing acts and increasing their *boulesis*. Only Vanessa and Sita had nothing concrete to do. Sita explored more of her house by delving into the dark recesses of the library, the tower, and the Vault. She normally had a dreamy look on her face, and when asked about it, she would say only that she was thinking. Vanessa, on the other hand, wandered around aimlessly, not satisfied with anything she found to do.

She was wandering down by the front gates one day, halfway through the break. Sunshine shone overhead, but there was a threat of clouds on the horizon, just above the trees. Thinking there might be rain soon, she began to turn back to the house when she stopped, pulled up short by an odd feeling.

Someone approached the mansion, someone unfamiliar and male. The ground told her that much, but it couldn't tell her who it was or why they were coming. So she waited.

A man broke through the tree line at the edge of the road. He wore black pants and a loose blue tunic. Dark black hair flowed just to his shoulders. Vanessa's breath caught in her throat—this man had the most beautiful gray eyes she had ever seen, as gray and stormy as the clouds rolling just past the horizon.

The man approached the gate at an easy amble. His mouth stretched into a wide smile when he saw her. "Hello. Are you the lady of this house?"

Vanessa nearly melted on the spot. That voice, that gorgeous voice, was smooth and seductive, and she could tell that this quality was entirely unintentional. She tried to pull herself together and steady her breathing, but it was so hard when all she wanted to do was melt. "No, I'm not. I'm here on vacation with my friends. Sita owns this house."

His gray eyes shone brighter at the mention of her name. "Sita? I think I know her. Can you let me in?"

The girl shook her head, unable to break away from his eyes. "No, I'm sorry, I can't, only Sita can let people in. It being her house and all." Vanessa felt her heart beat faster, and she felt unable to control even the blood flowing in her veins. Her cheeks turned bright red. "I can get her, though, if you'd like."

The stranger smiled. "That would be great."

Vanessa stood away from the gate and rubbed the ring Sita had made. She narrowed her concentration to the web of rings and followed the thread connecting her to Sita. Giving the thread a little mental tug, she saw Sita look up and mentally follow the thread back down to the gates. Vanessa turned her head so Sita could look at the man standing there. She felt instead of heard Sita's squeal of excitement and wonder. With a scowl, Vanessa broke the connection and turned back to the man. "She's on her way."

They didn't have to wait long. Sita came barreling down the path, blue skirts flying behind her and threatening to trip her up. She was barely out of breath when she reached the gate, her hair tousled, cheeks rosy. "Thanks for getting me, Vanessa," Sita said. She couldn't take her eyes off the man. Vanessa, who hadn't stopped staring at him, knew how she felt. "Owen?" Sita asked.

The man grinned and made Vanessa's heart skip a few beats. "Yes, Sita. I finally found you." He set a hand on the locked gate. "Will you let me in?"

Sita stepped closer, but she paused just as she was about to touch the lock. Her face lost the dreamy quality and became serious. "Wait . . . you've infiltrated almost all of my dreams for the past few months. You're part of the reason my boyfriend broke up with me a month ago. And now here you are, standing at my front gates, when no one else knows I'm in Corá. How did you find me?"

"You dream more vividly in Corá." He shrugged. "It was easier to track you. And I happened to be here instead of on Earth."

The conversation, so intimate despite its seriousness, jarred Vanessa into jealous action. "Sita, I don't think you can trust him. If he can cross the planes, how do we know he's not from Imbri Mors? He could be a plant."

Sita shot her a humorous glance. "Well, if he's a *plant*, you would know, wouldn't you?" Vanessa blinked, not understanding, until Sita scuffed the grass with one foot and Vanessa got the joke. She chuckled while Sita looked back to the man. "I need to know if you are who you say you are. I think I can use our connection to look into your mind. Owen, open your mind to me."

Owen sat down on the ground. Dust and dirt immediately clung all over his immaculate trousers. "In a heartbeat." He closed his eyes and lowered all shields, a smile to his lips. "Though you should know, I'm completely open out here now. If I get attacked, I'll blame you."

The girls glanced at each other, trying to decide if he was joking. Finally Vanessa shrugged and Sita turned back to the stranger. She closed her eyes and shrouded her face in a blank expression that reflected the level of her concentration. Silence descended on the three young people with only the constant wind through the trees as company.

Vanessa watched Owen's face contort at times, and Sita broke into a sweat. Concerned, she was about to touch Sita's shoulder when the other girl broke from the spell. Sita reached out and touched the gate. "Come in," she said over her gasps.

Immediately Owen rushed through the gate. Vanessa could tell he had put his shields back up, since she couldn't so much as read an emotion on the surface of his mind now. She was about to ask if they were OK when Owen gathered Sita into his arms and held her close. Sita leaned back to stare into his eyes. "It's about time you found me," she whispered. He only smiled and pressed his lips to hers.

Vanessa's world seemed to have lost its bottom. Her knees felt like jelly, her stomach did flip-flops. The clouds felt like they hung over her head and cast all of her world into shadow. Breath that had come easily now drew labored and harsh. Before either one of the lovers could see her, Vanessa fled up the path into the mansion.

Ariene and Roxie were in the sitting room when someone came barreling in through the front double doors, not even bothering to close them behind her. They saw Vanessa sprint up the stairs, tears streaming down her face. "'Nessa?" Ari called. The only reply was Vanessa's door slamming shut.

Roxie set aside her book on the couch beside Ari's chair. "What's wrong?"

Ari shook her head and strolled to the front doors. "Don't know," she said. Roxie followed. They both stopped in front of the open doors and saw in the distance what had made Vanessa run. Ari winced. "Uh oh. I don't think this one's going to end well."

Rox looked out the door over her shoulder, studying the kissing couple. "Yeah, I can guess. Vanessa jealous?"

"Yep. I hope she didn't fall for him the moment she saw him. That'll just make it worse."

"No kidding." Roxie stared up the stairs toward the second floor while Ari closed the doors. "I think it's just better to hope that no one gets killed this time."

Ari sighed. "I think so, too."

The rain broke late that night. Most of the women awoke to the crashing and rumbling of thunder overhead and the lashing of rain on the windows, and so they did not sleep well at all. The next day, everyone stayed inside and tried to find ways of amusing themselves that didn't involve the outdoors. Sita introduced Owen. Vanessa sequestered herself in her room.

Owen followed Sita around the mansion. She took him everywhere, and they were both disappointed that the rain kept them from the grounds and the tower's roof. Sita gave him the full tour: the lower sitting rooms, studies, music room, and kitchen, the armory and ballroom on the first floor, the second floor and third floor rooms, the library, and the sitting rooms and miniature dining rooms of the East and West wings. Both wings sat at diagonals off the sides of the house to stretch far back behind the main wing. The library was Owen's favorite, and was perfectly content to sit with Sita for hours in the library. Owen took particular delight in watching Sita's face light up with each new thing she showed him, and her happiness filled him with joy.

They ended up in one of the tower rooms. "I'm pretty much the only one allowed in here, even though there aren't any magical locks on the door," she said. The room they stood in was almost empty. Only a table and chairs stood inside, and a carpet decorated the floor. Sita sank onto the carpet.

Owen followed. He loved watching her move. "Maybe you should think about putting a lock on, then. This could be your private sanctuary."

She smiled. "Maybe." He leaned against the wall and pulled her to him. "I'm glad you found me." Sita leaned her head on his shoulder and chest, one hand against his heart.

He grasped that hand and kissed it. "I'm glad, too."

"Why were you looking for me?"

His smile faded. She was getting close to subjects he really didn't want to discuss. "I was looking for other people like us. People with wings. I was able to search peoples' dreams. I found you by accident, but once I found you, I knew I had to find you. When I finally talked to you, I just knew. I fell in love with you."

Owen felt her smile against his chest. "Do you have any family?" she asked.

"No," he said. He hoped his tone conveyed his distress. "Not anymore."

Sita sat up, and he sighed. He wanted her warmth back against him. "What do you mean? What happened?"

He bit his lip. "Do you have family?"

"Yeah, I have a sister, and an aunt and uncle, though I don't really talk to my cousins much." She tucked loose hair behind her ear. "I love my sister, though. She wants to move here."

"Well, I don't have family anymore, that's all."

She sighed. Her eyes penetrated deep into his before she lay back down on his chest. "I wish you would tell me. This is the second time I've asked, and the second time you've refused to answer. If we're going to be together, I should know more about you."

They sat in silence after that. Owen pulled her onto him so her body lay cushioned on his and he wrapped his arms around her.

Sita waited. He could feel the chill of her displeasure radiate from her body. Finally he sighed and caved. "I had family," he said. His voice remained quiet and blank. "I gave them up."

"Why?"

"They . . . I told them about my wings. And my magic. They despised me. I ran away, years ago."

"Any siblings?"

"One brother. Both parents were alive when I left. Last time I checked, they still were. I could care less whether my brother is dead or alive. But I want to find him."

She raised her head. "What do you mean?"

Owen closed his eyes. "When I left, my brother vowed revenge on me, for 'destroying our family,' as he says. I want to find him and clear things up. But he disappeared."

Sita studied his eyes. He knew she didn't believe him about wanting to find his brother for any good reason, but she believed the rest. "I'll help you, if I can."

He grinned down at her. "Thanks. But I think this one's on me." He decided it was time to change the subject. "Though there is another way to make me very happy."

She laughed and raised herself up carefully onto hands and knees. She stretched up and kissed him. Thoughts of his brother and family slipped away into the depths of his mind as his hands explored and her kisses deepened.

Sita pulled the both of them down to the large, formal dining room behind and to the left of the main stairs for lunch around noon. Roxie had the idea of pulling out the finer cutlery and using them at least once during their vacation. With Sita's permission, she set it up for lunch, and dinner would be served in the formal room that night. Everyone showed up except for Vanessa, who still hid in her room. Roxie fidgeted and glanced at the stairs a few times. "Should we take some food up to her or something?" she asked when they sat down to eat.

Ari shook her head. "Nah. If she's hungry, she can come down and be civilized instead of pouting up in her room. Besides, she has two feet, let her get it herself if she wants it." She dished out portions of ham onto her sandwich. "And I'm not exactly inclined to be nice to her right now." Sita's mouth twitched downward but she stayed silent.

The others simply continued eating, their mood palpably dimmer. Ari mentioned that the rain looked to be letting up. They all brightened, and soon began a loud conversation.

Sita felt through the connection of their rings that Vanessa was sitting on the stairs and listening. It also transferred the other girl's anger, so intense Sita thought they should all be on fire right now. She glanced at her friends but no one else appeared to have noticed. Sita felt Vanessa sneak into the kitchen, filch some meat and bread from their lunch, and sneak back up the stairs. Owen slipped his hand under the table and found hers to give her hand a squeeze. She turned and smiled at him. He grinned at her before returning to his enormous stacked sandwich. With a chuckle, she watched him eat. She heard the chatter of her friends only as background noise while she watched her new boyfriend.

Lunch was almost over when Sita began to feel a sense of unease at the base of her neck. Her skin felt clammy and the hair on her arms stood on end. Owen noticed and was about to reach out to her again when Sita stood up. "I'll be right back," she said to the group. They looked at her in surprise, but she left before they could question her.

Satisfied they wouldn't follow, Sita hurried into the hall and up the wide stairs. She turned left and strode down the hall to Vanessa's closed door. A sense of foreboding grew stronger and a chill of nerves ran from her head to the base of her spine. Raising her hand, she was about to knock on the door when it was yanked open and Vanessa glared out at her. Sita jumped.

"Hey, Vanessa," she said, trying to figure out what unnerved her. Vanessa only stared, her blue eyes cold and unforgiving. Awkward, Sita stood there and clasped her hands behind her back. She looked away from Vanessa's gaze. "Look, I just wanted to see if you were OK. Are you hungry? You can come down and eat with us if you want."

Vanessa blinked. She grabbed a jacket nearby and pushed Sita out of the doorway. Sita scrambled back out of the way as Vanessa closed the door. "Come to the fields with me, Sita. I want to talk to you."

Sita forced herself to breathe and tried to think of some other suggestion. Nothing came to mind. So nodding her assent, Sita followed Vanessa down the stairs and out the front door. She clamped down on the instinct to turn and run back to the house and reminded herself that Vanessa was still her friend.

They walked out into the fields. Vanessa led Sita out almost to the trees on the far side of the mansion. A small hill now stood between Sita and the house. She glanced over her shoulder and saw nothing but wet green grass shimmering in the drizzle—the house disappeared behind the hill. Thunder cracked overhead, and lightning brightened up the horizon.

While Sita was distracted by the noise, Vanessa spun around and threw a right hook at Sita's face. It connected with her jaw and sent Sita flying backward to land in a heap on the ground. Pain flared and grew in her cheek and jaw until she felt as if her entire face were one throbbing mass of pain. "What the hell was that for?" Sita said as she massaged her jaw. She got to her feet just as the skies broke.

At once they were drenched, their clothes stuck to their bodies in uncomfortable ways. Vanessa pulled off the jacket and threw it aside. "That was for humiliating me in front of the others!" she shouted. "We're gonna have it out, right here, right now!" She saw Sita's hesitation and laughed, her eyes shining in malice. "What, are you afraid of me? The great and powerful mage is afraid of *me*?"

Sita lost her hesitation. Her face hardened and she glared at her roommate. Lightning struck again, much nearer this time. It threw Sita's face into relief and made her skin as white as marble. "No, I'm not afraid of you. But we'll fight without magic, or we won't fight at all. Deal?"

The other blond shrugged, eager to be on with the fight. "No magic. Deal."

Then the fight began.

Vanessa closed with Sita, throwing as many punches as she could without regard for where they landed. Sita held up her arms and tried to avoid the blows. She landed a few hits of her own on Vanessa's body when the other girl took too long to strike. After Sita got a fifth hit in, Vanessa let loose, yelling in incoherent rage as she did. She tripped Sita and followed her to the ground, tearing at soaked hair, clothes, skin. She kicked and hit any part of Sita's body that was unprotected. Blood welled on Sita's arms from Vanessa's scratches to blend with the rain and flow off her body. Sita kicked up at Vanessa's back and legs, her blows connecting in enough places that she could feel Vanessa's attacks weakening.

Finally, Sita had just enough of an opening to reach up and hit Vanessa hard in the face. Vanessa let go, shrieking in time with the thunder overhead. Sita clawed her way to her feet again in the slippery mud and grass.

"Why the hell do you hate me so much?" Sita screamed. It was hard to hear anything over the pounding of the rain on the earth's bare back. She staggered from pain. "What have I ever done to you?"

Vanessa staggered as well and now sported a bloody nose. She panted and pushed her tangled curtain of hair out of her eyes. "I hate you . . . because you're better than me," she said between growls of thunder.

"What?" Sita shouted.

"I hate you!" Vanessa screamed back. "I hate you because you're *better* than me! You've got a great family, you're smart and pretty and always so damn *nice*. And you're powerful, you have more power than I could *ever* hope to have, no matter how hard I work!" Her voice was raw now, grating around the blood trickling down her face and into her mouth. "I hate you because you have people who love you no matter what. You have a great boyfriend, and awesome teachers, and all that *damn* power!"

Sita interrupted. "You hate me because you're *jealous*? This is all because of *jealousy*?" she shrieked.

Vanessa's eyes glinted cold and hard. "As I said, I hate you because you have everything I want. You've never really been my friend. I don't hate my friends."

Sita shook her head. "I guess you're right. I can't be friends with someone who hates me."

"I want you gone," said Vanessa. "I want you gone!" Sita, taking the opportunity to catch her breath, didn't bother to reply.

Vanessa rushed at Sita, screaming and her fists ready for contact. Sita stood still. *I want her gone from my room and the group.* Time seemed to slow. She watched Vanessa grow larger in her vision, hate-filled blue eyes burning into hers. *But Vanessa . . . she wants me dead . . . she knows it's the only way she can win.*

The strengthening rain lashed at both women as Vanessa attacked and Sita dodged, each looking for the opening that would end it. A cold wind pushed and pulled at them *She's getting close to breaking our fight rules and using her magic!* A tear slid down her face, hidden in the rain. *I don't want to hurt her!*

Sita threw a punch at Vanessa's midsection. The impact sent Vanessa flying to land hard in sticky mud. Still, she climbed to her feet with a groan. A rumble of thunder roared overhead and deafened them both. Lightning flickered nearby and the sky screamed once more as the light disappeared. *This is getting dangerous,* Sita thought. She shoved her drenched hair out of her eyes. *Looks like I might have to end it after all.*

As if the thought had conjured them, Robert and Ka'len appeared on the field, their faces as blank and still as stone. Ka'len stood by Sita while Robert tried to calm Vanessa down. He ended up freezing her body when she tried to hit him in the groin.

Rob walked back to Sita, trailing Vanessa behind him with his magic. "Let's get out of here," he shouted over the rain's percussion. Ka'len nodded and grabbed Sita's shoulder. Both men transported the fighters back with them.

They landed in the entrance hall of the mansion. Water dripped from all four. Vanessa's eyes fixed on Sita—the only part of her body she could move thanks to Rob's binding. Her normally clear blue eyes were full of red hate. Sita met those frightening eyes. "Vanessa," she asked. "Why don't you just go and join Darci? At least then you could fight me and try to destroy me without destroying the others with your hatefulness." Sita spun on her heel and climbed the stairs. When she reached her own room, she locked the door behind her.

Rob released Vanessa. He watched her stumble without sympathy. "What the *hell* were you doing, Vanessa?" His voice was low, soft, a growl that frightened anyone who heard it. "I know very well that *you* started it and how you were going to finish it! The entire fight was written over that field for anyone to see." He crossed his arms over his chest and leaned closer, his growl malicious. "Would you mind explaining, Vanessa?"

Vanessa looked away from him, her mouth thinned into a stubborn line. Her fists clenched and unclenched—her rage was barely controlled. Her body visibly shook from the intensity of it.

"Well?" Rob shouted. Ka'len remained silent. Both men knew the other girls watched and listened, but Ka'len's quick thinking kept them away and invisible due to his shielding. *Vanessa will not know her friends are watching, while they will be informed but out of the way,* thought Ka'len.

This time Vanessa answered. "I hate her. I hate her so much. I just . . . I just wanted to . . ." Her mouth twisted into an unattractive snarl. "I wanted to prove that I'm as good as she is. I'm better than her!" She shouted at the top of her lungs. The noise echoed back at them in the silent hall. "*I* should be the leader of our group, not *her*! I deserve it! I'm stronger, I'm prettier, I'm better . . ."

Robert stopped her with a magical gag, his eyes hard and unforgiving. Vanessa clawed at her mouth, her eyes wide in shock and she worked to breathe. "All I'm hearing from you right now is 'me, me, me.' You are all *partners*! You *must* work together! And you were, you were all doing so well!" He turned away from her, his soft voice floating over his shoulder. "If you cannot work as a team, then you cannot be *on* this team, am I clear? And *I* am the leader. I always have been." He began to walk down the hallway to his own room. "You have one night to decide if you can be part of this group or not. If not, you are to leave in the morning and you *will* be moved from the suite. Got it?"

Her silence was all the answer he was going to get. He continued walking until he disappeared up the stairs.

Ka'len stared at Vanessa a moment more and wondered which path she would choose. He planted thoughts in each of the watching girls' heads to make them go back to their own rooms. He made sure they were inside before he dropped his shield. Then he popped out of the room, as if he had never been there at all.

Vanessa was left to make her way to her own room, in a quiet hall, alone in a quiet, echoing room.

Vanessa was gone the next morning.

The house was quiet that day. Owen went into town to find something to brighten Sita's mood, and the others kept to themselves. Sita shut herself in her room and stayed there, not even coming down for breakfast. Ka'len had disappeared last night, and Rob was nowhere to be found in the morning. Both men had apparently taken their leave without saying good-bye.

There was no response that afternoon when Roxie knocked on Sita's door. She knocked again. No sound inside. Concerned, she tried the handle and pushed on the door. It opened. Roxie poked her head into Sita's room. *It's empty?* She withdrew, confused, and walked down the hall to Ari's room instead. She felt nothing from Sita through her ring—apparently, Sita had figured out a way to block her emotions from the rest when she really wanted to do so.

Ariene lay on her bed, spread-eagled on her back. Roxie walked in and plopped down on the soft comforter, jiggling Ari. "Have you seen Sita at all?" Ari blinked and fished a crumpled note from her pocket, which she handed to Roxie.

She took it and unfolded it Sita's scrawled writing decorated the page. She gawked at Ari. "Where was this? When did you get it?"

Ari shrugged. "I found it on her door. Maybe an hour ago," she said. She stared at the ceiling with blank eyes.

Geez, she's like a zombie! Roxie slapped her friend's arm. "And you didn't *tell* anyone?" she cried. "Sita went off to the top of some bloody mountain, by *herself*, she could *freeze* to death, and you don't *tell* anyone?" Her voice echoed behind her as she rushed from Ari's room, frantic. She grabbed her jacket and Sita's coat from the mud room off the kitchen. "If she's dead or injured, I'm blaming you, Ari!" she shouted, her voice bouncing off the walls and up the stairs.

Roxie grumbled, angry at both Ari and Sita for being stupid. She stopped and glared at the tiny Misty Mountains far away in the distance. *Now, which one is Sita on?* After a few more minutes of indecisive staring, she chose one. *I'll start with the tallest. Who knows, maybe I'll get lucky on the first try.* With a growl and a grimace, she clutched Sita's coat with one hand while she closed her eyes and willed herself to be at the top of Mount Nam, the tallest in the range.

A cruel and chilling wind tousled her hair. She opened her eyes to see the mountains around her and a speck far in the distance that must be the Grenol Hills and the mansion. Snowflakes fell slow and soft to the earth. She glanced around for Sita, but there was no sign of her. Snow crunched underneath her sneakers as she walked. "Sita?" Her voice echoed, unhelpful in its reply. "Sita! Are you here?"

Rox searched the peak while trying not to look down at the long fall. The icy wind began to sting her skin, even through her coat, and froze her lungs with each breath. She rubbed her arms. *I need to find her soon, or I'll freeze myself.* She rounded a blind corner and there she was, the gray rocks a perfect cover for Sita's still body. "Sita!" Roxie ran to her, slipping a little and getting snow in her shoes. "Sita, girl, didn't you hear me calling?"

Sita sat in the snow on the peak of Mount Nam, her arms clutched around her legs and her head on her knees. The bright wings folded around her made her blend into the whiteness of the snow. Roxie stepped closer to see there was a small circle around Sita completely devoid of snow, and she didn't appear to be cold. "Sita?" Roxie said, her voice almost lost in the whipping wind. Her hand reached out to rest on Sita's back.

"It's my fault," Sita said. "It's my fault our group is breaking, Rox."

Roxie knelt down beside her friend. She draped the jacket over her exposed shoulders. "It's not your fault, Si. You couldn't have stopped Vanessa. *She's* the one who couldn't deal." Sita reached up and touched Roxie's freezing hand. Her power warmed Roxie as well. More snow melted.

"It's my fault," Sita repeated. "I should have seen it, I should have stopped it."

"Why?" Roxie snapped. "Why should you have seen it?"

"Because I help lead when Rob isn't here. Leaders see those things! By missing Vanessa's pettiness and hatred, our group lost one more member. We can't afford to lose any more!"

"If *you* should have seen it, then we *all* should have seen it!" Roxie shouted, as much as to be heard above the wind as from anger. "We're a family, so sometimes we're blind to each other's faults!" She relented and eased over to lean against Sita's stiff feathers. "You can't blame yourself for Vanessa's mistakes, or for anyone else's. It was her choice, her actions. She knew the difference between right and wrong. And *that's* what makes the difference. As for Darci, that was no one's fault. It was . . ." her voice faltered. "It was in a way Darci's own weakness that took her from us. There was nothing we could do about that. Nothing."

Roxie sat beside Sita, her arm draped over Sita's back and glossy feathers. Sita put her head on Roxie's shoulder while salty tears escaped down her cheeks to be blown away on the uncaring wind. "But we're still broken, Rox. Our family is breaking," Sita whispered, her voice laced with enough power to be heard.

"I know." Roxie stood and held out her hand for Sita. Sita sighed and unfolded herself, her wings sweeping behind her before she took Roxie's hand. The sudden return of blood to Sita's knees made her sway. Roxie waited until Sita had hidden her wings and shrugged into her jacket before saying, "Let's get back." Sita nodded.

They disappeared in the howling wind and swirling snow.

∞

Darci sat at the enormous desk, her feet draped over the side of her chair. She fingered a dagger, watching how the dim light played over the blade. The white feather was still tucked behind her ear. Sandara and Alan sat in front of her on the other side of the desk. She grinned. They were tense.

"I want you to do something for me," Darci said. She looked at Alan sidelong, waiting for his response. Her lips parted in a feral grin.

Alan's face betrayed his struggle to remain calm, and his fingers found the amulet around his neck. "Anything, my queen. What do you require?"

Rolling her eyes, Darci sat up straight. "Oh, stop kissing my ass, Alan. I'm hardly a queen." Faint waves of black humor washed over the two professors as Darci chuckled. "But I do require something of you. I want you to devise a way to capture my old friends."

Sandara blinked. "Capture?" she asked. "Only capture, or kill as well?"

"If I wanted you to kill them, would I not have said I want you to kill them?" Darci's voice was too sweet, and dangerously soft, even with the multi-toned layer of her power added to it. "No, I want you to capture them only. Find out what they plan to do. If you can, keep them trapped for days, even weeks." She leaned back into the high leather chair, balancing the knife perfectly on one finger. "However, I don't think that will be possible. Sita is too powerful for either one of you to defeat."

Alan grimaced. "But my lady, how can she be so powerful? She couldn't even stop you . . ."

Darci slammed the knife on the table, her black eyes blazing. Alan shrunk back. "Do not question me!" she screeched. "She has power above the blue as well! She could snuff both of you out in a second, with ease, and barely scratch the surface of her power!" Satisfied that Alan was sufficiently cowed, she sat back in her chair. The dagger found her fingers again. "No, you couldn't hold her. I'm the only one strong enough to defeat her. And I will need to do so if we are to win anything. Her side will try to use her to their advantage much like you are trying to use me."

The two professors swallowed hard. Sandara blinked again and managed to keep her face stoic. Darci glanced over to her and saw her effort. She only nodded in approval of Sandara's attempt at stoicism.

"You will do as I ask. Capture and torture my 'friends.' Dismissed."

Chapter Thirty-Two
Trapped

Owen walked into his house. The blue paint on the outside looked just as chipped as it always did. The place had a familiar smell, like roses mixed with laundry detergent, that stuck with him. No one was home.

He shut and locked the door. The stairs looked freshly vacuumed, which meant his mother must have been in a bad mood last night. Owen tip-toed up the stairs in the silence of the house.

His room sat on the left side of the hallway, the door shut with a finality that always twisted his heart. He turned the doorknob and stepped inside.

It looked as it always did. Just as it had the day he'd left, except for the imprint of his mother's weight on his bedspread. The curtains continued to keep the window blind to what happened on the inside of this room.

The closet was closed as well. Owen opened it and pulled out a fresh shirt. He dropped his old, dirty shirt on the pile of clothes at the bottom. Those clothes had been sitting there for years, and his mother refused to touch them. She left everything as it was the day he left.

Owen glanced across the hall. That room was closed as well. He ignored the impulse to cross the hall and enter, but he needed to hurry up and get out of the house before any of this family decided to come home. He figured he had maybe another hour before his father returned home from work.

The duffel bag he carried with him lay on the floor. His journal was inside, along with a pen and a clean shirt from his closet. The comb in his bag needed to be replaced, as some of the teeth were missing. But he could get another at Sita's.

Owen stared around his old room. It looked cold and empty, despite all the possessions of his years spent here. There was nothing else he needed. But there was one last thing he wanted to do before he left for good.

He walked into his parents' room. It looked as cold and empty as his. Owen pulled out a feather tucked into his hair. The white feather gleamed in the scant light coming through the windows on the far side of the bed. He laid it on the bed covers.

Then he returned to his old room and pulled out a note from his pocket. His mother would read it, he knew. If she chose to show it to his father and sibling, then she would, but he didn't care as much about those two. His father hated him for his wings, and his brother . . . his brother couldn't understand Owen's reasons for showing them in the first place. His brother hated Owen without even understanding why. But his mother meant more to him.

His note waited on the mussed covers where his mother sat. He picked up his duffel, walked from the room, and closed the door.

An hour later, he was back in the other plane, at his small house in the middle of nowhere. He lived alone outside the small town of Ceran, in the peaceful forest near the borders of Gennaios. His small cottage was a two-room building, with one bedroom and the remaining space open as a kitchen, dining room, and living room bundled in one.

Owen unlocked his cottage and threw his duffel bag into the bedroom. He grabbed an apple off his counter and sat down on the hard wooden floor. His back leaned against the front of a chair. He closed his eyes and settled into a straight-backed position against the chair.

Calling up the gray-hazed world of dreams, Owen allowed a last fleeting thought of seeing Sita in three days before he plunged into the world between dreams and reality. He had a brother to search for, and he would not waste the power he had given his soul to obtain.

∞

All the girls were very happy, after ten days of fighting and being around each other non-stop, to arrive back at school. Roxie and Ari dropped their bags into their room and flopped on the couch to enjoy the feeling of normality. Skylar and Estelle popped their heads into the suite when they returned to say hello, but both remained in their room to unpack and rest.

Only Sita seemed to want to be elsewhere. Her room now stood empty on one side. Vanessa had cleared out her things. Sita dumped her suitcase on the bed. "Well, at least she didn't trash my side," she said. The wind rattled the windowpanes—her only answer. She unpacked with care and tried to ignore the stares of accusation and shame that came from Vanessa's empty half. She wished Owen had decided to come along.

Robert walked in and leaned on the doorframe. "How does it feel to be here now, without her?"

Sita glanced around the room. Everything looked dull, limp. Ordinary. "Feels a little lonely."

He sat down in her desk chair and gave her a knowing look. "Are you blaming yourself for what Vanessa did?"

Sita picked up the jacket from her suitcase, shaking it out before throwing it over to the closet. "A little. Why?"

"You shouldn't. She brought it on herself."

She sighed, clutching the clothes she pulled from the bag. "I know. But I still can't help but wonder, you know? I wonder if maybe I would have seen something earlier and been able to prevent it." She shoved the shirts into the drawer. "The group seems to be falling apart because of me."

Rob's brow creased. He crossed his arms on the chair back and rested his head on them. "How do you figure that?"

"Well, I didn't tell anyone about the voices in my head. Which only happen occasionally now, they've mostly stopped. But what if I had said something? Could we have helped Darci? And Vanessa, if I had found out earlier how she felt, maybe we could have talked things out. Cleared up the misconceptions."

"None of this is your fault. I've told you that before. It's as true now as it was then. Darci couldn't save herself, and there was nothing we could've done for her. She's gone, and we have to accept that, or we'll never get anywhere. As for Vanessa . . ." Rob stood and helped her lift the bag up to the top shelf of the closet. "As for her, she knew what she was doing was wrong. She knew what would happen. She chose to act the way she did, and she chose to leave. I gave her that choice." He met Sita's wide blue-green eyes with his own somber brown. "I gave her that choice the night she fought you. I told her to change or leave. She chose to leave." Rob brushed Sita's cheek. "It's not your fault she made that choice. It's her own."

Sita sniffed and sat in her new extra chair. She pulled the blanket there up over her shoulders and curled up. "I wish Owen were here," she said in a soft voice.

"Who?"

She frowned. "Oh, um . . . he's sort of my new boyfriend." A chill emanated from the other end of the room, so strong that Sita could feel it even in her reverie. "Didn't I introduce you when you stopped by the mansion? After Vanessa was . . . ah, handled?"

Robert merely shook his head. "No. And this is the first I'm hearing about him." He paused and moved his gaze to his fingers. "When did this happen?"

"Not that long ago. He showed up at the mansion."

The silence from Rob's side of the conversation stretched to the point that Sita felt awkward and embarrassed. "So . . . let me get this straight. You met this guy not that long ago when he showed up one random day at the mansion. You let him in and just said 'Hey, we should date!' and so you did?"

Sita winced as his voice rose as his summary went on. "No! I'm not stupid! I've met him before."

"Where and when?"

Now she glanced to the floor and clasped her hands behind her back. "Um . . . a couple of times in my dreams."

Rob didn't respond right away. Sita snuck a look at his face and realized he couldn't answer her straight away without shouting. He fought to collect himself. Why he would be so upset over her love life, she had no idea, but it was starting to annoy. "Look," she said. "I know what I'm doing, OK? It's not like he's a complete stranger. My magic didn't sound an alarm or anything. And I can date anyone I want, thank you very much, even if he *is* a complete stranger."

He said nothing in response to that. "And where is he now?"

"He said he had some things to take care of and then he would come here. He said it would only be two, maybe three days."

Rob watched her face closely, and what he saw there must have alarmed him a great deal, because Sita saw his eyes widen and the blood drain from his cheeks. "Do you love him?"

Sita said nothing at first, her face stoic. Rob waited, his arms still crossed, his eyes veiled. Finally she looked up. Her eyes shone bright, lit up like twin suns. "Yes. Yes, I love him. More than I ever loved Eric, or any other boyfriend. He's my match."

Rob rose to his feet and kept his eyes away from her. "I thought you would say that."

The flash of blue light shocked Sita from her thoughts. She raised her head to ask what he meant only to realize Rob was gone.

∞

Ariene lay on her bed to watch the ceiling. Her classes this semester were different from Roxie's and Sita's, and gave her an hour to herself twice a week. Usually she slept, but today she couldn't. Her mind was too heavy with thoughts of Darci and Vanessa. The Psychology 201 textbook lay open on her desk. It waited for her to come and read some more, its accusation almost overwhelming. So she turned on her side and faced the wall instead.

A knock on the door forced her to turn. "What?" she called.

The door opened and let Rob in. "Hiding out, or trying to sleep?"

"Both." Ari slid down off the bed. She shivered in her t-shirt. The early April weather wasn't quite warm enough for the shorter sleeves, so she grabbed a blanket off her bed and wrapped it around her. "I have this hour to myself, the others are at class."

"Ah." Rob climbed up onto Roxie's bed and took a seat. "I have news for you ladies. I've got another mission lined up for you."

Ari grinned and pumped a fist in the air. "Finally! It's about time we saw some more action! It's already been a week since spring break! Way too long between assignments."

Rob laughed. "I thought you'd be happy. This one is pretty easy, but necessary. I don't think you'll have any problems with it." He reached into his jacket and pulled out a sheet of paper. "Here, I wrote everything down. Show it to the others. You've only got two days to get ready." He disappeared.

She caught the papers and unfolded them, reading each word with care. She heard the door of the suite open and close, and her suitemates walked in. "Guys, we have a mission!"

The other two heard her and rushed into the room. "What is it? What're we doing?" Roxie asked.

Ari held out the paper. "We have to go to a field almost an hour outside town. There's going to be some kind of transfer, I think. Rob wasn't too clear on what would be there, just that we would spy on what went on and report back immediately."

"Any fighting?" Sita said, looking over Roxie's shoulder to read the paper.

Ari shrugged. "Rob didn't say anything about it, so I don't know. I would guess the rules are the same as last time, only fight if we have to."

Roxie nodded. "Makes sense. And this is in two days?"

Sita groaned. "Great, I have a ten-page paper due that day. This is not going to go well."

"Just remember to get your homework done before then," Ari said. She took the paper back from Roxie. "It shouldn't be too hard if you already know what you're doing."

Sita spread out her hands, her lip turned down in a pout. "But I don't know what I'm doing! I haven't even picked a topic yet! And it's due in two days!"

Roxie laughed. "Then you've got two days to figure it out, haven't you?"

∞

Two days later the group piled into an old and battered van for the drive to the field. Where Rob had found the van for them, Sita didn't know, but she was glad she didn't have to drive the clunker. They left just after dinner, taking care to act as if nothing were out of the ordinary. They changed into darker clothing in the van while Ari drove, weaving in and out of traffic in a rush to get there on time.

She stopped the van five minutes away from their destination. The trio filed out of the vehicle and checked their surroundings. Bushes concealed much of the field from the roadway, and more bushes and small trees dotted the landscape on the way to the field. Ari locked the van and followed her friends. Roxie led the way by staying as far in the bushes as possible. The others followed behind, keeping an eye out on all sides for the enemy.

The field appeared in front of them ten minutes later. Roxie stopped them on the edge of the clearing to check the directions. "This isn't right," she whispered back. Sita slunk forward to see. "There's something in the field, taking up most of the space. Rob said it would be empty, there's supposed to be some kind of transfer . . ."

Sita clapped a hand on Roxie's shoulder. "Calm down. We'll figure this out, and if we have to, we'll leave. Just stay calm." Roxie nodded her understanding and returned to studying the field. Large hedges grew from the ground, just inside the field's border. Roxie could see nothing beyond the hedges.

Sita shrugged. "Won't know until we get there. Let's see if there are any openings we could use to see what's inside." Silent nods answered.

The women took slow steps forward and watched everything around them. Sita spread out her magic in a blanket on the ground, her favorite form of enemy detection. There was nothing there.

They were about halfway around when the enemy attacked.

Men rushed from the woods to shoot at the trio with guns, arrows, and magical attacks; attack after attack hurtled toward the three women. Roxie cried out and ducked behind Sita and Ari as the first wave hit. Ari turned her hands into lion's paws, her teeth into fangs. Sita held up her hands and created a shield.

But the enemy had planned for this. One of the men stepped forward, a leer on his face. He pulled out a lighter and lit a rag on fire. Once it caught, he strode straight up to the edge of Sita's barrier and threw the fiery rag in.

It landed just before Sita's feet. With a gasp, Sita tried to put it out, but it resisted her magic. She looked to Ari and Roxie, her eyes wild. "We have to get out of here! It's a trap!"

Another burning rag sailed through the shield, almost hitting Ari in the face. They backed up until their backs hit the hedge. Seeing no other course, Sita turned around and blasted a hole through the hedge. She ducked through, Ari and Roxie close behind.

Ray Alan watched the group fight their way to the center of his maze. He chuckled with glee, excited about the prospect of finally finishing off the little nuisances. Grinning in malicious pleasure, he turned to the woman waiting at his side. "They are almost to the core. Let's go greet them, shall we?" He pushed a button on his control panel and walked out of the room with Sandara.

Roxie hunched over, breathing in gulps of air. She clutched her wounded left arm to her side and looked up at her friends. Sita had just blasted the men running toward them with a massive globe of power that rolled right over them and flattened every attacker in sight. "That won't last for long, but at least we get a breather for a minute." She looked around. "Ari, are you OK?"

The other woman waved a weary hand back at her. "I'm fine, but I'm reaching my limits," she said in gasps.

Sita was the only one of them still really standing, though a long wound on her arm from a knife graze oozed blood. "I've still got my reserves, I can go on. But how are we going to get out of this one?"

As if in reply to her question, the ground began to shake. Roxie looked down, then realized that the trembling ground formed a great square around their group. She jumped to her feet. "Look out!"

And the ground fell out from underneath them. The earth swallowed them all into the gaping hole before sealing itself up again.

Ariene landed in a heap, the air knocked from her lungs. Pain shot through her arm. She scrambled to her feet in the semi-darkness. "Rox? Sita?" she called. There was no answer except the echo of her own voice. She clutched at her aching arm. Taking a deep breath, Ari closed her eyes and changed them into the eyes of a wolf. The semi-darkness cleared in her night vision. Stumbling forward, Ari spied a figure in the distance. As she got closer, her face blanched, and she began to tremble.

In front of Ari, ten feet away, stood Roxie. Her eyes were vacant, her hair matted with blood, her clothes drenched in the thick red liquid as her heart pumped it out of her body. Her fragile pale skin was scored all over with claw marks—the marks of Ariene's favorite tiger shape. Roxie's hand stretched out to her, every finger broken and twisted, her mouth open in a scream of agony as she pled for Ariene to help her. Ari reached for her hand—and Roxie vanished.

Ariene tottered, confused. She turned around only to see Vanessa crawling toward her, moaning and dragging her charred and tortured body over the floor, hands reaching out for aid. Ari's eyes opened wide, her mouth uttered an anguished half-scream, and she ran away.

Professor Alan studied the windows that looked into each of the rooms. Sandara sneered next to him. "It looks like the trap worked. They're stuck in the illusions generated from the rooms."

He smirked. "Indeed. And greater men than they have been broken by those rooms." His expression faded when he looked into two of the rooms. "Though it seems those two will have to be taught a lesson. They haven't succumbed to the visions quickly enough for my liking." Alan looked back to the operating board. The rooms were definitely operational, and should have sent the two young women into the hallucinations by now, as the other room had for Ari. He looked back to the windows, perplexed. "Why haven't they . . ." he wondered to himself, not bothering to finish the thought aloud.

Alan pursed his lips. "Yes, I think a lesson is in order. Sandara, would you kindly watch the other one for me? I'm going to go deal with those two myself."

Sandara turned to the windows with obvious merriment. "Of course, Professor. It would be my pleasure."

Roxie shuddered in the chill, rubbing her arms to warm herself. A dark hallway presented itself to her, the roiling mist on the floor lit by some unknown source of dim light. She tried to see what was down the hall, but could see nothing. Her ankle lanced with pain as she rose to her feet. *I must have landed on it when I fell.* She tested it and took a few steps. *I'll be all right as long as I don't have to run.*

Limping down the hall, Roxie looked at the walls. There were no doors. She sighed and kept walking.

A figure began to materialize in the mists. Roxie squinted. When she saw the face she frowned, confused. "Allen? What are you doing here?" she called. She hobbled on her injured ankle as fast as she could toward his still-distant figure. "Allen?" she called again, slowing when she neared him.

The sight that greeted her eyes froze her. Icy tendrils of dread wrapped themselves around her heart and froze her lungs. She stared at the vision before her. Allen had clearly been tortured, his body covered in blood, his limbs distorted. The face she remembered so well had contorted in agony and frozen that way. He moaned and reached for her.

Roxie remained in place, unable to do anything but gape at the nightmare in disbelief. She shook her head and shut her eyes, willing the torture to end. When she opened them again, Allen was whole, unharmed, and smiling at her in that angelic way of his. Roxie took a step away, her hands raised as if to fend off a blow.

A deep chuckle echoed behind her. She whirled on her good leg. A second figure stood in the mist and laughed at her. "You should be very afraid, Roxie," the deep male voice advised. "Why aren't you afraid?"

She gulped. Her stomached clenched. "I'm not afraid of you."

His tone held a hint of annoyance. "Didn't I just say you should be?"

Roxie crossed her arms. "That's what all the villains say. And they all turn out to be wrong."

The man came closer, wraithlike. "Ah, but I am unlike any other villain you have faced, Roxanne. Because I know your deepest fears, and I have the power to make you actually live those fears."

Roxie lifted her chin, jaw clenched. "You have no power over me."

He chuckled. "Oh? Then turn around."

She turned.

Ariene had finally run as far as she could. She knew the bodies followed her, but she could run no more. Hands on her knees, she broke down and wept. "I'm a coward, I'm a coward, I'm a coward," she whispered to herself as her nightmare crawled nearer.

Sandara watched all of them through the windows. She saw Ari and Roxie crumble under the weight of the mind manipulation rooms. She smirked. "So you weren't as strong as we thought you were," she commented to the silent control room. "Such a pity." And she laughed.

Sita lay in a heap. Loose feathers floated around her. Her wings ached abominably from whatever she hit on her way down the hole. She sat up and tried to gain her bearings. The air smelled musty and dank, as if it had been closed for a long time. It made her cough, and the sound echoed around the room. She felt her head and groaned. *I must have hit my head, too. Damn, this hurts!* Her wings fluttered behind her as she scrambled to her feet.

A deep laugh echoed off the walls. Sita glanced around the place, but could see nothing in the darkness. "Who's there?" she called, turning in a slow circle. "Come out!"

A man walked through the mists. His slow claps wrenched at Sita's nerves and she felt her muscles tighten all over her body. "Bravo, Sita, darling. I didn't expect you to come through that fall unscathed. You're stronger than I gave you credit for." He walked closer, hands behind his back. "I'll bet you're wondering what's going on, aren't you?"

She backed away from him as he continued to walk closer. "Who are you?" she said in a growl. A knife came to hand from her boot—one of Rob's gifts. "Don't come any closer." Her left hand began to glow a soft purple.

He chuckled. "You think you can hurt me? How sweet. You're like a kitten, Sita. You have claws, but you don't know how to use them."

She gripped the handle of the knife tighter. "Were you the one who seduced Darci away from us?" she asked. Anger boiled just beneath the surface. It felt like her skin would be on fire any second, and the anger grew each moment she held it in check.

The man nodded. "Why, yes, dear, I am." His teeth flashed in the half-light for a moment as he smiled. "As I will you." He reached for her.

Roxie barely held the scream inside as she turned back around and saw what the man meant. Before her, every single person she cared about lay in a massive pile, their bodies bloodied and torn, eyes blank and glazed. The abuse on the bodies grew worse, the most horrific corpses on the top. Those top corpses had the faces of her dearest friends, and Allen lay at the very top.

She looked away to keep the bile from coming to her mouth. Her stomach heaved and she fought away the impulse to vomit. Once she found her equilibrium again, she looked back, thinking it couldn't get worse than that.

It could.

Roxie watched, held captive by the man behind her, as each one of her friends was killed by a look-alike Roxie, and each one died screaming her name. She stood in the man's crushing embrace, frozen and helpless, while icy tears stained her pallid cheeks. As soon as the torture stopped, he let her go. She stumbled away from him and turned, trying to see his face. "What kind of monster are you? *Who are you?*"

The strange man laughed. "Why, Roxie, don't you know me? I'm your dear teacher, Professor Alan, remember?" He stepped out of the shadows.

Sita twisted away from the man's attempts to grab her, slashing at him with the knife each time he came close enough. He leapt out of the way only to attack again with a speed that surprised her. Teeth clenched against the pain, she rose into the air. Both wings and flight muscles screamed at her in pain as the man underneath her looked up and grinned. "You're not getting away from me so easily, Sita." With a twist of his hand he cast a magical net.

Sita tried to counter the net, but it was too late—the threads of magic wrapped around her and brought her to the ground with a crash. She struggled and tried to slash it with her knife and her magic, but it was no use. The man stepped forward to cradle her prone, bound form in his arms. Sita shivered—it felt like being in a spider's web, with the spider preparing to wrap up its prey for later.

The man carried her struggling body further into the shadows. Feathers were painfully pulled out to leave a glowing white feather trail as she twisted and turned in the net. He sat down on a chair, which Sita didn't remember seeing earlier, and sat her on his lap. He grasped her chin in cruel fingers and shook her face. "Watch, and listen, my dear angel. This is important."

Sita tried to breathe, but the net was wrapped tightest around her ribs. She watched like he told her to, unable to do anything else. Visions passed before her eyes, controlled by the man who held her, and his arms tightened as she began to cry. Sita could feel the happiness that emanated from him, and it sickened her. "What do you want from me?" she whispered at last.

He removed his hand from her chin. "Why, Sita, don't you know? Haven't you been hearing all those doubts running through your mind for quite some time now? Months, in fact." Sita's eyes narrowed. Her lungs demanded more air and she gasped for breath even as the realization sunk in and made it more difficult to breathe. "Doubts that you're good enough? Doubts that your friends are true? That you're going to wake up one morning and find that it has all been a dream? That your boyfriend doesn't really love you at all."

The man grinned down at her. "Doubts that the power you have is really there, and not some figment of your imagination? And what of your wings? Doubts that they will actually continue to be there for you, that you haven't made all this up? Or my favorite part," his voice turned bloodthirsty, "you have doubts that the darkness you feel inside of you will be held at bay. That you aren't really the good girl you always thought yourself to be. That one day, you will become just like Darci—a betrayer to her only friends, a queen of the Darkness." He chuckled. "You doubt that you can fight the Darkness forever."

Sita felt the net loosen and the man dumped her on the floor. She wriggled out of the magical ropes and gained her feet. "You're wrong," she said in the steadiest voice she could command. "I don't have those doubts anymore, because I figured out whose voice was whispering those things to me. I know who I am."

He smiled at her. "But you don't, Sita. I can see it in your eyes." He grasped her wrist and pulled her to him. She was close enough to see every fine wrinkle around his eyes and mouth. His breath smelled stale, and his eyes held no warmth. "You have those doubts, and one day, you will succumb to them, because you are weak, and cannot resist their seductive call. You are not a leader, you are a follower, on the bottom rung of the ladder! You will not be able to control your power. One day, you will turn from your friends, from the light, and that's when I will be waiting.

"One day, you will be *just like Darci.*" His smile was predatory, victorious. "And on that day, my dear Sita, you will be mine."

Sita wrenched herself from his grip and ran from the echoes of his laughter. A realization dawned on her as she fled. *If it echoes, then it means there are walls around here somewhere. If I keep running as straight as I can, I'm bound to find one sooner or later.* So she ran, listening for the man's steps behind her, but they never came. She thought she could feel his breath on her neck, but when she looked behind her, there was nothing except the mist. She ran.

Finally, Sita found a wall, literally by running into it. The mist was so thick that she didn't see the wall until it was too late. She slammed into it and bounced to the ground. Stunned, she opened her eyes and realized the wall was actually clear, not stone or wood. *Plexi-glass maybe?* she wondered.

Sita looked through it and, by either sheer luck or the man's manipulations, was able to see one of her friends through it. Ariene knelt on her knees and wept uncontrollably in the grip of her own nightmare. Shocked at the sight, Sita regained her wits and banged on the wall, trying to get Ari's attention. But Ariene turned away. Sita realized that Ari faced her own demons, and wouldn't hear her.

Ariene rose to her feet and set her shoulders. This wasn't like her. She would never run from a fight, nor would she ever not take responsibility for her actions. If her animal instincts had gotten the better of her and made her cause these people damage, then so be it. Ari would face the consequences with honor and humility. She wiped the tears from her cheeks. "I will not run. I will not run!" she screamed, settling into a fighter's crouch. "Come and get me, if you want me." Ari waited until the tortured people caught up to her and formed a ring around her. She looked into Sita's eyes, but something was wrong. *Sita's eyes aren't brown! They're greenish!* Startled, Ari looked around, and found something wrong with each one of her "friends." Growling in pain, she realized the trap and pulled out a dagger. "I am not a coward!"

Sandara watched as Ari rose and began to move. Alarmed, she took a closer look at Ari and Roxie before she pressed a bright red button to page Alan. It would let him know that something had not gone according to plan. "They're resisting," she grumbled to herself.

Roxie stared at the man now in front of her. "Professor Alan?" she asked. "Why?" She turned to look at the vision still in front of her, then turned back to him. "How could you?" she growled as she lunged for him, knife in hand. He disappeared before she could reach him. "I won't be like that! I won't turn against my friends, and I *will not* let them die without a fight!"

Alan's disembodied voice echoed around her. She spun as he spoke, but could not spy him. "I'm so sorry, my dear, but it appears I have to go. I have an urgent matter to attend to." His laughter grated on her ears.

Angry now, Sita turned and flew into the air to retrace her run back to the man. *I will not be his play thing!* "We aren't here for your amusement, you asshole!" she shouted, hoping to attract his attention. She spotted him in a clear area through the mists. He turned around in surprise. Sita gathered her power and shot bolts of purple lightning at him, hoping to incinerate him where he stood.

He deflected the attacks with ease, not even an eyebrow raised. "My, my, we are in a temper, aren't we?" he called to her.

"What do you want?" she screamed.

A blast of unseen power shot her down from the air. Another blast hit her when she touched the ground to slam her against the nearest wall. Alan pinned her to it in an instant. "What do I want?" he growled at her. "I would be a king, Sita, ruling over everything I can grasp. I would have returned to me what I have lost. And I want you as my servant, as Darci is now."

Sita struggled in vain to break free from his power-enhanced grip. Then she stopped and stared into Alan's mad eyes. His nearness disgusted her and made her want to cringe out of his grip. "Darci isn't your servant! I will send you back to whichever Hell you crawled out from, you demon!"

His deep throaty laugh echoed around her, the sound grating on her ears. He leaned even closer. His eyes bored into hers while his grip tightened. "I think not. I think you will be joining me in that Hell, Sita, as my loyal dark servant. You cannot defeat me. You are too weak. Your loyalty, your friendships—those are your fatal weaknesses, Sita. I am stronger, because I have no loyalty to anyone but myself and my masters, and I have no friends."

In the other rooms, the two young women heard his words echo around them. Each stopped what they were doing to listen. Then they heard Sita's answer:

"If I didn't hate you so much, I might pity you. You can't defeat me. You can't defeat *us*. Those weaknesses you despise are our strengths. We will beat you."

Violet magic streamed from her fingers, fueled by her anger, to break the hold his power had over her. Before she could attack again, he grinned at her and said, "We shall see, won't we, my pretty angel."

And he vanished.

Sita let loose her rage. Bolts of magic charred the walls and burned away the mist. The lightning broke through a window on one side. Sita ran to it and climbed through. Her rage faded while the violet-colored storm continued in her former cell when she realized she had found the control room, and could see her friends through the windows.

A glance at the panel revealed all the controls she would need to free her friends. She paused when she found a note and a present for her. Sita scanned the note and then ripped it into a hundred tiny pieces, her mouth frozen in a snarl. The black rose on the panel gleamed in the bright white lights, taunting her. The words of the note ran through her head:

You will face the darkness eventually, Sita. And on that day, you will join me.

With a scowl, she pressed the buttons and set her friends free.

Chapter Thirty-Three
The Council

Robert waited for them that night. He sat on the couch like a sack of potatoes, a boneless lump. Owen had returned. He sat next to Robert, his gray eyes in shadow, keeping vigil with the other man. Owen glanced over at Rob. "If you don't like it, why do you let them fight? They'd never do it if you didn't push them in the first place."

Rob thought about it for a while, his eyes steady on the door. Finally he answered. "Can you hold the wind? Can you stop the rain?" A smile crept onto his face. "I could no more hold back the ocean than I could stop them from fighting. It's true, I did introduce it to them in the first place." Rob's face grew downcast and sad. "But now they've gotten a taste of the enemy, they won't give it up. So I sit here like a wife waiting for her soldier to come home." Owen snickered.

At half-past nine, the girls stumbled inside, tired and snappish. The two men helped them inside. Rob made sure they were all right and then left them alone to head off elsewhere and avoid their wrath. He could have stayed—the trio was too tired and sore to pick another fight, and once they cleaned themselves up, they went straight to bed. But he decided to leave Owen to bear the brunt of the scathing tongues and weary females. He knew Owen let him, since it meant he could then spend more time alone with Sita.

So instead of sticking around, Rob went into Corá. He headed straight for the capital after stopping by his little house on the outskirts of Torthal to freshen himself up. The capital wasn't far away from his place, and he could make good time traveling from there.

The capital, Lampros, always amazed him when he entered the gates. Surrounded on all sides by a single circular wall, the gates stood at the four cardinal points. He entered through the eastern gate, reserved for travelers and non-merchant peasants. The northern gate was saved mainly for the army, while the western and southern gates were reserved for merchants and nobles.

All the gates were at least the height of three men. Robert stared up at them and marveled at the enormous wood-and-metal structures. The wall itself was thick enough to withstand a siege, and Rob wondered exactly how thick it was. It looked to him to be almost the length of a car, but he was never sure.

Inside the gates were two guard barracks that framed the roadway in somber gray. Rob knew the tactic was meant as a warning: misbehave and you'll be thrown out. He ignored the threat, as he knew many of the soldiers personally by now, having drunk in the taverns with a good number of them. He strode past the barracks with a wave to the soldiers sitting outside and continued on, his hands now stuffed in his pockets.

The dirt street wound through the poorer neighborhood. Rob passed along the outskirts of the slum and the hovels. The smell of trash and unwashed bodies clung to the place, and other smells he couldn't place but didn't want to know of burned his sense of smell. Young children in rags watched any travelers with greedy or pitiful eyes, and quite a few begged along the street. He always wondered why the planners of the city had allowed the slums to be so obviously conspicuous on a main road, and he could never figure it out. It ran counter to every other city he had ever been in. As always, he shrugged and continued up the road. This roadway passed through progressively nicer neighborhoods as it moved out of the poorest area into the lower merchant's and laborer's area and then into the minor nobility and wealthy merchant class's homes.

Rob kept walking until he found the turn to the nobles' district. The road began to climb upward and curve into a circle around the finer town houses of nobles and court hangers-on. His feet began to ache—the cobblestones of this road were hard on the feet, and he felt sorry for the horses that had to traverse this particular street. He kept walking, watching as the city began to be lain out before him from the heights of the royal hill, until he reached the gates of the palace itself.

The guards stopped him at this gate, swords held in a wary gesture. Rob rolled his eyes. He had been here many times, and even knew these two guards personally. Yet they always stopped him, made him show his identification, and made him wait until someone could verify he was supposed to be there.

Rob handed over the medallion that identified him as a guest of the Council. "Hello Tom, Shane. Nice day today, isn't it?"

The guards gave him brief smiles. "Sure is, Robert," replied Tom. "Sorry we have to do this every time. You know the rules."

Rob smirked. "Yeah, yeah, I know. It's fine."

Finally the guard commander verified his intentions and allowed him through. Rob waved to Tom and Shane and followed his new guide inside the palace gates.

His page-boy guide led him straight to the Council chamber, keeping up a steady pace through the stone hallways until they stopped in front of the door. The page bowed to Rob and opened one door, announcing him as he did. Robert waited for the page to stop speaking before he walked into the enormous room.

All nine Councilors sat around a half-circle table, with Queen Catherine sitting as mediator. It was custom that the ruler of the country the Council was hosted by sit in on the discussions and act as a mediator. The Council changed countries every ten years, moving in a pattern from east to west and north to south. Gennaios, Catherine's country, was in its third year as host.

Robert bowed low. The cavernous room captured all sound, and his steps echoed when he was given permission to take a seat next to the table. The First Councilor, Dagwood Shale, greeted him with a wan smile. "It is good to see you again, Robert. How have you been?"

"I have been well, First. Thank you for your consideration."

"And are you here to join our discussion of the war, young Robert?" asked Yuriyi Vasgel, the Seventh. His half-closed eyes held only mild interest.

Catherine interrupted. "I invited him here, Councilors, out of consideration that he is the mentor of the Aligerai, of whom you have all heard a great deal lately."

The Councilors nodded. Abikanile, the Eighth, leaned forward, her ebony skin gleaming in the low lamplight. "What can you tell us that is concrete about the Aligerai, Robert? We have heard little but rumors and stories since they emerged last autumn."

Robert swallowed. This was not exactly what he had come to discuss. He cleared his throat. "Well, I can tell you that they are no longer five, but three. Darci deserted for Imbri Mors, and Vanessa chose to leave."

Murmurs echoed around the room, reflecting either the confusion or the thinly-veiled happiness of some councilors. Robert's eye was drawn to Khaden Whed, the Fifth. Her red lips moved from a small frown to a smirk. He watched her from the corner of his eye as he continued to speak. An uneasy feeling grew in the pit of his stomach with every second. "The remaining members work well together, and I foresee no further problems of that nature. However, Imbri Mors has been causing them a great deal of trouble in addition to their other operations. They attacked the Aligerai, as you call them, when I sent them out on a reconnaissance mission just yesterday."

The Sixth, Dimitryo Ovugel, stood up, his speech cloaked in a heavy northern accent. "Vat do you mean, zey attacked ze Aligerai? I deed not think zey could reach zat far."

"It's exactly as it sounds, sir," Robert replied. His palms moistened from sweat and nerves. "Imbri Mors must have planted some false intelligence into the mix, because I had believed I was sending them on a simple and easy recon. It turns out that was a trap, designed to capture but not kill the Aligerai. They have all returned safely, though not unscathed. The enemy also has at least one Ripper, and possibly more." A few Councilors gasped, and even Catherine paled at the news that Imbri owned Ripper devices.

"This is outrageous!" shouted the Fifth. Robert's eyes narrowed. There was just the hint of a triumphant gleam in her dark brown eyes, though nothing showed on her face. "The enemy can apparently walk up to the front door and demand anything they want! They almost got our most powerful weapons! What next? It is time for more drastic measures, Councilors, and this only proves it."

"Calm down!" said Dimitryo. "You exaggerate, surely, Khaden. Ze enemy vill not be able to touch us! Not vith ze Aligerai at our backs!"

Khaden leaned forward, the other councilors content to watch and listen and whisper among themselves. "Sixth, if the Aligerai are captured or killed, how can I be exaggerating? Imbri Mors has already tried this once. What makes you think they won't try again?" Silence descended. "We need to get them to a safer place. Somewhere far from the long arm of the professors."

Catherine rose from her center seat. "Enough." All eyes turned to her. "You are too . . . enthusiastic . . . about this proposal, Fifth. We cannot force these young women from their homes, their very world. If they help us, they must do so willingly. We cannot force them, or we are no worse than our enemies."

The First nodded his graying head. "Agreed. Robert, can you tell us what kind of powers these young ladies have? We still have no real idea of what they are capable of."

Robert bowed his head in respect. "Certainly. The remaining Aligerai are Sita Newbury, Roxanne Dalton, and Ariene Sandford." He hesitated. "Sita is the only one who is a color mage."

Dimitryo frowned. "I do not understand. Vat is a 'color mage.' It is not a term ve use."

"A color mage is the kind of mage who can use magic in a very general way," Robert said. The others listened in silence, as this was information they already knew. "Other magicians are known as 'type mages,' and they are limited in what their powers can do. For example, Roxanne is limited to powers with animals. Her power can do nothing outside of that sphere."

The councilor nodded. "I understand, thank you."

Khaden scoffed. "Humph, type mages. Useless creatures. Inferior to color mages. That we should rely on these half-mages to save our world, it's ridiculous . . ."

The Council broke into immediate uproar. The Sixth and Eighth shouted her down, while the Fourth and Third looked red in the face and mutinous. Three of the Councilors were color mages, and another two were type mages. Khaden paled and sat down, clearly disconcerted by the upheaval.

The First stood again, a harsh sscowl on his face and his expression fierce. "Khaden Whed, that is enough. You are not to speak in this session again unless your opinion is asked for specifically, is that quite understood?" Khaden nodded. He turned back to Robert, his features relaxing. "Thank you for explaining, Robert. Now, back to the matter at hand, please.

"Regardless of whether the Aligerai help us or not, we must confront the problem of Imbri Mors. They cannot continue their mass killings, either in Corá or on Earth, and the revelation of the Rippers only compounds the situation." Nods all around, though Robert noticed Khaden's was barely perceptible. "It is my belief that we must begin mobilizing for a war immediately."

Robert winced as all at once the Councilors began to shout again, either agreeing with the First or crying for another plan. He glanced at Catherine. Her eyes were shadowed, her face sorrowful. The Councilors would debate through the night, so he settled into his cushioned chair to watch and wait.

It was early morning when Robert staggered through the door of the suite. He looked haggard and as if he hadn't slept the night before. Which was true—he hadn't. Ari was the first to see him. "Robert!" she cried, hurrying to him. She helped him get to the couch. "Are you OK? What's happened to you?"

"Oh, nothing that a night of good, solid sleep won't cure," he said. He sank into the couch cushions, looking even more morose than when he walked through the door. "I have some very important news for you all. If no one's in class, I need you all here right now. Will you get the others?"

Ari nodded. She fetched her suitemates out of their rooms. Owen joined them from Sita's room as well, and Rob saw no reason to exclude the man since he already knew about Corá. They all converged at just about the same time, their voices fading to nothing when they saw Rob's appearance. "What happened?" Roxie asked, settling a hand on Rob's shoulder.

Rob sighed, a deep and mournful sound. "The Council met last night, and Queen Catherine of Gennaios asked me to attend. I agreed, and went there right after I made sure you were all OK." He leaned his head back on the cushion, closing his sore eyes. "They asked me for news of you, and I told them what happened yesterday. They were outraged, of course, and that only lent some weight to their decision, I think."

"What decision?" Roxie asked. Her hands twisted around each other. "What aren't you saying?"

He held up a hand to her. "Patience. I'll get to it. They deliberated for hours, and could apparently come up with nothing better. They asked the question of what to do about Imbri Mors."

Sita sat down hard in the closest chair, making it onto the cushion by inches.

Robert massaged his temples. He sighed in resignation—the pain was just as insistent as before. "After talking all night, the Council came up with a decision. Battle is their solution."

Silence greeted his announcement. His girls stared at him in shock and amazement, and not a little fear. Owen's gray eyes were blank and hard, revealing no fear or surprise. Rob was sure he had known all along what the decision would be. Ari spoke first. "You're sure? This is really going to happen?"

Robert nodded and she cursed. She slumped onto the couch as the rest of the group claimed their own seats.

Roxie spoke next, her hands now clenched and white in her lap. "Who's going to lead our side? The Council?"

Ari barked a harsh laugh. "Let's hope not. They take so long to make a decision that we'll lose the first battle before they even decide to strike!"

Rob held up his hands, a signal for them to quiet down. "No, not the Council. The Council will be the authority, but someone else will actually lead the army."

"So they will choose the leader?" Sita asked. Owen took her white-knuckled hand in his own.

"Yes," Rob replied.

Sita crossed her arms over her chest and leaned into the chair's soft back. Owen scooted a little further away, seeing the angry light in her face. "And this army? Who exactly will be fighting? And *where*? I mean, we can't exactly fight *here*! Do you know how many innocents will get caught in our magical cross fires?"

Their mentor nodded. "I know, Sita. That's why the Council decided to take the battle to our separate plane. There are plenty of uninhabited plains and valleys and such that the battles will not harm any of our peoples. I can't say as much for the land, though," he said with regret. "But that is their decision. As for who will be fighting . . ." Rob looked uneasy at this part. He glanced around, hoping someone else would say what he never wanted to.

Sita caught on first. "Oh, no. Oh, *hell* no. No! We aren't soldiers!" she cried as she found her feet. "We may have fought a couple of skirmishes with our personal enemies, but that doesn't mean we can fight in a *war* like this! The Council must be insane! Did they go flying too high in the atmosphere or something?" She stalked around the room, fury radiating from her.

Roxie shook a little, but her expression was determined. Ari put on a stoic mask and watched Sita pace. Owen leaned against the far wall, arms crossed over chest, taking it all in. Rob was pale as milk, but he spoke anyway. "Yes, the Council has asked that any available fighters be ready to go when they call. And they mean *everybody*." He paused, uneasy. "Well, their 'request' was more of an 'order,' actually."

The prowling young woman stopped. "They ordered everyone to fight," she stated, her voice devoid of emotion. "They actually had the gall to order something like that?" Her voice rose into shrieks of rage. "They are ridiculous. No one is trained for war!"

Robert stood and attempted to calm Sita down. *Plus, her voice is hurting my ears. Why do girls have to shriek so high?* He grasped her arm when she came around the couch and held her steady as she was forced to halt. "The Council knows what it is doing! True, no one in Corá has seen war for many years, but we have enough time to do training and practice before the battle begins!" He shook her. "We have to fight, Sita. With an entire army behind us, our small 'skirmishes,' as you called them, may not have been worthless after all. We have knowledge of our enemy that the rest of our friends and the Council do not have! We can help, and we can fight." Sita, most of her anger controlled now, sank back into her seat, her face sullen. Owen reclaimed her hand again and she deflated, the burning fury seeped from her at his touch. "We may not be experienced in war, but we do have some experience dealing with this enemy."

Ariene spoke up this time. "So who will be leading this little army of ours then? Who are the choices?"

Rob looked uneasy again. "Well . . . originally, the Council wanted Sita . . ."

Sita's head snapped up in outrage. "*What!*"

Robert shushed her. "But I told them no. Emphatically. I knew you would never agree, and told them to pick someone else. They actually listened, for once," he said the last under his breath. He resumed. "So their choices now are down to two. A Chular by the name of Samuel Knox—for some odd reason he has a human name—and a Bal'tari named Jun-Scrie. Personally, my money is on the Chular. He's very capable at leading his own people, and he seems to have made a study of war and fighting through the years, as a kind of hobby."

The girls were subdued now. "So they want us to fight," Roxie said, her voice steady but soft. Everyone looked at each other as Rob nodded. Roxie leaned back on the couch in an unconscious imitation of Sita's own movements a few minutes earlier. "Can we meet this commander, when he's chosen? I wouldn't mind knowing who's going to be giving us our orders, you know."

Rob nodded in agreement. "I'm sure I can arrange something."

Sita spoke again, her voice much more subdued now. "Are the other . . . organizations joining us in this, or are they holding to their secrecy and staying out?"

"The Council ordered everyone, Sita, and that means *everyone*. They'll be joining us," Rob replied. *And that's going to be just great. Twenty or more different groups fighting together. Instead of simply fighting on the same side of the fence, we all now have to actually work together.* He shivered slightly. *That's kind of a scary thought . . .* Rob let the thought trail away as he continued. "There are roughly twenty different groups out there that will be joining us and the soldiers already in Corá. As I'm sure you can imagine, that can cause some various problems when it comes to keeping loyalties secret from the other organizations." Owen's pupils contracted to pinpricks. Rob noticed his stiffness, and his own eyes narrowed in thought, but he let it pass.

Roxie chewed on her lower lip. "So Allen will be fighting too?"

Rob softened as he looked at his best friend. "Yes, Rox, he will."

Sita sighed, leaned her head on Owen's shoulder, and held her hands to her face. "I guess we fight, then. But if the Council asks us to do something stupid, that's where I draw the line."

∞

Vanessa crawled through the tall grass. Rain fell just in front of her face. She pulled her backpack closer and reached out with her gift to touch the grass on the other side of the curtain of water. There was nothing wrong with it, exactly, but there was just the faintest hint of rot, of death. Of something not right.

She reached out her hand this time and held it under the water, feeling the cold drops sting her skin. Vanessa hissed and snatched her hand back. The earth raged inside that watery circle, and Vanessa was unsure about walking in there. Gathering her pack and what courage she had, she stood up and walked into the rain.

Instantly she was soaked, and very cold. This wasn't the warm spring rain she was used to at this time of year, this was the rain of mountain winters, icy and relentless. The manse was a long walk away, and she knew people would see her coming long before she got close. She just prayed they wouldn't strike at her before she could talk to them.

Matted yellow hair blew into her eyes. Vanessa pushed it back and pushed onward. Half way to the house a cry went up, barely audible over a crack of thunder. Vanessa jumped. Realization dawned that she was the tallest object in the field other than the manse fifty feet away.

Emerald power reached out and yanked her up to the house, dumping her on her bottom onto the front stairs. Coughing, Vanessa regained her breath and her feet. She rose only to look straight into Sandara's eyes. "Well, well, what have we here?" the tall woman asked, her eyes gleaming in the dark. "This is indeed a surprise. Darci says you are to be welcomed here, and brought straight to her. Follow me, Vanessa."

Vanessa, soaked and not a little frightened, followed Sandara inside the door. Two men shoved the doors closed behind her, cutting off the current of cold wind at her back. She relaxed a trifle and studied the manse that now surrounded her. Sandara headed toward a grand staircase that curved up one side of the entrance chamber. The foyer was smaller than Sita's, and the entire house seemed to be dark and drab. Vanessa followed Sandara, noticing how threadbare the carpets were, how tattered the walls and draperies, how dusty the furniture. Overall, she thought the place depressing.

Sandara led the girl up the stairs and to the left, down a long hallway and up another set of smaller stairs. She stopped in front of a wooden door placed at the top of the stairs and rapped once. Not waiting for a reply from within, Sandara opened the door and stood back, motioning for Vanessa to enter first.

She did so as she swallowed hard and clenched her hands. This room was as depressing as the rest of the manse, furnished with shelves and books, and a massive desk to one side. Her breath caught in her lungs when she looked to the desk, for there sat Darci, lounging as if she cared nothing for the world. Vanessa froze in the middle of the room, hypnotized by Darci's eyes.

Darci looked up. The black eyes met Vanessa's blue, and Vanessa felt as if she drowned in a wave of darkness. The voice chilled as much as the eyes, if not more so. "What do you want, Vanessa? I can hardly believe the others know you're here. They wouldn't allow it," Darci said. The multi-toned voice made Vanessa quiver.

"Th-they don't know I'm here," Vanessa replied. She set her backpack down, taking time to gather her wits. She felt that if she didn't, she could lose everything to this creature before her. "I left them behind. I'm no longer with our former friends."

Darci studied Vanessa. "And what do you here?"

"I want to join you."

Harsh laughter echoed around the room. Darci leaned on the desk, laughing hard. "You wish to join me?" she said once the laughter receded. "You would betray them so quickly?"

Vanessa's mouth twitched in the shadow of a frown. "I betray no one by coming here, Darci. They betrayed me by kicking me out."

Darci considered her. "Vanessa, I get the feeling you would betray your own mother if it kept you safe and alive. By even being here, you do betray everything you and our former 'friends' stand for. Make no mistake about that."

"I want to join you," Vanessa said again.

Darci gave a very theatrical sigh and leaned back into the leather chair. "I see you are determined. But what can you offer me that would make me overlook your former allegiance and take you on?"

This time Vanessa smiled, wide and cruel. "I can give you information on the so-called Aligerai."

Darci's black eyes shone in the low candle light. Vanessa waited while she thought it over. Finally she looked deep into Vanessa's eyes and smiled as well. The blond allowed herself to relax a bit. "Tell me."

So Vanessa did. She talked for hours, with Darci smiling the entire time. Sandara stood near the door and listened, glancing every now and then over to Alan on the other side of the room. Once Vanessa began fumbling for things to say, Darci cut her off. "You've told me more than enough, Vanessa. I'll have someone show you to a room where you can sleep. You're welcome here." She waved a hand at the door and a servant came to lead Vanessa away. Exhausted, Vanessa could only follow.

The servant led her through narrow halls and shadow-filled rooms. There were a lot of other men about, and Vanessa kept her eyes from resting on any of them. They all gave her the shivers, and seemed to follow her too much with hungry eyes. The thought of it made her queasy.

The thought of Darci made her queasy. How such a small, quiet girl could transform into that . . . that creature downstairs, Vanessa would never know. *She's scary*, she thought. *Scarier than she ever was at school.* Vanessa closed her blue eyes long enough to collect herself before they opened again to follow the man leading her.

More men passed in the hallway. A few of them leered at her. Vanessa bit her lip. *Gross.* She thought back on the meeting instead. The professors looked like nice people, but Vanessa thought they were capable of doing everything Rob and Sita said they were. She frowned. *I don't care if they were right. I'm on the professors' side now. They have to treat me better than that. Right?*

A room came up on her right. The manse was a maze, and Vanessa knew she would effectively be a prisoner from now on. She would never find her way out of the place without someone stopping her. The servant opened the door.

Inside was a small room, with a small bed and a small dresser. The décor was as depressing as the rest of the house. Tan walls looked rotted and old. The rug on the floor looked as if it had accumulated hundreds of years of dust without ever once letting go of even a particle. Vanessa sniffed—the air smelled stale.

The servant prompted her inside. Vanessa nodded her head at him and did as he indicated. "There is a bathroom down the hall to the left," he said. Then he walked away, closing the door behind him.

She dropped her bag before the dresser. She would unpack later. For the moment, she was tired, and dirty, and even with the disgusting décor of this place, she knew she needed to rest somewhere.

Vanessa flopped down on the small but soft bed and fell into a deep sleep.

When the blond girl was gone, Darci returned her attention to her two professors. "Call off the attacks on the humans."

Alan's face went pale. Sandara bit her lip. "My lady, I can't stop attacking the humans," Alan said. He tried not to cringe when her black eyes focused on him. "There is more to this situation than you know, and . . ."

"How many gems are full?" Darci interrupted.

"How many, my lady?"

Darci glared at him, her eyes narrowing to thin slits. "You heard me, Alan. How many are full?"

"Almost half of our cache, which gives us five thousand full gems."

She studied her nails, which allowed Alan to relax out of sight of her direct gaze. "Five thousand full gems. And you need more?" He nodded. "Too bad, Alan. Whatever it is you're planning for those gems will have to wait until this battle is done." She gained her feet, her form blending with the dark shadows around her. "Besides, I do believe the *Pur* can be satisfied with five thousand souls, at least for the moment. Don't you agree, Sandara?"

The other woman stared at the floor, caught between two opposing powers. She clasped her hands behind her back. "Yes, my queen. I believe they can."

Darci bared her white teeth and faced Alan. "You see, even your second-in-command agrees. Do as I order, Alan, or accept the consequences of insubordination."

Alan, taking a deep breath and praying he wasn't about to provoke the mage, said something else. "May I ask why I am to stop the killings?"

"Because I say so!" Darci growled. Her eyes, if possible, grew even darker to hold no light at all. Alan backed off, lowering his eyes and settling into as submissive a posture as he could. Darci relented. "You are to stop this because we need to concentrate on more important things. Things like getting rid of the Aligerai, and winning the war that is about to begin."

The professors remained silent, bowing their heads. Darci smiled at them. "But I do have one final attack for you to accomplish." Alan's head lifted in hope. "I want the Aligerai to fight in this battle. We must give them the encouragement to do so. Attack their school in any way you see fit." She was about to send them away when she thought of something else. "Oh, and take Vanessa with you. She could tell you the easiest and most crowded place to attack students. You have not set foot on campus for quite some time, after all. Make this happen in the next three days."

Bowing, Alan and Sandara slipped out of the room. Darci smiled and sat back down at the desk to enjoy the game being played.

∞

Vanessa followed behind Alan and his men. The daylight had already begun to fade. She glanced round at her fellow students but saw no one familiar in the paths of her old school.

Professor Alan gestured his followers to hide against a wall. They lined up, waiting for his next command. Vanessa was now grateful for the training Robert insisted the girls go through. If she hadn't had that, she would have had a much harder time keeping up with these men. Alan walked back to Vanessa. "Are you sure dinner is over by eight?"

She nodded. "Yes, I'm positive. The doors close at seven-thirty, on the dot, every night. Stragglers are allowed to finish, but no one else can come inside. The only people that should be left are the staff."

Alan grinned. "Good. That's perfect." He held his hand out to one of the five men in his group. "Hand me the fuse." The man hurried to do as told and pulled out a long, thin piece of fuse from his pack. He gave it to Alan. The professor pointed to another man, a frightened looking blond. "You. I want you to light the fuse after I've placed it and we've all cleared. We'll wait at the rendezvous point we discussed earlier, on the other side of campus. Be sure to meet there. Once this goes off, we are gone." The men and Vanessa nodded in silence.

The blond man followed close behind Alan as the professor checked for onlookers, then led them all to the back of the dining hall. They paused at the emergency back door. Alan handed the fuse to the blond man and held out his hand for the circular object held by another man. This lackey handed it to his master with all due haste, glad to be rid of the thing. Alan smirked and held a hand over the ball. The object glowed blue for a moment.

Satisfied it would stay lit, Alan took the fuse back and connected it to the ball. He set it down next to the door and handed a match to the blond man, who audibly gulped. "Remember, wait until we are all out of sight. I need time to get to the rendezvous point and set up the gate. Run there immediately after you have lit this." The man nodded and leaned against the wall, watching the others run away from the building.

When they were just out of sight, he knelt down and struck the match.

Vanessa was just behind the last man when the ground shook. Alan stopped, having just reached the rendezvous. He began to open the gate. Vanessa dared not look back, afraid of what she would see.

Professor Alan had opened the gate and was shoving the men through the red portal. He grabbed the sweating blond man just as he ran up and pushed him through. He reached for Vanessa's arm but she shoved him away. "Go! I'll follow!" she shouted.

Shaking his head, Alan frowned but went through the gate. Vanessa stepped to the threshold and was just about to step through when she made the mistake of looking behind her.

The ground had stopped shaking, but now she knew why it had shaken in the first place.

Half the dining hall was blown away.

The rest was in flames.

Chapter Thirty-Four
A Terrible Way to Die

The young women heard the explosion as silence, then a deep boom followed by the rush of air. Only then did they hear the noises, the sound of crashing stone and wood into rubble on the stricken earth. Then came the flickering of orange light through the windows onto the walls. The ground shook underneath their feet, their building. Shouts in the halls made them get up and look outside as well.

They were shocked to find the dining hall half-gone, the hall obliterated where they had been not thirty minutes before. Sita held one shaking hand to her mouth. "Imbri Mors did this," she whispered into the silence. "They set a bomb."

"The real question is why. Why would they attack here?" Roxie said. She watched the fire trucks finally show up, alarm bells clanging. Students streamed out of buildings to watch, held back by the line of campus policemen. "What was their objective?"

Roxie glanced at her roommate in exasperation. "They wanted to strike at us, of course, to goad us into fighting."

Sita snorted. "They wasted their time and an attack. We've already decided to fight."

"But now they've made us angry," Ari replied. Her lips curled into a silent snarl, her fingers grew and changed into claws. "We'll have our own revenge for their attack on our school. On our people." The snarl left her voice, to be replaced by another emotion. "I hope Jack wasn't in the cafeteria." He had eaten dinner with them but lagged behind to finish his meal.

Sita gasped, hearing the fire alarms going off in their building. "Well, we'll have to wait for our revenge. We need to get out of here. They need us gone in case the fire spreads. Let's go to my house."

The somber duo followed Sita through their own gate into Corá, leaving the fires behind for the night.

They returned the next morning having spent a sleepless night in the fine beds of Sita's mansion. The fire was out now, but twenty people were dead. Only one was a student. The rest had been kitchen staff. With three weeks left in the semester, the school decided to set up temporary food service in another building and asked the remaining two dining halls to pull double duty. Ari paced around the suite and snapped at everyone until Jack answered her phone call and stopped by to check on her. Then she calmed down, to everyone's relief.

Every room in the hall was quiet. Music rarely played, and movies were out of the question. Books and papers were everywhere. Most students had a wild but tired look in their eyes that warned away anyone sane. Skylar and Estelle divided their time between their own room and the suite, partly to give comfort to their friends, and partly to take comfort in being with a group. The whole of the university alternately buzzed or fell silent in the final weeks of that semester, weighed down with grief and fear and the pressures of a continued scholarly existence.

Allen took to sleeping on the couch in the suite. He told the girls his floor was too loud to get any decent rest, but his eyes and manner betrayed him. They all knew he was there to protect them, afraid Imbri Mors would try something closer to home. After a week of this, Sita finally traded rooms with Roxie to let the couple take over her old room. She bunked with Ariene, glad now that she wouldn't wake up to the sight of a man snoring on their couch in the mornings.

Owen came back, terrified when he heard of the bombing. He barged into the suite one afternoon in a panic. "Sita? Sita!"

She ran from her new room. "What?" she said, running to him. "I'm fine, Owen. Nothing happened to any of us."

The wild look in his eyes faded. He swept her up in his arms to hold her tight. "I was so scared when I heard, I came as soon as I could."

She smiled up at him, her face glowing with joy at seeing her lover again. "Well, I'm glad you're back. I've decided that you're not allowed to go back to your house ever again. If you stay here, you won't fret about me, right?"

He laughed and hugged her close again. "Right. Which is why I'm glad you decided that, because I decided the same thing." Owen held her away from him to better look at her, checking over her body for any sign of injury. "You're really not hurt?"

Sita shook her head, unable to contain the smile creeping over her lips. "I'm really not hurt." Owen grinned and kissed her, in love with the feel of her lips, the smooth wetness of her tongue. She chuckled and kissed him just as deep, clinging to him and letting his sweet kiss chase away the nightmares of the past weeks.

Finally she pushed him away. "All right, all right. I have a lot of studying to do, and less than a week until the first test. You'd better let me get back to it, or we'll have more troubles than we can handle on our hands." He laughed loud and let her go, watching her return to her room until she shut the door. Then he slumped onto the couch and turned on a movie, eventually falling into unburdened, dreamless sleep.

∞

The suite was quiet that early morning two days after Owen returned, with all the others still asleep. Roxie and Allen lay passed out on the couch in the common room. Even Ariene had passed out in one of the chairs. Sita chuckled and shut the door on them. She turned to find Owen behind her, waiting for her. With a smile Sita ran to his arms.

Owen kissed her, relishing the taste of her sweet mouth. She smiled up at him, and kissed him again. "Do you really have to go?" she whispered.

He leaned his forehead on hers and sighed. "Unfortunately, yes. This is something I *must* take care of." He kissed her again, then pulled away. "And besides, you have finals next week. You can't afford to have me around. I'm a very big distraction, after all." He winked at her and she laughed. Through the swirl of gray mist rising around him, he could see her face. She looked sad, but a smile sat on her lips. Then he disappeared from her room, and Sita's face faded from his sight.

Owen materialized in the ballroom of a small mansion building. He dropped his pack beside his feet and bowed, though his bow was barely respectful to the people seated behind the long table in front of him. He glanced at the center seat as he rose. The table was visible, but the people seated behind it were not. Their bodies were hidden in the inky shadows that clung to the room and absorbed everything inside into darkness.

Owen tucked his hands into his pockets and folded his luminous wings behind him. "You called?" he asked.

A man's deep voice spoke from the gloom. "You have not paid your debt to us, Owen. We deemed it time to remind you of this fact."

Owen shook his head, his face stoic. "I haven't yet found the person I am looking for, *Professor* Alan. He is still eluding me. Finding him has proved as difficult as I predicted it would be."

A sadistic chuckle echoed around the room when Alan laughed. Owen's eyes narrowed. "But you *have* found the person you were looking for. She's by your side constantly, isn't she?" The man stood and his hands became visible in the yellowing light when he leaned on the table.

It was a battle for Owen to keep his face blank, but some of his trepidation showed through the mask. Alan grinned, his mirth felt if not seen. "She isn't who I'm looking for," Owen replied, his voice harsh. "You know I'm looking for my brother."

"But isn't she the person you have been looking for all your life? Your match, your partner, your love," Alan teased.

Owen shook his head in flat denial. *This can't be happening!* "It's not her! I'm looking for my brother!"

Alan's voice became cold. "Nevertheless, you have found something you seek. The terms of our deal were clear. We give you 'the means to find the person you seek,' and you . . ."

Owen's eyes widened in horror.

". . . you will aide us in destroying the enemy."

"No!" Owen screamed, his wings batting behind him. "I will not! You tricked me!" He grabbed his pack and tried to disappear, but Alan and his cronies activated their barriers while he was distracted. He scrambled toward the door, but the guards stopped him. Red shockwaves of electrical pain coursed through his body. He screamed and slumped in their tight hold. The two guards dragged him up to the table in front of Alan.

Alan's pale hand snaked out and grasped Owen's chin, jerking his face up to meet his eyes. "You will do as you are told, Owen. The terms of our agreement were clear, and you agreed to them."

Owen's body may have been numb, but his mind was fully awake. *No! How could I have been so stupid! No no no no no! What have I done* . . . He managed to open his mouth and get his voice to work. "My brother . . ." he whispered.

The shadowy man behind the table cackled in pure sadistic glee. "Oh, Owen. You simple, naïve fool. We knew where your brother was all along. We know where *everyone* is!" Owen's eyes widened at the implications of Alan's statement. Alan saw the knowledge in his eyes. "Oh, yes, Owen. We knew where you were all this time. We knew what you were doing. We know where your little girlfriend and her friends are. We know *everything*."

"You leave her out of this!" Owen managed to cry, mustering enough strength to struggle against the guards, who sent another electrical charge through him. He fell limp again.

A female voice spoke this time, purring in satisfaction. "Remember when you promised to aide us in destroying our enemies?" The voice penetrated his mind with gentle probes, as if it were trying to seduce him into agreement. "Our main enemy, Owen, is your girlfriend." He felt her triumphant smile, and he knew what she would say next. "And you are going to kill her for us."

Owen raised his head, his mind finally numb to what was happening. He still found enough of his spirit to fight back one more time. He kicked at the guards, straining against them. "I will *never* help you monsters!" he screamed in agony. The guards hit him a third time, and this time Owen was unable to recover. Conscious but in a great deal of pain, Owen allowed his captors to drag him away.

Alan stopped them. "Oh, you don't have to push the knife into her heart yourself, much as I would enjoy that. But there are other ways to kill and torment a person. Let me demonstrate. Giles, would you bring Eric Madison up please?" A man stepped from the shadows and held his hands up, palms toward an empty wall. Orange power streamed from his hands to form a frame on the wall. A picture appeared there on the giant magical window. Alan faced Owen. "You see, Owen? Your brother is there. We've known where he is all this time, because he is one of us." He gloated when he saw the horror form on Owen's face as the picture firmed and showed something he never wanted to see. He screamed in denial as the guards dragged him from the room.

The screen showed his brother Eric with his arms around Sita, kissing her passionately.

∞

Sita sat upright in her chair, jolted from the strangest dream. Cold sweat trickled down her back between her shoulder blades. The sensation caused her to shiver. Grabbing her robe, Sita jumped up from her desk and the hard pillow of books and hurried out into the common room.

She made her way to the kitchenette and began to make herself some hot chocolate. While she waited for the water to boil, she replayed the dream in her mind. As she did, she felt her hands grow cold and a shiver travel up and down her spine. The robe did nothing to dispel the chill she now felt.

In the dream, she had seen Owen on a journey to a place far away. He was surrounded by mist, and the dream itself was almost in black and white, it was so dimmed. He arrived at his destination . . . but the people he had intended to meet were not the people with whom he met. These people were bad, horrible people, the kind of people who would sell their mothers if it were to their own advantage. And in the dream, Owen was taken by this enemy and eaten by the mist.

Sita's hands shook as she moved the whistling kettle off the heat.

First, she had a dream about Darci being kidnapped. Next, Ari had a dream about Vanessa turning on them. And now Sita had another dream, but about Owen instead of her friends. All of this added up to one conclusion in her mind.

The dream was true.

As her legs turned to jelly, Sita sank to the floor, her back pressed hard against the counter. Just then, she heard a door open. Roxie came out of her room, yawning, and headed for the fridge. She paused when she saw Sita. But she only paused for a moment before she hurried to Sita's side. "What's wrong? What happened? Are you OK?"

Sita shook her head and tried to speak, but her first few attempts only resulted in her mouth flapping open and closed. Then she cleared her throat and told Roxie about the dream.

Roxie listened and held Sita's hand while she spoke. When Sita had finished, Roxie bit her bottom lip and met Sita's eyes. "Si . . . do you think it might be a trap? They've gotten into your mind before. Could this be the same thing?"

Nothing could be said in answer to that, so Sita instead turned away and shuffled into her room. She pulled out a duffel bag and began shoving shirts and pants into it, as well as anything else she could find that might be useful. Roxie watched. "What are you doing?" she asked.

"I'm going after him." Sita grabbed another pair of socks and rammed them into the pack as well. "I'm not leaving him in their hands. Do you know what they'll do to him?"

Roxie stepped in front of the door. "You're not going anywhere."

Sita stopped packing. She raised her head to look deep into Roxie's eyes. Rox held her ground. "Who are you to stop me." Sita picked up the bag and slung it over her shoulder, approaching until she was almost nose to nose with Rox. "Move."

"No."

Sita glared at her. "Move!"

"No." Roxie reached out and yanked Sita into her arms, wrapping her in a fierce embrace. "You have to stay here. We'll find him together."

That broke Sita from her panic. She dropped the bag to thud down at their feet. Tears broke through her defenses and she sobbed in Roxie's arms.

Rox held her close until she could cry no more, until the controlled vengeance began to replace the sorrow and fear in Sita's eyes. "You have to stay," Roxie repeated. "We need you to, or *we* can't hold on. You hold us together." She wiped her thumb over the damp cheeks, wiping away the salty tears held there. "Besides, you still have finals. If you don't take them, you'll fail. You know that."

"I'm not taking those inane tests," Sita said. She pushed herself out of Roxie's hold. The contents of the duffel bag spilled onto her bed as she upended it. "There are more important things than school."

"You have to take those tests, Sita. You can't skip out of this one."

"No." Sita ran a brush through her tangled hair and scrubbed at her smeared face with a towel. She felt like her heart would never beat again, but the traitorous organ did beat. "How can I concentrate enough to take a final when my boyfriend is in the hands of the enemy? It would be pointless, so why bother?"

Rox put a hand on Sita's shoulder. She fell still under her friend's hand and wilted a little. "Sita. If you don't take the finals, this entire semester would have been a waste. Can you deal with that?" She smiled at the back of Sita's golden head. "I know you. You would feel guilty later on. Though, I don't know, you might want to skip them just so you'll have something to blame Owen for when he comes back. You'll need to have some kind of reason for beating him senseless, after all."

Sita snorted, the tension leaking out of her shoulders. "OK, OK, I'll take them. But I'll probably fail anyway." She realized something was missing. "Where's Ari? I just realized she's not here."

"I think she fell asleep on the couch. I saw her behind a mountain of books."

"Oh." Sita tugged at her lip. "Well, she can stay there for now. We can wake her up for breakfast later."

"Much later," Roxie said. "It's three in the morning!"

∞

Professor Alan stood in front of the group, talking to Sandara. She nodded at something he said, then began constructing a gate into Corá. They had been at the small one-room apartment for days, weeks even, ever since the attack on the school. Vanessa was very sick of sleeping on a cot in the walk-in closet. So she was very glad when Alan announced to the five men that Sandara had brought word of the impending battle, and they would be traveling to the campsite as soon as they were packed.

Sandara activated the Ripper, then beckoned Vanessa forward once the gate's red edges began to appear. "Vanessa, dear, have you ever been to battle before?"

"No, never. It's not really the sort of thing normal people do here on Earth."

"Then perhaps you should stay at the manor with Darci. I'm sure she would love your company."

Vanessa shivered at the thought. "I would prefer not to. I can help in the battle. I'm skilled with calling plants, after all, and as long as the soldiers are on the ground, I can take them out."

Sandara's brows rose a fraction. "Really? That's very interesting. I will talk to Alan about it. Perhaps we can use you after all."

The gate into Corá opened fully and the eight members began to step through at once. Vanessa stayed at the end of the line. A strange sense of foreboding about the gate settled into her stomach and chest and made her start to sweat. She licked her lips. If something were going to happen across the opening, she wanted to let as many people go before her as possible—less chance of being attacked that way. She stood still as Ray Alan and Sandara passed her, talking in an undertone while they stepped through. It was finally Vanessa's turn. She closed her eyes and walked in.

She hated the feeling of stepping through the portal. One step through and she hung in space, carried through only by the momentum of her stride. Her stomach did flip-flops, her eyes saw only darkness, and an ethereal breeze pulled at her hair and clothes. Her mind refused to acknowledge the fact that for this one moment there was no ground beneath her feet.

Vanessa emerged onto the other side, gasping for air and stumbling while the vertigo wore off. But her feeling of foreboding only increased, and she looked around, searching for the source of what felt like impending doom.

Alan gave the order to head out to the base. "We need to get there quickly, before anyone notices our presence." The group began moving off to the west. No one paid any attention to the girl in the back.

Vanessa shuddered when the gate closed behind her. Sweating, she moaned as nausea overtook her and she dropped to all fours. Her vision blurred. Sandara heard her and looked back, brow furrowed. The woman placed a hand on Ray's shoulder. He turned and stopped to watch the girl.

Sweat poured from Vanessa's pores, drenching her clothes in a matter of seconds. She fought to stand, but the nausea forced her down. Her lungs couldn't take in enough air and she was left gasping. With another deep moan, she coughed up blood. The dark red stained her now-ivory face. A voice, deep and mighty, whispered in her mind. *You, Daughter, are corrupt. You taint this land with your deeds, you poison Me with your thoughts. You are not welcome here any longer.*

Pain as she had never felt before lanced through Vanessa's body. A high, terrible scream erupted from her throat. The sound frightened the Imbri members and scared away every animal in a mile's range. Everyone stopped to watch in shocked silence. Vanessa continued to scream and scream and the pain consumed her body and narrowed her world to nothing but pain.

Vines covered in wicked thorns sprouted in the middle of the path. They reached for Vanessa with hungry fingers. She screamed when they cut into her feet and wrapped around her ankles gently, as a lover's touch. Blood, bright red against her pale skin, dripped onto the emerald grass in lazy trails. Fighting the nausea, Vanessa rose and tried to fight off the vines, screaming louder when they twined up to her knees.

"Please!" she cried. "Please, no, take them away!" Her hands were cut to shreds when she tried to pull and tug at the vines. She began to cry in terror. "Don't do this to me, oh please, I'll change, I swear!" She sobbed harder and shrieked when the voice echoed in her mind again: *I have seen your heart, Vanessa. You are not worthy of the power you have been given. You will never change.*

Alan and Sandara watched, fascinated, as the vines overtook the girl's efforts and had her cocooned in thorns, still writhing and pleading in despair. Vanessa could no longer move anything but her voice.

The ground beneath her feet trembled and opened wide, a huge earthen yawn. Vanessa, encased in the black plants, blood mingling with the grass, plunged into the cavernous hole, her scream echoing up to the others.

Then the ground closed.

To Alan's eyes, it seemed the hole had never been there.

Shaken, Sandara turned to Alan. "Was that supposed to happen?" she asked, her voice quavering.

Alan slowly shook his head. "No. No, it was not." He stared at the spot a little bit longer. The pieces slowly began to come together. He looked at his flock as he came out of his reverie. "Come. We need to get out of here. Let's move." The Imbri, confused and frightened, moved off again.

The ground quivered in anger, and the voice spoke once more, heard only by those equipped with the magic to hear Her.

It is done.

∞

They all felt it when Vanessa died, in the middle of finals week, around ten in the morning.

Sita was leaving her fourth and last final when a burning sensation on her finger forced her to bend over and bite her lip to keep from crying out. She tried to hide the glowing band from any curious eyes. She almost fell to her knees, but the pain faded fast. Through the ring's connection, she could feel that the same sensation had woken Roxie and Ari, who had been sleeping in for once. They also cried out in pain. Sita felt through Roxie that Allen had sat upright in bed next to her when she shouted and reached for a knife that wasn't there.

A minute later and the rings were back to normal, as cool as when they had been put on. But now, instead of five gems, there were four. The tiny emerald had fallen out while the rings burned. Sita reached down and picked it up from the ground, tears welling up. "No." She began to run back to the suite, ignoring the strange looks she got from her fellow students. "No!"

Sita rushed into her suite a few minutes later, barely out of breath. "What happened?" she cried. "Does anyone know anything?"

"I don't know what happened, except for the scene I saw when the ring glowed," said Ari.

Roxie's head lifted. "I saw something, too. What did you see? Maybe we all saw the same thing."

Allen passed out cups of water while Ari recounted what she had seen. "It wasn't very long, but I saw Vanessa . . . well, it looked like she was being eaten by vines. But that doesn't make any sense."

"I saw her in Corá, with some other people, but I can't be sure who," Roxie said. Her eyes were red-rimmed and weary. "And then I saw the ground swallow her up." Allen sat down next to her and grasped her hand. "I think Vanessa's dead."

Sita sank into the armchair by the door. "I saw a combination of the two. Vanessa was wrapped up in vines, watched by a bunch of people, and then the ground opened and took her." She ran a hand over her face. "I think it's safe to say she's most definitely dead."

The group fell silent. They could think of nothing more to say. Tears dripped down their cheeks to land on cold hands or unfeeling cloth. "What should we do?" Sita whispered. "We can't leave her there."

Allen spoke up then. "I can talk to Rob about it. He might know how to find her . . . her body. We'll think of something." The others nodded and settled into their grief, grateful that this semester of death was over tomorrow morning.

Sita took off her necklace and stared at Vanessa's gem in her hand. She pulled out a drop of magic and attached the gem to the setting of her quartz crystal. It would stay there until she found out what had happened.

Chapter Thirty-Five
Gods Reveal All

The suite was empty. Everything was packed, down to the last piece of clothing and pin. Blinds hung over lonely windows, and the air conditioner hummed for no one in the late spring air. The girls were gone.

Far away in Maryland, Sita propped an empty duffel bag on her bed. The appearance from school to home took little from her but she was still exhausted. Getting home was easier now they could all teleport themselves, but their baggage took more out of them all than they thought. Sita knew the others would be in as much pain and exhaustion, if not more. Sita had arrived home the day before her sister's graduation from high school. The ceremony had been beautiful, and Marie was so happy to be out of school at last. Sita had taken her out to dinner the night before, as a graduation party. They stayed up late celebrating at home.

Marie stood in the doorway to Sita's room, still dressed in her pajamas. "You just got back two days ago and now you're leaving again?"

Sita closed her eyes. "Yes, Marie, I'm leaving again as soon as I get a few hours of sleep."

"Why?"

"I have to go into Corá. Some things have happened that they need my help with."

"I want to go with you."

"Absolutely not."

Marie stamped her foot and crossed her arms. "Why not? School ended yesterday for me too, you know. It's summer, I have nothing to do, and I want to help."

"Have you decided about college yet?"

Her sister shifted on her feet, studying the carpet. "Well, not exactly . . ."

Sita patted her on the arm. "That's settled then. You're better off sitting here and trying to figure out what you're going to be doing now you're done with high school."

Marie groaned. "You're such an idiot!" she shouted.

"I am not!" Sita replied after her retreating back. "I have things to do, then I'll be back! With any luck, I won't be gone very long."

"Why can't I go? I've been there before!"

"Because it's war!" Sita shouted back. "And I will not take my little sister onto a battlefield!"

Marie fell silent at last. She stared back at Sita with widened eyes. "War? What do you mean?"

Sita shoved her luggage off her bed and sat down in the space created. She rubbed a hand over her eyes. "Remember those attacks that were all over the news, the ones that killed hundreds of people at a time?" Marie nodded. "Those are the people we're fighting. They've moved the battle into the other plane, though I'm really not sure why—they might have actually heard our arguments about innocent people—and we're going to fight them there." She bowed her head. "And Vanessa died. We have to find her body."

Her sister sat down beside her and placed a hand on her arm. Sita grasped it, holding on tight. "I need you here. I need to know you're safe. If I take you there with me, I won't be able to concentrate long enough to do what they need me to do." Sita touched her sister's porcelain face and wiped away the solitary tear that slipped down. The pillow called for her, so she stretched out on the bed, Marie beside her. "You'll be safe here. I need you here. And try to think of what you want out of life, hmm?"

Marie finally nodded her assent. "All right. But only if you do, too."

"What do you mean?" Sita's eyes were half-closed already, sleep coming on too fast to fight.

"Come on, Si. Do you really think you'll be working here for the rest of your life?" She chuckled as Sita's eyes closed completely. Sita drifted in the haze of half-sleep and could still hear Marie's soft words. "You and I both know you're gonna end up in Corá." Her sister stood. "And so will I."

Robert showed up later that afternoon. He popped into Sita's living room and scared Marie badly enough to make her scream.

Sita came running. "What's wrong?" She relaxed when she saw it was only Robert. "Is it time, then?"

He nodded. Sita ran upstairs for her pack. Marie took that opportunity to steal Robert aside. "It's Rob, right?" His brow creased but he nodded. "Look, just please watch her for me? Make sure she doesn't get hurt? I want her back."

Rob smiled. "Of course."

A loud trampling down the stairs announced Sita's reemergence. "I'm ready, let's get going."

Rob took Sita's arm. "We might be gone a long time. I honestly don't know how long this will take. With luck, no more than a month. And I found a trace of where Vanessa's body might be."

Sita pursed her lips and handed her pack to him. "I have everything I need in there, and I can get more from the mansion if I need it. Did you get the others already?"

"You're the last."

"Good. Just let me say good-bye."

Rob half-bowed and walked into the kitchen. Sita pulled Marie to her. "I'll be OK. I promise."

Marie struggled not to cry and held Sita tighter. "If you don't come back, I'll track you down and kill you myself." Sita chuckled into her sister's red hair. Marie let her go.

Sita ran a hand down Marie's cheek. "I'll be back. I promise you that. And then we'll have the rest of the summer to relax. Maybe I'll even take you into Corá when I get back."

"You'd better."

Marie looked down at the floor, tears overwhelming her vision. When she looked back up, both Sita and Robert had disappeared.

Robert took Sita to an enormous field. Neat green rows of tents checkered the grass, and soldiers in varying uniforms roamed through the lines. Cooking food in the mess tent and at small firepits outside some of the tents sent delicious smells wafting through the air. Horses neighed and pawed the ground off to the left as the pair passed one of the picket lines. Cart donkeys brayed when someone got too close. The sound of metal on metal came from all sides of camp: soldiers practiced their skills, farriers shoed horses and forged new horseshoes, the smiths mended armor or weapons. It would have been cacophony if the camp hadn't been so spread out. As it was, Sita wasn't sure she would ever find her way around without a guide. The camp had been organized in a grid, but it wasn't easy like following a street grid, as there were no signs at all in the camp. Pennants and flags flapped and snapped in the breeze over some of the more important tents.

From the corner of her eye, Sita studied the side of Rob's face. She shoved her hands in her pockets, pack slung over one shoulder. "You know, I heard what Marie said. About you watching out for me."

"Oh?"

"She's just worried. I don't need you to look after me or anything."

"I disagree."

She stopped in her tracks. "What?"

"I disagree. I think you do need someone to look after you. Otherwise, you might do something stupid. Like date someone who just mysteriously shows up at your gate. Or try to go haring off after that same stranger because he gets kidnapped, probably as a trap for you." She gaped at him. Robert snorted. "Yeah, I heard about that from Roxie. She told me because she was worried."

"Oh would you stop being so jealous?" She kept her voice down. Soldiers surrounded them now, and she didn't want the whole camp to hear this argument.

Apparently, neither did Rob, as he did the same. "I'm not jealous, I'm right. You need us to watch your back and save you from doing something stupid."

"I don't need you! I don't need you or anyone else, and I don't need anyone to save me or anything. I'm fine!"

"Yes, you do. You want us, and you definitely need us."

"I don't need saving."

"You need us around to save you from yourself! You don't need us to save you from some enemy. You need us to save you from yourself!"

There was nothing more she could say to that. Clearly, he was unwilling to change his mind, and she didn't feel like continuing the argument. So she bit her tongue hard and followed him to a set of tents set off to one side close to the middle of the camp. These tents were a paler green, and larger than the soldiers' tents.

Roxie lounged on a stool outside, a book in her hands. She looked up when their shadows reached her feet. "Well, it's about time you got back here." She closed the book and beckoned them inside. "We've been waiting." The pair followed her inside.

Ariene sat on one of the cots inside the tent. She smiled when Sita and Robert walked in and made room on the beds for them. Rob remained standing, so Roxie took the last seat. "OK, here's how this works. We have three tents for our own use. Allen and I will share one. The other two you ladies can divide up as you will. And once Sita sets her pack down, I can take you all to look for Vanessa's body. I think I might have found where they came into Corá and that's likely where she is."

The women nodded. "So, who's sleeping where?" Sita asked.

"Ari and I are comfy here," Rox spoke up. "So it looks like you get your own tent."

Sita rubbed her hands together and grabbed her bag. "Great. I'll go put this away and then we can go." She was about to leave when she paused just inside the tent flap. "It looks like rain. Might want to grab a jacket or a spare cloak."

Her tent was luxurious compared to what she thought a normal soldiers' tent would look like. Two cots lined the walls, covered with sheets and plain fleece blankets. A small traveling desk stood off to one side, and a small dining table faced the door. Sita shrugged—if someone wanted them comfortable, she was hardly going to complain.

She strode to the right-hand bed and upended her bag over it. Two simple dresses fell out, along with two pairs of thin trousers and undergarments. A hairbrush, a toothbrush and paste, a journal, and a pen fell on top of the clothes. She gave it another shake. An old book fell out, along with two gleaming stones.

Once she made sure the bag was empty, she threw it onto the bed and grabbed the two stones. Each landed in a pocket of her cloak. *I'm glad now I thought to bring this from the mansion. It's easier than jackets.* She threw the cloak on over her jeans and shirt and walked out of her tent.

The others waited outside. When Sita emerged, Robert began walking off. "Let's go. We have to be back before nightfall and it's at least an hour's walk."

Almost exactly an hour later, they arrived at a small clearing. Robert led them through it by following a dirt path that bisected the grass and headed into the woods. Rain began to drizzle down. He stopped halfway through the field. "This is it. This is where the disturbance was felt most, so I figure this is where they came through. We can start here."

Fanning out, the group began to search. Sita walked forward down the path bit by bit. The cold sprinkle of rain kissed her skin and made her shiver. This place felt different. Not only did it look ethereal, it *felt* ethereal, as if they walked the boundary of another world. Even the air smelled different than it had walking along the path. The air here tasted sweeter, and smelled of flowers and spring. Sita eyed the ground, noticing how vibrant the green grass appeared. No animals strayed too close, and only far-off birdsong assured Sita that any animals even lived in the woods. As she began to notice more of the world around her, she also felt a growing vibration from her ring—as if it responded to whatever it was she felt in the clearing.

An idea came to her. If she could trace the vibrations of the ring she made, she would find Vanessa. She hummed a sorrowful tune under her breath to herself while she concentrated on the ground beneath her and on finding the magical vibrations of her ring.

The earth shuddered beneath their feet. They all staggered and fought for their balance. Frightened birds burst into flight from the woods. Sita stopped humming to look around after she regained her balance. The worn dirt road snaked further through the trees, but she could feel a tingle in the air now that wasn't present earlier.

A small mound of earth broke free from the grass to rise from the forest floor in front of Sita, a mound of dirt that soon became a tall, thin pillar. It grew until it reached the height of Sita's waist. Then it stopped.

The women stood still, silent and dumbstruck. Robert ran a sweating hand through his hair, awed at the sight. A chill wind blew among them, making their flesh prickle and the drizzling rain dance. Sita stepped closer, calm and composed. On top of the pillar of earth lay a sparkling gold ring with four gems in it.

Sita reached down and picked up the ring she had crafted, her eyes sad. Turning to her friends, she held out the ring for them to see. "I told you all these rings could never be taken off." She looked at each in turn, face full of sorrow. "If this ring is here, then Vanessa is definitely dead."

"Do we know how she died? Was it Imbri?" Estelle asked.

Robert paced around the pillar. "I'm afraid we can't know that for sure, but it's probably a safe bet that she went to Darci and asked her for shelter. I don't think Imbri would kill her though . . . the better question is how did the earth move like this?"

"You don't think . . . you don't think Vanessa is still alive down there, and it was her doing it?" Roxie asked.

Sita shook her head. "No, she's not alive. I'm sure of that. Not with her ring sitting here in my hand."

Ariene inched closer. "Well, then, what happened?"

Rob was about to answer when he was interrupted by mist. Swirling mist came from nowhere, directly above the pillar of earth. The drizzle of rain lessened to only a few drops and the breeze died. The mist, an eddy of reds, purples, and blues, began to take the shape of a woman.

Everyone stepped back. The mist began to solidify. The outline of a woman, wreathed in the thin rainbow mist, became clearer. Green hair the color of the grass under their feet hung to the woman's waist, changing from dark emerald to light green as it fell. The gown the woman wore changed colors constantly. It clung to her shape and flowed down to her ankles. The colors were as bright as the finest flowers in spring, and every color of the rainbow played over the rich fabric.

But it was the eyes that captivated the Aligerai most. Those eyes, set into a finely sculptured face that put any movie star to shame, reflected countless ages of time. Stars shone there.

The woman, fully formed now, stepped down from the pillar and touched a foot to the earth. The grass suddenly grew taller. "I can tell you what happened," she said. The voice coming from that full mouth startled them all—it sounded both masculine and feminine at the same time. It had an ethereal quality that echoed through everything, as if she spoke from a great distance. Sita felt the echoes reverberate within her own soul.

Sita looked closer. The woman's face had at first looked incredibly beautiful, the finest specimen of female beauty she had ever seen. But on a second glance, she could see how that same face was also very masculine in its lines, the features changeable. Sita met those eyes with caution, afraid that she would lose herself in the stars. "Who are you?"

"Do you truly not know me?" she asked. She turned to Rob. "You should be able to say who I am, Robert Gordon. You have known me for many years."

Robert bowed deep, not daring to look at her face the way Sita did. "Yes, ma'am, I know who you are. I thank you for all you have done over the years."

The woman gave him a soft smile. "You are a good man, Robert Gordon. I am glad to have you in my service any day. Your vow of protection has held true, and for that I thank you." Robert stayed bowed. She turned to look at the group of young women around her. "As for the rest of you, I can tell you what happened to this girl. She is buried here, by my doing."

A collective gasp rose from the group. "What? Why?" Roxie asked.

"She was corrupted. Corrupted by greed. By hate. Her very presence here tainted the land." The woman strode over to Roxie, staring her square in the face. "With her magic tied to plants and the land, if she is corrupted, then so is everything she is tied to. I could not have her here. She would have tainted me."

Sita finally put the pieces together. "Oh my god. You're . . . you can't be . . ."

The woman grinned now and floated to Sita, the grass growing behind her as she came closer. "Ah, the Awle Heir has figured it out. Wonderful, my dear." She brushed a finger over Sita's pale cheek. "Yes, I am Corá. I am the embodiment of the land, of this entire world." Her face changed, became less beautiful and more vengeful. "If someone threatens my very existence, I will negate them if at all possible. I will not become like my sister, Earth."

Sita's brow creased. "What do you mean, like Earth?"

"Have you ever seen Earth's embodiment? Her human form? No. And you likely never will." Corá twined her fingers through her green hair, still focused on Sita. "Gaia, or Earth, my twin, is dormant. Her magic has long been lost, stolen away by greedy human mages who wanted more than the Mother gave them. I will not let that happen to me." She reached out to touch the ring in Sita's hand. "Vanessa wanted more than was given to her. The greed and hate in her heart reached down into her very soul. She was corrupt. She was, unknown to her, killing whatever vegetation and land she touched. She was harming me. What would you do, if someone were making you ill?"

Roxie snorted behind them. "Well, I wouldn't kill them, that's for sure."

Corá whirled around to peer at the brunette, her gaze piercing. Roxie swallowed. "I would not be so certain of that, my dear Roxanne. There are depths to you that you will not admit, even to yourself. Especially to yourself. I have seen your dreams, your heart, and your soul over these past few months. Ever since you stepped foot on my soil, I have known you all." The mystical woman then refocused on Sita and reached into the young woman's pockets, pulling out the two gems there.

Sita held herself still while Corá studied the gems, running her hands over the rough surfaces. "Angelite and celestite. Very wise choices for you. These stones like you very much. They are happy with you." She replaced the gems. "They are filled with your magic already. Surprising, since gems normally take many years to attune themselves with a person. What will you do with these?"

"I don't know yet. But these two were stolen from Imbri Mors. Two less of these in their hands is only a good thing."

Corá smiled, the expression grim. "Yes, Imbri Mors. Odd that you should mention them."

"How so?"

"They are a blight on my skin. An open sore, a wound to my people. Yet I can't seem to be rid of them."

The woman circled Sita, like a vulture or hunter circling its prey. Sita held still, watching her from the corner of her eye. "Let me guess. You want us to do it for you."

"Yes." The multi-toned voice came out in a hiss, the face contorted into lines of fury. "I cannot kill them myself. I can only make them miserable."

Skylar stepped forward. "Excuse me, but if someone as powerful as you can't kill them, what makes you think we can?"

Corá lost her fury and smiled again, beatific and angelic. Sita was reminded of a young horse—they could be all fire and heel one minute, but docile and eager to please in the next. "You have strengths to you that others do not possess. You have many hidden qualities, hidden depths, that make you endure long past the time when you should have given in. Your presence here is proof of that much."

"Forgive me, Corá, but why can't you get rid of them yourself?" Sky said.

The strawberry lips curled into a snarl. "With their combined magical skills, they have been able to thwart any attack I throw at them." She fell into a sullen look, her shoulders drooping. "You must remember, Aligerai, that my strengths are in nature. I can throw any number of tornadoes, hurricanes, floods, earthquakes, and fires at them, but those attacks come at a cost. Not only to me, but to the land and my people. Ridding myself of them on my own would cause more harm than good." She spread her hands wide, pleading. "Which is why I need someone to do it for me, so I don't harm those I am trying to protect. You understood the dreams I sent you and you acted on them. This gives me hope."

Sita blinked in surprise. "*You* sent the dreams Ari and I had?"

The goddess looked almost offended at the question. "Of course. Who else would send you dreams?" Then she sighed and deflated a little. "Will you help me?"

The group fell silent then. Rob remained off to the side. Sita watched the looks on her friends' faces, watched them glance at each other in turn, and saw them each come to a decision. "Your luck is in, Corá. We're already fighting them," Ari said. "We'll do our best to help you."

Corá chortled and clapped her hands together. "Excellent, excellent! Thank you." Sita bowed her head and closed her eyes with a soft sigh. Corá turned to her. "Sita, my child, what is wrong? Does this decision displease you?"

Sita looked up from her study of the ground. "No, it doesn't. I'll fight against Alan and Sandara. They have my boyfriend, and I want him back." She wrapped the cloak's edge closer around her. "But ridding you of Imbri means only one thing: Darci's death. And her death can only be accomplished at my hands. Sorry, but that doesn't make me very happy."

The others quieted. They had not realized that piece of the puzzle before. Corá floated closer until she stood just in front of Sita. A slender finger reached to touch Sita's face. "You are truly amazing, Sita. There is far more to you than meets the eye." Sita met Corá's gaze and her breath caught in her throat at the wonder she saw there. "Do not feel guilty when you must fight Darci. There is more to that situation than meets the eye as well."

"What does that mean?" Sita pushed the warm finger away, her annoyance plain. "My friend's death can only be at my hands, by my doing. No one else stands even a chance at beating her, and you tell me I shouldn't feel guilty about it? Hardly."

Corá tapped Sita's cheek with her palm. "Don't get smart, girl. As I said, there is more to Darci's situation than you know. You will discover all in due time." She stalked back to the pillar of dirt, her hair turning a strange shade of greenish-brown when she stepped onto the disturbed earth. "Meanwhile, you have all agreed to aide me in ridding our world of Imbri Mors. I hold you to your oath. And in return, I will do everything I can to aide you in the battle tomorrow, and in future battles to come."

Robert bowed again when she looked to him. "Robert Gordon, watch over these women. They are dear to me, now and always. As are you, so be sure you do not die tomorrow, or I shall be very disappointed." She vanished into the rainbow mist once more.

The group stared at the pillar. Sita fingered Vanessa's ring and breathed deeply before slipping the jewelry into her cloak pocket. The drizzle started up once more. Stunned silence hung around them.

Finally Rob broke their reverie. "Well, that was exciting. We know what happened to Vanessa, we know where she is, I say it's time to head back to camp. Dusk comes quick in these woods."

Roxie stopped him just as he turned to lead. "Wait. Shouldn't we put up a marker or something?"

Ari nodded. "I think so. She needs a headstone." She looked at Sita. "Can you make it?"

"Me?"

Ari rolled her eyes. "Well, you're the only one with magic that can create things, you know. The rest of us are a little bit limited, thanks."

Sita had the grace to blush. "Right. Well, I don't know how good this is going to be. I'm not as good as Vanessa was at working with earth, you know."

"Just try," Roxie said.

"All right, all right, give me a minute." Sita knelt down on the damp ground, the rain beginning to soak her cloak. She laid her hands on the earth and pursed her lips. The pillar began to shake and change. It hardened from the soft dirt into a two-foot-high gray stone. Sita paused for a breather before raising a glowing finger to the stone. She traced the words out in purple against the rock, then she pushed the magic into the marker. The words were engraved there, a hint of violet still clinging to them:

VANESSA MARIE YEAGER

One of the five Aligerai from Earth
Buried here by Corá herself
Rest in peace

Chapter Thirty-Six
War

Soldiers streamed around the sopping manse. They formed into units and began the long march to the battleground. Alan watched them go while his own underlings scurried around the house to make things ready for departure. He sighed in regret—one more troublesome thing to worry about before he could think about leaving.

Once he saw the last of his soldiers depart into the mist, he turned from the windows and stalked back into his office. He took off his jacket and flung it into the chair. His office was quieter at the moment—Sandara had already departed for the field to oversee the last of the army arrivals. He smirked. It was quite nice to have a woman around to do the woman-work. Darci had disappeared at dusk yesterday, and no one had seen her since. Alan wasn't worried, though. How could his queen resist the conflict to come?

He chuckled to himself and downed a glass of brandy. Wiping his mouth on his hand, Alan walked from the office and down to the first floor where his prisoner waited for him.

The door was strong, and nothing short of Darci's power could break the bird-man inside out of his cell. Alan unlocked it and walked in, shutting the door behind him. Owen sat on the ground in the farthest corner, shrouded in darkness, the only light coming from his small, barred window. Alan stalked over to stop just short of the man's outstretched feet. "There is to be a battle tomorrow, Owen." No reply. Alan frowned. "What do you think will happen when your lover finds you have joined our ranks?"

Owen's hoarse voice echoed in the stone chamber. "You will never make me fight against them. I'll die first."

Alan grabbed Owen by the neck of his shirt. "I think I could arrange that." He flung Owen against the wall, forcing the bird-man's wings behind him where they wouldn't be able to buffet the good professor. He pinned Owen there, his hand bruising the tender flesh of Owen's neck. "You are worthless now, Owen. You couldn't help me while you lived and breathed, but your death will help us by rendering Sita absolutely useless, just like she was when your brother left her. Her grief when she finds out you're dead will consume her, and she won't be able to fight against us anymore. We will win!" He pushed harder, forcing Owen's airway almost closed. Owen tried to gasp in air, barely getting enough.

An eerie green glow caught Owen's attention from the corner of his eye. In Alan's hand there sat an orb of green magic, crackling like electricity. Owen recognized it for what it was. "No . . . no, please! Are you insane? That . . . will kill . . . anyone within . . . a mile's radius!" Owen just managed to gasp it out as Alan's grip loosened.

The evil smile on the professor's lips reflected the charged globe in his hand. "That's not a problem. Why do you think I would care, Owen? I've already decided to kill you, and so I shall, in this manner, right now. There is no changing my mind."

He threw the glowing ball high, sending a lance of his own blue magic into it. The bolt of Alan's magic activated the globe, and it expanded. Alan forced Owen's head up, to watch the orb as it swelled and grew larger than a man. It rotated in the air, circular now instead of a globe, and turned into a flat disc that opened into another world. Owen could see nothing but darkness on the other side.

A timid knock on the door yanked Alan's attention away. The door opened to reveal his most junior aide. "Sir, everything is ready . . ."

The boy would never speak another word. Alan enveloped him in cobalt power, cutting off his voice and hauling the boy over to the edge of the glowing vertical circle. Just as the boy was about to fall in, Alan removed the magic. The boy screeched, the sound high and piercing. He tottered on the edge, his arms wind-milling. Then he toppled over, his screams cut off in a sudden rush of acrid air.

Alan dragged Owen over as the disc floated further down, nearly going through the floor. It crackled and hissed. "You saw what I did with my aide. And he only displeased me. Do you think he survived Metanoia, the plane of Chaos? Do you think he survived *that?*" Owen didn't answer. He stared into the darkness of the gate, the glow washing his features in a sickly olive color. Alan dragged him even closer, at the very lip of the gate now. "Do you think you will survive?"

He shoved Owen forward.

Owen screamed as he fell into the gate and disappeared into the darkness.

∞

The day after Vanessa's body was found, Allen came to Roxie. She followed him out of the tent and beyond the line of sentries. He led her hand in hand to a more secluded grove of trees. "What's going on, Allen?" she asked. His hand felt clammy and nervous, and it was making her sweat with nerves of her own. "Tell me what's wrong."

She knew he was trying to hide something, because his brown eyes gleamed with a quality like fear. Allen pulled her close against his chest and wrapped his arms tight around her. "Roxie . . . you know I'm fighting tomorrow, right?"

"Yes," she said in a whisper.

"And I'm not gifted."

She scoffed. "You don't have magic. That doesn't mean you aren't gifted."

The feeble defense made them both smile. "Roxie, I just wanted to spend a little time with you before tomorrow happens."

Rox laid her head on his shoulder and sank into his embrace. "I know." She felt his muscles tighten. She had to steel herself to ask the next question. "Are you scared?"

Allen stayed silent for a long time. He simply held her, and she let him take what comfort he could. Eventually he answered. "A little."

She raised her head to look into his face. "Only a little?"

"OK, maybe more than a little." He rested his forehead against hers. "I just don't want to leave you."

A tear threatened to slip from under her closed eyelid. "Oh, Allen." She kissed him. "You'll be coming back to me before the sun sets tomorrow. I know it."

"I love you."

Roxie smiled up at him, hiding her own fear. She wasn't used to hiding her emotions, and it was harder than she thought possible to do it now. But she would do anything for him, even this. "I love you, too, Allen. I always will."

They stayed in the grove for another hour, holding each other in silence. Roxie was afraid to say anything else that might betray her own fear. She knew he needed to hide his fear and if she expressed her own, he wouldn't fight tomorrow. And she knew his division of men needed him on the field. After another deep kiss, Allen led her back to her tent and kissed her good-bye.

Roxie watched him walk away and felt a twinge in her heart that she thought would feel like a knife twisting over and over. When she could see nothing more of his blue tunic, she walked inside her tent. Ari and Sita waited for her. She walked in and they stopped talking.

Ari reached over to lay a hand on Roxie's shoulder. Rox grabbed on as if it were a lifeline. "He's going to fight," she said into the silence.

"Are you OK?" Sita asked.

"Of course not. How could I be OK with this?" Roxie sighed and sat on her bed next to Ari. She leaned back and changed the subject. "We don't really know anything about them at all, do we? What kind of sick and twisted people could torture us like they did? Could kill all those people, or start this war?" Ari's face paled next to her. Sita was silent. "Si, what do you think?"

Sita pursed her lips. "I think I don't want to know anything more than I need to about them."

"What? Why?"

"Because if I know nothing else about them, it's easier to hate them. I don't want to know that they were tortured or warped as children. I don't want to know that their family was murdered before their eyes, or they were banished, nothing. All I need to know is that they are now twisted, sadistic killers intent on our deaths."

Ari crossed her arms and frowned. "But aren't you sinking to their level?"

"No. The only way to kill them is to hate them. Compassion will get me, get us, killed this time." Sita closed her eyes, and Roxie suddenly knew what this was about. "If I know nothing else about them, then I can hate them, easily and without remorse. If I know them, I couldn't kill them. Hating is the easiest way to stopping it all."

Ari spoke up again. "But are you sure it's the right way?"

"When am I ever sure?"

Roxie broke into the silence. "Sita, you know it's not right. You know better." She looked deep into Sita's pain-filled eyes. "Killing them won't bring Owen back. Revenge never solved anything."

Sita stood and headed for the tent flap. She spoke over her shoulder before she headed back out into the rain. "But it makes me feel better." The tent descended into desolate silence after that.

Robert came by in the late afternoon to lead them over to the command tent near the heart of the field. Roxie walled away her emotions and followed him and her friends. Men flowed around the small group until they came to the middle of camp. Guards surrounded the command tent. They stopped the group just as the women and Robert came within sight of the tent. Rob held up a paper, which the guards took to read over. Satisfied, they let all four of them through.

The command tent was a surprise. It was plain and the same dull green as the other tents, but flew more banners, and had four guards posted outside the entrance, two on each side. Without those flapping pieces of cloth and the somber set of soldiers, Roxie wouldn't have been able to tell the difference between this tent and the lowest soldier's.

This set of guards stopped them as they were about to enter. "Papers?" one of them asked.

Robert again held out his paper, which fluttered in the breeze. The guard was about to take it when a giant horned head popped out from inside the tent. "Let them through!" boomed the head. The girls jumped. "I have been expecting them." The soldiers saluted the head as it disappeared back into the tent. They stepped aside to let Rob through.

The inside of the tent was as dull and plain as the outside. It looked as their own tents had first looked, with cots hidden behind a privacy screen and tables. The only difference in this one were the number of tables—there were at least four, and all much bigger, holding all manner of maps and books and weapons. They all stopped just inside the entrance.

Samuel heard the guards outside stop someone. "Damn fools, when I say I want to see someone, I expect to see them at once." He popped his head out the tent's opening to see a small group of mostly women halted by the guards. "Let them through!" he bellowed. It was always fun to make his soldiers jump, and the jumps from the women were incredibly satisfying. "I have been expecting them!"

He stomped back inside with a glare to Catherine. She had a smirk on her face that meant she was trying not to laugh. Samuel sat in his chair and waited. A young man walked inside, followed by three young women, all around the same age. He studied them. Each was a mage, which set his teeth on edge. Their power was obvious, even to the ungifted such as him.

Robert bowed at the waist. "Queen Catherine, Commander, I have the pleasure of presenting the Aligerai to you." He stepped aside and the young women could now all see that there were only two people in this tent. The queen sat on their left, her brown trousers and dark green tunic allowing her to blend in with the surroundings, only a fine silver circlet on her head to mark her rank. On their right was a Chular—a creature that called to mind images of the Minotaur, a great bull-headed beast with only the vaguest hint of humanity.

Samuel smirked at their obvious curiosity at his appearance. "So, these are the famous Aligerai?" the commander said. His voice was surprisingly quiet, considering the volume he had used outside the tent, but it was a deep bass that was pleasant to listen to. The great head snaked lower. "They do not look like much to me."

Robert hid a smile, but one of the women, a blond, decided to interject and answer the commander. "We aren't famous," she said. "And we didn't even really know we were given that silly name until we got here and Ka'len told us."

The commander bowed his great shaggy head to glare at her through half-lowered eyelids. "Do not get cheeky with me, mage."

A tense silence fell over the group until Robert again stepped forward and said, "Ladies, this is Samuel Knox. He's the Commander of the Queen's Army. We'll be reporting to him and Queen Catherine through this battle." He introduced each of his girls and then turned back to face the huge commander. "Commander, please tell us where we can do the most good."

Samuel snorted. "Mages. Uppity creatures. Think they can tell you what to do whenever they want." He looked over the young women again. "Which one of you is the one with purple magic?"

The same one who had been so forward a moment ago paled and raised her hand. Samuel fixed on her. She met his stare, holding the gaze until he dropped his eyes. "Well, you will do, at least." He cleared his throat. "I will try to keep you out of the fighting as much as I can. I know you do not necessarily fight willingly, nor is this exactly your battle. So I have decided to hold you all in reserve." Samuel pulled a map of the field off the table and held it up for them to see. "My command will be here—" he pointed to an area on a high hill, "—but the main fighting will be around here." This time he pointed out a wide area below the hill, large enough for both armies to fight with room to spare.

All of the young women nodded their understanding, some with more relief than others. Only Sita looked dissatisfied. "No offense, Commander, but you're going to need us." Samuel snorted in surprise and dropped the chart, his eyes wide. Sita stepped forward to look again at the map. "Especially if Darci shows up. Then you won't just need us, you'll need *me*. And besides . . ." She let the plans fall back to the table. "I *will* be fighting. I have a debt to settle with Alan and Sandara that I will have fulfilled, or there will be hell to pay."

Samuel's eyes narrowed. "What is this debt?"

He watched in alarm as Sita changed from a furious but contained woman into a seething tower of rage. He glanced at her friends, but they looked at ease, so he tried to force himself to calm down. It barely worked. "They stole my Owen," she growled, her lips curling into a snarl. "I will make them pay for what they did to me, and if they've hurt him, I will make sure they are sent to the deepest hell that exists. They killed Vanessa, and they seduced Darci from us, which I cannot forgive them for. I'll make them pay for that, too."

The commander nodded once, which seemed to placate the fury standing before him. "I will see to it that I send you against them. Rest assured, you will have your debt paid in full by tomorrow if I have anything to say about it." He gulped as the young woman deflated, the rage and magic contained again.

Queen Catherine took that moment to intervene. "As we are now all acquainted with each other, I think it best that we look to other things. Why don't I have an aide show you back to your campsite and you can rest for the day. We attack at dawn. You'll need all the sleep you can get tonight. I suggest you turn in early."

Knowing a dismissal when they heard one, the young women and Rob bowed to the leaders and followed an aide back outside. They left only relief in their wake. Catherine glanced at the Chular commander. "Well. They're an interesting bunch, aren't they?"

"If you say so, Majesty," Samuel replied. He sank onto his camp stool and picked up the edge of the map. Something about the young mage gave him the shivers. "But I believe I will stay out of that mage's way if she catches sight of Alan or Sandara tomorrow. I do not think she will care about who is in her way then."

"I think you're right."

Dawn came all too soon for the Aligerai. Nightmares plagued their sleep, allowing them no more than a few hours of solid, deep rest. They awoke to horns bugling in the foggy air. Robert came to each tent to make sure they were all awake. He was nearly decked by Ari, as he had needed to shake her shoulders to wake her up. She apologized in her half-sleep and rose to dress. Soldiers rushed in a controlled kind of chaos all around the girls' tents, running to grab weapons and form into their units. Then they marched off to the awaiting field.

They were finally ready. Robert jerked his head in the direction of the flow and they trailed behind him, waking up more with each step. The soldiers gave them a wide berth. Sita, having slept very little last night but strangely not very tired, paid attention to her surroundings. The birds of the far-off woods should have been singing up the sun—there was complete silence from the forest. Smaller animals, such as squirrels or chipmunks, should have been darting everywhere in the camp, scavenging for tidbits. None could be seen. Even the trees themselves appeared to wait, not daring to move, watching the men march to battle in eternal green silence.

Sita reached into her pocket and felt Vanessa's ring. *You were supposed to be here, Vanessa,* she thought. *I know we didn't really get along, but you were one of us. You should have been here.* She pulled out the ring and watched it wink up at her in the light of false dawn. Her necklace swung from her neck, the quartz still keeping watch over the emerald from her own ring. Now she knew what had happened. She could lay the gem to rest.

She took her necklace off. The gold of the ring would look out of place with the silver, but it couldn't be helped. Sita slipped Vanessa's ring onto her chain. Then she took the emerald between her fingers and separated it from the quartz. Letting her feet guide her, Sita sunk into her magic and created another space in the ring big enough for one last gem.

The emerald fit perfectly in the hole she made. Sita pushed it in until it would be secure and then cut the magic. It looked the same as the other gems still in Vanessa's ring. Sita re-hung the chain around her neck and felt goose bumps kiss her flesh where Vanessa's ring touched. *I won't forget you, Vanessa.* Tears threatened to rise, but a bitter thought made her mouth twitch into a smirk. *The only thing I need now to make it complete is something of Darci's. Then I'll have a whole little collection.*

A rainbow mist caught the corner of her eye. Sita gazed at it and saw Corá appear there for the briefest moment. The goddess raised her hand in blessing and disappeared. The wind tousled their hair, making the others shiver. *Do not be frightened,* Corá whispered in Sita's ears. *Darci is not here. She did not come. Today is not the day to fight her.*

Sita turned her face into the breeze and smiled, knowing Corá would both see and feel it. "Thank you," she whispered, and felt the invisible hands caress her face a final time.

Roxie looked back to see Sita's dreamy expression. She shortened her stride to fall back beside her friend. "Sita, are you all right? Maybe you should sit this one out."

"I'm fine, Rox. I'm fighting today, no matter what anyone says." Her eyes lost their dreamy look and hardened. "I will make Alan return Owen, or I'll take his life. That's all there is to it." Roxie shivered and let Sita get lost in her thoughts, walking beside her in silence.

Rob led them to the hill from which Samuel Knox would command. He was already there, surveying the troops and making sure they were in position. Queen Catherine stood beside him, holding maps. They turned when they heard the group approach.

"Ah, yes, glad to see you all made it," the commander said. "I realize it is earlier than many of you are undoubtedly used to."

"We'll manage," Ari replied. She marched to the edge of the hill to look down at the troops below, arranged into neat units. The enemy could be seen in the distance, across the wide plains. "When will the call be given?"

"As soon as the sun rises," said Catherine. "We hope the enemy won't be expecting an attack quite so early. Maybe we can catch them just a little off guard."

"I would not count on it," said a disembodied voice. Catherine and Samuel both drew their swords, looking around wildly for the source. Ka'len appeared next to Sita. She only raised an eyebrow. "Hello, my dear. How have you been?"

Sita ignored the pleasantries. "Where have you been? I haven't seen you in ages."

He scoffed. "Oh, hardly ages, my dear. But I am afraid we shall have to catch up later. The first stroke of war will be landing very soon."

Samuel edged forward, lowering his sword only a trifle. "And just who are you?"

Catherine smirked and settled a hand on the commander's arm. "Peace, Sam. He's Ka'len Lera. I'm sure you recognize that name."

The Chular commander lowered his weapon, but kept an eye on the old man as Ka'len bowed to them both. "Majesty, Commander, I do apologize for arriving in such an unceremonial way. I have come to offer my services, if you will have them."

The queen smiled now. She held out her hands to the mage, which he grasped. "You are most welcome, Ka'len. We are holding the mages in reserve for the moment, so we may not require your magical skills. But you have seen battle before, and I for one would be very happy to have your tactical advice."

"As you wish, Majesty," Ka'len said, winking at the queen. "We shall catch up later as well, yes? It truly has been ages since I have seen you, Catherine."

The sun replied for her, diverting all of their attentions. The field was bathed in red-gold, the sun itself a crimson red on the horizon. Just the barest sliver peeked above the trees, but it was enough to wash the plain with bloody light. Samuel took the great horn hanging from his hip and blew, sounding the signal for the march.

Below them the soldiers began to walk, marching across the open plain with purpose. From the height of the hills, the commanders could see the enemy begin to stir. "Looks like we didn't steal much of a march on them after all," Samuel muttered under his breath. "Ah, well. We should still have superior numbers."

Ka'len glanced at the Chular from the corner of his eye. "I wouldn't count on that, Commander."

They watched in agonizing silence as the two armies marched toward each other, rattling their weapons and shouting war cries. The queen's army paused when they were just outside of half a mile's range. Everyone on the hill could see the general riding up and down the front lines, shouting encouragement, but his words were lost to the wind. He spoke only a little, for his soldiers were lusting for blood halfway through his speech. He finished talking and pointed his horse north, staring down the enemy's swords. Then he spurred his fine horse onward and led the men in a charge, the enemy following suit.

As the sun rose in bloody witness, the two armies converged in the middle of the plain.

Even from on the hill, the carnage was terrible. For all her bloodlust and desire to find the professors, Sita was very glad they weren't actually on the field. The red uniforms of Imbri blended with the gray of the queen's soldiers, and the green or blue uniforms of the various shadow groups. Sita could see only the mass of seething, screaming, dying humanity. After a while, she couldn't stomach any more of the death on the field and turned away.

Ka'len stood close by her. She knew he saw her disgust. "Sita, this is necessary."

"Is it really?"

He frowned. "I believe so. Do you believe Imbri Mors would rest until they accomplished their plans?"

"No."

"Then this is necessary. It is the only way to stop them."

Sita bit her lip and turned away from him as well. "Ka'len, I don't like it. So many people will die today. If there was a way to prevent it, we should have taken that path."

The old man stepped closer and settled a hand on Sita's shoulder. "If there were any other way, Catherine would have found it and taken it. This war is taking place in her land. She had the final decision."

Sita nodded. A wind blew up around them. Sita could feel Cora's touch in the breeze, and the slight contact soothed her distress. She looked up to see Samuel Knox studying the battle with an intensity that frightened her. He barked an order at the man standing next to him. The mage, a tall man with sandy hair and a pleasant, handsome face, listened to the words and twisted his fingers in a complicated symbol. Sita knew he cast a spell. "What's the mage doing?" she asked Ka'len.

Ka'len followed her gaze and explained, attracting an audience of the other Aligerai. Each officer had a bubble around his head that one of the army mages created. Colorless, thin enough to allow enough air to breathe, and private for the officer the bubble belonged to, the bubbles constituted the warfare message system of the army. Those bubbles allowed a magical passing of orders—the commander would speak the order to the mage, who would then cast a spell after the commander's words. The spell sent the orders straight to the bubbles around each officer's head, and they would hear it.

They watched Samuel give another order. A report was transmitted back to him through the mage, who had a receiving bubble around his head. The officers could also give a report to the commander by speaking a keyword to activate the privacy mode, giving the report, and then repeating the keyword to make his or her voice heard publicly again. Sita returned to the battle below. From the corner of her eye she saw Ari squint and look closer at the armies. She guessed Ari changed her eyes into hawk eyes. That seething mass of enemy looked much bigger than their own army, and she knew Ari tried to see how far they stretched beyond what they could plainly see. Ari caught her breath when the change in her eyes firmed and she could see again. "Commander!" she cried. "Commander, they outnumber us . . . at least eight to one!"

Samuel whirled to glare at her. "How do you know that?" He shook his head. "Never mind. You can explain later. Can any of you come up with something to help us?"

Roxie stepped forward. "The animals in the forest can help us, if I can get them to come."

The commander nodded. "Do it."

Ka'len grabbed Roxie's arm as she passed him. "Be careful. Do not get too close to the fighting. Their archers could pick you off."

She patted his hand. "Don't worry. I just need to get to the woods." Roxie was preparing to leave when Sita noticed something. The brunette breathed deep and rose a few inches off the ground.

Sita watched with a puzzled brow. "Rox . . . when did you . . . you're flying?"

Roxie laughed, the light in her eyes dimmed by the carnage below but still bright. "I've been practicing with my *boulesis*."

Robert swept her up in a giant hug, twirling her while she laughed again. "That's great! When did you figure out how to do it?"

"Why didn't you tell us?" Ari asked right after him. She sounded indignant.

Ka'len shooed Roxie away. "Hurry, Roxanne, there is no time to waste."

Roxie smiled at them and blushed. She rose another couple of inches and shouted over her shoulder. "I finally got it a few weeks ago, and I practiced when you guys wouldn't see. I didn't want anyone to see me fall on my face that many times!"

Sita chuckled. "So that's what those bruises on your legs are from. I was wondering."

Roxie's blush deepened. "I fell a lot." Then she zoomed away into the forest below the rise to call the animals.

While Roxie mustered her animals, Ariene transformed into a robin and flew away to watch from above. Sita saw her flap over the army twice before coming back. She returned to her human body. "The animals are going to work. They're distracting some of the enemy." Ari glanced at Sita. "I didn't see any sign of Alan or Sandara, Si. Maybe they won't show up."

Sita glared. "They'll show. They won't be able to stay away."

The other woman cleared her throat. "I'll just go keep an eye out for Allen. His soldiers are in blue, so he's pretty easy to spot.

And he has a bubble around his head." Sita tried to smile but only managed half of one. Ari winked at her and transformed again into a robin and flew away.

The battle continued for hours. Ka'len waited with them, while Sita stood nearby and listened to the commanders and the shouts from below.

Sita watched for signs of Imbri officers. Ari came back periodically to report on the movement of both sides. Sita twitched every time the other blond came back for a landing. Samuel forbade Sita to use magic to fry any of the officers that Ari saw, preferring to keep her magic in reserve. Ka'len kept one hand on her shoulder at all times. "You cannot be everywhere, Sita," he said. "And in this, you must obey your leader. He knows how to best use the resources at his disposal. If he says you are in reserve, then you must listen."

"I know, Ka'len. But he promised me Alan and Sandara, and I won't let that promise be broken. If I see them, I'm going in after them." She returned to scouring the battle scene below her. The back of the army was engaged now, with Allen and his blue comrades entrenched with Imbri red.

Of the Aligerai, Sita was the only one to remain on the hill. She stood in silence, her arms crossed over her chest and a stoic expression on her face. An itch in the middle of her back began to bother her. She tried to ignore the sensation, but as the battle wore on, the discomfort grew. Finally, she could stand it no more—she sighed and allowed her wings to burst from her back.

Ka'len skipped to the side, a black look on his face. "Sita! A little more caution, please. I would rather not be hit by your wings."

This drew a chuckle and a bit of a smile from her. "Sorry," she said. Whispers from behind caught her attention and she turned to see the aides and even some of the officers staring at her in shock. Apparently, the rumors of a winged woman had been only that— rumors. The confirmation of her standing before them caused some surprise, even in the midst of a battle. The commander and the queen both kept their attention on the fight, though Samuel did tell Sita to lower her wings to keep from making herself a target.

She complied and went back to watching the soldiers. Ari flew back and forth with reports. The archers and some of the knights took out a number of the Imbri officers, but still there was no sign of Alan, Sandara, or Darci.

The battle raged on. Imbri lost ground first, with the Gennaian forces pushing the enemy back. But after a few hours, the men began to tire, and the Gennaian line moved backward toward the hill. Outnumbered eight to one, the Gennaian soldiers had known this wouldn't be a short fight, but this lasted longer than anticipated. The fighting remained far enough away to not pose a serious threat to the hill, but Samuel did stiffen as it raged closer.

As the sun traveled into late afternoon, it became apparent that the forces were more evenly matched than either side would like. Imbri fought like possessed men, and many Gennaian soldiers fell to their passion. Every time it looked as if the Imbri line would falter, somehow they found new energy, new strength, and their bodies fought on. But the Gennaian army had training and discipline on their side, and the knowledge that they defended their homes and loved ones from this enemy. Their strength and desire to win only grew as the battle wore on, even as their bodies grew more and more tired.

Finally, a break in the Imbri line drew all attention on the hill. Samuel shouted for the men to push their advantage, and the message was quickly relayed by the mage. The Gennaian soldiers pushed, and soon the Imbri army had turned tail to retreat. Samuel gave his final order for the day: follow only to the edge of the plain. Then retreat back to the hills to a spot further south and make camp.

Sita's brow furrowed. "But how can they make camp? The camp is here. No one packed anything this morning," she said to Ka'len.

"Not to worry. The aides have been busy the last few hours," he said. "Samuel is excellent at reading a battle. He knew hours ago how this one would end. He passed the order to one of the pages, and the aides and camp helpers have since been packing and moving camp to the new location. Even our tents have been packed and moved."

"If I'd known that, I would have put away my dirty clothes." Ka'len guffawed.

Catherine and Samuel joined the two mages. "No sign of Alan or Sandara," said Samuel. "Or of Darci. Perhaps they will show when battle resumes."

"When will that be?" said Sita.

The queen glanced to the commander. Sita felt like they were silently communicating about her, but couldn't quite put her finger on what they said to the other in that glance. "I expect Imbri will take a day to treat their wounded. They will also need to make sure all their soldiers are still armed. Roxanne's animals were very good today at stealing arrows and small weapons." Catherine smiled. "I daresay their archers will be scrambling to make more arrows tonight."

Sita returned the smile, but her heart wasn't quite in it. "So we'll probably have tomorrow to rest, then?"

Samuel nodded his great shaggy head. "Aye. Most likely. We could also use the reprieve to fetch and tend our wounded. More soldiers were wounded today than expected." He turned to Catherine. "We should also send word to the castle that we need more healers out here. The group the Healers Guild sent with us is not adequate."

The queen nodded, her brow pinched in anger. "Oh, yes, I will be having words with the guild. They will send reinforcements tonight or I will fine them for dereliction of duty."

With that, the queen and the commander turned away, talking softly about the plans for tomorrow and the day after. Sita cocked her head and turned to Ka'len. "I thought wars and battles and such were less . . . structured. This one seems to be very organized."

Ka'len sighed. "Normally, you would be right. But this is only the beginning, the first foray into this particular conflict. Alan and Sandara are not seasoned commanders in battle, nor do they have any truly talented war leaders on their side. They may have studied war command, but this does not give them a good grasp of how to lead a battle or orchestrate a war. We can use that to our advantage by using their inexperience to buy our own men time to rest." One hand tugged at his beard. "It is odd, however, how their soldiers kept finding renewed energy. I may suggest Samuel consider sending a mage to look into that."

Sita nodded her understanding and took one last look at the churned fields stained red with blood before she followed Ka'len down the hill to the new campsite.

Even with no battle the next day, no one slept in. An hour after the sun rose, Roxie found her way to the picket lines to help with the horses and mules, while Ari went to the archers to practice catching and stealing arrows in her bird form.

Sita woke when Ari and Roxie did. Unlike her friends, she found very little to help with. Her liking for animals and horses was appreciated, but unneeded with Roxie there. She could help in the healers' tents, but the reinforcements had arrived late in the night, and she was told thanks but no thanks when she offered her help. And, unlike Ari, she could not turn into a bird.

So, bored and a little hurt at not being needed, Sita made her way out of camp. She crossed the sentry line, with the sentries warning her not to stray too far, and made her way into the trees to practice some magic and burn off a little steam.

Samuel would have killed her himself had he known.

Relative peace reigned in the camp. Soldiers fixed weapons and rested their bodies and minds. The horses were forced to rest and their own wounds tended by animal healers. And the wounded humans were patched up by healers and sent back to the tents.

A few men and mages were given the sad and unlucky task of digging graves for the men killed the day before. To everyone's relief, there weren't many dead, comparatively speaking. But there were enough dead that the grave diggers kept busy from dawn to dusk by carting the bodies out to a secluded area and digging the graves. The diggers made a map of where each body was placed and gave each grave a number. The number corresponded to a list of the deceased. Headstones would be placed later, after the battles were finished.

Samuel gave the order at dusk that all soldiers should be assembled and ready to move at dawn. The next battle would begin across the plains, where the Gennaian army had chased Imbri the day before. Movement in that direction had been sighted, but the enemy remained far enough out that there would be no attack that night. The soldiers gave a rousing cheer at this news, and even Sita felt a spark of anticipation and thrill run through her veins. It was difficult to sleep that night, with some soldiers singing battle songs over the campfires and the entire camp filled with a sense of purpose and energy for the coming day.

He also, very discreetly, asked one of the mages to scry on the Imbri forces and try to find out how their men had found their renewed energy.

The next morning, the soldiers assembled and marched out across the fields, ready to meet Imbri further out. The commanders and queen would climb to the top of another hill, further south than the hill from the first battle, and watch the carnage from there. If the Gennaian army accomplished its goal and forced Imbri to retreat again, the commanders would lose the advantage of the hills as the conflict pushed further into the Winding Plains and away from the Grenol Hills. They would have to make do with setting up command on the plains.

All could see the forces of Imbri approach. On the Winding Plains, very little could be hidden. For miles there were only the long grasses of the plains. The lonely plains town of Frindam appeared as a speck in the distance, and the South Road and West Road the only break in the grasses. Catherine had ordered Frindam's evacuation, just in case the fighting reached that far into the plains, and had ordered some of her nobles to send some of their personal guard to block the roads into the Plains far enough out to prevent innocent civilians from passing into the middle of the fighting. On a very clear day, the far-off Hargol Hills that marked the end of the Plains could be seen.

Imbri approached the Gennaian army and soon the two met in a clash that could be heard even from the hills. Sita winced and turned away. Ari and Roxie repeated their feats from the first battle, though Roxie had a more difficult time staying hidden. If the battle moved into the center of the plains, she would have a much harder time using her gifts near the fighting. Wounded soldiers began to trickle into the camp around midmorning.

Sita, as last time, remained chained to the hill by Samuel's orders. She felt him keeping an eye on her.

The second battle followed much the same pattern as the first. Samuel and his commanders took advantage of Alan and Sandara's weakness to draw the Imbri forces into a false sense of victory, then increased the ferocity of their attacks when the enemy soldiers got sloppy. Soon the Imbri army began to blow the horns for a retreat. Gennaian soldiers cheered and, with a renewed vigor stemming from impending victory, chased the enemy further into the Plains.

Samuel soon called them back and ordered that a new camp be erected in the Plains. He tripled the number of sentries and outriders. Few slept peacefully that night as the feeling of exposure in the grassy plain swept over them all.

For a week, the pattern remained the same. Fight, rest, fight, rest. Sita grew bored and frustrated at being kept on a leash. She even snapped at Ka'len, who scowled at her and told her to stop acting like a child. The rebuke toned Sita down a little bit, but only so much.

During the entire week, there was no sign of Alan, Sandara, or Darci. In the middle of the fourth battle, Sita growled this fact aloud. Samuel overheard and offered his theory that the professors likely would not appear until they felt like they needed to get their hands dirty in order to win. So he would force them to get their hands dirty by whittling down their army.

Sita still didn't like it.

The only real highlight was Samuel's mage returned with news. Through his scrying mirror, the mage had seen how the Imbri men found their renewed energy.

"They have some kind of connection, my lord," he said to Samuel. The entire command could hear him speak, even as he gave his report over the sounds of battle. "A connection back to their commanders. And they are sent pure energy . . . I know not what else to call it, my lord." The mage wrung his hands and shifted from foot to foot. Samuel growled low in his throat. The mage began to sweat. "It is as if they are feeding on raw, untainted energy. I know that somehow it is transmitted to the soldiers from the commanders, because the energy comes from further afield, but I can tell no more than that, nor any means of stopping it."

Queen Catherine clenched her jaw. Sita shoved her hands in the pockets of her cloak as she listened. "It's coming from Alan and Sandara, then."

Now Samuel curled one great hand into a fist and stared out across the plains as if he could summon the professors to him in that glance. "Then the only way to stop the energy flow," he said.

"Is to kill Alan and Sandara." He pointed a finger into Sita's face as she opened her mouth to speak. "No! Do not even ask." The commander then proceeded to ignore her and continued to watch his soldiers fight. Sita stalked to the other end of the camp.

Listening to the battle was the worst part, and it was the sounds that soon haunted Sita's nightmares. Men's screams as they took an arrow, or a sword cut, or were thrown by the horses. The terror some felt upon being injured and trapped on the battlefield was conveyed in their screams. Horses whinnied their fear and pain, and Sita felt their deaths keenly. Some of the injured men could have been saved if they had made it to the tents, but some were trapped on the field until an enemy killed them or the battle itself crushed them.

It was the screams that struck Sita to her core. Not the sights. Not even the blood-scented wind. It was the screams.

After another week of near-constant fighting, the men were injured and exhausted. Imbri Mors' commanders pushed their soldiers relentlessly, and the Gennaian force had been hard pressed to keep up. Still, the Gennaian army had pushed the Imbri force to just beyond the middle of the Winding Plains and held them there, unable to gain more ground but also unwilling to give up any. The Hargol Hills rose as a green and brown smudge in the distance to the south. Samuel gave the order to rest for a day, and so they did. Sita sat in her tent and played with magic to keep herself amused. Her area of tents was quiet, with her friends out being useful and Robert and Ka'len off elsewhere.

Then she heard a noise. It sounded like shouting, but the shouts were too far away for her to make out clearly. Curious, she rose from her cot and emerged from the tent. It was hot today, and the sun beat down on the Plains much stronger than it did in the hills. Sita wiped a hand across her brow and turned in the direction of the shouts.

It came from the south, the direction of the battlefield. Sita hurried into an aisle to better see what made the noise. When she saw, her mouth went dry and she froze in place. Mounted scouts thundered back to camp on their horses, the riders shouting and waving at the sentries and soldiers on foot. Finally, she made out what one rider said. "Imbri is attacking! Hurry! They come this way!"

Soldiers scrambled to gather weapons and assemble into units. Samuel bellowed orders and strode to his own position. He held a great axe in his hands, ready to take on any enemy that made his way to the camp.

Sita fetched her knives from her tent and ran to join Samuel. She slid one knife into her boot and one into the sheath at her hip. Trousers had definitely been the right choice for today; a skirt would have held her up.

The Gennaian army quickly assembled and marched out, the cavalry charging ahead to draw any immediate attack and allow the foot soldiers to catch up. Samuel roared, which earned some extra speed from the horses and soldiers both.

Catherine soon joined Samuel and Sita outside the camp. "How far away are they, Sam?"

"Too close, Majesty. Too close. When the scouts return, I will question them on how the enemy was able to get this close before a warning was sounded."

"But how far, Sam?"

Samuel paused before answering. His eyes narrowed as he studied the clash of the cavalry with the Imbri vanguard. "We are not in immediate danger, Catherine. However, we cannot afford to lose any ground."

A hawk burst from the tents. Ari took to the air and followed the soldiers, who now ran to meet the Imbri line. She circled overhead three times before returning to camp. Sita raised an arm for her to land on. Ari tried to be gentle, but her claws still bit into Sita's arm and drew blood. "They have the same numbers as they did yesterday," she said. "But this time, I think I saw Alan and Sandara."

Sita's heart skipped a beat. "Darci?"

Ari shook her hawk head, the human lips pursed. "Still no sign of her."

Catherine sighed. "She may not participate in the fighting. Or they may be holding her in reserve. It is difficult to say."

"But the professors have come out to play." Samuel grinned, a bloodthirsty gleam in his eyes. "Excellent. This may be the start of their final push to win."

Sita's stomach clenched. The professors were in play. Her pulse quickened. She would find them soon and take her revenge.

Ari's lips transformed back into a hawk's beak. She squawked and flapped her wings once. Sita launched her back into the sky, and Ari winged back to the battle as fast as she could go.

Footsteps behind her made Sita turn. Robert hurried up, a dagger in one hand. "What's the news?" Sita caught him up on what they knew and he grinned, as bloodthirsty as Samuel. "Good. Maybe this will end today."

They waited and watched in silence. Ka'len joined the group soon after Robert had, and other mages and commanders also joined their silence. Samuel gave orders to his mage, who relayed them to the field. The battle twisted and turned, writhing across the face of the Plains as if it were an animal in its death throes. Sita nearly gagged as the wind turned and blew the scents of blood and gore and death into their faces. The sun beat down on their heads, adding to the discomfort of all on the Plains.

Soon Sita noticed that the Gennaian army faltered. The soldiers made more mistakes, which the Imbri soldiers took advantage of. The line on the right wavered, as if it were about to break and allow Imbri to gain an advantage and outflank the Gennaian force. Samuel growled and beckoned to Robert. "You're going in. Do what you can."

Robert nodded and pulled his sword. He took a long look at Sita, who returned his stare, before he sprinted out to join them. Magic already gathered at his fingertips, and soon he joined the mages in casting spells from the edges of the battle.

Samuel again beckoned, this time to Ka'len. "Can you do anything to aid from here?"

"Of course. I am very good with distance casting."

"Then do it."

Ka'len began to work, his magic joining Robert's attacks on Imbri. But Ka'len also worked some magic to shore up the Gennaian line, lending the men strength.

Sita waited for Samuel to beckon her forward as well, but he did not. He went back to issuing orders to the waiting mage. Grinding her teeth, Sita crossed her arms and waited.

The battle raged on into the evening. A full moon rose over the Plains, its light bright enough to see by. The battle continued, with neither side gaining much ground. Sita and the others fought off exhaustion, and she knew that if she was tired, the men were triply so. Samuel did his best to bring the fight to a close, but every time the Gennaian men tried an attack that should have made an end of it, the Imbri army would somehow counter and keep the armies engaged.

Around midnight, Samuel began to swear. "Alan and Sandara have something to do with this. The last attack should have been able to create a wedge down the middle of Imbri Mors and divide the force. Yet somehow, it did not. Not even the diversion with the cavalry riding out and around made any difference." He growled and paced, his eyes never leaving the battle. "The professors have something to do with this. It must be their magic."

"Then let me go after them," Sita said. "Let me fight them. I can bring this to an end."

But Samuel shook his great head. "No, I need you here in case Darci shows up. Or unless the professors break through and make their way here. So you stay here, Sita."

Sita ducked her head to hide her expression. Her hands clenched at her sides. Ka'len, his magical attacks paused hours before to save his energy, put a hand on her shoulder as much to reassure her as to restrain her.

The Gennaian men gained some ground and pushed Imbri back, but it wasn't enough to end the battle. The men were clearly exhausted. Some simply dropped from exhaustion, to be crushed under the hooves of the horses and the weight of the battle. Others died when their reflexes slowed so much that they could no longer parry or strike efficiently.

Samuel sent out the orders around camp to round up every last able-bodied aide and remaining soldier in the camp. He ordered them to take up weapons and organize into units. Only the few aides too young to be pushed into battle were held back. Then he sent them out as reinforcements, with Ka'len adding a little extra magic to their weapons for a slight advantage.

Catherine paced, as restless as Sita. Once or twice, Samuel growled at her, but still she paced. The queen also kept her gaze fixed on the battle. "Let me go, Samuel. Let me ride out and meet them."

"No."

"Then at least let me send my bodyguards to aid the men."

"No."

The queen growled, the sound nearly as ferocious as one of Samuel's own. Clearly, he had heard the queen's growl before, as it didn't faze him at all. "Samuel, you waste resources by keeping them here!"

The commander glared at his queen. "Catherine, if the enemy breaks through, I need your bodyguards to take you back to the castle. Bound and gagged and slung across a horse if need be, but they will remove you from the Plains if Imbri wins. I will not risk you to a fight such as this one where you are not needed."

Catherine huffed and continued her pacing.

The night wore on. Sita felt her eyelids struggle to close, but she stubbornly refused to sleep. People died on this field. How could she sleep while they fought and died? So she stayed, Ka'len still holding her shoulder. Goosebumps decorated her exposed arms. Nights on the Plains could be very cold, and she hadn't expected to be out during the night when she left her tent earlier.

Another hour passed before a tinge of grey began to lighten the deep darkness of night, and the moon's brightness began to fade as it sunk toward the horizon. Still the fighting raged on as false dawn began to bring the world to life. Sita's eyes adjusted easily to the slow shift in light. The temperature began to warm just slightly as well.

Samuel studied the changes and gave more orders to the mage. "Dawn," he said. "This must end today. The men are too weary for more." The rest nodded assent.

As the light brightened, the group of commanders and mages received the first good look of the battlefield since dusk the previous day. Sita's stomach churned when she saw the carnage. So many men had died, so many horses . . . and with the blood and gore and distance, the tunics blended into each other, making it hard to distinguish from that distance how many of the fallen were Gennaian or Imbri. Still, the number of fallen and wounded men shocked her. Nausea swept from her stomach to her head, and she held a hand to her mouth and closed her eyes to keep down the meager contents of her stomach. It was then that she realized she hadn't eaten anything in quite a while, not since the queen's aides had brought a tray of food for dinner sometime yesterday.

Rays of orange and gold burst from the horizon and the sun crested the earth. Its light hid the clouds above and turned the sky fiery. Even during the horror of battle, Sita saw the dawn and felt wonder at its coming.

The sun's light brought renewed vigor to the men of both sides. It was as if they all sensed the end of the battle would be near, and now they just wanted to finish it so they could rest in the sun's rays.

A man stumbled out of the press and back to the commander's stand. Sita watched his approach, curious as to whom it was. When she realized it was Robert, she strained forward and called his name. Rob stumbled many times, and his sword drooped in his hand, but one of Samuel's aides hurried out to meet him and help him back. He stumbled once more before he reached Samuel. The commander leaned down to hear Rob's muffled report. All that Sita caught was "My magic is spent. Captain Vahora sent me back." before the wind carried his words away.

Samuel listened carefully to what Rob had to say, then nodded and growled and turned to another aide. The young man supporting Rob led him over to Sita and Ka'len, who helped him to sit. "How bad is it?"

"It's bad." Rob looked up at them with dull eyes. Gore covered most of his body and blood stained his face. Sita couldn't stop staring at him, horrified by the sight of him. And the smell off his clothes made her gag. Her friend slumped against the earth and closed his eyes. Ka'len kept hold of Sita's shoulder but put the other hand on Rob's bowed head.

Green light brightened the field in the very center, washing the soldiers in the sickly color instead of the now-golden light of the sun. All attention focused there. Another green flash, and then a blue, lit up more soldiers. Every time the lights appeared, twenty of the queen's soldiers fell.

"It's them!" Sita said. All eyes turned to the field. Men staggered and fell away from the fight on both sides, and Samuel sent the last of his aides to help shore up the line. "It's them, let me go!"

Ka'len and Robert both clamped down on her arms and shoulders. They managed to hold her as she fought to be freed.

"Samuel, let me fight!" Samuel glanced once in her direction, but when he saw that Ka'len and Rob held her back, he ignored her.

Rob climbed to his feet and pulled both her arms toward him, turning her to face him. "Sita, stop it! Damn you, stop! This isn't the time to go haring off."

"Yes, it is! It's them, and I have to get out there!"

Robert shook her hard. Ka'len managed to keep his grip, but it was a near thing. He said nothing as Rob shouted at Sita. "Will you listen for once? You need to stay here."

"No!"

"God, stop acting like a petulant child!"

That shut Sita up faster than anything else could have. She felt the words as a slap to the face, and beneath the shock bubbled anger. It rose in her until she felt the anger fill her chest and reflect in her eyes. Rob took the opening her silence created. "You need to stay here. You can't go out there, it's too dangerous. They're looking for you. They're trying to flush you out. You go out there, you'd be playing right into their hands!"

The anger filled Sita to the brim. She resumed her struggle, and this time she felt their grip loosen, just slightly. Just enough. "I need to be out there, fighting them, because they attacked me! They attacked *us*, and I have to fight them if I'm going to get Owen back!"

"Damn it, Sita, you're going to get us all killed." Rob pushed all his weight into his hold on her arms, and Sita staggered, but it wasn't enough to hold her down completely. "I've said it before and I'll say it again: you need to be saved from yourself, you fool!"

Sita snarled, fighting against Ka'len's iron-hard grip on her shoulders. "No, Sita! We need you here," he cried. She lunged forward, her eyes filled with violet. Ari already winged back to tell them what Sita now knew: Alan and Sandara had finally shown up.

Just as Ari was about to reach the commanders, Sita wrenched free of Ka'len and Rob's hands. She released her wings in one painful rush, causing some of her skin around the wing stems to crack and bleed, and pushed off from the ground. Ari squawked and dove out of Sita's way. She had to flap her hawk wings hard to stay aloft. Sita rushed past her, murder in her eyes, and headed straight for the center of the battle.

Eric lunged. The sword in his hands plunged deep into the man's chest. Blood spurted from the wound and the man fell. Eric was covered in dirt and gore, his face so streaked with filth that no one recognized him. He fought in the thick of things, near the middle of the field, following his leaders while they walked through the soldiers and took them out with a mere wave of the hand. He grimaced. If only he could do that. That wouldn't be so bad.

He struck another man over the head, knocking him unconscious. Eric felt another attacker behind him. He spun around and thrust his sword forward, catching the man off guard. The surprise in the soldier's eyes cut to Eric's heart.

The battle wasn't supposed to be like this. It was supposed to be clean, with the soldiers fighting in units, with the leaders staying out of the way and directing when needed.

It wasn't supposed to be like this.

Eric cried out in pain when an enemy's sword sliced into his arm. He kept it only because the other man was knocked off balance by other fighters. Eric swung his own sword into the man's stomach to spill his bowels into the trampled and bloody mud.

Green lights flashed from the corner of his eye. Eric turned his head to look. Alan and Sandara had begun their attack. Eric set his mouth in a grim line and fought on, keeping an eye on his masters, and trying not to watch the enemy's leaders or look for a sign of white wings in the sky.

Sandara enjoyed herself. The Gennaian soldiers had at first rushed her, thinking her an easy kill. But then she smiled, held up her hands in front of her, and called on her power. It spread around her in ecstatic waves for thirty feet, killing any queen's soldier that it touched. Alan, his blue magic accompaniment to her own, walked beside her in the same manner.

Together, the professors cut a path through the queen's army, heading straight for the commanders' camp. They took it in turns to attack, Alan lighting the soldiers' fear-filled eyes with blue, then Sandara illuminated them all in light of palest green.

As the light touched the soldiers, their bodies felt weightless, and they hung in suspended time and space. It was almost a pleasant feeling, but the soldiers panicked when they realized their weapons would not move; their arms would not lift swords, their legs would not carry them from harm. As the panic set in, the weightless feeling began to ebb, and all they felt was pain. Fire lanced through their limbs, and their chests felt crushed. They each felt as if they would be pulled apart, as if they would drown in the sea of pain that engulfed them. Some succumbed to the pain soon after it began.

They were the lucky ones.

The magics of Alan and Sandara pulled the remaining men limb from limb.

And the souls of those unlucky men, suffering slow and agonizing deaths, were harvested into the stones each professor carried. The souls of any man who happened to die on that field, whether friend or foe, was carried by their magic into the stones waiting back at the Imbri camp.

A third of those thousand gems were already full.

The power, the sheer power, contained in those gems was intoxicating, and Sandara wanted more, wanted to feel the life force of those humans drain into her and make her stronger. It was a wonderful, powerful feeling.

An unexpected shadow crossed Sandara's path. She looked up, blood not her own oozing over her face. She saw Sita in flight, aiming to gain altitude and then plunge down straight at Alan and herself. Grinning in bloodthirsty glee, Sandara raised her hand, took aim, and fired a bolt of green.

Sita's limp body fell from the sky.

Chapter Thirty-Seven
What Love Can Do

Sita's body fell from the cloudless blue sky.

The soldiers, from both sides, paused to watch the gleaming white wings, the streaming golden hair, as the woman plunged to her death in the middle of their fight.

The Aligerai gave a collective cry of anguish that echoed around the silent field. Every man shivered at that cry, hearing the soul-deep pain of two women in the cores of their own souls. That pain was almost more real than their own wounds, their own exhaustion, and all watched with bated breath the fall of the bird-woman.

Ariene, still in hawk form, landed on Ka'len's outstretched arm, setting down only long enough for Ka'len to launch her back into the air, back in the direction of battle. She transformed into an oversized eagle as she flapped into the air and flew as fast as she could for Sita's prone form plummeting toward the battle below.

Everyone held their breath when they saw the bird streak across the sky toward Sita.

Ariene strained, her world narrowing to the plight of her friend. Sita fell fast, too fast for Ari to get beneath and catch her on her back. Adjusting her angle just a bit, Ari strove forward and finally reached the point above Sita. Then she tucked her wings and dove. She followed Sita's path, her weight lending extra momentum. Her claws extended, her lungs burned from the strain, her wings beat even harder . . . and she caught Sita's shoulder and waist to grip her tight in trembling talons.

Relieved, Ari pulled out of the dive just as they came within range of archers. But no one shot at them. As if Sita's renewed safety were the signal, the fighting began again, and the archers had more pressing worries than the giant bird and her burden.

Eric saw it all from below, held his own breath as Sita fell, and breathed a huge sigh of relief when Sita was safe again. He didn't have time to wonder about his sudden feelings, however; more soldiers rushed at him. But he began working his way closer to Alan and Sandara's area.

Ari flew away from the battle, setting down off to one side. She plopped Sita onto the soggy grass, trying to avoid jostling her too much. She lost her bird shape and became human again. Sita lay very still on the ground, and Ari's heart drummed loud in her ears when she saw no movement. "Sita?"

A flutter on Sita's face caught her attention. "Sita!" Ari bent down and grabbed Sita's shoulder. "Sita, are you OK?"

Sita groaned and attempted to sit up. Ari held an arm behind her friend's back and helped her sit. Sita put a hand to her head. "That hurt."

"It should. Sandara threw something at you, you passed out, and I had to come rescue your butt. I caught you in mid-air, which, by the way, is pretty awesome, if I do say so myself."

Sita grimaced and pushed herself up from the ground. Ari pulled her up and held her steady as she regained her balance. "Thank you, Ari," Sita said. "I owe you one."

"Damn right you do. Now let's get you back to the healers. Maybe they can help with those cuts you have. Sorry about those, by the way. My talons are kind of sharp."

"I'm not going back."

Ari frowned. "What do you mean?"

"I mean, I know where Alan and Sandara are, and I won't let them get away. Now that I know what to expect, I can guard against it. Let me go, Ari." Ari clutched her arm tighter. "Let me go. I have to do this."

"You shouldn't go alone."

Sita smiled and extricated herself from Ari's grip. "I have to. This is my fight. And I can't have you guys around when I unleash the big magic, now can I?"

Ari was about to reply when Sita shoved her out of the way and climbed back into the air, a translucent lavender shield encasing her entire body. Ari watched her go, growling in frustration. "Fine, then," she said. She changed back into hawk form and took to the air again as well. "But I'm keeping an eye on you from now on."

419

Sandara saw her coming again and unleashed another bolt of power. It rebounded off Sita's shield this time and came back to Sandara. The woman shrieked and dove out of the way, shoving Alan to the ground. The green bolt hit the dirt where Sandara had been standing and made a crater there thirty feet wide. The professors looked up and swore. Sita came in for a landing.

The soldiers cleared away, by common consent, and confined their fight to areas outside a forty-foot circle of the mages. Sita was glad—she didn't want her own people getting hurt in this fight. So she set up a thin barrier around that forty-foot range, enough to keep the enemy out and the magical attacks inside. And keep Alan and Sandara trapped inside with her.

None of them saw the young man who fought at the edge of the barrier and watched their fight while battling to keep his own life.

Sita smiled, a cold and chilling expression. The professors climbed to their feet, wary, while Sita stood before them and waited. "Hello Alan, Sandara. It's so wonderful to see you again. And under such pleasant circumstances." Alan swallowed hard. "I believe you took something from me. I want it back."

Sandara sneered. The blood on her face and matted in her hair marred her good looks. "And what would that be?"

The winged woman's face lost any trace of humor, of kindness, and turned into a hard mask of rage. "You took my Owen from me. Return him, and I will leave you to the battle around you."

"And if we don't?" Sandara asked. Alan glared at her to shut up.

Sita's white teeth gleamed in the sunlight. "I'll murder you and leave your corpses for the vultures."

Alan stepped in front of Sandara, forcing her to stop talking. He put on his most charming, oily smile. "I'm afraid we can't return him to you, Sita, but perhaps we can come to some other arrangement. You liked Eric quite a lot, didn't you . . ."

Violet fire surrounded the two Imbri, cutting off Alan's words. Sita had heard enough. She gathered her power and threw more fire at them, trying to cover them both with it.

But Sandara was faster than she anticipated. The woman pulled two emerald daggers from the back of her trousers and cut through the magical fire as if it were nothing. Sita felt a tremor in her chest and her belly clench as Sandara jumped out of the circle of fire, leaving Alan to his own devices inside. She threw one dagger at Sita's feet, distracting her, then the other straight for her heart.

Sita's instincts kicked in. She lunged to the right to avoid the dagger. It caught her sleeve and drove her into the ground, where it pinned her in the soft earth. Sita grasped the handle and tried to pull it free, but it only worked itself in deeper, stinging her palm and fingers with every touch. She tried to pull the fabric apart and escape that way, but her clothes were too well made, and the tear from the dagger was now buried in the ground with the dagger's tip.

Sandara gestured and sent fire around Sita, mimicking Sita's attack. The lime-colored light cast a sickening pallor to Sita's cheeks. Her violet eyes glared up to meet Sandara's own dark blue. The older woman flashed a cruel smile and gestured again. The dagger began to glow, and Sita screamed, feeling her power draining away.

"Yesss," hissed Sandara. "Yes! The power! Oh, Sita, you have so much of it! Why not share a little?" She cackled and Sita's power drained into her own body, just as it had in Thirka.

Sandara, laughing all the while, threw lime-green bolts at Sita, hitting her in the legs, the waist, the chest. Each time Sita screamed louder, harder, longer. The pain began to override her mind, began to take control. Between bolts, she tried to reach for the dagger, for the power, anything that could make it stop. But nothing came.

The pain clouded her thoughts and made her mind fuzzy. Sita bit her lip hard enough to bleed in an effort to keep control. "Is power all you care about, Sandara?" she said through the pain. Gasping, she mustered the last of her strength and lashed out with her magic at the dagger, forcing it from the ground and away from her. Coughing and bloody, Sita sat up on quivering hands and knees, feeling exhausted and drained.

Sandara snarled. "You little bitch. Yes, I want power, I want to be the most powerful sorceress in all the worlds, and you will give me your power or you will die! And then I will have your soul . . ." Sita had to end it now. The older woman, with her dark blue eyes burning brilliant in her pale and gory face, raised both hands in a slow and deliberate gesture. Sita looked up and watched, as if in a dream, and recognized the gesture for what it was: a killing blow. And not a merciful, swift one.

The bird-woman's eyes widened. She pushed onto her shaky knees and tried to rise. But her strength was almost gone. When that failed, she dropped the shield encircling their small clearing and tried to gather the magic to her. But she knew it wouldn't be enough.

Sandara threw her most powerful attack at Sita, still on her knees and unable to shield. Sandara screamed in triumph—

—until a shape interposed itself between the magic and Sita. The shape, a man carrying a sword, cried in pain when the power hit him in the stomach. Blood spattered outward over half the clearing, coating Sandara and Alan in the red stickiness of arterial life.

Sita surged forward and caught the man as he fell. "Eric!" she cried. "Eric, what are you doing here? Why?" She felt tears carve tracks down her face and a sob lodged in her throat. "Oh, Eric."

He reached for her face, but his hand dropped. "Sita . . . I'm so sorry . . . I had to . . . tell you . . ." he gasped as his breath and blood rushed from him. Eric drooped in Sita's shaking arms, his breath wheezing one last time from his lungs. His eyes stared into Sita's until they glazed over and could see no more.

Sita clutched the torn body to her and sobbed over him. "Why, Eric?"

Sandara stood watching the girl, covered in gore and gathering her power once more. She chuckled and sneered down at the couple. "He loved you, didn't he. Ha! Look at where that got him. A horrible death in the arms of his beloved!" She cackled like a mad woman.

Sita glared at her, tears still in her eyes and a fierce look on her face. "You vile woman. You killed him. So I'll kill you."

Her eyes became violet once more, and she set aside Eric's body. Sandara threw attack after attack at Sita, but each one glanced off the younger woman's shield. The sporadic green light illuminated Sandara's wide and frightened eyes, etched her terrified face into Sita's memory.

Purple light outlined Sita's hands and grew in intensity until it was almost white. Sandara finally had to look away. She held her hands in front of her, trying in vain to ward Sita off.

But Sita felt no mercy now. She grasped Sandara's shirt, burning holes in the woman's skin. Sandara screamed. "Where is Owen?" Sandara shook her head, pleading for mercy. "Where is he?" Sita snarled, shaking Sandara like a rag doll in her hands.

When Sandara could only whimper, Sita huffed and laid a hand over the woman's face, forcing her power inside the professor's body and granting her a swift but painful death.

She allowed the body to fall to the ground and turned her attention to Alan. He was still surrounded by her violet fire. She commanded the circle to widen, stopping it just short of Sandara's body and giving Alan a ten-foot wide oval to move in. "You will tell me where Owen is. Tell me, and I'll give you a quick and painless death."

Alan shrugged, looking for all the world as if he were completely unconcerned. "Well, that's hardly an incentive to tell you, is it? Now, if you were to let me roam free if I spoke, then perhaps we could come to an arrangement."

"I don't think so."

He met her eyes, his own shadowed and cruel. "Then I guess you'll just have to beat it out of me."

Sita clenched her fists in rage. "You're going to tell me before you die!"

The battle began.

Alan was much more skilled than Sandara. Sita found herself blocking more of his attacks than she could dodge, and he never let his emotions sway him as Sandara had. He fired bolt after blue bolt at her, aiming for all parts of her body.

Then he got creative.

Massive sapphire spheres the size of Sita's body rolled at her in an attempt to overwhelm and crush. She dodged them and forced them to dissipate. Long, sharp wedges of blue ice rained down on her from above—Sita countered by bouncing them off her shield and back at Alan, who made them disappear with a twitch of his hand. He sent blue fire at her. She met it with waves of violet. He attacked from below the ground. She took to the air and fought on two fronts as his pillar of blue erupted from the ground and he sent bolts of blue lightning at her from above.

Nothing could penetrate her violet shields. Her power was the stronger in this battle, and both knew it was only a matter of time.

"You may defeat me," Alan said through gritted teeth. He threw everything he had at her. "But you will never defeat the *Pur*. They are ultimate, timeless, and all-powerful!" He began to laugh, the sound breathy and harsh, and Sita saw a gleam of desperation come to his eyes. "With all my plans coming together, Imbri Mors will rule all. We will be the power behind thrones, the brain behind science, the hand behind all things. I will lift the world out of the ashes and into a more perfect, more beautiful place. One in which I will be a king, and answerable only to my masters, the *Pur*, who are like gods. They hold our souls in their hands, and I will deliver those souls to them with a glad heart for safekeeping and rebirth. They hold my soul highest above all, a god among mortals, immortal and glorious. And I will finally, *finally*, have returned to me what I have lost! You can't defeat them! They will end you. And Darci, my Queen, the Darkness Incarnate, will set them free. And they will change the worlds into the ultimate Paradise of Hell!" Sita set her face in a stoic mask and concentrated solely on the attacks, the defense, the kill.

Alan shot another attack at her. The beam of magic grazed Sita's face and cut a few strands of her hair in half. "My dear angel," he said. "You've finally joined me."

Sita's lip curled in disgust. "I haven't. I'm against you. Don't you see me trying to kill you?"

Laughter erupted from Alan, craggy but loud. As unwise as it was, Sita paused when she heard his laugh. He sounded almost manic. "You have, Sita! You've joined the Darkness!" He spread his hands wide and a wave of blue magic poured from him. Sita dodged just in time. "You've killed Sandara in cold blood. You're trying to do the same to me. You're letting your revenge win. Don't you see, my angel? You've joined the Darkness today." He flung his left hand into the air and a net formed above her. It floated down in an attempt to trap her, but Sita disintegrated the spell with a swipe of her violet magic. "Taste the Darkness, Sita, let it in. It's so sweet, so rewarding. And the best part? You have to kill me in cold blood, too. You'll only bring yourself closer to me when you kill me! You've become one of us, and our blood is your baptism!"

Alan laughed again, the hysterical sound grating on Sita's ears and nerves. "Oh, shut up, you fool," she shouted at him. "I'm not on your side."

The final straw came when Alan attempted to attack and disintegrate Eric's body, sending rays of deadly light straight for him. Sita, aware of his intent, never looked away from the professor. Instead, she waved a careless hand toward Eric's still form, giving him a shield, and waved another hand at Alan, encasing him from head to toe in lavender.

She strode forward, her face stoic but her violet-filled eyes alight. Alan glared at her and sneered. He raised a hand to attack, but Sita beat him to it. A slash of light bit deep into Alan's neck and chest.

The amulet Alan never took off went flying, the gold chain sliced by the attack. Eyes wide, Alan stumbled, blood flecking his pale skin as he tried to recover. Sita saw his eyes follow the amulet before they returned to her. He raised a hand and whispered something that sounded like a name.

Sita snarled and sent a concentrated bolt of dark purple straight into his heart.

Professor Alan lay dead at Sita's feet.

Sita allowed her magic to fade. Quivering limbs and a pounding heart reminded her that her body would make her pay for all of this. She stood still, unable to move as her mind worked to process what had just happened. Combat continued to roil around her outside her thin barrier of magic, but with her victory, the Imbri forces soon turned tail and attempted a retreat. The Gennaian army followed to rout the enemy. Taking to the air, Sita flew in slow deliberateness back to the camp, carrying Eric's lifeless, heavy body in her trembling arms and Alan's amulet in one hand.

Her friends gathered around her. The battle was won. Sita, however, did not share their elation with the victory. She felt numb. She stared at the field of dead bodies and the blood on her hands and clothes. With gentle care, she slid Eric's body to the ground and closed his sightless eyes. Then she turned her back on him and walked away.

Her heart felt like it would stop beating at any moment, as if it would pound itself into oblivion. Tightness in her chest threatened to steal her breath away and squeeze her heart in its tracks. The ground felt like it swayed beneath her feet. "Owen," she whispered. Owen had disappeared, and she knew Alan had done something to him. But the professor was now dead, the secret of Owen's whereabouts gone to the grave with him.

Sita kicked at the ground. Something inside her snapped and she came out of her despair. Far-off screams reached her ears, and she wondered who screamed. Then she realized it was her, and she fell to her knees and pounded on the earth, punctuating each blow with another yell. Her throat felt raw, but the bleak emptiness in her core remained. Her friends backed away, uncertain and confused. She allowed the emotions to sweep over her and she screamed and screamed, over and over again, until every person on the battlefield heard her and trembled.

"OWEN!"

Darci rifled through the drawers of Alan's desk. She skimmed the papers, hunting for something that had been bothering her for a while now. Her dark eyes flashed in the dimly lit study, reading over words that had nothing to do with her hunt.

She reached the end of his papers, even going so far as to lift every single one out and make sure there were none trapped on the bottom. Darci replaced them all with care—his filing system had been quite complete, after all. The thunder echoed her frustration and she stood from the chair, studying the desk. Her quick hands darted over every inch of the dark hardwood.

Finally something clicked underneath her fingers. A hidden drawer popped out from the side of the desk, so cleverly concealed that she had never noticed it before. She brushed around the desk to see what was inside. More papers. Groaning, she lifted the thin sheets out and brought them closer to the lamp—the faint and spidery handwriting was difficult to read.

When she finished reading each sheet of paper, Darci chewed on her lip and reclined in the large chair, thinking hard. She had guessed there might be something like this involved, but to have confirmation of her suspicions was worrying. These creatures might be beyond her power to control.

But if Sita helped me . . . yes, if Sita helped me control them, we could rule the world.

Darci grinned into the yellow lamplight and pulled out fresh papers. She had plans to make.

Chapter Thirty-Eight
The Bitter End

Alexander Knight settled himself in his chair. He studied the papers on his desk. They detailed the events of the last two weeks, telling him in excruciating detail about the short war and the aftermath.

Knight sighed. The girl was perfect, but she thought for herself too much. That scene when she fought Imbri Mors alone . . . he nearly had a heart attack at that point, and forced himself to calm down until he finished reading.

Knight stood and paced around the edge of his office, clasping his hands behind his back. The girl was rash, selfish, and stupid, at least in battles. That could be a problem, a kink in his plans for her. He would need to get her to calm down while outside school, need her to almost sequester herself. If she kept that dangerous free will, that ability to think for herself, without regard to his plans . . . that could be very bad indeed.

The cabinet against the wall opened a crack. A light shone from inside, white light that called him closer. He knew what lay inside that cabinet, had collected it himself. He knelt down and opened the door to reveal a shard of diamond as large as two hands together that shone with the brilliance of the full moon at night. He smiled. This diamond had been very difficult to fill all those years ago.

He set the diamond back in the cabinet and closed it. The diamond's resident constantly tried to free herself. He must not allow that to happen . . . she could warn Sita, or the other surviving Awle members that he knew must be out there somewhere.

Alexander Knight sat back on his chair and picked up a quill, sliding over a piece of thin parchment. He began writing out new orders for Robert and Allen, the diamond and its occupant at the forefront of his mind.

∞

The battles were over. The Council met the day after, arguing among themselves over what to do next. Queen Catherine kept her army at the ready, though the commander did allow a rotating schedule of leave time for the soldiers. Samuel Knox and Catherine managed to convince the Council not to disband the armies gathered from other nations, over the strenuous protests of Khaden Whed. All celebrated the fact that Alan and Sandara were now dead.

Eric's body was buried outside Sita's mansion the day after the war ended. After she had slept for a few days, Sita created a small tombstone for him with only his name and dates as label, and set him to rest underneath the willow trees near the lake. She thought he would like the view. Purple crocuses, like the ones he had given her so long ago on the day she first found Corá, lay in a blanket over his grave.

Now Sita stared out her window in her mansion. The lights stayed off when darkness fell. The windows stayed open even as the air grew cool. Her skin prickled in the chill, and without even thinking about it she rubbed her arms with her hands, trying to stay warm.

The gleam of gold reflected in the window's glass. She reached down and fiddled with Vanessa's ring. The gems winked up at her. Sita sighed and let it drop against her chest. In her other hand she held the amulet that had once hung around Ray Alan's neck. As if it could tell her the man's secrets, sometimes she would hold it and ask it to speak to her. But she heard nothing. With a sigh and a frown, Sita set the amulet aside as well.

A knock on the door echoed around the room and Roxie let herself in. She wrapped the blanket she held around Sita's shoulders and hurried to close the windows. "Sita, come on. You can't wallow in here forever." She settled a comforting hand on her friend's shoulder. "We'll find him. I know we will."

Sita shrugged the hand off, pulling the fleece tighter around herself. Roxie, a frown marring her pretty face, sighed and stepped back. "I am not wallowing, thank you," Sita said. Roxie cocked an eyebrow. "I'm remembering. Our victory wasn't everything I wanted it to be. Yes, we won the war. But we lost Darci. Then we lost Vanessa, and again when she died. I lost both boyfriends, one of them twice. It's just . . ."

"Bittersweet?"

"Yeah. You could say that."

Roxie stood in awkward silence behind Sita, unsure of what to say. Sita picked up her earlier train of thought, voicing it aloud for Roxie's sake. "But mostly, I'm planning."

"Planning what?"

An ugly sneer twisted Sita's beautiful lips. She turned away from Roxie to stare out the window into the darkness. "I'm planning how to get my boyfriend back, and . . .

"How to get my revenge."

Far away in Corá, Darci saw Sita's face, heard Sita's words. She sat back in her plush chair, shrouded in the comforting darkness. A single long white feather swished through the air in her fingers.

She laughed.

ABOUT THE AUTHOR

Kira R. Tregoning began writing stories from a young age and began to attempt novel writing at the age of eleven. Fantasy stories have always been a favorite, and her personal library is dominated by fantasy, sci-fi, and mythology. Kira is a graduate of the University of Maryland with degrees in Classics and Linguistics. She is currently hard at work on the next book in The Aligerai series and another unrelated story.

Visit her website at: http://theworldofcora.wordpress.com

Facebook: www.facebook.com/kiratregoning

Twitter: @KiraTregoning

Reader feedback is always welcome!

Find out about new releases by signing up for Kira's newsletter at:
http://eepurl.com/3mLh9